You cha

with th

Before the elv

It must live, and i

for the [illegible]

An elf's ambition can be no less dangerous than a [illegible]n's.

I give myself to you, Shevarash. A weapon in your hands.
Use me well.
And an elf's vengeance can be even worse.

The Bracer is a priceless relic of antiquity,
as are Ynloeth's shattering swords.
Thousands of years' worth of elven magic has been lost.

The sentient sword would not suffer its companion blade
the pleasure of a kill.
Drizzt Do'Urden finds a new enemy
in the weapon of a trusted friend.

The Knights of Myth Drannor had met baelnorn before,
and knew it for what it was.
Not all elves are content
with but a thousand years of life.

You weep for the dead, elf? Be at ease.
I will leave your bones here
with the rest of this dry old wreckage.
And now they Return to their ancestral homelands,
and find only war.

Welcome to the most
ancient realms in Faerûn.
Welcome to the Realms of the Elves.

THE LAST MYTHAL
Richard Baker

Forsaken House

Farthest Reach

Final Gate
June 2006

REALMS ANTHOLOGIES
Edited by Philip Athans

Realms of Mystery

Realms of the Deep

Realms of the Dragons

Realms of the Dragons II

Realms of the Elves

Realms of War
November 2008

Realms of the Elves

The Last Mythal Anthology

Edited by
Philip Athans

The Last Mythal
REALMS OF THE ELVES

Published by Wizards of the Coast, Inc. FORGOTTEN REALMS, WIZARDS OF THE COAST, and their respective logos are trademarks of Wizards of the Coast, Inc., in the U.S.A. and other countries.

Printed in the U.S.A.

Cover art by Adam Rex
First Printing: February 2006
Library of Congress Catalog Card Number: 2005928113

9 8 7 6 5 4 3 2 1

ISBN-10: 0-7869-3980-X
ISBN-13: 978-0-7869-3980-0
620-95462740-001-EN

U.S., CANADA,
ASIA, PACIFIC, & LATIN AMERICA
Wizards of the Coast, Inc.
P.O. Box 707
Renton, WA 98057-0707
+1-800-324-6496

EUROPEAN HEADQUARTERS
Hasbro UK Ltd
Caswell Way
Newport, Gwent NP9 0YH
GREAT BRITAIN
Save this address for your records.

Visit our web site at www.wizards.com

Table of Contents

TRAITORS

RICHARD LEE BYERS

-25,090 DR

Rhespen Ash brandished his truesilver staff and shouted words of power. The magic cast up shields of wind and light, and hurled bright, crackling thunderbolts at the foes lurking in the green shadows between the trees.

It wasn't enough. The enemy wizards shattered his defenses quick as he could conjure them, volleys of arrows moaned through the air, and Rhespen's troops and their horses died.

If he'd had a chance to prepare, it would likely have been different, but the ambuscade had caught him entirely by surprise. He'd marched a small company of his master's warriors into the forest because some of the inhabitants—elves, his own People!—had sent a message requesting help to repel an incursion of trolls. He'd had no reason to suspect the missive had actually originated with rebels seeking to lure a portion of the royal army into a trap.

He glanced about to see how many of his predominantly human men-at-arms lay dead or crippled and how many remained on their feet. It looked as if the foe had neutralized half of them already.

The battle was lost. For a moment, Rhespen considered using sorcery to whisk himself to safety. But he owed it to his men to attempt a proper surrender and so prevent the destruction of any more lives. He murmured a charm to amplify his voice, the better to cry for quarter, and an enormous shadow swept over his beleaguered force.

His soldiers looked up, and cheered. Rhespen felt the same jubilation. King Orchtrien and his get were busy fighting in the great wars far to the southeast. Yet somehow, one of them had perceived trouble in the supposedly peaceful heart of the realm, whereupon Prince Bexendral had employed a spell of teleportation to rush to his vassal's aid.

Some of the enemy shrieked, bolted, or collapsed cowering at the sight of the gold dragon on the wing. Others shot arrows, or assailed the wyrm with darts of light and blasts of frost. Hovering, leathery wings beating and flashing in the afternoon sunlight, Bexendral didn't even appear to notice the attacks. He growled a spell, and sparks rained from the empty air to the forest floor, where they exploded into prodigious blasts of flame. Twisting the horned, wedge-shaped head at the end of his serpentine neck, the prince spewed a flare of his own burning breath, decimating the rebels and plunging the survivors into disarray.

Rhespen's men, suddenly keen to avenge their fallen comrades, hefted their swords and spears and ran toward the flames. The mad rush had no tactics or order to it, but what did it matter? Bexendral had come and his warriors couldn't lose.

Rhespen used his magically enhanced voice to shout to the rebels: *"Surrender now, or the dragon will kill you all!"*

◎ ◎ ◎ ◎ ◎

Huge as Bexendral was, his sire dwarfed him, and even though he'd served the king for a century, Rhespen always felt a pang of awe upon entering his presence. His heart beating a little faster, he marched the length of the vast, high-ceilinged hall, kneeled before the intricately carved cylindrical pedestal that served as a sort of throne, and laid his staff at Orchtrien's taloned feet.

Up close, the gold smelled of saffron, and his yellow eyes shined like lamps. "Rise, Milord," he rumbled. "Tell me what you've learned."

"Yes, Majesty." Rhespen drew himself to his feet. "Many of the forest folk are loyal. Only three noble Houses—Vilirith, Starfall, and Duskmere—took part in the treachery."

Someone snorted. Rhespen turned to see that, as expected, it was Maldur Breakstone. Burly and florid of face, long hair dyed a premature white to create the appearance of wisdom, the human mage gave him a glower.

"Did you wish to comment?" asked Orchtrien, beard of fleshy tendrils dangling beneath his jaw.

Grimacing, Maldur feigned reluctance. Then: "I don't mean to impugn Lord Rhespen's competence, Majesty, nor, obviously, his loyalty. But if he failed to notice that any of his fellow elves were plotting treason to begin with, are you certain you can trust his findings now?"

Rhespen stifled a surge of anger. "Do you, Milord, have any concrete reason to doubt them?"

Maldur shrugged. "Perhaps the truly important question is what to do next." He shifted his gaze again to Orchtrien, tilting his head back so he could look the reptile in the eye. "Majesty, I suggest you execute all the dastards implicated in the crime and confiscate their lands and property. If other elves are contemplating treason, perhaps the fate of the rebels will dissuade them. If not, well, the traitors still deserve the harshest punishment you can mete out, and you need wealth to prosecute your wars."

Rhespen frowned. "Majesty, I recommend a more merciful approach."

"Well, you would, wouldn't you," Maldur said, "considering that the knaves are your own race, and that it was mainly humans who paid the price for their treachery."

"I'm a servant of the crown before all else," Rhespen said, "and I grieve for the warriors who fell. I advise moderation because severity could sow unrest where none currently exists, and with war raging on our borders, that we can ill afford."

"You may be right," Orchtrien said. "Still, we must do something to deter the rebel lords from further folly. We will hold their children hostage, and you, Rhespen, will supervise their captivity."

"With respect, Majesty," Maldur said, "Lord Rhespen might find it a trial to manage prisoners of his own race. He might start feeling unduly sympathetic. Whereas I—"

"I want a sympathetic jailer," said the king. "I want the hostages to enjoy their sojourn with us, and to savor all the pleasures and wonders my court has to offer. That's the way to win their fealty, and when they one day ascend to their parents' estates, to put an end to this insane impulse to anarchy for good and all."

"Your Majesty is wise," Rhespen said. "But I hoped to journey south with you and fight at your side. Surely someone else—"

Orchtrien snorted, the exhalation hot with a hint of the fire forever smoldering inside him. "All my deputies are argumentative today. You will do as I have commanded."

Rhespen inclined his head.

Rhespen had friends among the ravens, hawks, and owls, and they kept him apprised of what occurred in the vicinity of the royal city. Thus, it was easy to intercept the hostages before they started the climb up the mountain highway.

To his surprise, the newest arrival had seen fit to travel in a coach with curtains drawn across the windows. Never had he known an elf to employ such a conveyance. It closed one off from the kiss of the wind, from the ever-changing sight and scent of verdure that was as vital to his kind as food and drink. Indeed, the mere thought of riding for days pent up in such a box made him cringe, and he wondered if the Count of Duskmere had sent an invalid to totter about Orchtrien's palace.

He kicked his gray palfrey into a canter, and his half dozen bodyguards clattered after him. Six was the smallest number protocol allowed. He meant to welcome the hostage like a cordial host, not a foe who feared hostilities.

The Duskmere retainers greeted him with glum faces but likewise with respect.

"Our mistress," said their chief, "is the Lady Winterflower."

Rhespen turned to see if, now that she had, in effect, been introduced, Winterflower would see fit to emerge from her carriage, pull back a curtain, or at least speak. She didn't.

"Is the lady ill?" he asked. "Or deep in Reverie?"

"I don't believe so," the servant replied.

Then perhaps she's hard of hearing, Rhespen thought. He swung himself down from his horse, advanced to the coach, and rapped on the door.

"Milady?" he said. "I'm Rhespen Ash, Royal Councilor and Magician, come to escort you into the Bright City and see to your comfort thereafter."

"Escort me, then," she said, still without revealing herself. Her soprano voice sounded sweet, yet cold, like a drink from a frigid spring.

"The weather is mild, and the view going up the mountain is spectacular. I recommend you ascend on horseback, or at least unshroud your windows."

"No doubt I'll have ample opportunity to observe the

walls of my prison once I'm trapped behind them."

His mouth tightened. He had no wish to vex her, but likewise saw no reason to tolerate the childish discourtesy implicit in her refusal to reveal herself. If he permitted it to succeed now, it would be that much harder to eliminate later on.

"Milady," he said, "I could never forgive myself if, through inaction, I deprived you of one of the fairest sights in Faerûn." He murmured a rhyme and swept a talisman through a mystic pass. Winterflower's retainers gawked and exclaimed in alarm, but the incantation was only a few words long, and he'd already finished before they could make up their minds to intervene.

He touched the talisman to the side of the carriage, and the top half of it faded from view. The startled driver appeared to be sitting on empty air, and Winterflower herself, to be riding in some sort of peculiar open wagon. Rhespen pivoted to regard her, and his eyes widened.

With their fair, clear skin and slender frames, most elves were pleasant to look upon, but even by the standards of their comely race, Winterflower was extraordinary. Her curls were soft, gleaming ebony, and her eyes, sapphires flecked with gold. Her features were fine, exquisite, yet somehow avoided the appearance of daintiness. Rather, they bespoke courage and intelligence.

She glared at him. "Had I been allowed to bring my grimoires and amulets with me into captivity, I'd wipe your feeble enchantment away, then punish you for your impudence."

He shook off his surprise at her loveliness. "Then I'm glad the king forbade you their use, and before long, you'll feel the same. Let's continue on our way." He whistled, and his horse, trained in part by magic, instantly left off cropping grass and came to him.

He rode beside Winterflower as the road switchbacked up into the mountains, past the minor bastions and watchtowers built to guard the way. He chatted about the sights they encountered, and she responded—or failed to—with a silence and an expression as stony as the crags rising around them.

Until Dawnfire came into view. For elves were famously susceptible to beauty, and despite herself, she caught her breath. Her features softened.

Orchtrien's capital was both a city and one vast castle, the whole hewn from the living rock of the mountaintop, then refined and polished like a cameo. Not an inch of it was plain, dingy, or poorly proportioned. At the crest of every spire, framing every window, and etched into every section of wall, finely wrought ornamentation delighted the eye.

"We'll ride out early one morning so you can see it at sunrise," Rhespen said. "The stonework catches the red and gold light like a mirror."

Winterflower scowled, struggling to break the spell of the vista as he himself had earlier exerted his will to cast off his astonishment at her loveliness. "I hate to think," she said, "of all the toil that went into creating that monument, simply to feed a dragon's vanity."

"It's a city. A good many folk who aren't dragons live there and enjoy it, too. By nightfall, you'll be one of us."

"I wonder how many poor slaves fell to their deaths in the carving of it."

"Orchtrien doesn't have slaves. He has subjects, the same as any king. You'll see."

She sniffed, and still half visible and half not, the coach clattered onward.

A patrol comprised of Orchtrien's personal guards recognized Rhespen and stepped to the side of the street, clearing the way for him and his companions. Clad in gilt armor, the warriors were tall, lanky men with blond hair and tawny eyes. Their skin had a golden cast as well, and in some cases, a faint patterning suggestive of scales. Winterflower studied them as her coach rolled past.

"Those," said Rhespen, "are half-dragons."

"I know what they are," she snapped. "Orchtrien's bastards, or the bastards of his dragon sons. Abominations engendered by the rape of elf and human women."

He shook his head. "Rape? Milady, I can't imagine how you come by such lurid fancies."

"Do you claim the women have a choice?"

"Yes. Though admittedly, I don't recall anyone refusing. The rewards are considerable."

"What reward could adequately compensate a woman for lying with a gigantic serpent? They accept the horror and shame because they dare not refuse."

"Gold wyrms can change their shapes. They visit their mistresses in the forms of males of their own races." He grinned. "Otherwise, I'll grant you, squashing could be a problem. But the two of us, gently born and newly acquainted, ought not to speak of such coarse matters. Your new home is just ahead."

The column passed through an arch in a wall adorned with flowers, bumblebees, and hummingbirds rendered in mosaic. On the other side, in the very heart of the city, towered a wood of oak and shadowtop. High in the branches hung dwellings constructed on multiple levels, some portions enclosed, others, simple platforms. White, blue, and amber lamps glowed in the twilight, and the scents of cooking tinged the air.

"This is the Elf Quarter," Rhespen said. "You can imagine all the hard work and potent sorcery it took to transplant these trees to the top of a mountain, just so people like us would feel at home."

"In other words," she said, "Orchtrien wounded a true forest to create this unnatural place. That doesn't surprise me. His marauders kill trees every day to clear more of his cursed farmland."

"The army must eat, Milady, the entire kingdom must, and the unfortunate truth is, forests don't yield as much food as grain fields. I assure you, the king intends to leave the greater portion of the woodlands intact."

"Every particle of soil, every leaf, every twig of our homeland is sacred, Milord. If you still possessed the soul of an elf, you'd know it, but I fear it shriveled in you long ago."

Rhespen felt a twinge of incipient headache. "We can discuss these matters later, at our leisure. For now, let me install you in your new residence, and I'll leave you to your rest."

◎ ◎ ◎ ◎ ◎

In the evenings, Winterflower took to singing from one of the open platforms high in her shadowtop. Her repertoire, comprised of laments and dirges, was as cheerless as her conversation, but so lovely was her voice that her neighbors still made it a habit to stop and listen. Over time, word of her performances spread, and even folk who were not elves began to wander into the quarter at dusk to partake of the free entertainment.

So perhaps it shouldn't have been any great astonishment when the king himself asked for a song, but nonetheless, it caught Rhespen by surprise.

He turned from the table where he dined with the hostages and looked across the hall, to the pedestal atop which Orchtrien crouched over his own wagon-wheel-sized plate of beef and bowl of red wine. "I beg your pardon, Majesty?"

"I've heard about the nightingale of the Elf Quarter," the dragon replied. "Please, Milady, grace us with a song to celebrate my victory over the Red Triumvirate."

Inwardly, Rhespen winced. Some of the rebels' offspring were adjusting well to their soft captivity, but Winterflower remained as scornful and unyielding as ever. He feared she'd refuse Orchtrien's command, and so earn punishment. He'd never considered the gold to be especially cruel by nature, but his master still possessed a regal pride, a dragon's pride, and was little inclined to tolerate disrespect.

Rhespen groped for an excuse to offer on Winterflower's behalf. She rose from the table before he could think of anything. "As Your Majesty commands," she said. She walked to the patch of floor before the throne, took a breath, and began to sing.

Her song, a mournful ballad, was lovely, and cast its spell over everyone in the hall. Rhespen sat as captivated as the rest, until he realized how the lyrics might be construed.

He could only hope that no one else would so interpret them. Many of the folk in attendance didn't even speak Elvish, and others were surely content to enjoy the song without analyzing it for provocative implication. Perhaps, he thought, it would be all right.

Then a disembodied fist made of blue phosphorescence shimmered into existence. It smashed Winterflower in the face, flinging her to the floor.

Rhespen sprang to his feet, knocking his chair over in the process. He called for his staff, and the length of white shining metal appeared in his hand.

Sneering, Maldur rose as well. He didn't summon his own staff—perhaps he'd never mastered that particular knack—but light flickered and oozed inside the gems he wore on either hand.

"You surely noticed," the human magician said, "that the song told of a mad, vainglorious king, and the calamities his misrule inflicted on his subjects."

"It's an ancient song," Rhespen replied, "dating back to a time before elves even walked this world."

"Nevertheless," Maldur said, "she surely intended it as a veiled comment on His Majesty's reign." He glared down at Winterflower. "Didn't you, Milady?"

Rhespen stared at her, silently imploring her with his gaze: For once, curb that bitter tongue. You could forfeit your life by admitting to such a thing.

She peered back at him, then lowered her eyes and said, in a meeker voice than he'd heard her use hitherto, "As Lord Rhespen said, it's simply an old song with a plaintive melody. I meant nothing by it, and apologize if it offended."

Rhespen gave her his hand and helped her up. He glared at Maldur. "It's you, Milord, who should beg forgiveness."

"Nonsense," the human said. "It's plain she intended the insult even if she now lacks the courage to admit it, and in any case, I don't apologize to rebels."

Rhespen pivoted toward Orchtrien. "Your Majesty, you placed Lady Winterflower in my charge. Thus, I'm duty-bound to defend her honor."

He actually expected the dragon to forbid any semblance of a duel, for both he and Maldur were valuable servants, and Orchtrien would find it inconvenient to lose either one of them. But the gold surprised him.

"You two have been squabbling for years," Orchtrien said. "I'm tired of it. So I give you leave to settle your quarrel. We'll have a martial entertainment to celebrate a martial triumph."

Servants cleared away the tables and chairs nearest Orchtrien's dais, creating a space sufficiently large for a pair of mages to hurl destructive energies back and forth without inadvertently blasting an innocent spectator. Rhespen and Maldur stood at opposite ends of it, and the king cried, "Begin!"

Rhespen declaimed a word of command, drawing a pulse of light from his staff and wrapping himself in a protective enchantment. At the same time, Maldur twisted a ruby ring a half-turn around its finger, and a halo of red luminescence outlined his body. The human too had activated a mystical defense. Rhespen wondered exactly which ward it was, and what sort of spell could punch through it.

Maldur rattled off an incantation. Rhespen didn't recognize the precise spell—every wizard had his own secrets and obfuscatory tricks—but he could tell the human invoked the powers of the storm. That might be all right. From past observation, Rhespen knew his opponent liked flinging thunderbolts about, and had accordingly conjured a ward that was particularly effective at blocking them.

He plucked a pair of teeth from one of his many pockets, flourished them, and recited a rhyme of his own. He and Maldur finished at the same moment.

Maldur thrust out his hands, and a dazzling streak of lightning burst from his fingertips. As Rhespen had hoped, the twisting flare terminated harmlessly several inches from his chest.

But the booming, deafening string of thunderclaps that accompanied it hammered him like a giant's war club. He reeled, fell, and still the unbearable noise pounded on, smashing his thoughts into incoherence.

At last the cacophony subsided. Dazed, he struggled to lift his head and take stock of the tactical situation. It was about as bad as could be. He'd conjured a dozen pairs of fanged, disembodied jaws to fly around Maldur and harry him, but whenever one of the manifestations tried to bite its target, the human's protective corona of scarlet light withered it from existence. Confident of the efficacy of his defenses, Maldur had simply ignored the darting, wheeling jaws to start reciting another attack spell.

Which was to say, he had gained the advantage. If Rhespen attempted an incantation of his own, the human would almost certainly finish first, and strike another potentially devastating blow. Rhespen would do better to release another of the spells stored in his staff, a process only requiring a moment.

He spoke the appropriate word, and only then realized he wasn't gripping the truesilver rod anymore. He must have dropped it when the thunder staggered him. He peered about, spotted it, reached for it, then Maldur completed his spell.

A ragged shaft of shadow leaped from the human's upraised hand. Rhespen flung himself across the floor, rolling, trying to dodge the burst of darkness. The edge of it grazed him even so. Cold pierced him to the core, and an unnatural terror howled through his mind.

He denied the fear, refused to let it overwhelm him, and Maldur started yet another spell. Shaking, half frozen, Rhespen fumbled his staff into his grasp, gritted out a word of command, and clanged the head of the weapon against the floor.

A good portion of the marble surface jolted and shattered into pieces. The upheaval couldn't knock Rhespen down. He was already on his knees. But it threw Maldur onto his back, jarring the breath out of him and making him botch his recitation.

Maldur instantly started to raise himself back up, and an ignorant observer might have concluded that Rhespen hadn't accomplished much. But in fact, he'd altered the tempo of the confrontation and deprived the human of the momentum that allowed him to attack repeatedly without fear of reprisal.

The two mages jabbered rhymes. Rings dripping sparks, Maldur punched the air, whereupon an unseen force slammed into the center of Rhespen's chest and knocked him back a step. But he refused to let it spoil his magic. On the final syllable, a tingle ran over his skin, and he was as invisible as the top half of Winterflower's carriage had been.

Praying that Maldur didn't already have some sort of enchantment in place to augment his natural senses, Rhespen dashed forward. He swung wide before charging straight at his foe. Had he stayed on the same line, the human might easily have struck him with another spell despite the handicap of casting blind. His elven boots, possessed of a virtue that stifled noise, made no sound on the jutting chunks of broken floor.

Rhespen's disappearance took Maldur by surprise. He hesitated for a precious moment, then brought his hands together and lashed them apart. The topaz rings on his thumbs flashed.

Instinct warned Rhespen that he mustn't trust invisibility to protect him from this particular magic. He threw himself down.

Blades of yellow light leaped out from Maldur's body toward the four corners of the hall, like the spokes of a radiant wheel suspended parallel to the floor. If Rhespen hadn't ducked, one of them would inevitably have pierced him.

As soon as they winked out of existence, Rhespen jumped up and scrambled onward. Three more strides carried him into striking distance, and he swung his staff at Maldur's face.

Since the human couldn't see the threat, he made no effort to parry or evade, and as Rhespen had hoped, the scarlet aura provided scant protection against a purely physical attack. Metal rang, and Maldur's knees buckled. Blood started from his gashed forehead.

Visible once more—it was a limitation of the shrouding spell that making an attack dissolved it—Rhespen kept bashing. Maldur fell, curled into a ball, and tried to cover his most sensitive parts while gasping out a rhyme. Then, abruptly, he heaved himself onto his knees. A needle-toothed mouth gaped in the palm of each of his hands, and he snatched for Rhespen's body.

Rhespen jumped back, and the fangs in his adversary's left hand ripped his doublet and shirt but not the flesh beneath. He struck another blow with the staff. Maldur collapsed and lay twitching. Rhespen raised the rod high to drive the butt end down at the human's throat like a spear.

"Stop!" Orchtrien roared, the sudden bellow nearly as overpowering as the crash of Maldur's thunderclaps.

No! By all the powers of earth and sky, Rhespen had earned this consummation. It wasn't fair to balk him. Still, drawing a deep, quivering breath, he made himself lower his weapon and pivot toward the throne.

"Majesty?" he panted.

"You've avenged the affront to your charge's honor," said the wyrm, "and in the process, you and Maldur have provided a splendid entertainment." He gazed out across the hall. "Have they not?" So prompted, the company applauded.

"I'm grateful to have pleased you," Rhespen said, trying to hold resentment out of his voice. "Yet I thought you gave Lord Maldur and me leave to seek a final resolution to our quarrel."

"And so you have," Orchtrien said. "You've tested yourselves against one another, vented your ire, and from this night forward, you'll cease your bickering and work harmoniously together."

Rhespen inclined his head. "As the king commands."

Over the decades, Rhespen had stuffed his residence full of furniture and works of art produced by a dozen races with their diverse cultures and aesthetic sensibilities. Some articles had been presents from the king, some gifts from petitioners eager to curry favor with an influential royal official, and still others treasures he'd purchased for himself as his tastes grew increasingly cosmopolitan and eclectic.

In contrast, Winterflower's residence was purely elven, the furnishings sparse, forms and lines deceptively simple, yet every item beautifully conceived and flawlessly crafted. She'd evidently tossed out everything fashioned by any other sort of artisan, and as she conducted Rhespen onto one of the open platforms, he experienced an unexpected pang of nostalgia for the small forest settlement of his birth.

She led him to a bench that afforded a clear view of the stars through a gap in the branches overhead, poured him a cup of dry white wine, and they sat quietly for a while, savoring the vintage and the glories of the night sky.

Eventually she asked, "Why do you and Lord Maldur dislike each other?"

"Rivalries are common at a royal court. People vie for the king's favor and the most lucrative appointments. Maldur and I each possess the same skill, wizardry, so we have good reason to feel we're competing with one another in particular. Beyond that, each of us has always championed his own kind. He exhorts Orchtrien to rule in a way favorable to humans, while I push for policies that would benefit us." He smiled. "So despite your low opinion of me, perhaps I'm not such a dismal excuse for an elf after all."

"Elves shouldn't have to beg a wyrm's permission to live as we please."

"You've made it painfully clear that you think so. You actually did choose that song to insult Orchtrien, didn't you?"

"Of course. You knew it from the start." She hesitated. "Why, then, did you defend me?"

"As I explained at the time, it was a question of honor."

"I believe that, but I also suspect there was more to it."

He grinned. "You're shrewd. Had I allowed Maldur's accusation to stand unchallenged, it would have made me the lax, incompetent dolt who permitted one of my charges to malign the king, and he would have been the faithful deputy who disciplined you after I neglected the task. I couldn't permit the court to come away with such an opinion."

"But what if Orchtrien comprehends that I truly intended the mockery? Isn't it conceivable you've forfeited his trust by protecting me? Mightn't it have been more prudent to abandon me to my fate, even at the cost of some humiliation?"

He sipped his wine and looked at the stars. "Well, conceivably. I considered that, too. Perhaps what tipped the scale is that for some perverse reason, I like you, Milady, despite the way you curl your lip at me."

At the periphery of his vision, she lowered her eyes. He thought she colored, too, though in the dark, it was difficult to be certain. "I know I shouldn't take out all my frustrations on you. It's just that sometimes I feel as if they'll tear me apart if I don't express them somehow. I hate the way things are!"

"There are still lands left where elves hold supreme

authority. I suppose that if you and your kin find Orchtrien's rule unbearable, you could emigrate."

"It would mean forsaking forests we cherish. Abandoning them to the woodsman's axe. And suppose we could establish a new home elsewhere. How long would it be before one dragon prince or another conceived an ambition to add it to his domain?"

Rhespen sighed. "Not long, perhaps. A century, if you're lucky? Faerûn is changing. The dragons are bringing the entire continent under their sway, despite all that other races can do to resist. I daresay it would be happening even faster if the wyrms didn't so often contend with one another.

"The inevitability," he continued, "leaves us elves with a clear choice. We can aspire to an honorable estate as the dragons' vassals, or defy them and suffer. I infer that you, Milady, don't truly wish the latter, or you would have owned up to insulting the king."

"I should have. Any of my brothers or sisters would have. But after Maldur's magic struck me down, and he accused me, and that huge golden horror fixed me with his gaze, I knew I didn't want to die. I fear I'm a coward."

"No," said Rhespen. "You're wise. For why should you throw your life away on an empty gesture?"

She gazed out across the city with all its myriad lights. "Perhaps if we elves could set aside a measure of our pride, we'd recognize that our lives can still be fulfilling under Orchtrien's rule. Perhaps I could learn to be happy in this place, if some kind friend would teach me of its joys."

Rhespen felt his heartbeat quicken. "Milady, that's all I've ever wanted."

Orchtrien gave Rhespen a cheerful draconic grin, which, to the uninitiated, would have seemed a terrifying display of fangs as long as swords.

"We won!" the king declared.

"I know, Majesty," Rhespen said. He no longer followed the tidings of his master's various wars as avidly as he once had. But he was a royal deputy, and still needed to stay informed. "I'm told the warriors of the green cabal fell back in total disarray."

"They did indeed," Orchtrien said, "and afterward, their lords had no choice but to cede all their holdings east of the river."

"That's splendid." It occurred to Rhespen to wonder just how many men-at-arms the gold had lost to seize the territory in question, but he decided not to inquire as yet. Let the king savor his triumph. They'd have time to assess the current state of the army later on.

"We'll go back next year, or the year after, and push the greens out entirely," Orchtrien said. "Chromatic drakes treat their subjects like cattle! Compassion demands that we bring their poor thralls the enlightened rule of a metallic."

"Your Majesty is generous."

"Tell me how you've managed in my absence. I trust there have been no further acts of insurrection."

"None."

"I knew securing hostages would solve the problem. How are the prisoners faring?"

Rhespen smiled. "They've adjusted well. Indeed, they've become so enamored of life in Dawnfire that, when the time comes to send them home, we might have to prod them forth at spear-point."

Orchtrien laughed, suffusing the air with warmth. "Even the lovely Winterflower?"

Yes, Rhespen thought, to say the least. Over the course of the past two months, Winterflower had immersed herself in the life of the city and the amusements of the court with a relish that astonished him. It was as if she, a creature of passionate extremes, must either hate or love her captivity, and upon recognizing the bleak futility of the former course had committed herself heart and soul to the latter.

Or perhaps it was her affection for him and desire to share in his life that accounted for the change. For though both had tried in vain to stifle the burgeoning feeling—it was reckless for a jailer to grow overly fond of his prisoner, and her kin, still rebels at heart, would scarcely have approved—a tenderness had flowered between them. Indeed, for his part, it was a love deeper than he'd ever felt for any other woman.

But he saw no reason to discuss such intimate matters with Orchtrien, so he simply said, "Even her."

"I intend to host a revel to celebrate our conquests," said the gold. "She must attend, and sing again." His yellow eyes shined brighter. "Something less suggestive this time. I prefer to avoid the inconvenience of any more shattered floors."

As Rhespen and Winterflower approached the arched doorway with its frame of gems and precious metals, her face turned pale, and the blue, gold-flecked eyes rolled up in her head. Her knees gave way.

Rhespen caught her before she could fall. Heedless of the curious stares and questions of other nobles en route to the ball, he carried her into a velvet-curtained alcove provided to serve the requirements of overstimulated revelers desirous of a moment's quiet, or lovers in need of a trysting place.

He set her on a divan, then murmured a petty charm of enhanced vitality. It proved sufficient to rouse her, and her eyelids fluttered open.

"What's wrong?" he asked. "Are you ill?"

"Afraid," she replied.

He took her hand. Her fingers were cold. "Of what?"

"Need you ask? I haven't seen Orchtrien since the night I insulted him."

"But I have, and I promise, he has no wish to punish you."

"How can you be certain? Perhaps this is a cruel game. He invites me to a dance, I enter the hall anticipating only merriment, and the torturers seize me."

Rhespen shook his head. "I've told you before, you've listened to too many gruesome stories. I've heard them too, tales of whimsical atrocities perpetrated by dragon tyrants, and I daresay some of them are true. But true about reds, or blacks, or greens. The golds possess a nobler temperament."

"Orchtrien marches company after company off to perish in his wars. He was willing to risk your death for a moment's diversion, with never a thought that such an attitude was callous or unjust. We're lesser creatures in his eyes, to exploit as he sees fit."

He sighed. "I thought I'd weaned you away from such notions. I hope that in fact, I have, and it's just anxiety stirring up their ghosts."

She took a deep breath and let it out slowly. "Well, perhaps. I want to believe you. I know you wouldn't bring me to him if you thought he meant me harm."

"Of course not. So compose yourself, and we'll make our entrance. The sooner we do, the sooner you'll see that everything truly is all right."

As they descended the wide marble stairs, the rich but lively harmonies of the orchestra rose to greet them, while dancers spun and leaped on the floor below. Most wore some garment of cloth-of-gold, golden jewelry, or both in honor of the king, and in the aggregate, moving as one in time to the music, they resembled gleaming statuary sprung to joyous life.

It was a splendid sight, but Rhespen could tell Winterflower was still too frightened to appreciate it. She clenched his forearm as if to keep herself from plummeting into an abyss.

On such an occasion, etiquette didn't require newcomers to pay their respects to the king immediately, but Rhespen still thought they needed to get it over with. As soon as the music stopped, he led Winterflower to the center of the floor, where Orchtrien had stepped and whirled at the heart of the dance, and where he still stood chatting with his erstwhile partner, a youthful, auburn-haired human beauty newly arrived at court.

To participate in an amusement like the dance, the dragon had to change form, and tonight he'd chosen the semblance of a handsome elf with blond hair, golden eyes, and skin the color of bronze. When he noticed Rhespen and Winterflower approaching, he pivoted in their direction. In so doing, he turned his back on the human lass, who made a sour face at the sudden loss of his attention.

"My friends!" the dragon said.

Winterflower curtsied, and Rhespen bowed. "Good evening, Majesty," the wizard said.

"It is now that this lady has seen fit to grace us with her presence," Orchtrien said. "What will you sing for us, my dear?"

"A new ballad," said Winterflower, stammering almost imperceptibly, "to commemorate your victory over the green wyrms. I composed the tune myself—well, tweaked an old one, really—and one of the court poets helped me with the lyrics."

"It sounds splendid." He studied her features. "Yet you don't seem particularly eager to perform it, or to be here at all."

"I . . . I'm told that many singers feel faint before they take the stage. Your Majesty's court is an illustrious and demanding audience, and I'm not even a bard, just a girl with a habit of warbling for her own amusement."

"You're too modest," Orchtrien said. "I also worry you're less than completely forthcoming. I hope you're not afraid of me, Milady."

Winterflower hesitated. "Only to the extent that any subject fears the displeasure of the king."

"Well, stop it," said the drake. "I summoned you to Dawnfire to forge a bond of friendship between us, and so you could teach me to be a better sovereign to your people."

“Surely Lord Rhespen is well qualified to explain our needs.”

“Oh, he does his best, but you possess qualities he lacks.” To Rhespen’s surprise, Orchtrien shot him a wink. “I’d love to hear your song now, assuming you feel up to it.”

“Of course, Majesty.” Though she masked it well, Rhespen could tell she was eager to embrace any excuse to distance herself from the gold.

Winterflower climbed onto the orchestra’s platform to sing, and they, master musicians all, began to accompany her with the second verse. As before, the performance was fine enough to engage every listener, but this time, the sentiments expressed were so unobjectionable that not even Maldur could take them amiss.

“Delightful,” murmured Orchtrien, amber eyes subtly aglow to reveal the drake within, “and the scent of treason clinging to her makes her all the more so.”

Rhespen felt a twinge of uneasiness. “Majesty, I swear to you, Lady Winterflower’s no traitor.”

“Nonsense. All the hostages are rebels at heart, or at least they started out that way. That’s why we caged them here, to subdue them. By gentler means than we usually employ, but still. You’ve managed the first stage admirably, and now that the wars are done until spring, I’ll undertake the next.”

When the song concluded, Orchtrien applauded loudest of anyone, and gave Winterflower a gold bracelet cast in the form of a coiled wyrm. He then led her to the center of the floor for several dances in succession, while various other ladies struggled to swallow their jealousy.

The dragon drew his captive close and whispered in her ear. Winterflower looked to Rhespen with trapped, frantic eyes. From across the hall, Maldur gave him a smirk.

Rhespen climbed the stairs to the archway, balked, then forced himself onward. A hundred years, he thought, I've served him faithfully for a hundred years. That surely counts for something.

Beyond the doorway was a round stone platform surrounded by a parapet, with a chill autumn wind whistling across. By nature a creature of mountain peaks and the boundless sky, Orchtrien had incorporated several such high, open perches into the city, and repaired to them whenever walls and ceilings came to seem oppressive.

Rhespen crossed the platform, kneeled, and set his staff at the gigantic reptile's feet. Despite the gray clouds sealing away the sun, Orchtrien's scales still shimmered.

The dragon snorted a wisp of smoke. "Such stiff formality when it's just the two of us! You must intend to ask for a very great boon indeed."

Rhespen rose. "Yes, Majesty."

"Petition away, then."

He wanted to, but it was difficult. Though he fancied that he didn't lack for courage, over the course of a century, he'd cultivated the habit of pleasing his master, not annoying him.

Perhaps he could ease into the matter at hand. "You frequently invite Lady Winterflower to join you in one diversion or another. You've sent her a series of costly gifts. You don't pay nearly as much attention to the other hostages."

Orchtrien chuckled. "The other hostages are nowhere near as charming. Nor is any of them the darling daughter of the Count of Duskmere, who, according to your inquiries, was the chief dragon-hater among the rebels. Imagine his vexation when he hears I've seduced Winterflower to be my mistress. Or if she bears him a half-gold grandchild!"

"I thought you hoped to win the affection of the rebels."

"Of the young ones. I believe we must settle for compelling the obedience of their elders."

"Perhaps so, Majesty, but . . . . Let me say it straight out.

I love Winterflower, and she reciprocates my feelings."

The dragon cocked his head. "I had no idea."

"I suspected not. You've been away, and we've done our best to keep our bond a private matter between us."

"Under the circumstances, I suppose that's fortunate."

"Majesty, do you understand what I'm trying to say? To you, Winterflower would be the diversion of a season, or a year, to put aside as soon as she starts to bore you. I aspire to spend the rest of my life with her."

"So you wish me to indulge my appetites elsewhere."

"Yes, Majesty. Indeed, I beg it. The realm is full of women who would give anything to be your mistress."

"Or yours, Royal Councilor. Perhaps that's what ails us both, for where's the sport if the quarry races eagerly toward the hunter? Whereas Lady Winterflower presented you with a challenge, just as she now flinches at the sight of me."

"Maybe that was what first stirred my interest, but at this point, my sentiments are far more profound. Thus, I implore—"

Orchtrien snorted. "Enough, my friend. I hear your plea, and will conduct myself accordingly."

By dint of magic, Rhespen could have floated from the ground up to the door of Winterflower's residence as effortlessly as smoke rising from a fire. Or shifted himself through the intervening space in the blink of an eye. Instead, he chose to trudge up the steps spiraling around the trunk of the shadowtop, because he dreaded the conversation to come.

He still found himself in Winterflower's presence before he could think of a gentle way to present his news, and the welcome in her face twisted into dismay when she registered what was no doubt the dazed, stricken look on his own.

"What's wrong?" she asked.

"This morning," he said, "the king gave me a new commission. It seems he's decided it would be advantageous to make some effort to prosecute his wars through the winter months. I'm to lead a company across the eastern border to harry the dominions of the greens. To raid, burn houses and barns, and steal or destroy food."

"Leaving me behind."

"Yes. When I told Orchtrien that you and I had fallen in love, he seemed sympathetic, but apparently it isn't so."

"In fact, he's punishing you for having the audacity to ask him to leave me alone."

Rhespen shook his head. "I don't know. He may think he's buying me off. That's the common practice when the king or one of the princes wants to bed some wretch's wife. They give the cuckold a fine appointment that takes him away from court, so he needn't witness what's occurring. And the fact of the matter is, before I met you, I begged repeatedly for such an opportunity. With the kingdom perpetually at war, fighting is the surest way to win the highest honors and the most profitable offices."

"You're saying you couldn't refuse."

"No one may refuse a royal command."

"I can't stay here alone as the target of that creature's lust. Let's run away. Tonight."

"We could try, but he'd find us."

"You don't know that!"

"Yes, I do. Do you understand why the drakes are conquering the world? It isn't their physical prowess, mighty though they are. It's their magic. They possess arcane secrets unknown to elves or men."

She took a deep breath. "Give me one of your spellbooks, then."

"You know I can't do that. If it was discovered in your possession—"

"Don't you see, I can't let him force me! I never could have borne it, and now that you and I . . . He'll be vulnerable in the form of an elf, and if I catch him by surprise—"

"No! No matter what shape he wore, you wouldn't be a match for him, and in any case, it won't come to that. I told you before, he wouldn't stoop to rape."

"I fear that even now, you refuse to see him for what he is."

He took her hands in his own. "Promise me you won't do anything foolish. Rather, use all your tact and womanly wiles to put Orchtrien off without offending him, and wait for my return."

She studied his face. "Can you promise you will return?"

He forced a confident smile. "Of course. By that time, the king, bored with laying futile siege to your chastity, will have turned his attentions elsewhere, and I'll ask your father for your hand."

The eastern sky was lightening to gray, but it was still black in the west. Rhespen squinted, straining to spot a telltale flicker of motion against the stars.

Serdel, the stocky, grizzled veteran who served as his second-in-command, peered alongside him.

"See anything?" the warrior asked, evidently clinging to the hope that the keen eyes of an elf had noticed something imperceptible to human sight.

"Not yet," Rhespen said.

He supposed it was ironic. At the start of the summer, Prince Bexendral had rushed to his servants' aid without even being called. This time around, Rhespen had carried the proper spell to send a message to his distant masters ready for the casting, and had employed it as soon as calamity struck. Yet now, no one had responded.

It made him wonder if Orchtrien truly had dispatched him on this errand in the hope that he would die. Though he hadn't admitted it to Winterflower—he'd needed to calm her, not agitate her further—he had some reason to suspect so. Winter warfare was notoriously hard and dangerous. That was why civilized people generally eschewed it. The king, moreover, had sent him forth with a relatively small raiding party, ostensibly because a larger one would find it too difficult to forage sufficient food and hide from the enemy.

But despite freezing temperatures, howling blizzards, and the meager strength of his command, Rhespen had executed his commission with considerable success. Until one of the green drakes, possibly despairing of the ability of its minions ever to catch the marauders laying waste to the border marches, forsook the warmth and other amenities of its palace to address the problem itself.

The wyrm had attacked by surprise, in the middle of the night. Rhespen estimated that it had slaughtered half his men. Others, terrified, had scattered and were lost to him. He'd somehow managed to keep the rest together and to retreat with them under the cover of a conjured darkness and other sleights intended to hinder pursuit.

But he was certain that wasn't the end of it. The green would surely track them, and likely find them before the sun climbed into the sky.

He raked his fingers through his hair, struggling to devise a plan, then said, "We have to assume that for some reason, His Majesty didn't hear my call, which means we need to look after ourselves. Divide the men into four groups. Have them lie down and bury themselves in the snow there, there, there, and there." He pointed to indicate the proper spots.

Serdel frowned. "Do you think that will fool a drake, Milord?"

"Not by itself, but it's a start. Now move! The wyrm could appear at any moment."

As soon as the men-at-arms covered themselves over, Rhespen summoned several whirlwinds to smooth away the telltale signs of their burrowing. When the spirits of the air completed their work, only the footprints the soldiers had left prior to their division into the four squads remained.

He then conjured the illusion of fifty frightened warriors scurrying along, fast as the snowdrifts and their exhaustion would allow, at the terminus of the trail. Because the insubstantial phantoms couldn't make new tracks, the display had to remain more or less stationary, with the individual figures stepping in place, but he hoped that wouldn't be a problem. Dragons flew so fast that the green might well spot and overtake the illusion before it noticed the column wasn't making any forward progress.

The object was to give the reptile safe targets on which to waste its magic and poisonous breath. Though adult, it wasn't as huge and ancient as, say, Orchtrien, which meant it didn't command as many spells, and that its lethal spew took longer to renew itself after repeated discharge. It had already been profligate in its use of those resources during the initial attack. If Rhespen could trick it into exhausting the rest—

He smiled bitterly. Why, in that case, it would still be a wyrm, the most fearsome creature in the world, a behemoth quick and nimble as a cat, with scales as protective as plate, and claws and fangs capable of obliterating any lesser being with a single slash. Dragons sometimes killed each other, but it was preposterous to imagine that elves and men could do it.

Still, better to try than die a coward.

He summoned a spirit of earth and bade it lie quiet inside a patch of soil near his illusion, took up a position behind a gnarled, leafless birch, and shrouded himself in invisibility. After that, there was nothing to do but wait. He wondered how Winterflower fared, and if she would ever learn how he'd met his end.

Then the green came hurtling out of the north.

Its eyes glowed yellow, it appeared more charcoal-colored than green in the wan dawn-light, and hornlets jutted like warts from its brow and chin. A drake's senses were so sharp that it was by no means certain that either the warriors' covering of snow or Rhespen's own masking spell would keep it from detecting them, and he held his breath until the creature's headlong trajectory made it clear that it was intent only on the illusion.

He made the phantom warriors shriek and cringe, and when the reptile swept over them and spat its fumes, collapse as if the lungs had rotted in their chests. The green wheeled, snarled words of power, and tendrils of filthy-looking vapor oozed into existence among the figures on the ground. Rhespen commanded more of his puppets to stumble and drop.

But not all of them. He had to leave the green something to attack with tooth and talon, a reason to plunge to earth, and he needed the cursed reptile to do it soon, before it perceived the true nature of the targets he'd conjured to befuddle it.

It dived. It slammed down with a ground-shaking impact that would have pulverized any genuine creatures of flesh and bone caught underneath. It clawed and bit at several more of Rhespen's phantasms, at which point it unquestionably discerned their lack of substance.

He shifted the focus of his concentration to the waiting elemental, and the spirit exploded up out of the ground. A massive, almost shapeless thing compounded of rock and mud, it possessed an eyeless, featureless lump of a head, and long, flexible arms like enormous snakes with three-fingered hands at the ends. Its lower body was just a legless, undifferentiated mass linking it to the earth, but that didn't constrain its mobility. It could slide wherever it wished like a wave flowing on the surface of the sea.

It rushed the surprised green, seized hold of one of its batlike wings, and tore and twisted it, just as Rhespen had instructed. He knew his agent, mighty though it was, was no match for the dragon. But if it could deprive the green of its ability to fly before it perished, that would eliminate another of the reptile's advantages.

The green tried to wrench its wing up and out of the elemental's hands, but the spirit of earth maintained its hold. The drake contorted itself to bring its foreclaws and fangs to bear. It ripped chunks of its attacker's substance away.

Rhespen decided he needed to help his servant. He declaimed a spell and swept his staff in a mystic pass. A mass of snow rose from the ground, congealed into a long, glittering icicle, and flew at the green.

The spear of ice pierced the base of its neck, and the shock of the injury made it stiffen and falter in its attack. The elemental, or what was left of it, heaved on the wyrm's now-tattered wing, and bone snapped. A jagged stump of it jabbed outward through the reptile's hide.

The green tore the elemental to inert clods and stones with a final rake of its talons. Then, hissing in fury, crippled pinion drooping and dragging, it rounded on Rhespen, who'd relinquished his invisibility by flinging the frozen lance.

He should have been terrified, but he realized with a pang of surprise that he wasn't. Rather, relished the success of his tricks and the green's resulting discomfiture. Perhaps the prospect of his imminent demise had unhinged his reason.

The wyrm lifted its head and cocked it back. Its neck and chest swelled repeatedly, pumping like a bellows. A foul scent suffused the air, stinging Rhespen's eyes. Evidently the creature believed it could muster one more blast of venom.

Rhespen snatched a little cube of granite from one of his pockets, brandished it, and rattled off an intricate rhyme. The green's head shot forward, its jaws gaped, and at that instant, he declaimed the final syllable of his incantation. A plug of stone appeared in the back of the dragon's mouth. Instead of jetting forth at its intended target, the wyrm's breath spurted uselessly around the sides of the obstruction.

The green's head jerked up and down as it tried to spit out the stone that choked it.

"Now!" Rhespen bellowed. "Hit it now!"

Like the elemental before them, his men-at-arms

surged up from their places of concealment. As Rhespen had insured by their placement, and the positioning of his illusion, the dragon fought in the center of the four squads.

Spears and arrows flew. The majority glanced off the dragon's scales, but some penetrated. Raising his staff high, Rhespen created a mesh of sticky cables to bind the wyrm's head to the intact wing lashing atop its back. The idea was to hinder the green in its effort to retch the stone out, but its thrashing tore the web apart immediately.

The green's jaws clenched, the obstruction at the back of its mouth crunched, and it spat out the granite plug in fragments mixed with ivory shards of broken tooth. It oriented on one of the groups of warriors and took a stride, commencing its charge.

Rhespen conjured a burst of raw force, barely visible as a colorless ripple in the air. The attack jolted the green, bloodied its flank, and made it stumble.

"Over here, stupid!" he shouted. "I'm the one you want."

The maddened wyrm pivoted and ran at him. Rhespen stood his ground for as long as he dared. Every moment the drake focused on him was another moment his warriors could assail it in relative safety.

When it was several strides away, he released another of the spells bound in the truesilver rod. The enchantment of levitation shot him skyward like a cork bobbing to the surface of a pond.

The green's fangs clashed shut just below his feet. It reared up on its hind legs, snatched and narrowly missed again with its fore claws, then he rose too high for it to reach.

Meanwhile, arrows pierced the drake. When their missiles were exhausted, the men-at-arms drew swords, readied axes, screamed war cries, and charged in to cut and hack at their foe. No doubt they were afraid, but they also knew aggression was their only hope. If they didn't kill the green, it would surely slaughter them.

They instantly started dying. The dragon struck and caught two at once in its fangs. Its talons raked out the guts of a third, a flick of its tail pulped the torso of a fourth, and a swat from its wing broke the neck of a fifth. Yet the soldiers' blades gashed it in its turn, and its blood spurted to darken the snow.

Still floating above it—a position that allowed him to attack it without fear of striking his allies—Rhespen hammered it with spells of flame and blight. It kept on fighting. The elf took a chicken bone from one of his pockets, snapped it, and declaimed yet another incantation.

The green stumbled and shrieked as a number of its own bones fractured. The legs on its right side gave way, toppling it. It writhed, seemingly attempting to scramble back onto its feet, but it evidently couldn't accomplish that or anything else. Not yet. The pain of its internal injuries was simply too great.

Rhespen suspected the dragon's incapacity would only last a moment, but it provided an opportunity, and the men-at-arms took full advantage. Howling, they plunged their weapons into the green's body over and over again. Rhespen split its flank with a screech of focused noise.

The green thrashed. The warriors had to scramble back to avoid being crushed. Rhespen assumed the reptile would rise. But in fact, its convulsions gradually subsided, until at last it lay motionless, and the gleam in its yellow eyes dimmed away to nothing.

The warriors stared at the huge, gory corpse as if unable to believe what they were seeing. Then one cheered, and the others followed suit, the jubilant clamor echoing from the snowy hillsides.

Rhespen floated back down to the ground to join them, whereupon Serdel thumped his fist against his chest in salute. "Hail, dragon slayer," the soldier said.

The air was blessedly mild. The trees were putting forth tender new leaves, and meltwater murmured down the mountainsides in glistening torrents. It was all lovely, but on that day, though he was an elf, Rhespen had no inclination to stand and savor the sight. He was too eager to see Winterflower.

His men were equally eager to greet their loved ones and partake of the ease and rewards they'd earned, but that still didn't mean they could ascend the road to Dawnfire at speed. Over the course of the campaign, they'd lost the hearty war-horses they'd started out with to the weapons of their foes and the hardships of the season, and replaced them with whatever mounts they could steal. Those nags had been of indifferent quality to begin with, and hard use and hunger hadn't improved them. Their riders were lucky they could make the climb at all.

Before beginning, Rhespen dispatched a messenger from the fort at the foot of the mountains to ride ahead with the report he'd written and news of his impending arrival. He had a responsibility to inform Orchtrien of the outcome of his mission as soon as possible, and besides, if Winterflower learned he was mere hours away from the Bright City, perhaps she'd ride down to meet him.

But in fact, it was Maldur, dyed silver mane gleaming in the sunlight, who met him three quarters of the way up the highway.

"Welcome home, Milord," the human wizard said.

"Thank you," said Rhespen, perplexed.

Following their duel, he and Maldur had made some effort to obey Orchtrien's command and bury their rancor, but the dislike still simmered beneath the surface. Thus, it seemed unlikely that Maldur would volunteer to escort his rival into the city, yet it would be just as odd for the king to order one of his principal deputies to perform such a trivial task.

"According to your dispatch," Maldur said, "you performed brilliantly. I bring His Majesty's congratulations, along with clean garments, freshly groomed mounts, banners, and all the other appurtenances required to make a brave show as you ride to the palace in triumph." He waved his hand, sparkling with jewels, at the string of servants, horses, and laden donkeys behind him.

"That's excellent. The men deserve some acclaim for the job they've done."

"I'm sure." Maldur twisted in the saddle as if to give an order to the lackeys hovering behind him, then turned back around. "Oh, I nearly forgot. I have one more thing to tell you. A bit of news concerning one of the elf prisoners the king placed under your governance."

Rhespen's mouth felt dry as dust. "What is it?"

"For the past two months, Lady Winterflower has been the king's mistress." Until this moment, Maldur had kept his expression bland, but now a gloating smirk showed through. "The king thought it best you learn before entering the city. He thought it might forestall some manner of awkwardness."

"I . . . " Rhespen's fist clenched on the reins. "I'm not sure what you mean, Milord, but of course I appreciate the information. Tomorrow, or the next day, I'll have to check and see how all the hostages are getting along. For now, though, let's attend to the business at hand."

For the rest of the ride, Rhespen felt numb and sick. He told himself Maldur had lied, but couldn't make himself believe it. The human was spiteful, but also too proud to perpetrate a falsehood that must inevitably collapse as soon as Rhespen and Winterflower came together. In the aftermath, he'd look petty and ridiculous in everyone's eyes, including his own.

Even feeling as he did, Rhespen tried to acknowledge the cheers of the crowd, for his men's sake, and because it was an obligation of his station. It was obvious heralds had carried news of his exploits throughout the city—otherwise, folk wouldn't have understood what they were supposed to celebrate—and a good many people shouted, "Dragonslayer! Long live the dragonslayer!"

He steeled himself before entering Orchtrien's great

hall, but even so, faltered when he saw that the king had opted to preside over his court in the form of a bronze-skinned, topaz-eyed elf. There had to be a reason he favored that shape, and when Rhespen spotted Winterflower among the throng, it was plain what it was. She'd abandoned the clothing and jewelry she'd brought from her homeland, and likewise the love tokens he'd given her, in favor of all-new attire and ornaments agleam with gold. She smiled at him—he was, after all, the guardian who'd treated her kindly—but the expression betrayed no excitement and promised nothing. The warmth came back into her face when she returned her gaze to the dragon on his throne.

I truly have lost her, Rhespen thought. Grief and fury surged up inside him, and he strained to hold them in. Because he hadn't lost everything, no matter how it felt. He still had his position, the life he'd worked so hard to achieve, and he wouldn't throw them away with an hysterical outburst. He wouldn't give them—Maldur, Orchtrien, and Winterflower herself—the satisfaction.

He kneeled before the dais and laid his staff at his master's feet.

"Rise," Orchtrien boomed. "Rise, my friend, and let me look at you. Stone and sky, you're thin as a straw!"

"It's a pleasure to see Your Majesty again. As I hope was clear from my report, the warriors you gave me performed wonders in your service."

"As did you. You actually killed one of the greens, all by yourselves?"

"We had little choice. I called for help, but neither you nor any of the princes appeared to succor us." He hadn't meant to bring it up, but somehow it slipped out anyway.

Orchtrien hesitated for a heartbeat then said, "The message never reached me."

"Of course, Majesty. I assumed that for whatever reason, the magic failed."

"Be glad it did. Your victory over the green demonstrated your prowess as nothing else could. In a month or so, when we march to war in earnest, you'll be one of my chief marshals."

Rhespen reminded himself it was what he'd always wanted, and struggled to appear grateful. "Thank you, Majesty. I'll strive to be worthy of your trust."

Orchtrien smiled. "But not immediately. You've striven enough for the time being, and now I want you to relax and enjoy yourself."

Relax and enjoy himself. In its way, it was a royal command, and Rhespen endeavored to obey it like any other of Orchtrien's orders. He choked down delicacies that weighed in his stomach like stones, guzzled drink that tangled his feet and tongue but only darkened his mood, and bedded ladies and servant girls whose affections left him feeling lonely and hollow even at the moment of release. Through it all, he smiled and chattered as the court expected, and whatever the entertainment, be it banquet, hunt, ball, or play, endeavored to ignore Winterflower's presence.

But a royal favorite had no reasonable hope of avoiding proximity to the king's mistress, and besides, for all his intentions to the contrary, Rhespen often found his eyes drawn to her. He supposed it was the same impulse that prompted a person to pick at a scab, or to probe a sore tooth with his tongue.

So it was that he stared after her as Orchtrien escorted her out of a masked revel. She apparently said something flirtatious, because the transformed dragon laughed and took her in his arms. As they embraced, Rhespen could see Winterflower's face with its winged half-mask of white swan feathers over his master's shoulder. For just a moment, it was as if a second mask dissolved away behind the first, and she regarded him with the same desperate, miserable expression she'd worn the first time the king danced with her. Then her eyes sparkled once more, and her amorous smile returned. His arm around her waist, Orchtrien led her onward, no doubt to the bed they shared.

At the center of Dawnfire stood the royal palace, a sprawling hive that was home to a legion of servants, guards, and courtiers. Within that complex rose the high keep containing Orchtrien's personal apartments, and the quarters of those he wanted closest. Prowling the benighted garden adjacent to the tower's southern aspect, inhaling the fragrance of brunfelsia, Rhespen pondered how best to slip inside, and wondered too if he was mad.

Wasn't it likely that, half-drunk as he'd been, he'd imagined Winterflower's momentary change of expression? Even if he hadn't, even if she was secretly unhappy, what could he do about it? Nothing! Whereas he was all too likely to forfeit his life by probing any further into the matter.

Yet something inside him demanded to know the truth. He shifted his shoulders to work the tension out, gripped his staff, and strode to the keep's primary entrance.

At the top of the steps leading to the arched double doors, a long-legged pair of half-dragon guards saluted. "Milord," they said in unison. "The king isn't in residence tonight," the one on the right continued.

"I know," Rhespen said. He'd chosen tonight for this harebrained escapade precisely because Orchtrien had flown south to confer with barons busy recruiting and training warriors to replace those slain in last year's battles. He drew twin pulses of power from his staff. The half-dragons swayed, and their eyes opened wide, as the magic touched their minds. "But I need to retrieve an important document I left inside. So please, admit me."

Ordinarily, they might not have cooperated, his rank notwithstanding. But thanks to the charms he'd cast, they trusted him completely, and made haste to swing open the small door set in the middle of the huge, dragon-sized one on the right.

Once they closed it again, leaving him to his own devices, he took a wary glance about to make sure nobody else was watching. No one was, so he whispered the words to veil himself in invisibility, then stalked onward, his elven boots muffling the sound of his passage through the sleeping tower's hushed and shadowy chambers.

Orchtrien invariably installed his mistresses in the apartments directly above his own; it was an open secret that a concealed staircase connected one bedchamber with the other. As he approached the entrance to Winterflower's suite, Rhespen was disheartened to see that no additional sentries guarded the way. Their absence cast doubt on the forlorn hope that the king was somehow compelling the elf girl to serve as his concubine.

I could still turn back, Rhespen thought, *before I humiliate myself or worse.* Instead, he touched the head of his staff to the door. The lock clicked, disengaging, and the panel swung ajar.

He closed it behind him and stalked on through the darkened apartment. He found Winterflower lying on a couch in front of an open casement, immersed in Reverie or simply staring into the gloom. Whichever it was, she bolted upright as soon as he dissolved his spell of concealment.

"Milord!" she exclaimed, glaring. "Are you insane, to intrude here?"

"Probably, for I perceive that I'm unwelcome."

"Of course you are."

"From which I infer that the look you gave me meant nothing."

"I don't even know what you're talking about."

"Then I'll leave. Unless you'd care to scream for the guards." He realized he didn't much care if she did or not.

"I should. You've betrayed the king, compromised me—" Her face twisted. She snatched hold of his hand and squeezed it hard. "What am I saying? Forgive me!"

He shook his head. "To forgive, I need to understand."

Still clasping his fingers, she rose. "You're a true wizard, not a dabbler like me. I assumed you could tell. After he sent you away, Orchtrien labored tirelessly to seduce me, and always I refused him, even when he hinted that my 'ingratitude' might prompt him to hurt my kin. Until finally, weary of coaxing and threatening, he laid an enchantment on me."

"To alter your affections?" Elves possessed a degree of resistance to magic that clouded and altered thought, but of course no one was impervious to dragon sorcery.

"Yes. Most of the time, I adore him, and yearn for his touch. Only rarely do I remember myself, and my true feelings, and only for a little while." She smiled bitterly. "So you see, there's the real reason no maiden has ever declined to become his harlot."

"It's monstrous."

"I don't suppose Orchtrien sees it as any different than when a person like us trains a hound or a horse. At any rate, I'm glad you know. I wouldn't want you to believe I forsook you of my own free will. Now you truly should go, before you're discovered. Just be happy, and remember me."

"I won't abandon you to this slavery. We'll run away together."

"As you once explained to me, Orchtrien would find us, and all the more easily since I'd struggle with all my strength and wits to make my way back to him."

"I'll lift the curse."

"I know you'd try, but you also told me that neither you nor any other elf commands magic to rival Orchtrien's."

He felt queasy with helplessness, then an idea struck him. It was reckless, mad, but perhaps that was what the situation required.

"No," he said, "not yet."

"What do you mean?"

"For the time being, it's better you don't know, lest you succumb to an urge to tell Orchtrien. It's better if you don't even recall I was here." He twirled his hand through a mystic pass, touched her forehead, and caught her as she fainted. "Forget, and endure a little longer."

Like Orchtrien's personal residence, the sanctum where he and the princes practiced their sorcery was a tower with gardens growing all around. Over time, the forces leaking from behind the thick granite walls had warped the blossoms and shrubs into growths unknown to nature. As Rhespen prowled along, making his reconnaissance, a pine tree writhed, and the needles clashed softly, as if they were made of metal. Pale, fleshy flowers with lidless eyes at their centers twisted to watch as he passed.

Before the high iron door stood the semblance of a dragon shaped from the same metal. Though motionless at the moment, Rhespen was sure it would spring to life if anyone approached too close, and that when it did, it would take more than a spell of friendship and a halfway plausible excuse to make it step aside. He also suspected that a simple charm of invisibility wouldn't deceive it.

Best to avoid it entirely, then. The only way to accomplish that was to shift himself through space and into the spire blind, with no foreknowledge of exactly where he'd end up. He might appear right in front of a second sentinel. He might even materialize in a space already occupied by another solid object, and thereby injure himself.

Still, it seemed the best option, so he whispered the proper words and sketched a mystic sign. For a moment, his fingertip left a shimmering trail in the air.

The world shattered into scraps of light and dark, and the fragments leaped at him, or at least that was how it seemed. Then he stood on a stone floor in a shadowy chamber.

He turned, looking for threats, and saw nothing but walls, doorways, and the iron portal with, presumably, the dragon statue still oblivious and inert on the other side.

The absence of immediate danger was only marginally reassuring. Confident of their prowess, Orchtrien and his progeny used only warriors and walls, commonplace measures, to protect their residences and thus their persons. Indeed, one could almost surmise that the golds only bothered with bodyguards and such because they comprised part of the customary pomp and display of a royal court. But they'd taken greater care to preserve the arcane secrets of dragonkind, and Rhespen suspected the iron wyrm wasn't the only guardian—or guardian enchantment—they'd emplaced to foil intruders.

Could he cope? He supposed he'd find out soon enough.

He veiled himself in invisibility—it might help and likely wouldn't hurt—and quickened his eyes with the ability to perceive mystical forces. He'd hoped the enhancement to his vision would enable him to avoid magical snares and likewise help guide him to his goal, and so it might, but only if he peered carefully. Over the centuries, arcane power had so permeated the very substance of the keep that every surface and stone seemed to shimmer. It would be difficult to pick out particular patterns of energy from the overall glow.

He stalked onward, through a succession of conjuration chambers, where artisans or magic had inlaid complex pentacles in gold, silver, jade, onyx, agate, and lapis lazuli on the floors. Many of the forms, and the symbols inscribed along the arcs and angles, were strange to him. He could have gleaned a great deal from them, but only if he'd had the leisure to study them for months or years. As matters stood, he needed a more readily accessible source of knowledge.

It didn't appear to exist on the ground floor, but he explored the area thoroughly without discovering a ready means of ascending to the levels above. Squinting, he scrutinized the ceilings with his magesight, and finally found a hanging whirlpool of phosphorescence that indicated the presence of an illusion. Appearances to the contrary, that particular patch of ceiling didn't exist. Rather, it was an opening, the first of a series positioned one above the other. A creature as huge and agile as a wyrm could easily employ them to scramble up and down.

Rhespen used a spell of levitation to accomplish the same thing. He explored the second story, where kilns, alembics, shelves of jars and bottles, and mazes of glass tubing attested to studies in alchemy, then started floating up to the third. He was partway there when he heard a soft dragging overhead. From long experience, he recognized the whisper of a dragon's tail sweeping across a floor.

A heartbeat later, the darkness above Rhespen changed. It had shape and solidity, and it plunged at him. The gold couldn't spread its wings and fly through what were, for a creature of its immensity, relatively narrow openings, but it was too impatient to climb or float down. So, confident that it could weather the shock of impact, it had simply jumped.

That meant Rhespen had only an instant left to haul himself out of the way. No handhold was in reach, and the charm of levitation could only carry him straight up or down. He bade it jerk him upward fast as it could, until he could plant his hands on the alchemical level's ceiling and pull himself along it like a fly crawling upside down.

As soon as he cleared the opening, the dragon plummeted by, so close he could have reached out and touched it. He only saw it for an instant before it plunged on out of sight, but even so, he recognized Prince Bexendral.

The important question, of course, was whether Bexendral had noticed him. It was entirely possible, his invisibility notwithstanding. A dragon's nose was sharp enough to catch his scent, and its ears, to register the pounding of his heart. He waited motionless, scarcely daring to breathe, until he heard the iron door groan open and clang shut. Evidently the prince hadn't detected him. Perhaps Bexendral had been preoccupied, or maybe he'd simply hurtled by too quickly.

Rhespen struggled to calm his jangled nerves, then

ventured onward until, nearly to the top of the keep, he found the library.

One great chamber occupied the entire floor. Some of the books and scrolls were of conventional size. Any elf or human scholar could have managed them conveniently, and Rhespen inferred that drakes capable of changing shape must have written them. Most of the volumes, however, were huge, and composed of substances more durable than parchment, ink, and leather. One wyrm had etched its lore on copper plates stitched together with a silver chain. Another had scratched glyphs onto octagons of teak, while a third had employed oblong sandstone tablets resembling the lids of sarcophagi. When Rhespen examined the collection with his magesight, it shined as though aflame.

He took an eager stride forward, and only then noticed the shifting stripes of crimson light masked by the general blaze, at the same moment that a gate between worlds yawned open. He couldn't see it, but he felt it as a gnawing, nauseating wound in the fabric of reality. Then something surged through.

For an instant, he mistook it for a dragon, simply by virtue of its size, for it was big enough that no smaller chamber could easily have contained it. But its shape was altogether different, with nothing of a drake's grace or beauty. It was a towering, bipedal mound of a thing, with a lashing prehensile tail terminating in a coal-black stinger, a dozen mismatched, many-jointed arms sporting one or more talons, and a head that was virtually all mouth lined with row upon row of tusks. Despite Rhespen's invisibility, it oriented on him immediately.

He'd never encountered such a horror before, but from his studies recognized it as a ghargatula, which was to say, a sort of devil. Evidence that Orchtrien, for all his pretensions to being nobler than the chromatic wyrms, wasn't above trafficking with infernal powers.

Frightened as Rhespen was, that insight steadied him, rekindled his anger at Orchtrien, and reminded him of the rightness of his cause. I slew the green, he told himself, and I can kill this thing, too.

But he'd need protection. He rattled off an incantation and sketched a glyph on the air. Figures identical in every way to himself, three-dimensional reflections created without the instrumentality of mirrors, sprang into existence all around him.

The ghargatula's sting whipped around its massive body and struck one of the images, popping it like a soap bubble. Good. That meant the gigantic fiend couldn't tell the difference between the real Rhespen and the false ones.

Of course, at any given moment, it might still target the genuine article by chance, and even if it didn't, it wouldn't take it long to obliterate all the phantoms. As the ghargatula crouched low, compressing its ungainly form, to destroy a second illusion with its fangs, Rhespen declaimed another spell, whereupon he started shifting rapidly back and forth between the material world and a higher level of reality. During those moments when he was elsewhere, the devil shouldn't be able to touch or even see him.

Like the phantom duplicates, the trick was a useful but less than perfect defense. Rhespen could only hope that, functioning in tandem, they'd prove sufficient. He brandished his staff and hurled a blast of flame at the ghargatula.

As far as he could tell, the attack had no effect. The devil eradicated another illusion with a jab of its claws.

He battered it with conjured hailstones. That didn't appear to hurt it, either. Obviously, like many spirits, it was essentially impervious to certain forces. But he couldn't remember which ones, and could only pray to discover its vulnerabilities by trial and error before it succeeded in landing an attack.

He splashed it with steaming acid, and that was useless, too. It still squatted low, and its gaping jaws leaped at him. He smelled its fetid breath—actually felt the points of gigantic fangs as they snapped shut on his body—then he was a wraith once more, and the teeth passed harmlessly through him. He scrambled clear of the ghargatula's mouth before his body could slip back into the sphere of solid matter.

He pierced his foe with darts of force, and at last it hissed and jerked in pain. He cast such spells for as long as he could, then switched to bright, crackling flares of lightning. The thunderbolts charred it and made it convulse.

Yet when Rhespen expended the last of his lightning, the behemoth was still on its feet. Its flanks heaving, arms and stinger lashing, it lunged forward.

Rhespen retreated. Glancing about, he saw that he only had a single duplicate left. His jumps between planes were slowing as the enchantment that enabled them ran out of power.

If the gods were kind, he might have time for one more spell before the ghargatula plunged its fangs, talons, or stinger into him. But perhaps that was all right. With his weapons—the effective ones, anyway—all expended, he only had one more tactic, one final forlorn hope, to try anyway.

He raised the truesilver staff in both hands, high above his head and parallel to the floor, and declaimed the opening phrases of his spell. He tried to make the cadence and intonation precise, and to invest the words of power with all the concentration and willpower he could muster. To believe that the magic would prevail was the only way to make it perfect, and he was certain nothing less would do.

The ghargatula reared above him, and hurtled down like an avalanche, jaws spread wide. He chanted the final word of his incantation, and green light suffused the devil's form as if it were burning from the inside out. In an instant, its form dissolved, leaving only a luminous haze behind to fade gradually away.

Panting, trembling, Rhespen marveled at his luck.

Killing the ghargatula would have been a considerable feat, but as far as he was concerned, he'd accomplished something even more extraordinary by returning it to its own infernal domain. That had required breaking the enchantment that summoned and controlled it, which was to say, overcoming Orchtrien's mystical power with his own.

It shouldn't have worked. The gold was by far the superior mage. That was the point of the whole lunatic enterprise. But because of the element of chaos intrinsic to sorcery, it was theoretically possible for any magician to break the enchantment of any other, and tonight he'd proven the theory valid.

Which, he realized with a stab of alarm, didn't mean he was out of danger. He'd activated a ward that had unleashed the ghargatula on him. What if the same magic had also alerted Orchtrien that an intruder had entered the library?

Rhespen listened for sounds emanating from elsewhere in the keep, and heard nothing. With his mystical sensitivities, he examined the ether around him. It didn't appear that anyone was about to teleport into the chamber.

So apparently he was all right. He flourished his staff and shifted and molded the ambient patterns of magical force as a painter might swirl and blend paint on a palette, recreating an approximation of the red bands he'd noticed before. They were inert, but if one of the golds glanced around the room with magesight and didn't look too closely, he might think the broken ward was still intact.

Rhespen extracted a series of tiny objects from his pockets and set them on the floor. He waved his hand over them, and they swelled into normal-sized pens, bottles of ink, and blank books. He then called on certain spirits of the air, who revealed their presence by taking up the writing implements and beginning to copy the contents of several of the dragons' grimoires. The quills flew and the pages turned with supernatural rapidity.

⊛ ⊛ ⊛ ⊛ ⊛

Rhespen set his hand on Winterflower's head and whispered words of power that sent the shadows spinning around the darkened chamber. Every magician learned spells to dissolve the works and break the bindings of another, but he felt at once that this one was different. His arm burned with power straining for release.

On the final syllable, it blazed from his flesh into hers. She jerked, but afterward eyed him uncertainly.

Assailed by doubt, he asked, "Do you feel any different?"

"I . . . think so," she said.

"The counterspell was supposed to break Orchtrien's hold on you. I was certain—"

"By the Winsome Rose, you're right! I'm myself again! It just took a moment for me to realize." She threw herself into his embrace, and for a while, they were too busy to talk. But finally she asked, "How? How did you kill him? Did you take him in his sleep?"

He blinked in surprise. "I didn't have to kill him to liberate you. The magic cleansed you all by itself. I stole his secrets to obtain the proper counterspell. They're right there." He nodded toward the haversack containing the copybooks, shrunken again for ease of transport, where it sat on a chair with his rod leaning beside it.

Now it was her turn to seem nonplussed.

"It will be all right," he assured her. "I now possess all the lore Orchtrien does. I haven't crammed every bit of it into my head yet, but it's in that bag, available for use. That means we can run far away, and he won't be able to track us. I can block his attempts at divination."

She gave her head a little shake, as if to snap her thoughts into focus. "That's wonderful. How will you sneak the secrets—and me, of course—out of the city?"

He grinned. "That's the easy part. I have a spell of teleportation stored in my staff. Grab anything you wish to carry with you, and I'll whisk us both away."

"I only want my jewelry box." She turned to fetch it, and something banged. Rhespen realized it must be the door, flying open and smashing into the wall. Running footsteps pounded toward the bedchamber.

Startled, he hesitated. Dazzling light blazed, filling the air, blinding and disorienting him. When the glare died, his tortured eyes could just make out, through floating blobs of afterimage, Maldur, ivory wand in hand, and the several half-dragon crossbowmen he'd brought along with him.

"These fellows," the human wizard said, "are watching you closely. Start murmuring an incantation under your breath, begin an occult gesture, or ease a hand toward one of your pockets, and they'll shoot."

"How did you know?" Rhespen asked. He didn't really care how, but if he could get Maldur talking, gloating, it would give him time to try to figure a way out of his trap.

He told himself there had to be a way. It was ridiculous to think that he, who had defeated a ghargatula, might prove unable to cope with half a dozen humans. But actually, he knew such could easily prove to be the case. Wizards were mighty, but only when given a chance to bring their powers to bear. When not, they were as vulnerable as anyone else.

"When you came home," Maldur said, "and found out that this damsel had become the king's whore, it broke you. I have made a study of you and could tell, no matter how you tried to hide it. I watched with satisfaction to see you wither away, but you didn't. The iron came back into your nature, and at the same time, you started to betray signs of exhaustion. I inferred that you were visiting Lady Winterflower at times when the king was elsewhere, but no matter how hard I tried, I couldn't catch you sneaking in or out. Not until tonight."

"Because," Rhespen said, "I haven't been coming here. I spent my nights in study of new magic. Tendays ago, I sneaked into the golds' tower of magic and copied all the grimoires."

Maldur's eyes widened. "Impossible."

"No, merely difficult. The lore I stole, all the secrets of draconic sorcery, is in that pouch." He nodded at the haversack.

Rhespen was reasonably sure Maldur would turn in that direction. The white-haired man was, after all, a magician, surely avidly curious, jealous of the arcane might of the wyrms no matter how he tried to suppress such dangerous feelings. He hoped the guards would reflexively shift their eyes as well.

Because he only needed to distract them long enough to speak a single word of power. He whispered the first syllable, and crossbows clacked. Pain stabbed into his guts.

His knees buckling, he denied the agony long enough to grit out the remaining syllables. Magic chimed through the air, and his enemies dropped. The half-dragons were quite possibly dead, or failing that, unconscious. But thanks, perhaps, to some talisman or enchantment of protection, Maldur was merely stunned. Shuddering, blood streaming from his nose, teeth bared in a snarl of effort, he shook his head and managed to raise himself to his knees.

He struggled, too, to level his wand.

Rhespen attempted a second spell and immediately botched it. The excruciating fire in his midsection, the trembling of his hands, and the choked rasp of his voice, made precision impossible. But if he could get his hands on his staff, perhaps he could still shift Winterflower and himself away from here before Maldur recovered sufficiently to stop them.

He looked for Winterflower, and rejoiced to see that she'd already had the sense to pick up the staff and the haversack, too. Then she released the teleport spell he'd bound in the rod and vanished.

He goggled after her in astonishment and horror, until a blast of force from Maldur's wand slammed him into oblivion.

◎ ◎ ◎ ◎ ◎

Rhespen woke lying on a rack, his wrists and ankles manacled to the torture apparatus and a vile-tasting leather gag in his raw, dry mouth. Such restraints were an effective way of ensuring that a magician couldn't cast spells.

He wondered if he could have cast them in any case. A healer had evidently tended the multiple puncture wounds in his guts. Otherwise, he might well have succumbed to them already, or failing that, remained unconscious or delirious. But they still throbbed so fiercely he could scarcely bear it, and he felt as weak and feverish as he was parched.

He lay alone in the dungeon for what seemed an eternity, until he wondered if a slow, agonizing, solitary death by thirst was the punishment Orchtrien had decreed for him. But finally footsteps sounded on the stairs. Rhespen turned his head to see the king himself, wearing his elf shape, descending.

Orchtrien extracted the gag from Rhespen's mouth.

"Maldur begged me to put him in charge of your interrogation and punishment," said the gold. "I'm considering it."

Rhespen tried to answer, but his voice was inaudible. Orchtrien unstoppered a leather bottle and held it to his lips.

"I'm told you must content yourself with just a swallow at first, lest it make you sick."

Despite his pain and fear, the cold water sliding down his throat gave Rhespen a moment of bliss, the last such he might ever know.

"Thank you, Majesty," he croaked.

"Thank me by answering my questions truthfully. It may go easier for you if you do. You told Maldur you copied my grimoires. I'd hoped it was simply a lie, a distraction, but I've since discovered that something broke my ghargatula's tether, so I suppose it must be true."

"Yes."

"And Winterflower absconded with the texts."

"Yes." Abandoning Rhespen in the process. He could only assume she'd been too panicked to linger long enough to dart across the floor, grab his hand, and carry him along with her.

"Where did she go?"

"I don't know. We hadn't decided on a destination."

"Curse it, anyway! Why did you betray me, Rhespen? Haven't I given you everything?"

"Everything but what I wanted most. When I begged for that, you sent me away to die."

"No!" The gold hesitated. "Well, all right, that possibility was in my mind. I wanted her, and no hunter likes it when someone tries to balk him in the pursuit of his chosen prey. I was annoyed with you, but by no means certain you'd die. I thought it more likely that your exile would simply cure you of your infatuation and your impudence. And that if you succeeded in your mission, the rewards would more than compensate you for the loss of a woman, however fetching."

"If you didn't want me dead, why didn't you respond to my call?"

"If I, or one of the princes, had crossed the river, all the greens, and all their warriors, would have turned out to fight us. I wanted winter raiding, not all-out war."

"And such strategic considerations aside, you were chastising me, even if it wasn't supposed to result in my demise."

"Just so. But when you returned victorious, your punishment was over. I wasn't angry anymore. I meant it when I lavished honors on you. Why couldn't you put the episode behind us?"

"Perhaps I would have," Rhespen said, "in time. But then I learned that Winterflower hadn't yielded to you of her own free will. You chained her mind and spirit with the foulest sort of sorcery."

Orchtrien stared at his prisoner in seeming amazement, then laughed. "My poor friend. My poor fool. Mind you, I'm not much better. She cozened me as well. She convinced me she truly had come to love me."

"She . . . what?"

"I give you my word as a king and a gold dragon, I never cast any sort of spell on the lady, certainly not a coercion as abominable as that." Orchtrien sighed. "In retrospect, it's easy enough to see what happened. When Duskmere and his confederates lured your company into a trap, it was a useless, ill-considered tactic, born of anger rather than guile. But after Bexendral defeated them, they began to exercise their wits, and when I demanded hostages, they sent us a spy and a witch, to accomplish whatever harm she could. To that end, she established a liaison with you."

"No. That can't be. She despised me at first. I had to win her trust and affection."

"She made you think so, and me as well. She had to. Given her pedigree, we would have grown suspicious if she'd warmed to us too easily, and as I observed previously, her initial disdain made us prize her subsequent affection all the more. I wonder if she also used enchantment to make herself more appealing."

"She had no grimoire."

"That we discovered."

"If she'd cast a glamour on herself, one of us would have noticed. She had some rudimentary magical skills, but she wasn't a true wizard."

"Or so she told you. She was adept enough to snatch up your staff and use it instantly. Either way, it doesn't matter. Once you succumbed to her charms, she could attempt various ploys. She could try to wheedle secrets out of you, or subvert your loyalty and turn you into a rebel, too."

"Until you sent me away and took her for yourself."

"Yes. I daresay she had mixed feelings about being a royal mistress. It must have been difficult for her, loathing me as she did. She must have lived in constant fear that I, with my discernment and arcane powers, would unmask her. Yet she was in a still better position to spy, or even attempt regicide when I seemed most vulnerable, though she never mustered the nerve and stupidity required for the latter."

"Until I came home."

"Yes, whereupon she tried to manipulate you into serving as her assassin. Without suggesting it directly, of course. She knew you almost certainly wouldn't succeed, but even if I killed you, the realm would be the weaker for it, and perhaps she imagined that the ensuing commotion would provide her an opportunity to escape with whatever secrets she'd discovered.

"Unfortunately," Orchtrien continued, "her dupe succumbed to her blandishments as usual, but didn't behave precisely as she'd expected. You too went digging for secrets, in a place where she herself would never have dared to intrude. Now she's carried all that lore away, and I'll have to put off marching against the reds to recover it."

"Majesty," Rhespen said, "if what you're saying is true—"

"Of course it's true! Why would I bother lying to a creature in your situation?"

"Then I've wronged you, my benefactor, my liege lord, in thought and deed, and I beg for the chance to atone. Let me help retrieve the books."

"Traitors," Orchtrien said, "don't get second chances."

He jammed the gag back into Rhespen's mouth.

After Orchtrien's departure, Rhespen lay struggling to disbelieve the dragon's assertions. He couldn't. They made too much sense.

Winterflower had made him her pawn, led him into treason and stripped him of his honor and everything else he possessed, then abandoned him as soon as it became expedient. The shame and humiliation of it were unbearable.

But he had to not only endure but transcend them.

Otherwise, he'd rot and suffer in his cell until the king's servants either killed him there or led him forth to the scaffold.

That might happen anyway, because Orchtrien had every right to think him helpless. But in point of fact, Rhespen had long ago bound himself to his staff. The link was what enabled him to call the rod into his hands.

He'd always spoken a word of command to facilitate the process. His captors no doubt assumed it was a necessity, and it was entirely possible they were right. Rhespen hoped, however, that if he exerted all his willpower, and simply articulated the word in his thoughts, it might suffice.

He made the attempt repeatedly, while spasms wracked his guts, and shame, fury, and dread gnawed at his concentration. For what seemed a long while, nothing happened. Then the cool, rounded rod materialized in his left hand.

Its sudden appearance startled him, and for an instant, he was terrified that he'd fumble and drop it, whereupon the clang would summon a guard, or else he'd lack the mystical strength to draw it back into his grasp a second time, even though it was just a pace or two away. He gripped it with all his meager strength and succeeded in holding on to it.

In addition to the temporary spells he stored in it based on his anticipation of his needs, the rod possessed a few permanent virtues. One was the power that had unlocked the door to Winterflower's suite. He invoked the same attribute, and his shackles flew open. So did the buckle securing the gag.

He stood up. The dungeon spun, pain stabbed through his belly, and he had to clutch at the rack to keep from falling. He whispered his charm of renewed vitality. It steadied him and blunted the agony, but he was still weak. Truly potent healing magic was the province of the gods and their priests, and thus beyond the reach of even the ablest wizard.

Such being the case, he was in no shape for a fight, or

even to cast spells of any complexity. Fortunately, he still had several enchantments of stealth and disguise stored in his staff, where he'd placed them in case he needed them to sneak into Winterflower's apartments.

He veiled himself in invisibility. Then, employing his staff as if it were a crutch, he hobbled up the stairs, unlocked the door at the top with a touch of his prop, and passed on into the dank, torchlit corridor beyond.

Working on the reasonable assumption that Winterflower had fled back to her kin and the rest of the rebels, Orchtrien had marched his army into the forest where they dwelled, only to find their treetop towns and fortresses deserted. The Count of Duskmere had led his allies to some hidden stronghold deeper in the wood, and if the king wished to retrieve his stolen secrets, he had no choice but to pursue and attempt to track his enemies down.

As the trees and brush grew thicker, and the way more difficult, the royal army had to stop more and more often to rest and regroup. Whenever it did, Rhespen, cloaked in the image of a human spearman, slipped away by himself. His comrades thought nothing of it. They'd grown used to what they took to be his odd and solitary disposition.

The reality, of course, was otherwise. He needed solitude to perform his divinations. It would hardly do for the other warriors to catch him engaging in occult ritual.

With the tip of his staff, which now appeared to be a common lance, he scratched a mystical figure in the loam then stared at the round empty space at the center. It was a window, through which he hoped to glimpse the objects of his search. But nothing appeared, and when it became apparent that nothing would, his mouth tightened in frustration.

After carrying the copybooks away from Orchtrien's keep, he'd placed a ward on the forbidden texts that would warn him if anyone else found and touched them.

Winterflower, or one of her fellow rebels, had discharged the enchantment while Rhespen lay insensible in the dungeon. But he'd hoped that a trace of the link connecting the volumes to himself remained, and that the connection might enable him to scry for them where even the dragon monarch had failed.

But evidently not. He rubbed out the magical figure with the toe of his boot, looked up, and discovered a raven, head cocked, beady eyes bright, perched on a branch above his head. He caught his breath.

Anticipating that his divinations might fail, he'd convinced some of his friends among the birds to scout for him. The most difficult part had been making them understand that they needed to keep their distance until such time as they actually made a discovery. He couldn't let his fellow soldiers observe him conversing with ravens, either.

"What is it, Thorn?" he asked. After so many years of practice, the croaks and chirps were fairly easy.

"What do you think?" the raven snapped. "I found them!"

In his excitement, Rhespen nearly asked where, but caught himself in time. Thorn wouldn't be able to tell him, because he had no conception of the units of measurement elves and humans used, and Rhespen lacked any familiarity with the landmarks in this portion of the forest.

He glanced around, making sure once again that no one watched, then whispered an incantation, brandished a talisman, and dwindled into a creature virtually identical to the black bird overhead.

He beat his wings, rose into the air, and rasped, "Show me."

As it turned out, the rebel stronghold was nearby. But it was well hidden, and Rhespen suspected that without the aid of sorcery and flying scouts, the royal army could blunder about for a long while before discovering it.

It was a crude place compared to the settlements the elves had abandoned. Their former habitations were works of art, conceived for beauty as much as utility, constructed with painstaking care, and polished and perfected through the centuries. In contrast, it was plain that they'd fashioned their new treetop bastions in haste, and that concealment and defense had been their sole considerations.

Wearing his true body, and a shroud of invisibility, once more, Rhespen scrutinized the fortress, forming an impression of the general layout, then inscribed another scrying pentacle in the dirt. Because he was so close to the copybooks, a vision appeared where none had manifested before.

He beheld a number of elf mages absorbed in study of the pilfered texts, in a room where golden sunlight spilled through tall, narrow windows. The magic likewise gave him a sense of the chamber's location high in a shadowtop. At first glance, the gigantic tree, like its companions, resembled a pure manifestation of nature, untouched by artifice. But if a knowledgeable observer peered for a while, he began to notice the ramparts, the stairs, the places where the shadowtop had obediently hollowed itself to make halls and galleries, until he discerned that it was in fact the equivalent of a mighty keep, and the hub of a network of fortifications.

I know everything now, Rhespen thought. I can lead Orchtrien straight to the books. I should go back, reveal myself, and tell him so.

Yet he wasn't certain of that. The king had expressly refused him the opportunity to attempt to atone for his crimes, and if he simply offered information, might continue to treat him as a traitor. Orchtrien might believe that his own magic or aerial reconnaissance would have led him to the elves' stronghold in another day or so, and indeed, that was entirely possible.

But if I present him with the books themselves, Rhespen reasoned, surely that will constitute such an impressive act of restitution that he'll have no choice but to forgive me.

It would, moreover, afford him an opportunity to strike at some of the cursed rebels directly, not just slink about and spy on them. Since Winterflower had forsaken him, he'd had no opportunity to avenge himself on anyone, and his anger was a clenched, choking weight inside him.

He murmured an incantation. The world shattered, restored itself in a different configuration, and he stood in one corner of the elf wizards' sanctum. Thus far, he was still invisible, and despite the puff of displaced air, no one noticed his arrival. Thank the gods for open windows, and the breezes that blew through them.

He whispered words of power, brandished his rod, and power blazed from the end. The force was psychic in nature, incapable of disturbing physical reality but devastating to the ethereal substance of the mind. Some of the assembled scholars immediately fell unconsciousness. Others thrashed in the throes of epileptic seizures.

Either way, they no longer posed a threat, and he felt tempted to slaughter them all while they lay helpless. But perhaps that would be dishonorable, and in any case, it would be reckless to linger here any longer than necessary.

Instead, visible once more, he scurried about collecting the copybooks, making sure he found them all, shrunk them, and stuffed them in his backpack. Then he chanted the opening words of the spell that would whisk him back to the royal army.

During a necessary pause, he heard another voice whispering an incantation of its own. Alarmed, he tried to pick up the tempo and finish first, but the other spell-caster had too much of a lead.

She bobbed up from behind a table on the far side of the chamber, thrust out her hand, and a shaft of green light leaped from her fingertips. Rhespen tried to dodge, but was too slow. The beam struck him, and he experienced a momentary feeling of crushing weight, as well as a fleeting sensation that his feet had taken root in the floor.

He recognized what had happened. His foe had laid an enchantment on him, and while it lasted, it would keep him from fleeing the scene by magical means.

He lifted his staff to blast the female mage and so prevent her from hindering him any further. But before he could act, she flopped backward and sprawled motionless on the floor. Evidently, in the wake of the psychic assault, she'd needed a supreme effort just to cast the one spell.

Still, unlike her colleagues, she'd clung to consciousness, which suggested that she possessed more willpower and sorcerous ability than any of the rest. It seemed a bad idea to allow her to gather her strength a second time, and in any case, he was furious with her for complicating his escape. Still intending to smite her as soon as he had a clear line of sight, he stalked closer.

Then he froze, because the wizard was Winterflower. He hadn't noticed her presence hitherto because she hadn't been in current possession of one of the forbidden books.

Her sapphire eyes fluttered open. "When the staff disappeared," she whispered, "I feared you might try to find me. But I hoped that the wards from the dragon grimoires would keep anyone from scrying for us, as you promised they could."

"They did," he said. "I found you by another means, and now you're going to wish I hadn't."

"I didn't want to abandon you. It was just that the books were more important than anyone's life, yours or mine, and if I'd delayed for even another moment, Maldur might well have stopped me from taking them."

Rhespen laughed, though it made it feel as if something were grinding inside his chest. "You can't stop lying even when you know there's no longer any point."

"I'm not lying. After you fought Maldur to protect me, and I realized you were trying to help our people in your own way, I came to care for you, even though it was a mad, stupid thing for a spy to do. If we'd managed to flee together, I wouldn't have let any of my comrades hurt you. I would have done my utmost to convince you to stay with me and join our cause."

"I don't believe you."

"Kill me then, if that's your desire. I don't have the strength to stop you."

He leveled his staff, but for whatever reason, found himself too squeamish. "You won't escape so lightly. I'll take you with me when I leave, and turn you over to Orchtrien. Now hold your tongue, or I'll hurt you."

He recited a counterspell, but the anchoring enchantment she'd laid on him remained in place. The great charm of unbinding he'd discovered in Orchtrien's grimoires might well have dissolved it, but after the loss of the copybooks, he hadn't had a chance to prepare another such for the casting.

Well, no matter. Winterflower's binding would fade away on its own in a little while. Until then, he simply needed to avoid detection. Wary that his erstwhile lover might not be as helpless as she pretended, and that it might be a bad idea to let her beyond his reach, he hauled her to her feet and dragged her along with him to the door. A word and a touch of his staff sealed the panel as securely as the sturdiest lock.

"Now," he said, "we wait."

"Punish me however you want," Winterflower said. "I deserve it. But don't go back to Orchtrien. By his lights, your treachery was too grave a matter ever to forgive. He'll kill you whether you give him the books or not."

"You just don't want him to have them. You think that as long as they're in someone else's possession, even mine, a chance exists that somehow, someday, the lore will wind up serving the cause of insurrection."

"I'm trying to protect both you and the texts, you, because I love you, and the books, because they're vital. We rebel wizards devoted ourselves to mastering the wards against divination first of all, in the hope of shaking Orchtrien off our trail. Beyond that, we've scarcely begun to decipher the lore—I suppose that, after a century spent in the company of wyrms, you had an advantage in that regard. But we can already tell that here, finally, is our chance to oppose the dragons' might with a comparable strength of our own."

Rhespen made a spitting sound. "Nonsense. But suppose you could succeed, and establish an independent realm of your own. What makes you assume that kingdom, won by lies, theft, and seduction, would prove any better than what exists now?"

"Perhaps it wouldn't. But at least we elves would rule ourselves, according to our own philosophies and traditions. The forest would be sacred, and if our archers died in war, it would be to protect their own people and homeland, not to further a conqueror's dream of empire."

Rhespen felt doubt, and a sorrowing softness, ache inside him. Scowling, he struggled to extinguish them. "I told you to be silent. Another word, and I truly will smite you."

She sighed, bowed her head in submission, and they simply waited until cries of alarm sounded beyond the windows. He hauled Winterflower to the nearest one.

The opening was narrow, and the wooden wall was as thick as Rhespen's arm was long. But by virtue of an enchantment, the window provided a broad field of vision even so, albeit stretched and distorted around the edges. Beyond it, sentries scurried along the ramparts, or raised their weapons to the sky. A shadow flowed over them, and something immense and golden flashed above the treetops.

"Orchtrien," Winterflower groaned.

"Yes," Rhespen said. "I knew that if I could find you, he could, too, but I hoped it wouldn't happen as fast as this."

Arrows flew up at the gold. Most failed to pierce his scales, and he seemed to take no notice of the ones that did. He cocked back his head, snapped it forward, and spewed flame in such abundance that he must have an enchantment augmenting the quantity.

The rebels had surely laid wards to keep their stronghold from burning. Still, the sweeping column of fire reduced mighty branches and sections of trunk to charcoal and ash in an instant. Warriors leaped from their stations to escape the onrushing flame, and for the most part, achieved only a death by falling. Smoke billowed through the air, though not thickly enough to hide the brightness of Orchtrien's exhalation. It carried the odor of seared flesh.

But not everything burned. Some portions of the fortress, including most of the central shadowtop, proved resistant. After trying and failing to ignite them a second time, Orchtrien roared an incantation.

Rhespen experienced the same fleeting sensation of heaviness, of being stuck to the floor, with which Winterflower had previously afflicted him. He could tell from the way she grunted and swayed that she felt it, too. No doubt everyone in the stronghold had.

Orchtrien snarled another rhyme, whereupon a gigantic dome of rippling rainbows shimmered into existence over the fire-ravaged stronghold. The gold then wheeled and flew away.

"Curse it!" Rhespen cried. Orchtrien had made certain that no one could flee with the stolen texts again, either by translating himself through space or eloping in a more conventional fashion.

"It's the end," said Winterflower. She sounded almost matter-of-fact, but Rhespen could sense the anguish burning just below the surface. "All the lives we sacrificed. My degradation. My deceit and betrayal of you. All of it for nothing."

Rhespen drew a deep, steadying breath. "I wonder. . . . Orchtrien brought an army into the forest. He's gone to fetch it, and that gives us a little time. Let's see if we can put it to good use."

Just before dusk, the shell of rainbows vanished.

Orchtrien had to dispel it to bring his warriors close enough to threaten what remained of the rebel stronghold. His colossal form glided over the charred, spindly remnants of the trees.

It was time. Rhespen looked at Winterflower, and she at him. The moment stretched on until it became clear that neither knew what to say. He settled for giving her a smile, then exited the library, walked down a little corridor, and stepped out onto a small platform in the open air, still foul with drifting, eye-stinging smoke and stench. He cast a series of enchantments on himself, raised his staff, and flew up above the treetops, where Orchtrien was.

Some dragons, like Bexendral, could hover in place with a certain amount of difficulty. Orchtrien had mastered the trick of halting and floating effortlessly in midair, as if he were weightless as a cloud. He did so as he regarded Rhespen with his burning yellow stare.

"I assumed," the dragon said, "that, having escaped your cell, you'd run as far from me as possible."

Rhespen grinned. He felt as he had when he'd battled the green wyrm. He knew he should be terrified, but experienced a sort of crazy elation instead. It was exhilarating to defy one of the masters of the world.

"That might have been prudent," he replied, "but as you can see, you were mistaken. You often are, whether you realize it or not."

"I was certainly mistaken about you. Have you always been a traitor, then, in collusion with Winterflower from the start?"

"No. She had to trick me into it, and after you explained the ruse to me, I was appalled at my folly. As recently as this morning, my one desire was to win your forgiveness."

"Yet now it's plain, from your tone and manner as much

as the place where I find you, that you mean to oppose me. Why?"

"This may amuse you: I'm not certain myself. The sacrifice of all those warriors, year after year? The injuries to the woodlands? Your pet devil? The humiliation of my people, obliged to grovel to an overlord of another race? The humans who cheered me specifically as a 'dragonslayer,' a hint that they too chafe under your rule? Or perhaps I simply resent the way you treated me in particular. In any case, you're correct. I do stand with the rebellion."

"So be it, then." Orchtrien spat a stream of flame.

Rhespen brandished his staff, and the bright, crackling jet forked to pass him by on either side.

"It won't be that easy," he said, "While you were bringing up your troops, I passed the time preparing spells I stole from your library."

Unfortunately, even the great charm of unbinding hadn't eradicated the enchantment preventing teleportation, or obliterated the mystical barrier around the stronghold. But his afternoon of study had equipped him for arcane combat as never before.

Orchtrien lashed his wings and hurtled forward. Luckily, the enchantment of flight Rhespen had cast on himself made him just as quick and considerably more nimble in the air, and he whirled out of the way. At the same time, he rattled off an incantation and brandished a talisman shaped like a silver snowflake.

Enormous, sparkling, floating ice crystals leaped into existence directly in front of Orchtrien. As he streaked through them, their razor edges gashed his scales and ripped his leathery wings.

The dragon wheeled, roared words of power, and spat. The exhalation leaped forth in the form of dozens of winged serpents composed of living flame. Flying as fast as arrows, they spread out with the obvious intent of encircling Rhespen and attacking from all sides.

Recognizing that he had no hope of evading them

all, Rhespen called to the spirits of the air. Whirlwinds sprang into existence all around him then leaped to intercept the snakes. The vortices engulfed, shredded, and extinguished the creatures of fire.

Rhespen experienced an instant of satisfaction, which gave way to fear when he perceived that, while he was busy dealing with the serpents, Orchtrien had taken advantage of his preoccupation to attempt to close with him. The wyrm had climbed above him then furled his wings and plummeted, talons poised to seize and rend.

Rhespen whipped himself to the side. One of the dragon's claws caught a fold of his cloak and tore the garment from his shoulders, giving his neck a painful jerk. The scalloped edge of a colossal pinion swept past, nearly bashing him. Then Orchtrien was below him, turning, lashing his wings to gain altitude once more.

Lower still, all the way down on the ground, the royal army began its assault on what was left of the rebel stronghold. Tiny with distance, but the unnatural white of his long hair conspicuous even so, Maldur waved a line of warriors forward. Rhespen could only hope that one of his fellow elves would succeed in killing his longtime rival, because, the Black Archer knew, he was unlikely to find an opportunity himself.

Indeed, orienting on him anew, Orchtrien already required his attention. He hammered the dragon with a downpour of acid that seemed to do him little harm. Orchtrien riposted with a charm that turned a portion of his adversary's blood to fire and poison in his veins. Rhespen convulsed in agony, and rather to his surprise, the pain abated. The spell had injured him, perhaps grievously, but not enough to kill him instantly. Most likely one of his defensive enchantments had shielded him from the full effect.

As twilight faded into night, he and Orchtrien fought on, assailing one another with all the powers at their disposal, fire, cold, lightning, terror, blight, transformation, and madness. Meanwhile, warriors battled on the ground, and in each case, the struggle proceeded about as Rhespen had anticipated.

The stolen texts had augmented his powers considerably, but Orchtrien, who'd had centuries to master the secrets contained therein, was still the better mage, and in addition, possessed an overwhelming superiority in toughness and stamina that enabled him to weather attack after attack. Despite the damage to his wings, the dragon still flew as fast and maneuvered as ably as ever, still hammered his opponent with spell after spell. Blistered and frostbitten, his whole body aching, Rhespen was running low on magic, and questioned his ability to cast much more of it in any case. Pain and fatigue eroded his concentration.

The defenders in the trees were in just as desperate a condition. From the little that Rhespen had been able to observe, they'd fought well, but they needed more than valor to withstand their foes. Orchtrien had simply killed too many of them, and burned too much of their system of fortifications, before the present battle even started.

Sadly, there was nothing to be done about it. Nothing but keep resisting for as long as they could.

Rhespen conjured an animate blade seemingly made of inky shadow. It was all but invisible against the night sky, and as he sent it flying at Orchtrien, he dared to hope that even a dragon might not see it coming.

Orchtrien disappointed him by snarling a rhyme. White flame outlined the dark blade, and it crumpled in on itself and disappeared. The milky blaze, however, remained. It floated in the air for another heartbeat then flung itself at Rhespen.

He tried to dodge, and the streak of white fire twisted to compensate. It splashed against his chest.

The impact didn't hurt, indeed, he didn't even feel it, and wondered if somehow, miraculously, the spell hadn't affected him. Then he realized he was falling. The flame had burned away his charm of flight, and most likely, all his defensive enchantments as well.

With the aid of his staff, he could at least float and so keep from plummeting to his death. He could only move straight up and down, and had little hope of dodging his foe's subsequent attacks. He began to conjure the phantom duplicates that had confused the ghargatula. Then something slammed into his back, and he passed out.

When he woke, his various pains had given way to numbness. Yet he still had a feeling that something was hideously wrong, and when he looked down at himself, he found out what it was. Dark with blood, one of Orchtrien's talons stuck out of his chest. The dragon had gotten behind him somehow, struck, and driven the claw completely through his torso.

"Poor fool," Orchtrien said, actually sounding a shade regretful. "Did you really imagine that, because you killed a green, you could defeat me?"

"I did defeat you," Rhespen croaked, praying it was so.

Winterflower spent a month in the hut by the sea before accepting the grim truth that no one else was coming to keep the rendezvous.

After Orchtrien's initial assault, everyone had known the rebellion was doomed. But they'd dared to hope they could save the stolen texts, so other elves could employ them another day.

The question was, how? Orchtrien's first enchantment precluded the use of sending spells, and the shimmering, multicolored cage he'd dropped over the stronghold would prevent anyone from fleeing on foot until such time as his army surrounded the place.

At that point, however, the shell would come down. Accordingly, the rebels had entrusted one of the copybooks to each of a number of runners, who would employ magic, guile, and their knowledge of the terrain to try to slip past the advancing royal troops and vanish into the forest.

It might work—but not if Orchtrien oversaw events on the ground. His wizardry was too powerful, his senses too acute, and he'd be too intent on divesting his foes of their plundered lore. Therefore, Rhespen had volunteered to engage the dragon high in the air and keep him occupied long enough for his newfound allies to attempt their escape.

He'd managed it, too, even though it had surely cost him his life. The problem was that even so, none of the other runners had made it through the enemy lines. Maldur and his ilk had killed or captured them all.

So everyone else had died to salvage a single text—and what a text it was! Winterflower and the other runners had divided up the copybooks in haste, without paying any particular attention to who was getting what. Later on, when she'd had the leisure to examine the tome in her possession, she'd discovered it wasn't really a spellbook at all, but rather an abstract metaphysical treatise on the fundamental nature of dragons and their links to the forces of creation, to the elements of nature and the stars.

Thus, it couldn't teach her how to strip hundreds of people at once of the ability to employ teleportation, or how to imprison an entire stronghold in a bubble of force. It couldn't provide her with any sort of weapon or tool at all. Her mouth twisting, tears stinging her eyes and blurring her vision, she lifted it to fling it onto her mean little fire.

But she couldn't bring herself to do it, couldn't bear to concede finally and completely that all the sacrifice had been in vain. Orchtrien had kept the book locked away in his tower of wizardry, hadn't he? Surely that suggested it could serve some practical purpose.

She conjured a floating orb of soft white light, opened the volume, and started to read it again.

Eighty-nine years later, late in the spring, Orchtrien and his court repaired to the gardens to enjoy the balmy night air and the spectacle of the comet. Burning a fiery red, its tail spanning much of the heavens, it was a fascinating sight. Indeed, the dragon could hardly tear his eyes away from it.

Though everyone wanted him to—all the tiny, scurrying folk wheedling and whining for his attention. He reminded himself that it was part of being the king, and a part he usually enjoyed, but at the moment, that didn't make it any easier to tolerate.

In his present humor, the jabbering, blathering mites seemed as contemptible as gnats, and when he felt obliged to glance down at them, he discovered the light of the new star still colored his vision, as if he saw them through a haze of blood.

Something about that made him feel excited and uneasy at the same time. He shifted his gaze back to the sky, and a hand stroked his foreleg, startling him.

"Let's go to my chambers," a husky voice purred. He looked down at a human woman, and after a moment remembered she was his current mistress, though even then, her name escaped him. "I can show you better sport than this."

He picked up his foot and stamped her to paste.

For an instant, he was appalled at himself, then a wave of elation swept the previous feeling away. He licked up what remained of an arm and gobbled it, tasting human flesh for the first time. It was savory enough to make him shudder with pleasure.

But even so, it couldn't long distract from the even greater ecstasy of slaughter. He killed another human, and another, until he lost count.

Indeed, he lost nearly all sense of himself. He only vaguely comprehended and cared not at all that he was laying waste to his own palace. And once he ran out of prey there, he went on destroying his way across his own city.

Nor did he consider the implications when he smashed his way into the fortress where he'd quartered much of his army. Or register the pain of the wounds he suffered when the men-at-arms and war wizards, trapped and desperate, started fighting back.

Until the strength spilled out of him all at once, and he flopped forward onto his belly. Then a measure of clarity returned.

He tried and failed to stand. Struggled to muster another blast of flame and couldn't manage that, either. His sight dimmed.

Meanwhile, warriors stabbed and chopped at him. It shouldn't be happening. If he'd fought as he was accustomed to, using his intellect and magic, he could have crushed a dozen armies. But he'd engaged them like a rabid beast, and here was the result.

"The red star murdered me," he whispered.

Conceivably, someone heard. For in the days that followed, as all the wyrms in Faerûn ran mad at once, slaughtering those closest to them, their loyal lieutenants and warlords, first of all, destroying all that they themselves had built, people began to name the comet the King-Killer.

THE STAFF OF VALMAXIAN

PHILIP ATHANS

The 23rd Year of the Sapphire (-7628 DR)

The heat from the explosion seared Valmaxian's unsuspecting lungs from precisely five hundred ninety-eight feet, seven inches away. It burst into a perfect sphere of orange fire, traced with veins of red and flashes of yellow, and a painful white at its heart. It rolled out of its central point to a diameter of forty feet in the time it took for Valmaxian to close his eyes against the blast. He put his hands to his face and felt the shockwave tousle his long blue-green hair and whip his plain white satin robe around him.

"Oh, no," he breathed, then coughed once, trying to hold the rest of the coughs in.

The shockwave passed, but residual heat washed over him and drew sweat out of every pore in his trembling body to plaster the silk robe tightly to him.

"Well," his mentor said over a sharp exhale, "that was . . . less than successful."

Valmaxian let his hands fall to his side, his fingers balled into tight fists. He blinked open his eyes and waited for the spots to clear, listening to his mentor's footsteps approach. The spots cleared, and Valmaxian could see the fine gold inlays in the green marble floor. The gold traced a series of precise lines and arcs that marked the distance from the center of the room and defined various angles. It was how he knew with such precision how far away from the center of the blast he stood.

Valmaxian looked up, ignoring the scope of the enormous chamber. The domed ceiling soared twelve hundred feet above his head, the inside of the dome likewise marked with radii and calibrations. The round casting chamber—his mentor's private studio—was exactly two thousand feet in diameter, the centerpiece of the fifth largest building in the Western Provinces of Siluvanede, the kingdom of the Gold elves and all that remained of the past glory of mighty Aryvandaar.

Valmaxian's almond eyes settled on the thin form of his mentor, who stood at the lip of a bowl-shaped depression in the center of the room. The green marble there had been scorched black.

"Is it . . . ?" Valmaxian asked his mentor's still back.

"Your precision is improving, at least," Kelærede said, his voice echoing a thousandfold in the columned vastness of the casting chamber. "You've centered the fireball in a rather precise manner."

"The wand?" Valmaxian asked, knowing the answer.

Kelærede stood, turned around, but didn't look at his student. "You're young," he said, his voice devoid of accusation.

Valmaxian sighed and walked forward. His boot heels tapped out what sounded to Valmaxian like a funeral march. He came to the edge of the central bowl and looked across at a raised column that rose from the center to the height of the floor. On its eighteen-inch round surface lay a thin strip of molten silver, maybe a foot long. The metal still bubbled around the edges.

"Damn it," Valmaxian breathed.

"There will be other wands," Kelærede said.

Valmaxian turned and saw Kelærede standing next to a small table, pouring a glass of water from a sweating crystal decanter.

"It took the artisans of Guirolen House three years to craft that from silver mined from Selûne herself," Valmaxian reminded his teacher. "It cost a king's ransom."

Kelærede shrugged in that entirely too-forgiving way he had of shrugging and said, "Then it's fortunate that our own beloved king is not being held for ransom."

Valmaxian let a breath hiss out through his nose and said, "My failures amuse you."

Kelærede looked up, his face serious, and a cold chill ran down Valmaxian's still sweating back.

"Not at all," the older elf said, his quiet voice carrying well in the still air. "It is not the simplest thing, Valmaxian, though you seem to think it ought to be."

"It took the staff a tenday to prepare the bat guano alone," Valmaxian reminded him. "It was a waste."

"Yes, it was," Kelærede answered.

They looked at each other for a long second before Valmaxian turned back to the blackened central bowl of the casting chamber.

"I can't do it," he said. "Not this way."

"You can't learn from me?" the teacher asked. "You can't try, fail, try again, then—"

"What?" Valmaxian interrupted. "Then what? Fail again, try again, fail again, try again, fail again, and again and again until all the silver has been mined from the moon to the western continents and back again and I still haven't finished a single, simple, ridiculous little wand of fire?"

"The fact that you don't allow for the possibility that you might succeed is at the heart of why you fail, my son," Kelærede answered. "You've always been harder on yourself than I have been on you, and I'm known as a difficult teacher. You're quick to punish yourself, but like everything else you keep that punishment inside. I've been trying to show you that in order to create an item of true power, you'll need to give something of yourself, you'll need to open up and let some of what is—"

"There are other ways," Valmaxian interrupted again. "There's another way."

"My students and teachers alike consider it rude for a student to interrupt his mentor," Kelærede replied. "We've discussed that, Val, and I've made my feelings on the matter clear."

"I know," Valmaxian said, still looking down at the scorched marble.

The spell wasn't supposed to actually go off. It should have been absorbed into the rare silver wand. It was a simple task, but one he found himself unable to complete. Valmaxian, in his own eyes if not in Kelærede's, was a dismal failure. But he didn't have to be.

"Valmaxian," Kelærede warned, "you have promised me that you will not pursue that path—that you'll *never* pursue that path."

"I have," Valmaxian said, turning to offer a weak smile to his teacher. "I apologize."

Kelærede returned Valmaxian's weak smile with a strong one. "You're young and impatient, Val. You're merely five hundred years old—you know that, don't you?"

"You've told me."

"It's true," Kelærede said. "I could have made the same mistake myself at that age. When I was as young and frustrated as you are I might have done what you're considering doing now, but I didn't. I was warned away by my own teacher the same way I'm warning you now. Decades pass fast enough for our people, Val, and it may be decades before you are able to do what you set out to do today. It could be decades more before you're ready to go out on your own—a century maybe—but you will do it, Val. You will succeed."

Valmaxian looked up at the dome so far above his head and forced another weak smile.

"Yes," he said, "Yes, I will succeed. Yes, I will."

In a much smaller room, a tenday later, Valmaxian spread a scroll out on a rough flagstone floor. The scroll had been cut from a lamb's hide, carefully tanned to a nearly paper thinness. The writing on it was in Kelærede's careful hand. Only a handful of elves on all of Toril could have written the runes, sigils, and fell diagrams inscribed there.

He glanced around the simple chamber, checking one last time that everything was ready. The furniture had been moved out, a single thin taper burned in an iron candlestick, and he'd firmly shuttered the narrow arched window.

Valmaxian wore a common robe of rough wool. His hands were shaking. He drew in a deep breath and held it, counting to twenty before exhaling. He sat on his knees on the cold stone floor, a third of the way into the room with the single locked door at his back. In front of him, past the expanse of the scroll, was nothing: fifteen feet or so of floor then blank wall. The thirty-foot high ceiling seemed excessive for so small a room, but it was one of the reasons he chose it.

The gate would be twenty feet in diameter.

He rubbed his eyes, took three quick breaths, and started to read.

It was difficult going. The words were hard to say. Instructions not meant to be read aloud were interwoven with them, advising on proper cadence, tone, timbre, even earnestness and enthusiasm. Likewise there were instructions for the proper gestures. His hands and fingers had to move in a very precise way and at very specific intervals.

At least three times in the course of the minute it took

to cast the spell Valmaxian almost stopped. He knew he should stop but also knew he had to go on.

The last word echoed into silence in the still air and Valmaxian dropped his shaking, sweating hands to the floor. He didn't know what to do with them.

He blinked when the light first appeared—a soft violet traced with blue—and it didn't so much grow brighter as more plentiful. It formed a ball first, about the size of Valmaxian's fist. The young elf looked at it with increasing anxiety.

He'd started it, and there was no way to stop it.

The ball of light continued to grow. It was as big as Valmaxian's head when it started to spin. As it spun faster, the ball flattened out on top, becoming a whirling oval of blue-violet light. Flashes of white appeared, smearing into traces of brilliance. The light grew rapidly and became a flat disk that slowly tipped up on one edge. It held its place perpendicular to the floor eight feet from the tip of Valmaxian's nose. There was no heat, but the young Gold elf perspired all the same. He blinked but never looked away.

All at once the disk opened in the center and spun itself to form a ring. Beyond it, Valmaxian was able to make out irregular shadows. The light from the spinning ring interfered with his natural ability to see in the dark. He strained to focus on the space in the center of the ring, and after a few blinks he was sure he was looking at a wind-carved boulder. The curved rock had almost the shape of a woman, at least as tall as Valmaxian. The ring reached its full diameter of twenty feet and the violet light dimmed. Valmaxian saw more of the misshapen rocks loosely sprinkled across a broken landscape of talus and coarse sand. The deep red sky was striped with clouds of black dust whipped by a buffeting wind.

Another shape formed in the swirling dust: a shadow two heads taller than the tallest elf. It walked on two legs, swinging long, apelike arms at its side, its head and shoulders studded with irregular horns and spikes.

Valmaxian held his breath as he watched the demon step through the gate into his little room. The spell had been specifically designed to call but one creature from all the endless malignancy of the Abyss, one nabassu, one thing.

It looked like a gorilla, but with huge, batlike wings rustling behind it. Its broad, flat face was dominated by a wide mouth held open by two upturned tusks. Its little nose was pushed back between two startlingly intelligent, silver eyes that seemed to reflect the light of the candle and the spinning magic gate as though they were made of polished platinum. Grotesquely naked, its skin was blotchy and gray.

Valmaxian tried to swallow but couldn't. His throat closed tight. The demon noticed that and smiled, drawing back half a step.

"En—" Valmaxian started to say, then coughed. He made sure to keep his eyes from meeting the demon's. "En'Sel'Dinen."

A low growl rolled out of the fiend's mouth, followed by a drifting mist of green vapor. "Ah . . . you called . . ." the beast said, its voice like thunder heard from the bottom of a well.

"I am Valmaxian," said the elf, forcing a confidence into his voice that he didn't really feel.

"Well," the demon replied, "good for you. And Kelærede?"

Valmaxian managed to swallow finally then said, "He forbade me from calling you. I had to steal the scroll."

The demon made a sound that Valmaxian thought must be a laugh.

"I require your service," the elf said.

"Ah," said the demon, "and I thought this was a social call."

Valmaxian felt his face flush. He kept his eyes to one side.

"You know enough not to look me in the eyes," En'Sel'Dinen observed. "Kelærede—he's your master?"

"He is my teacher."

"And what has he taught you about me?" the demon asked.

"Enough," Valmaxian said, his eyes wandering over En'Sel'Dinen's misshapen toes. A tiny insect scurried under one ragged yellow toenail.

"Wealth, then, is it?" the demon asked. "Power? Magic?"

"Yes," Valmaxian whispered.

The demon laughed.

Valmaxian cleared his throat and said more clearly, "Magic. The others will follow."

The demon stopped laughing and leaned slightly forward. "Nothing comes without a cost," it said. "What are you willing to spend?"

"Anything," Valmaxian said. "I don't know."

"Neither do I," the demon replied, "but I'll think of something. A single sacrifice. A sacrifice to be decided later."

Valmaxian felt his own mouth curl up into a smile, though deep down he didn't want to smile. "Anything," he said again. "Anything."

The 76th Year of the Amethyst (-6964 DR)

The fireball exploded in the exact center of a circle formed by freestanding columns of bleached marble, simple cylinders each a thousand feet tall. The circular expanse of the interior was a floor of identical white marble a mile in diameter. Valmaxian sat on a ladder-back chair of polished mahogany far enough away from the explosion that his spidersilk robe wasn't ruffled by the wind from the shockwave. He couldn't feel the heat, either.

"Did you melt it?" Valmaxian asked in a quiet, relaxed voice.

An enchantment he'd created himself took hold of the soft tones and transported his voice clearly across the marble surface to the ears of Third Apprentice Yulmanda.

The apprentice, a Gold elf girl less than a century old, walked quickly to the center of the casting circle and looked down. Valmaxian heard her quiet sigh.

"That was the last of the silver from Selûne," Valmaxian stated without emotion.

Yulmanda turned toward him but kept her eyes on the floor. "Master, I—"

"*Failed!*" Valmaxian shouted, his voice rolling over the smooth floor like waves crashing on a beach. "You failed, because you are a stupid, useless girl."

"Master—"

"Shut up," Valmaxian roared, holding up a hand as if to hold back the sound from the apprentice's mouth. "Get out of here. Leave my studio immediately and do not return. Your father will receive a bill for the materials you so foolishly wasted. You're not fit to touch the Weave."

He heard the girl sob, even heard the first of her tears tick onto the marble floor at her feet. Valmaxian looked away, up at the deep azure sky over Siluvanede. He could tell the girl was trying to think of something to say, some defense that could save her place as one of Valmaxian's students—the most coveted position for the young Gold elves of Siluvanede. Valmaxian's studio was unparalleled. The items he enchanted there were sought after throughout the elf lands all around the High Forest and beyond.

Yulmanda didn't bother arguing. Crying, she walked quickly past him and to the broad steps at the edge of the casting circle. The steps would lead her a hundred feet down the elf-made tor on which the casting circle had been built. It would then take her the better part of the day to cross his compound and pass through the gates into the city proper.

As Yulmanda's footsteps touched the top of the stairs, Valmaxian heard another set approaching. He kept his eyes fixed on a single cloud lazily wandering across the perfect sky and waited for the newcomer to approach. It would be a long walk.

The wand that Yulmanda had ruined was, of course, a minor trinket, intended as a gift to a wealthy collector more interested in the rare silver than the enchantment. The collector had several of Valmaxian's finest pieces and had recently begun to collect his work to the exclusion of all others.

"Master Valmaxian," a voice behind him called.

"Who are you?" Valmaxian asked without bothering to look at the intruder.

"Piera—" the young elf started to say then obviously realized Valmaxian wouldn't care what his name was. "A messenger, sir, with disturbing news."

"The staff?" Valmaxian asked, his blood running cold. The look he gave the messenger sent the boy back two steps.

"Staff, Master?" the messenger asked, his face pale and his eyes bulging. "N-no, Master Valmaxian."

Valmaxian sighed and put a hand to his chest. His heart beat rapidly, and his palm was sweating.

"Master?" the messenger asked. "Are you feeling unwell? Should I fetch—?"

"Be still, boy," Valmaxian barked, turning his face back up to the azure sky. He took a deep breath and closed his eyes.

The messenger cleared his throat.

Without opening his eyes, Valmaxian said, "You are still here."

"Yes, Master," the messenger replied. "I was told to deliver a message."

"Then deliver it with haste and be on your way," Valmaxian said, eyes still closed, "or are they paying you by the hour?"

The messenger let loose a terrified chuckle and said, "Oh, no, Master. I am paid by the message."

Valmaxian let a long sigh hiss through his teeth and heard the boy take another step back.

"Master," the messenger said, "it's Lord Kelærede."

Valmaxian opened his eyes. The little cloud had passed

from his field of vision. He didn't look at the boy.

"Master, Lord Kelærede lies on his deathbed. He has asked for you."

Valmaxian rolled his head slowly to one side, his eyes straight forward so the boy tilted lazily into view.

"Kelærede's dying?" the wizard asked.

"Presently, Master," the boy said, nodding. "Or so I was told."

Valmaxian looked back up at the sky and the boy said nothing for the space of four rapid, ragged breaths.

Valmaxian said, "Well, then, I guess I must be off."

Kelærede looked fine. Valmaxian could see no difference in the elf's face, or in the fine veins on the back of his hand. It had been closer to seven hundred years than six hundred since Valmaxian had seen his former teacher, but the look of disappointment was as plain in Kelærede's eyes on his deathbed as it had been the day he'd turned Valmaxian out.

Valmaxian sat on a stiff-cushioned chair next to Kelærede's narrow, low bed. The old elf sat propped up with pillows. Valmaxian avoided the dying elf's eyes. Instead he looked around the simple bedchamber. They sat in silence for a long time. Kelærede's breathing came labored and slow, and his legs didn't move the whole time.

"You have done well," Kelærede said finally, his voice as thin as a reed. He looked the same, but sounded different.

Valmaxian nodded in response.

"I wanted to see you," Kelærede said, "one last time."

Valmaxian looked his former teacher in the eye and asked, "To make peace? After so long?"

Kelærede's breath whistled out of his nose and the old elf shuddered. "You could have been one of the finest craftsmen Aryvan—" The old elf stopped to cough, then smiled. "I was going to say 'Aryvandaar.' Old habits." He coughed again and said, "You could have been one of the finest."

"I *am* the finest," Valmaxian said. He sighed when he realized how he sounded. So much time had passed but Kelærede could still make him feel like a child.

"You made the bargain, didn't you," Kelærede said.

"I did what I had to do," Valmaxian answered.

"Regardless of the consequences?"

"Consequences?" Valmaxian asked. "The items I craft are the most sought after in Siluvanede. *That* was the consequence of my actions. I cast a spell—from a scroll you wrote yourself. I solved a problem using the Weave. Isn't that what you always taught me to do?"

Kelærede shook his head. "I always told you that you could be everything you ever wanted to be but that it would cost you something of yourself."

"I thought that was what you warned me against," Valmaxian replied. "You told me the demon would require payment, then you tell me I should have spent 'something of myself.' I spent all I needed to spend, and the bill has not come due in over six and a half centuries."

Kelærede coughed through a bitter laugh and said, "That doesn't mean it will never come due, and there's a difference between spending a single thin copper of your own essence every day and the price that En'Sel'Dinen will surely ask."

"And you would know, I suppose," Valmaxian said. "It was you who bound that demon to service the first time."

"And I who sent it back to the Abyss where it belongs," Kelærede said.

"It was my decision," Valmaxian said. He stood, his knees shaking. "I have been fine without you. You were holding me back."

"I was teaching you," the old elf whispered.

"You were wasting my time," Valmaxian almost shouted. His voice echoed against the bare walls. "You're wasting my time now."

"Am I keeping you from your work, then?" Kelærede asked. "I understand it's a staff."

The blood drained from Valmaxian's face, and he felt warm, though he knew he should have expected Kelærede to be following his work.

"A staff, yes," Valmaxian said. "It will be my masterpiece."

"Your masterpiece . . ." Kelærede said around a harsh laugh. "A masterpiece I hope you're prepared to lose. If En'Sel'Dinen knows it means anything to you, that's what he'll want."

Valmaxian opened his mouth to argue, to scream at the dying elf, but no words came out. His knees trembled, and he loathed the feeling. He forced himself to turn away from the bed.

"This disease has confounded all the priests. Every last one of them. My body has failed me so I Journey West, Val. This is the last time you will ever see me," Kelærede said to Valmaxian's back. "You can't tell me I was right? You can't promise me you'll undo what you've done?"

Valmaxian turned his head, but not enough to see his former teacher, and asked, "Is that why you sent for me? So that after all this time I could tell you you were right? Or were you hoping to hear that the demon had extracted some hideous price from me so that you could say 'I told you so'?"

"Is that what you think I want?"

"Isn't it?" Valmaxian asked.

"You were like a son to me."

"I'm not your son," Valmaxian said. "I never was."

He lifted one foot and it felt as if it weighed a thousand pounds, but when he lifted the other it felt a little lighter. He found himself storming out of the room. Kelærede said nothing to stop him. The old elf didn't laugh, cough, or call out.

Valmaxian passed through the door with his eyes down and brushed past someone in the corridor. He stopped when he felt a hand on his arm.

His eyes met the gaze of a young elf woman. Her long chestnut hair was pulled back and tied behind her head, her simple cotton blouse and breaches revealed a perfectly formed figure with slim hips and ample breasts, but her full lips were pressed into a tight line and her crystal blue eyes narrowed in accusation.

"You're Valmaxian," she said, her voice like music, though anger and resentment were plain.

For the second time that day, the second time in over six hundred years, Valmaxian was speechless.

The woman sighed and said, "What did you say to him?"

"I . . ." Valmaxian started. "Who are . . . ?"

"Chasianna," she said, folding her arms across her chest and setting her jaw even tighter. "He's my grandfather. He asked for you. He's spoken of you. You broke his heart."

"We had a difference of opinion," Valmaxian said. "That was a long time ago."

"A long time ago, maybe," she said, "but there's not a long time left to go. He wanted to make peace with you. I have no idea what you did or what he did . . . what happened . . . but I will not have him Journey West without having made his peace."

Valmaxian realized he wasn't breathing. He felt strange: embarrassed, angry, and ashamed all at once. He shook his head and said, "Do you know who I am?"

"I don't care who you are," Chasianna said. "I love my grandfather."

Valmaxian drew in a breath to protest. Chasianna tipped her head to one side, widened her eyes, and seemed ready for any response.

"You can go back in," she said, her voice softer, hopeful. "It's not too late."

Valmaxian closed his mouth, and that made Chasianna smile. He found his lips curling up to return her smile, and he glanced back at the door to Kelærede's bedchamber. Without a word to Chasianna he turned around and went back to the door.

"Say anything," she said. "Just say anything to make it right for him, even if it isn't right for you."

Valmaxian went back into the room and walked to the side of the bed. For the first time since coming back to his former teacher's studio that day he knew what he wanted and had some idea how to get it.

"Kelærede," he said.

The old elf looked up at him with eyes that seemed even more dull than they had only moments before.

"Kelærede, you were right," Valmaxian said. "I wanted more than I should have had. I wanted a life I wasn't willing to earn. I should have stayed with you. I should have taken the decades, if you thought that's what I required. I should not have stolen the scroll. I should not have summoned the demon."

Kelærede opened his mouth, but didn't say anything.

"Journey West, my teacher," Valmaxian said when he heard Chasianna step into the doorway behind him. "Journey West knowing that I will undo what I've done."

One corner of Kelærede's dry lips lifted to indicate a smile then the life slipped away from his face.

Valmaxian sighed, satisfied that both Kelærede and Chasianna had not only heard him but believed every insincere, lying syllable. Kelærede was dead, leaving only one true master.

The 78th Year of the Tourmaline (-6962 DR)

Valmaxian had had traced out on the marble floor of the casting circle in dwarven mithral an inlay marking out a gentle arc. Spaced exactly fourteen feet, eleven inches apart were five circles. Lines extended from the centers of the first and fifth circles that met at a point precisely one hundred and eighty-nine feet, eleven inches from the farthest of the small circles in the center of the arc. In each of the five circles stood a single, inexpensive clay golem. He'd told the featureless humanoid forms to stand still, and since they possessed no minds of their own, that's exactly what they did.

Valmaxian surveyed the scene from the top of one of the pillars upon which was built a small platform with no railing. A narrow staircase of elven steel curved from the platform and wrapped around the pillar all the way to the white marble floor a thousand feet below. Valmaxian had to look through a complex series of lenses hung on golden frames to see what was happening on the floor and be seen from there.

An apprentice—Merellien was his name—stepped out onto the floor, the staff cradled in the crook of his arms. He walked with care and haste across the mithral-traced marble, glancing up only once at Valmaxian, who offered him a curt nod.

Valmaxian smelled chypre and heard footsteps at the top of the stairs. He smiled, like he always did in the presence of Chasianna. In the two years since the death of her grandfather, they'd become all but inseparable. He turned, still smiling, and her beautiful face beamed. She stepped onto the platform next to him, touching his elbow. She was nervous about the height and the lack of railings, even though she wore the feather falling ring he'd given her months before. Valmaxian found that nervousness, like everything about Chasianna, charming.

"The staff?" she asked.

Valmaxian nodded and turned back to watch Merellien step into the circle at the point of the cone.

"Should I shield my eyes?" Chasianna asked.

Valmaxian chuckled and said, "No, no. No lightning this time. Just a spray of magic missiles . . . I hope."

"You hope?"

The apprentice looked up at Valmaxian, who nodded once. Merellien faced the golems, raising the staff in both hands in front of him. He exhaled, then spoke a single command word. Three jagged-edged bolts of blue-white light shot out of one end of the staff and flashed unerringly to the middle three golems. The first missile exploded onto the chest of the second golem, the second missile into the middle golem, and the third bolt burst onto the midsection of the fourth golem. The creatures jerked back, but remained standing.

"Damn it," Valmaxian sighed.

Chasianna said, "You can't expect a magic missile to kill a golem. Not just one."

Valmaxian rubbed his eyes, avoiding the expectant gaze of the apprentice so far below, and said, "That's not the point, though, is it? Only three of them came out."

"And it should have been five?" she asked.

"I know what you're going to say."

"You did it your way, didn't you?" she asked, though he knew she knew the answer. "You did it your fast way."

"My way works," he said then realized that she'd just seen it fail. "It has worked before. I'm just . . . it's . . ."

"Will you let me show you?" she asked.

He smiled at her and said, "You can't make it any worse."

Valmaxian held out his hand and mumbled a few syllables. The staff leaped from Merellien's light grip and soared up through the air and into Valmaxian's hand. He turned and handed the staff to Chasianna.

She took it with the respect Valmaxian felt the staff deserved. It was unfinished still, but it would prove to be his masterpiece. Chasianna placed it carefully on the floor of the platform and shooed Valmaxian back a couple steps.

She looked up at him and asked, "Magic missiles?"

He nodded, and she looked down at the staff, holding her left hand half an armslength above its smooth, polished surface. He watched her enchantment with enormous interest and unconcealed respect. An artist in her own right—certainly not as adept as he, but a capable mage—still, he doubted she'd be able to overcome whatever flaw it was in the staff that caused the enchantment to limit itself to the ability of the user. It should have been able to do what Valmaxian himself was capable of.

It took her a while, but Valmaxian watched her the whole time. When she was almost done she touched the staff and there was a flash of light that, even though he was expecting it, made Valmaxian flinch. The color drained from Chasianna's fine-boned face and her arm twitched.

Valmaxian stepped forward and fell to one knee. He touched her on the shoulder, and Chasianna twitched back. She looked up at him, and the dullness in her eyes made Valmaxian's flesh go cold. She was sweating, and she had a streak of gray in her hair where no such flaw existed before. Her hands shook, and when she spoke her voice was quiet and forced.

"It'll . . . work now."

"Chasianna . . ."

She smiled, leaning back and sliding into a prone position on the round platform. He helped her down, and made sure her head didn't strike the stone.

"How many times did he tell you?" she asked.

Valmaxian blew a breath out through his nose and glanced up at the overcast sky. "Nine hundred and forty-three times," he said. "I counted."

"I'm sure you did," she said, then coughed.

He shook his head and told her, "It's not the only way."

"Try it. Try the staff."

Valmaxian lifted the staff from the platform floor. It felt warm to his reverent touch.

"Merellien," he called, then tossed the staff at the apprentice. Valmaxian mumbled an odd-sounding word, and the staff drifted to slip easily into Merellien's hands.

The apprentice turned to the clay golems, lifted the staff, and glanced up at Valmaxian, who looked down at Chasianna. Though still weak, she smiled at him. Valmaxian turned back to the apprentice and nodded.

Merellien faced the golems, held up the staff, and repeated the command word. Five bolts of blue-white light shot from the tip of the staff, and one struck each of the golems dead center. Two of the automatons staggered back.

Valmaxian's heart leaped. One more functionality of the staff successfully enchanted and—he hadn't done it. It was Chasianna and her grandfather's ridiculous notions of self-sacrifice and transference of personal energies.

He turned back to Chasianna and saw that she had lost consciousness. Her breathing was shallow. He kneeled next to her and scooped her up in his arms. She smiled but didn't open her eyes.

Three nights later Valmaxian sat on the cool marble floor of his open-air casting circle, gently rocking the staff in his arms and staring up into the star-spattered sky. Chasianna had begun to regain her strength and he was able to get back to work, but the last day had been spent facing more dissatisfying results.

He knew he could have gone down the path that Kelærede and Chasianna would have had him take, the one that seemed to work for them, though in a way that held them back as well. Every time they put some parcel of themselves into the enchantment of an item, that was a part they lost. So they had to lose something to gain something. A zero-sum game never interested Valmaxian. It hadn't interested him six hundred years before when Kelærede insisted on it and it didn't interest him when Chasianna, in her own sincere way, did the same thing.

To add to the staff, he needed something more. To that end he had had two of his most trusted apprentices make certain preparations. Circles were drawn on the marble with fine chalk. Candles sat cold, but ready. Ready for a summoning.

It was something he hadn't done in what for even an elf was considered a very long time. The results of the first summoning had satisfied Valmaxian's needs for that long, but there was the staff, and that needed more.

Valmaxian set the staff on the marble floor next to him and drew in a breath to start the spell. Before he could utter even the first syllable, the gate opened. It was the same as the first time—the same colors, the same intensity of light and motion—but it happened faster, and it happened before he'd made it happen. He was not in control of any of it. The demon was just there.

"Valmaxian, my old friend," the creature said, his voice somehow still echoing though they were outside. "How can I be of assistance to you this time?"

Valmaxian put a hand on the staff and tried to make it stop shaking—his hand, not the staff. The staff just sat there, cold and indifferent.

En'Sel'Dinen's freakish eyes drifted down to the staff and widened. One corner of the beast's twisted mouth pulled up.

"Ah," it growled, "the staff. The Staff of Valmaxian."

Valmaxian's heart skipped, and he shook his head.

"The Staff of Valmaxian. . . ." the elf repeated. Yes, it would bear his name, Valmaxian decided then, and it would roar his legacy to the ages.

"What is your pleasure, sir?" the demon hissed.

"The retributive strike," Valmaxian said, taking up the staff and rising to his knees in front of the enormous creature. "The retributive strike, the Fire of All, the Will, the Ego, the Presence. It must live. It must be aware. It must know itself and its creator and it must revel in its own power and mine. It must live, and it must live forever, and it must be fit for the hand of a god."

The demon grinned, showing a horror of jagged fangs, and said, "A tall order."

"Worth anything," Valmaxian almost gasped. All restraint and even common sense fled him, replaced by pure ambition. "The staff will be worth a king's ransom—a god's."

The demon took a step closer, but Valmaxian didn't flinch.

"Those years past I asked for a price from you for what I gave," En'Sel'Dinen said. "Are you prepared to balance our ledgers tonight?"

Valmaxian scoffed, smiled, and said, "You have no—"

"I *gave,*" the demon barked.

Valmaxian stood, drawing himself straight, and lifted one eyebrow. "You served my master before me, then you served me. You'll serve me again."

"I claim my price, elf," was the demon's only reply.

Having no intention of giving the miserable, bound creature anything, Valmaxian shrugged and said, "Name your price, and let us be on with it."

The demon snorted a puff of noxious yellow fumes and said, "Chasianna."

Despite his confidence that the demon could hold nothing over his head, was bound by the spell to do his bidding, Valmaxian's blood ran cold.

"What did you say?" he asked.

"The girl," the demon growled. "Chasianna. You know of whom I speak."

"Why?" Valmaxian thought to ask. The fact that En'Sel'Dinen even knew her name started to shake his confidence.

"Her skin," the demon almost whispered. "Is it soft? Soft to the touch? Warm and pleasing?"

Valmaxian tipped his head, and the demon laughed at him. The sound made Valmaxian's stomach turn.

"You'll pay me," the demon said. "I am bound no more—was never bound to you. Your teacher, that bastard Kelærede, he tried to warn you, didn't he? Tried to tell you that you could never control me. He tried to tell you that anything gained from me would have a cost."

"Go back," Valmaxian said, a slight lilt in his voice betraying his lack of confidence. "Return to the Abyss, and come no more to this—"

"Fool," En'Sel'Dinen interrupted. "I will have her soft skin and her yielding lips and her heaving—"

Valmaxian coughed out the command word and the

shimmering darts of magic leaped from the tip of the staff, crossing the handful of paces between the elf and the demon in less than the time it took for Valmaxian to close his eyes against the sudden light.

It was too bright. Valmaxian knew that right away. The missiles wouldn't generate that much light.

He opened his eyes, blinking rapidly. The purple splotches cleared soon enough, and the demon was gone. The missiles might have hurt it, certainly hadn't killed it, couldn't possibly have disintegrated it, but it was gone.

"Chasianna," Valmaxian breathed, then turned and ran for the stairs, muttering the words to the spell that would take him in a flash to the home of the only elf on Toril he'd ever truly loved.

⊙ ⊙ ⊙ ⊙ ⊙

Valmaxian stepped into Chasianna's home through the last of a series of dimension doors, holding the staff out in front of him. He expected to see the demon En'Sel'Dinen there, expected that Chasianna and her house retainers would be fighting the creature off. He expected to join the fight. The last thing he expected was nothing, but that was exactly what greeted him.

The tastefully appointed sitting room into which he stepped was dark and quiet. A gold filigreed end table had been tipped over, a crystal vase shattered on the floor next to it, and a single long-stemmed lily lay already wilting on the damp rug.

"Chasianna!" Valmaxian shouted, letting his voice echo in the sitting room's domed ceiling.

He held his breath waiting for a reply, but none came. He scanned the room and saw nothing else out of place. The room was sprinkled with valuable antiques, some enchanted by Kelærede himself. Valmaxian had come to know every one of them, and none were missing.

He crossed quickly to the wide doorway that emptied into the foyer. He stepped out onto the checkerboard marble tiles, his boots clicking and sending a rattle of sharp echoes up the soaring stairway.

"Chasianna!" he shouted again, waiting as his voice followed the footstep echoes up the stairs. Again, there was no answer.

Something made him keep walking, stopping at the foot of the stairs. He'd opened his mouth to shout for her again when he heard it. At first it sounded like a scream, and that sent a cold chill racing down Valmaxian's spine. It wasn't a scream, though. It was a less natural, less elven sound. It sounded like wind whistling through—through what? Rocks? A narrow canyon?

Valmaxian didn't stop to think why he might have drawn that specific conclusion. Instead he raced up the stairs trailing his robe and the staff—held firmly in one hand, the other sliding up along the banister—behind him.

"Chasianna!" he shouted at least once more as he ascended the stairway.

His legs began to ache as he rounded the top of the stairs, but he ignored the pain. He came to the wide double doors—closed—to Chasianna's bedchamber and realized two things at the same time: the upstairs maid was not there to open the doors for him, and there was a bright red light—wholly unlike the warm orange glow of Chasianna's hearth fire—burning from under the door.

Valmaxian put a hand to the wrought-iron door handles and recoiled from the heat. He cursed and gathered up a corner of his robe, using it like a potholder to open the door. He stepped into a blast furnace.

Chasianna's personal suite was large, befitting a woman of her class. Where Valmaxian expected to see a wall some hundred feet in front of him, where the bed would be, there was nothing. It seemed as if the whole side of the house, with the servant's wing behind it, had been broken off. The room had been opened to the outside, but it was not Siluvanede Valmaxian saw there. The "outside" was a blasted landscape of sand and rock—dead, barren, and bathed in a blood-red light. The wind poured out of it in unnaturally sustained waves of near-blistering heat. The air held a foul odor—no, a thousand foul odors—and searing grains of white-hot sand.

Valmaxian stood at the doorway of his lover's bedchamber and stared straight into the depths of the Abyss itself.

"Chasianna!"

A figure stepped out from behind a twisted spur of wind-carved rock.

Valmaxian stepped forward, the staff tapping the floor next to him, and said, "Chasianna . . . is it you?"

A second figure eased from around another rock, then a third, and a fourth. Valmaxian stepped forward again, his heart beating rapidly, sweat beginning to pour from him in sheets.

More of them appeared from the sand-blown air of the Abyss. They were bent, bloated forms not unlike elves in that each had two arms, two legs, and a head. The comparison stopped there. None of them stood more than four feet tall. Their pale, gray skin shone almost purple in that hellish light. Their mouths hung open, revealing irregular rows of serrated fangs. From the tips of their chubby, almost childlike fingers grew long, heavy claws. There were more than a dozen of them, and when Valmaxian stopped moving they rushed forward.

Valmaxian thrust the staff out in front of him and spoke the now-familiar command. Bolts of arcane energy spat from the tip of the staff—five of them—and split into separate paths on their way to the bloated humanoids. Five of them fell, but the others came forward, so Valmaxian sent five more missiles into their midst and dropped five more.

He could kill many of them that way, but for every five that fell, seven or eight more appeared from the rocks and concealing wind behind them. Valmaxian spoke a different command. The first little demon that touched what Valmaxian had conjured in front of him recoiled in unhurt surprise from the solid wall that was there but could not be seen. The other little demons—dretches, Valmaxian recalled—railed against the wall, pounding at what looked like thin air, scratching at it, even biting it.

Valmaxian stepped through the gate and felt as if he was falling. The effect passed a heartbeat later and he was aware of the heat radiating from the coarse sand. It started to burn his skin, as hot as a summer sun, and he could feel it on the soles of his feet even through his sturdy boots.

Valmaxian looked up and caught the eye of a particularly bulbous dretch on the other side of the invisible wall. The thing bared its spiny teeth at him. Its eyes bulged and its nostrils flared. Valmaxian felt a shiver course through his sweating arms. He drew in a breath and held it, then realized the thing was using magic. Valmaxian shrugged it off. He would not be scared away that easily. He would not be scared at all.

Valmaxian smiled and started to utter the complex words of a spell. The dretch wanted to scare him, but Valmaxian knew how to scare people too, and he knew how to do it better. The spell rolled off his tongue, and his hands traced the intricate patterns in the air in front of him. Valmaxian could feel the energy burst out of him. He couldn't see anything, but he knew the dretch and several of its rotund companions could. They saw their worst nightmares, their most vile imaginings, the terror that consumed their hearts, smash into their fragile psyches and explode. They ran, losing their water on the burning sands, screaming, gibbering in some freakish Abyssal dialect that Valmaxian was glad he couldn't understand.

Not all of them ran, though. There was a way around the wall of force and a few of the dretches found it. That was enough to lead the others in that direction. Dozens more kept drifting out from behind stones, and a few even dug their way from under the sand like zombies rising from the grave. Valmaxian peppered them with glowing missiles of concentrated Weave. He dropped five at a time: five, ten, fifteen, twenty. . . .

One dretch got within a few paces of Valmaxian and spat out a cloud of gas. The vapor seemed to stick in the wind, moving with it but not as quickly as the sand that passed through it. It coalesced into a cloud of greenish gray smoke that looked like a miniature thunderhead. Valmaxian could smell the cloud from several paces away, and it almost made him gag. The smell was indescribable. Valmaxian rattled through another spell and held his arms out on each side of him. He roared an incoherent challenge, and a rush of wind spread out, knocking a few of the little demons off their feet and sending the roiling cloud of reek scattering into the blowing sand.

He'd had to concentrate at least a little to cast the spell, and in the time his attention was occupied a dretch drew sharp, jagged claws across his midsection. Valmaxian hissed in pain and struck out at the dretch with the staff. The fine weapon pulped the creature's head, spraying green and gray fluids across the sand in front of Valmaxian. Another of the little demons came up to take the headless dretch's place, and Valmaxian swung the staff around, smacking it into the thing's chest hard enough to shatter ribs, break skin, and spill out the fiend's stomach. It died squealing, then everything went dark.

It wasn't a natural darkness. It wasn't night, and Valmaxian wasn't blind. It was a darkness that only the Weave could create. Valmaxian reacted quickly. He could hear more of the things near him and getting closer. He hissed through a spell and felt his skin tighten, felt something touch him in an angry, violent manner, but it didn't hurt. There came a clang like something hard banging on steel. Valmaxian smiled, though it wasn't easy since his spell had turned his skin to iron.

A dretch grabbed his right leg, but Valmaxian couldn't see it. He felt another hand on his side, an arm beginning to encircle his waist. He muttered a command word, and the lighting returned to its normal dull red as he used the staff to kill the dretches that were trying to drag him down. Their brains were smooth and yellow.

With magic missiles he dropped a few more that had dared to come close under cover of the darkness. Valmaxian knew he had to face the fact that the dretches would always be more afraid of En'Sel'Dinen than they would be of him, no matter how many spells he cast or how many he killed.

The elf mage looked up and counted the dretches as they came at him. He dropped a few with magic missiles as they came too close, but he stepped back to buy himself time as well. He watched where they were coming from, how they all moved just a little bit to one side, how they congregated in the entrance to a narrow, windswept gorge. He saw them blocking his way, but only in that direction. Valmaxian was smarter than he needed to be to understand that the dretches were guarding the gorge—guarding the way to En'Sel'Dinen, and Chasianna.

Valmaxian turned that way and started walking. Some of the dretches in front were brave enough or scared enough to lunge at him. He killed some by smashing the staff into their heads. Others he killed with magic missiles. Some he killed with spells. The smell of the internal organs of the little fiends, their sweat, panic, and blood filled the stinging air along with the sand. Valmaxian didn't bother counting how many he killed. It might have been thousands.

It just went on and on.

The demon had torn off all of her clothes, and Chasianna's skin blazed red in the oppressive heat of the Abyss. Her hands were bound behind her back and she was gagged to keep her from casting spells. En'Sel'Dinen held her long hair tightly in one of his massive hands. A tear traced a path down one of her grimy cheeks, and her eyes were red and puffy. Deep cuts crisscrossed her arms, and her knees bled. Bruises blossomed all over her. She was a mess, but the fact that she was alive made her the most beautiful thing Valmaxian had ever seen.

"Demon!" Valmaxian called, tensing his chest to hold back a body-racking cough.

En'Sel'Dinen smiled. The dretches surrounding him scurried into hiding among freakish stone statues that littered the wind-blasted plain. The demon's silver eyes shone red in the deep orange light that seemed to come from the sky itself. There was no sun. There was nothing so logical and steadfast as that in the chaotic depths of the endless Abyss.

"Ah, Valmaxian," En'Sel'Dinen rumbled, "at last. Bravo on the dretches, my old friend. It's been hours since I've seen so many dispatched so quickly."

Valmaxian ignored the demon and looked at Chasianna. "Are you—?" he started to ask.

"She won't be answering, elf," the demon interrupted. "She belongs to me now—in body if not in soul."

Valmaxian, Chasianna's voice rang in the Gold elf's head, *blink if you can hear me.*

Valmaxian blinked, and Chasianna let her head fall in relief.

How are you doing this? Valmaxian thought.

"I was right about her skin, my friend," the demon growled. "It's soft as the guts of a dragon. But I will have to empty her willful mind."

He'll hear soon, Chasianna answered. *You can defeat him, but it will mean draining the staff.*

"I know," Valmaxian answered aloud.

En'Sel'Dinen looked down at Chasianna, the twisted smile fading quickly. "Bitch," the demon growled. "That little trick will be the first to go."

The demon opened his fang-lined mouth and leaned toward the girl at the same time he pulled her closer to him.

Valmaxian shouted a command word, and a flurry of white-hot spheres blasted from the staff and pounded into the demon with enough force to topple a keep on Toril.

The demon shrieked, more in surprise than pain, and tossed Chasianna to the burning ground.

The fiend spun on Valmaxian and screamed, "She's mine! You were paid in full!"

"I'm ending our arrangement, demon," Valmaxian said, "and I'm taking her with me."

En'Sel'Dinen lunged forward and his eyes blazed. Valmaxian felt his heart skip a beat, and a wave of pain twisted his chest and drove him to his knees. He tried to breathe in but couldn't. The skin on his face burned. His right hand tightened on the staff, causing his forearm to cramp.

"Heartstop," the demon said, "is what the humans on your world call it, elf. You have seconds to live."

Valmaxian couldn't speak, couldn't even stand. He looked up at Chasianna lying on the sandy ground, her eyes wide and terrified. He could almost see himself, weak and dying, reflected in those eyes.

He broke the staff.

Retributive strike—it was a power he'd hope to gain from the demon but had always had inside him. He could have added it to the staff's many powerful enchantments himself, but it would have required such a sacrifice of magic and personal energies that it would have left him with hardly the power of a novice spellcaster. He'd traded Chasianna's freedom, her body, and his own soul for it, but he had one chance to take it all back.

The staff broke apart, and the sound was almost enough to drown out the demon's scream.

Valmaxian felt a wave of cold wash over him. The pain in his chest eased just enough for him to force a gasp of air into his lungs. He felt a rough, hot hand on his shoulder, felt himself tossed to one side to land with a scraping skid on the coarse sand. He felt the staff fall from his hand. He heard the demon scream again, and there was a shouted string of words so arcane and foul Valmaxian's ears began to bleed from the sound of them.

"Chasianna," Valmaxian gasped, "I'm sorry."

The sound stopped all at once and silence fell over them like a shroud. The pain and tightness in Valmaxian's chest was gone, and he found he could breathe. The cold was gone too, replaced by the scorching dry air of the Abyss. Valmaxian spat out a mouthful of burning sand and coughed enough to make his vision blur. He blinked away the tears that filled his eyes and looked up. Chasianna struggled to a sitting position. New bruises, cuts, and scrapes covered what little of her hadn't been bruised, cut, or scraped before. She coughed too, but managed to catch Valmaxian's gaze. The gag hung off her face. She opened her mouth to speak, but it was the demon Valmaxian heard.

"That was very, very close, elf," the monster said, its voice somehow less forceful, quieter.

Valmaxian looked over at the source of the voice and had to struggle to keep from retching. The demon had been blasted into pieces—chunks really—by the force of the staff's retributive strike. Blood so dark red it was almost black had splattered everywhere, and one of the demon's powerful legs twitched on the sand a good ten yards from the hip it had once been attached to. The demon looked at Valmaxian with only one eye, the other lost to the ruin the left half of the creature's face had become. His head, attached to only one shoulder and one arm, rolled on the gore-soaked ground. The demon's torso had been split diagonally down the middle, and his right arm was nowhere to be seen. In his left hand he held the shredded, shortened remnants of the staff.

Valmaxian struggled to his feet, but found himself falling more than walking to Chasianna's side.

"You are a fool," the demon called after him. "What's left of your greatest creation will make a mockery of your wasted life."

Valmaxian ignored him. Pain flared in dozens of places around his body and he could feel a palpable sense of emptiness. Valmaxian would return to Siluvanede and his studio with less command of the Weave than any of his assistants, and no staff to show for it. He would indeed be ruined.

"Valmaxian," Chasianna said. "Untie my hands."

"Ruined," the demon muttered, with perhaps the slightest trace of regret. "The great Staff of Valmaxian in splinters."

Valmaxian struggled with the bonds, but Chasianna's hands soon came free. She drew in a breath and started to work a spell.

"Hold on to me," she whispered in his ear.

"Ruined!" the demon shrieked in impotent rage, unable to stand, unable to kill the two elves who were already fading from sight. "You have nothing!"

"Hold on to me," Chasianna whispered again as the sound of the wind faded around them. "We're going home."

Valmaxian closed his eyes, held on tight, and smiled.

The last sound they heard in the Abyss was the demon En'Sel'Dinen, lying in pieces on the sand, screaming, "You have nothing, elf! You have nothing!"

The demon was wrong.

NECESSARY SACRIFICES

Lisa Smedman

The Year of the Behir (1342 DR)

Corwyn followed the brunette down the narrow cellar steps, admiring the sway of her hips. She moved down like a dancer, in time with the music that filled the tap room of the inn above. The Old Skull Inn might have a reputation for drawing unsavory characters, but the women Jhaele hired to wait tables more than made up for it. This one had the most delicious laugh, and hips like . . .

Something was wrong. The brunette had stopped at the bottom of the stairs. She stood rigid, staring at something on the floor. Beyond her, in the darkened cellar, a shadow shifted.

Instantly sober, Corwyn drew his short sword. He stepped past her, sweeping her behind him with one arm.

A *twang* sounded from the far corner of the

cellar. Pain lanced into Corwyn's thigh. He didn't stop to glance down at the wound.

"Up the stairs," he shouted, giving the brunette a shove. At the same time, he marked a dim patch of white hair against ebony skin. Drow.

He charged, thrusting at the dark elf's chest. The drow dodged the blade with uncanny speed, simultaneously spinning and slamming a foot into the back of Corwyn's knee.

Corwyn stumbled, but managed to dodge the dagger that slashed at his arm. That it hadn't been a thrust for the vitals told him something: the dagger must be poisoned. Reeling back to his feet, the bolt in his thigh a hot point of pain, he somehow managed to catch the drow's wrist with his free hand. The wrist was sticky, coated in something that allowed Corwyn to maintain his grip. He slammed the dark elf's hand into the wall, and heard the knife clatter to the floor.

The drow spat a word at Corwyn—a curse. Then he wrenched his wrist free and spun. An elbow slammed into Corwyn's temple. Blinking stars, Corwyn staggered back, sword loose in his hand. He flailed with it as the dark elf retreated, and heard the sound of wood sliding against stone then only the sound of his own harsh breathing and feet pounding down the stairs.

His foot slid on something: Spilled blood.

That was when he looked down and saw the boy.

The Year of Moonfall (1344 DR)

Blowing snow stung Sorrell's face as he trudged through the forest. As the curtain of white shifted, the trees that surrounded him were screened from sight, then reappeared again. High above in the creaking branches, the elves of Cormanthor—his People—sat snug behind shuttered windows in their treetop homes, celebrating Midwinter Night. He caught the faint smell of mulled wine and onion-baked venison, and heard snatches of song over the shrill of the wind.

He drew his cloak tighter and shivered. For him, there would be no more singing. The ache inside him had stoppered his voice like a plug of ice.

He strode on, chin tucked into his chest, the club that hung from his belt swinging as he walked. Eventually, in the dusk ahead, a massive oak tree loomed. It had a trunk the size of a tower. A dozen elves with hands joined might just have encircled it. As Sorrell drew closer, he could see that the oak was utterly black, just as the songs had said. Its trunk, branches, and leaves—which had never fallen, not for five millennia—were as dark as a drow's heart.

Between two of the massive roots was a hole in the ground. Stairs, slick with ice, spiraled down into darkness. Sorrell paused at the top of it. He'd traveled so far, but he was finally there—and in time for Midwinter Night. After two years, did he still want to quench his sorrow in blood?

He reached under his cloak and slid a finger into the pocket of his shirt—the pocket over his heart—and touched a lock of auburn hair, tied with a frayed ribbon.

He touched the black bark. Brilliant white light flared around his hand, bright enough to reveal the dark shadows of the bones within his flesh.

"I give myself to you, Shevarash," he intoned in a voice made flat by grief. "A weapon in your hands. Use me well."

The air in the cavern beneath the oak stank of damp stone and earth, the smells of the Underdark. The cavern was large, but the black tree roots that twisted down through it made it seem tight and confined. Dozens of elves filled it: pale, willowy moon elves; sun elves with skin the color of burnished bronze; stockier wood elves like Sorrell—even a couple of wild elves with black tattoos on their bark-brown skin. All of the Dark Avengers were dressed in the ritual vestments of Shevarash's faith. Elven chain mail gleamed in the light of the candles they held, and blood-red cloaks draped their shoulders. Their faces were hidden by helmets with a fixed half-visor, revealing only their eyes and their grim mouths.

One of the *dhaeraowathila* led Sorrell to an altar at the center of the cavern. Weapons were piled around it in a heap: axes with broken handles, rapiers with notched blades, battered bucklers, splintered crossbows missing their strings, and hundreds of broken crossbow bolts. Drow weapons, all. Sorrell's breath lumped in his throat as he spotted a dagger with a spider-shaped pommel; a furrow in its blade held the remnants of poison, faded to a dull brown. The sight of it tore a sick hollow in his gut.

He climbed across the shifting pile of broken weapons, onto the altar. As he turned to face the *dhaeraowathila*, the elves in the cavern began to keen in voices both male and female. That there were women among Shevarash's faithful shouldn't have surprised him; Dalmara had been stronger than him, that terrible night.

The *dhaeraowathila* who had led Sorrell to the altar—a sun elf with hands criss-crossed with old scars—handed him a crossbow bolt fletched with bone-white feathers. Sorrell gripped it at both ends, crunching the fletches in his right fist. The barbed point cut into his left palm; the pain was sharp and clean—and welcome.

As the keening grew to a wail, the *dhaeraowathila* nodded. Sorrell lifted the bolt, then broke it across one raised knee.

The keening stopped.

"Sorrell Ilithaine," the *dhaeraowathila* intoned, "what do you seek?" His voice was gravelly, as low as a dwarf's.

The poisoned dagger atop the heap of weapons still held Sorrell's eye. He swallowed down the lump in his throat.

"Vengeance," he whispered.

The *dhaeraowathila*'s hand shot out, grabbed Sorrell's shirt. The priest pulled Sorrell's face close to his own. His eyes blazed from behind his visor. "Does your heart not burn?"

Sorrell managed a nod. A lie. His heart didn't burn. It was ice.

"Then shout!"

Sorrell reeled backward as the priest released him. He took a deep breath and clenched his fists tighter around the broken pieces of the crossbow bolt. He pictured the horror he'd seen in the cellar that night. The two he held most dear, dead.

"Vengeance!"

He raised the halves of the broken bolt and tipped back his head, shouting at the ceiling above.

"Vengeance!"

His body was rigid, tense. He expected something to break, to release the tears that were dammed up inside him.

It didn't.

Slowly, he lowered his hands.

One of the other elves stepped forward, handing the *dhaeraowathila* a helm filled with blood. The priest held it out. Sorrell glanced down, wondering whose blood it was, then decided it didn't matter.

He dipped the broken ends of the bolt in it then raised them to his face. He touched one to each cheek, just below the eye, and waited. Blood dripped onto his hands, and trickled down his wrists.

"Do you swear to serve Shevarash?" the priest asked.

"I so swear," Sorrell answered.

"To be his weapon of vengeance against the drow?"

"I so swear."

"To give no quarter, and to demand none? To carry the fight ever onward and downward? To continue on, until your own death should come?"

Sorrell gave a wry smile. Death would be welcome. A release. "I so swear."

"Never again to laugh, never to *smile*, until the day the last drow lies dead?"

Sorrell's jaw tightened. He could feel a blaze kindling in his own eyes. "I so swear."

With a savage yank, he pulled his hands downward, painting twin streaks of red down his cheeks.

Blood tears.

The *dhaeraowathila* lowered the blood-filled helm and said, "Then welcome, brother. Welcome to our war."

Sorrell waited on the veranda that encircled the High Council chamber. Snowflakes blew in through the veranda's latticelike outer wall and swirled around his boots. The floor shifted slightly as the tree branches that supported it bent in the wind. Sorrell's shoulders hunched, but not against the morning's cold. Tension bent him like a strung bow as he silently composed the plea he was about to deliver. His fists clenched. His entreaty had to work. It *had* to.

After a moment, a door opened. A wood elf with a high forehead framed with graying hair stepped out, shutting the door behind him. His clothes were of green velvet, embroidered with gold; on his right index finger was a gold ring with an enormous carved emerald: a council seal stone.

Sorrell touched his right hand to his heart and bowed low. "Councilor Rellithorn."

Hands clasped Sorrell's shoulders and straightened him. The older elf stared at the dried blood on Sorrell's cheeks. One hand shifted slightly, as if to wipe it away, then returned to Sorrell's shoulder. The older elf squeezed Sorrell's shoulders tightly, and for a moment Sorrell thought he was going to be drawn into a hug.

"Sorrell. Welcome home, nephew." The older elf he took a step back, reestablishing a formal distance. "What is so urgent that you insisted on interrupting an emergency meeting of the High Council?"

Sorrell's jaw clenched. "I heard about this morning's attack, Uncle Alcorn. Everyone in the temple was talking about it after the High Council summoned the *dhaeraowathila.* You're going to send one of the Dark Avenger war bands out." He touched the handle of his club. "I want to go with them."

Alcorn shook his head. "You're untrained. The war band we're sending won't take you—especially on a mission of such importance. The two attackers came through the portal that joins us to the Yuirwood; somehow, they discovered how to use it. They were part of a scouting party, and must be hunted down before they can return with this information to whatever drow city sent them. If we fail, Cormanthor could face an attack in force—and at the worst possible time."

Sorrell nodded. After six hundred years of debate, the High Council had finally come to a decision. Cormanthor, like Eaerlann before it, would be abandoned to the encroaching humans. The elves would retreat to Evermeet, a land the humans could never defile. Even then, preparations were being made—preparations that would all be for naught, if the drow attacked in the meantime.

Sorrell squared his shoulders. "The drow that was killed. I heard . . . " His voice dropped to a raw whisper. "They say his fist was blackened with pitch. Is it true?"

It took Alcorn a moment to meet Sorrell's eyes. "It's true."

Those two simple words punched into Sorrell like blows, leaving him slightly dizzy. He took a deep breath. "Uncle, can you not see the hand of Shevarash at work? Midwinter Night, and I am accepted into his faith. The very next morning, there is an attack by the same group of drow who . . . " He paused, choked down the emotion that clawed at his throat with fingers of ice. "Please," he pleaded, his script forgotten. "This might be my only chance to avenge Dalmara and . . . and . . . "

Alcorn's eyes softened. He glanced at the door that led to the High Council chambers, then back at Sorrell. "I'll see what I can do."

Sorrell returned to the room the Dark Avengers had assigned him. It was sparsely furnished, with only a chest to hold his belongings and a hard wooden bench for Reverie. The walls were of plain stone, bereft of the carvings and paintings that usually decorated an elven dwelling. He sat on the edge of the bench, twisting the leather thong that hung from the grip of his club, wondering if his uncle would follow through on his promise.

The answer came a moment later, when Pendaran, the priest who had initiated Sorrell into Shevarash's faith, opened the door. The *dhaeraowathila* wore a plain brown cloak and trousers, a contrast to the polished armor he'd worn the night before. The scars on his hands and the gnarled mass of scar tissue where the tip of his left ear had been attested to his many battles. Sorrell had heard that the sun elf had been an officer in Evermeet's cavalry before joining Shevarash's faithful.

Pendaran held a worn pack in his hands. He tossed it onto the bench where Sorrell sat, then folded his arms across his chest. His face and hands were a dull metallic gray, as if his skin had been painted.

Sorrell stared at the pack, realizing what it meant. He nearly smiled, catching himself just in time. "I'm going?"

Pendaran's wheat-blond eyebrows pulled down into a scowl. "By order of the High Council, yes."

Sorrell's heart beat a little faster as he rose to his feet. And so it began—his chance at vengeance. "You won't be sorry."

"We'll see." Pendaran nodded at Sorrell's club. "I noticed that your weapon is ensorcelled. Do you know how to use it?"

Sorrell lifted his club. Made of black thornwood, it only had a simple haste dweomer placed on it, but Pendaran was right in one respect: Sorrell knew this weapon. He'd spent months learning from the best fighters he could find, and more months smashing massive gnarlwood nuts, imagining each to be a drow head. Practicing hard, until the weapon felt as natural in his hand as a lute once had. He could hold the heavy club at arm's length, level with his shoulder, for an entire afternoon without so much as a twinge in his muscles. He was as strong as any warrior—a far cry from the man he had once been.

"I know how to use it," he assured Pendaran.

The sun elf nodded. "You'll be joining the Silent Slayers—the band of crusaders that I lead. You'll be club bearer."

"Shevarash's fifth and final weapon," Sorrell recited. "The club Maelat, which he carries together with Shama, his spear, and Ukava, his sling, when he appears in the guise of Elikarashe, as he is called in the songs of the Yuir." He nodded at the quiver at Pendaran's hip. "His other two weapons are the Black Bow, and Traitorbane, his sword."

Pendaran's eyebrows raised slightly. "For a novice, you already know a lot about our faith."

"I learned that from a song years ago. Long before—"

"Before the assassins of the Blackened Fist struck," Pendaran finished for him. "Your uncle told me why you're here." His eyes bored into Sorrell's. "That's why I agreed to take you. Not because of the High Council's orders, but because this is your fight." He paused. "You will have to do everything you're told, exactly as you're told, the instant you're told. Understood?"

Sorrell gave a fierce nod. "Understood."

Pendaran's eyes blazed. "We will have our vengeance. The drow have no mercy, and deserve none. They're vermin that kill man, woman and—"

Sorrell blinked in surprise. "They killed your *child*?"

"She may as well have been." Pendaran's mouth ticked with silent emotion. "Her name was Alfaras. She was a moon-horse. A loyal mount, fierce in battle—until a drow bolt found her heart."

Sorrell could only stare. How could the loss of a *horse* compare to—

"I raised her from a foal," Pendaran whispered. "She

came to me, willingly, from the herd. I rode her for nearly a century. One day, I'll ride her again. In Arvandor."

He turned and picked up the pack. "Inside is everything you'll need in the Underdark." He untied the main flap and pulled out a belt with a series of loops that held small metal vials sealed with waxed corks. "Potions for curing, and for neutralizing poison." He draped the belt over the chair, then pulled out a bandolier with larger loops that held rough-cut quartz prisms. "Flash gems. With a time delay. Speak the command word, throw one into a cavern or drop it down a rock chimney, then close your eyes for a count of three. Anything that's sensitive to light will be blinded long enough for you to kill it."

Next came soft leather boots, as new looking as the pack was worn. They were dark red, embroidered with thread-of-gold. Pendaran held them up, then let them fall to the ground. They landed without making a sound.

"Boots of silent striding?"

"More than that." Pendaran spoke a command word: "*Levarithin.*"

The boots gently lifted from the floor. Pendaran held out a hand, stopping them before they rose to the ceiling. "*Descenthallan.*" The boots sank gently to the floor. He stared a challenge at Sorrell. "You got that?"

Sorrell nodded. "*Levarithin . . . descenthallan.* Got it." The boots rose from the floor, then sank again.

"Good." Pendaran lifted a fine silver chain from the pack; dangling from it was a circle of what looked like clear glass. A ring. Unfastening the chain, he slid the ring off and handed it to Sorrell. "Put it on."

"Which finger?"

"It doesn't matter."

Sorrell slipped the ring onto his left index finger. The magical ring adjusted to fit, then seemingly disappeared. Sorrell could feel it, but couldn't see it.

"*Vanessaril* to become invisible," Pendaran instructed. "*Maniferril* to become visible again."

Sorrell repeated the first command word. Going

invisible was an odd sensation. He had to fight the urge to turn around and see where his body had gone. It left him feeling off center and slightly dizzy.

"*Maniferril*," he said, glad to be able to see his feet again.

"You'll get used to it," Pendaran said. "But don't come to rely on it. The Underdark's filled with traps and wards that will kill you just as dead, visible or invisible."

Sorrell lowered his hand. "How soon do we leave?"

"As soon as you've put this on." Pendaran pulled a metal jar from the pack and handed it to Sorrell. Like the potion vials, it was sealed with a cork. The wax seal had already been broken, and the outside of the jar was smudged with gray. It smelled like mud mixed with herbs.

"Magical armor paint," Pendaran explained. "Strip down, and smear it over every bit of your body—especially those bits you'd most like to keep."

Sorrell met Pendaran's eyes. The *dhaeraowathila* was testing him, seeing if Sorrell would forget his vow by smiling at the joke. The veiled reference to lovemaking, however, reminded Sorrell of Dalmara . . . and of children.

The lump of ice returned to his heart.

"Something wrong?" Pendaran asked.

Sorrell managed to shake his head. "No, sir." The title came unbidden to his lips; it fit. Sorrell met his eye and slapped a hand against the handle of his club. "I'm looking forward to splitting drow skulls."

"Good. When you've finished, join us near Shevarash's Oak. I'll be briefing the war band there."

Sorrell stood with the other members of Pendaran's war band near the portal, waiting as two elves swept it clear of snow. There was evidence of a recent fight. The snow that had fallen since then hadn't quite covered up the crystallized patches of red that were frozen blood.

Pendaran briefed his war band. "Two drow came through. One was killed, but the second escaped back through the portal. She was wounded—badly enough that she left a trail the half-elves could follow. It led to a cavern with an entrance no wider than a crack; the half-elves had to use magic to see inside it. They spotted a chimney in the rock, leading down to the Underdark. From the boot prints they found they estimate there were five drow in total."

Pendaran ran a scarred hand through his wheat-colored hair. "A scouting *thalakz*," he concluded, using a drow word. "One down, and four to go. And one of the four wounded, and slowing the rest down. Their leader, obviously, or they would have killed her."

As he listened, Sorrell stared at the other three members of Pendaran's war band.

Koora was a heavily tattooed wild elf, with dark brown skin and black, wavy hair, and the nervous, watchful air of a woodland creature that would startle at a sudden move. A small, dark blue gem—obviously magical—orbited her head like a restless fly. A sling hung coiled at her belt, next to a lumpy looking leather bag that probably held sling stones. Her feet were bare, despite the snow.

The other two—Nairen and Adair—were clearly related. They had the same triangular jaw, the same thin eyebrows that met in a **V** over a narrow nose. The resemblance was close enough that they were probably brothers—though Nairen, the one with the broadsword at his hip, was a full moon elf, and Adair, the one leaning on the short spear, was part human. Both were tall and wiry, with fair skin the color of cream and hair so black it shone a deep, silken blue. Nairen wore his in a neat braid that hung down his back, while Adair's was loose and looked as though it had been hacked to its shoulder length with a knife. There were threads of gray in it; Adair looked twice as old as Nairen. But half-elves aged faster. The two might very well have been only a year apart.

Both men were still young. Added together, their ages would probably barely match Sorrell's own hundred and twenty-six years.

Pendaran, however, was easily twice Sorrell's age, well into his third century of life. He was armed, that morning, with a bow that was black as night and strung with a blood-red string. A quiver at his hip, next to a sheathed dagger, held a dozen arrows with red fletching.

The sweepers moved aside with their brooms. The portal was a mosaic made from thousands of pebbles set into the forest floor; dark green stones formed a pattern of oversized leaves that spiraled in toward the mosaic's center. Only by stepping on the leaves in a specific pattern could the portal's magic be triggered. Sorrell had never used the portal before. He'd have to watch where the others stepped, or be left behind.

He expected Pendaran to set out immediately, but the *dhaeraowathila* was busy untying the strings of a small silk bag. The others in the war band gathered around him expectantly. They gave Sorrell sharp glances as he joined them.

Pendaran tipped the bag's contents into one calloused palm: five rings made of a brownish material that looked like carved horn. He held out his hand; Koora, Nairen and Adair each took a ring. Sorrell hesitated, then took the fifth ring. He slid it onto the second finger of his left hand, next to the invisibility ring. Immediately, his awareness expanded fivefold. He was aware of everything around him, as if he were looking and listening in several different directions at once. His mind filled with voices.

. . . filthy spider kissers. A male voice—either Nairen's or Adair's.

Five silver pieces says I take down more than you. Similar to the first voice, but deeper, more human sounding.

Good hunting. That voice was female, with the distinctive lilt of a wild elf. Koora.

Cut the chatter, Pendaran ordered.

The voices fell silent.

Pendaran turned to Sorrell. "To use the ring, imagine yourself speaking to the person you want to talk to," he said out loud.

Sorrell concentrated. *Like this*?

He saw Adair wince.

Not so loud, Nairen snapped.

Novices, Adair grumbled, shaking his head.

Sorrell gave the half-elf a sharp look. Adair had obviously intended him to hear that.

Let's go, Pendaran ordered.

Sorrell expected Pendaran to take the lead, but it was the wild elf Koora who stepped onto the portal first. Pendaran followed.

You're next, said Nairen, gesturing with a jerk of his head. *The new man goes in the middle, where he can do the least harm. Remember that.*

Sorrell shrugged off the comment. The Silent Slayers had worked together as a team for nearly six years—he'd overheard someone mention that the night before—and were obviously used to doing things a certain way. And Sorrell had yet to prove himself. He nodded and stepped onto the first leaf, observing where Pendaran placed his feet. Nairen and Adair followed.

Koora reached the center of the spiral and vanished. Then Pendaran. One moment the grizzled knight was just ahead of Sorrell; the next, he was gone. Only a faint shimmer in the air marked the transition. Sorrell hesitated for a heartbeat, then stepped on the center leaf himself.

It was as if he'd stepped into a cyclone. The world spun crazily around him, trees flashing past in a blur. Reeling sideways like a drunken man, he fell to his hands and knees. He glanced up and saw Pendaran staring down at him, a slight frown on his face. Sorrell scrambled to his feet, ignoring the scrapes on his hands—and on his dignity.

Nairen, then Adair stepped out of the center of the portal.

The mosaic they'd been transported to looked identical to the first, save for the fact that the leaves on it were red. Pendaran glanced around, then waved the group on.

Sorrell trudged along at the middle of the group, as

instructed. In the Yuirwood, it wasn't snowing. The ground was clear, though icicles tinkled in the branches above. And it was cold; Sorrell's breath fogged the air. In years gone by, he would have wrapped a cloth around his throat and mouth to protect his voice.

He inhaled, savoring the bite of cold air inside his lungs.

A short time later, an outcropping of granite could be seen through the forest ahead. Pendaran halted the group and pointed out a crack, no more than a palm's breadth wide, that ran up the face of the rock. *There it is.*

He glanced around, then whistled softly. A moment later, a patch of brown detached itself from a nearby tree. It was a half-elf, her hooded cloak and trousers the exact shade of the forest around them, her face and hands stained a mottled brown. Save for her bright blue eyes, Sorrell would have had difficulty spotting her, even close up. Her boots must also have been magical; she moved without making a sound. She held a bow with a nocked arrow in one hand. She assured Pendaran that nothing and no one—visible or invisible—had passed through the crack since morning.

Pendaran glanced at Nairen.

The wild elf stood with closed eyes, her arms extended toward the crack in the rock.

Pendaran nodded.

Adair leveled his spear at the crack and whispered under his breath.

Pendaran nodded again.

Nairen caught his leader's eye, shook his head.

Sorrell realized the Silent Slayers were talking to one another, comparing notes as they used magic to examine the cave. He felt like an outsider, watching a performance he wasn't allowed to participate in.

Join up, Pendaran said. *We're going in.* He repeated the latter, out loud, to the half-elf who had been standing watch in the forest. The woman saluted them, then resumed her vigil.

The other three Slayers each laid a hand on their leader's shoulder. When Pendaran glanced impatiently at him, Sorrell did the same. He noticed that the others were crouching slightly, and bent his own knees. Pendaran's lips moved in silent prayer, and he took a step forward. Sorrell felt a tearing sensation, as if his body had been yanked thin, and found himself standing inside a cave. The walls were jagged and rough; ice-split granite. Loose stone shifted underfoot. Sorrell started to straighten—

Watch your head, fool!

The warning was in Nairen's voice. And it was a heartbeat too late. Sorrell cracked his head on a bulge of rock that he hadn't noticed in the dimly lit cave. Wincing, he sank back into a crouch.

Koora squatted beside a hole near the back of the cavern, her hands extended over it, palms down. Adair and Nairen stood to either side of her, weapons ready. Pendaran scowled, then nodded as if he'd made a decision. Koora began to whisper: another spell. Not sure what was expected of him, Sorrell snuck a glance out through the crack in the rock at the trees of the Yuirwood. He tried to fix the image in his mind; it might very well be the last time he saw a forest.

Switch to Shevarash's sight, everyone, and activate your rings.

Sorrell heard whispered voices. Glancing over his shoulder, he saw the Slayers disappear from sight, one after the other. He was about to speak his ring's command word when something in the cave's entrance caught his eye. He at first dismissed it as a large bug, then realized it had a square shape. Curious, he took a step closer.

The moving thing was a tiny wooden chest, just the right size for a child's doll house, with eight legs that looked like they were made of stiff black string. As it crawled into the cave, Sorrell jerked his foot back from it.

What in the Abyss is that?

What? Pendaran asked.

Sorrell hadn't realized his exclamation had gone out

to the group. He started to answer aloud, then caught himself. No more mistakes.

On the floor near my foot. A tiny chest—probably magical, he guessed. *It looks kind of like a spider.*

He heard Koora whisper. Sparkles of magical energy streaked from where she had been crouched and crackled around the miniature chest. Its legs fell still.

Sorrell felt a hand nudge him aside. *Don't touch it.* Pendaran's voice echoed in his head.

Sorrell stepped back. He heard a slight rustle, and guessed that Pendaran was squatting to examine the miniature chest. A faint metallic rasp announced a dagger being drawn from its sheath, then he heard a pop that sounded like a cork being drawn. The miniature chest shifted slightly as an invisible dagger tip poked it. Slowly, its lid lifted. Inside was a bright red powder that rose into the air in a puff as the lid was raised. A stream of liquid appeared , pouring onto the chest from an invisible container; the liquid quenched the cloud and filled the chest, making the remaining powder hiss and bubble.

Poison spores, Pendaran announced.

Sorrell heard a rustle as Pendaran stood.

There will be more, the leader continued. *Following their makers, slowly creeping their way toward the chimney to tumble in and dump their poison on us. But by the grace of Shevarash, we have discovered them.*

Sorrell was certain the lengthy speech had been for his benefit: a morale booster. Or perhaps for the enlightenment of those around him; he heard low-pitched, grudging acknowledgement from the two brothers.

Find the rest of them, Koora, Pendaran continued. *Dispel them.*

Sorrell heard a female voice whisper a prayer. Sparkles of magical energy shot out of the cave's entrance and coalesced around tiny objects on the ground beyond. He felt someone move close—Pendaran.

Close your eyes, the leader instructed.

Sorrell did, and felt a fingertip touch each eye. A

whispered prayer followed. When Sorrell opened his eyes again, he could see the others again. Or rather, he could see the shifting auras that were their heat signatures. Their bodies were tones of red: a dull ruby where clothing masked body heat, bright orange-red on exposed faces and hands. White plumes bloomed at their noses each time they exhaled, quickly fading to yellow, then dusky orange, then purple-blue. Their extremities—ears and fingers—were blobs of darker, purplish red. Behind them, the stone of the cavern was dark purple, almost black, colder than the air that filled it. As they moved, fuzzy afterimages of lingering heat briefly streaked the air, then faded. Their boots left dull smudges of blue warmth on the colder ground.

The effect was stunning in its beauty—so riveting that for a moment Sorrell found himself starting to hum a tune under his breath and wondering how he would possibly convey it in verse.

Then Pendaran's gruff voice-thoughts ordered them into the chimney. *Weapons at the ready*, he instructed. *There's a larger cavern below. If we missed anything, we'll have a fight on our hands. Fan out as soon as your feet hit the floor.*

Sobered, Sorrell readied his club. He watched as Koora stepped onto the empty space above the chimney and sank slowly from sight. Pendaran followed. Then it was Sorrell's turn.

"*Descenthallan*," he whispered aloud, and stepped onto empty air.

As he drifted down into the tight confines of the chimney, gripping his club against his chest, he wondered if the warriors in the ancient songs had felt as frightened as he did just then.

The time for songs, however, was long over.

They traveled through the Underdark for a long time—it must have been well past Night's Heart in the

World Above—before Pendaran at last called a halt and set a watch. The trek had been exhausting and not what Sorrell had expected. He'd pictured the passageways through the Underdark as something like forest trails: a bit rough underfoot, and winding, but something that could be negotiated at an upright, walking pace. The reality was far different. They had clambered down slopes of jagged stone, squeezed through passages so tight that Sorrell had been afraid to inhale fully, lest he get stuck, used their boots to levitate up and down connecting chimneys, and crawled through caverns with ceilings so low they had to worm their way along on their bellies, nose to boot with the person ahead. They'd pushed themselves hard, stopping only once, and just long enough for Adair to murmur a prayer that filled their hands with nutbread and their leather drinking cups with water, a meal that was consumed in haste and silence. And still they were no closer to catching their prey; the drow simply had too good a start.

By the time Pendaran admitted that there was no point in running themselves to utter exhaustion, Sorrell was filthy, sweaty, and stumbling. He didn't complain when Pendaran chose him as one of the first, together with Koora, to be allowed to slip into Reverie.

It was over much too soon. Sorrell felt as though he'd barely begun his meditations when Pendaran shook his shoulder.

You're on watch, the leader said. He pointed down the passage. *Take over Nairen's position. He's about fifty paces back, at the mouth of the large cavern.*

Sorrell nodded, uncrossed his legs, and rose to his feet. Despite his fatigue, he was glad to stand a watch. Glad to be included. Stooping to avoid the low ceiling, he clambered back the way they'd come, his magical boots silent, even when they slipped on the rough stone.

When he got to the spot where the moon elf should have been he couldn't see anyone.

Nairen? he asked.

He stared down into the cavern. It was as wide as a tree was tall, and three times the height of a man. Its floor was dotted with dull red dots—luminescent, ball-sized fungi that grew in clusters amid the jumble of rock. They were bright spots of true color against the cold black-purple of the stones they grew upon. "Crimson spitters," Pendaran had called them. If disturbed, they released a cloud of deadly spores, similar to the ones the miniature chests had contained.

The drow had gone that way, but not along the floor. There were tears in the blue-glowing, fan-shaped lichen that clung to the cavern's ceiling where the drow must have brushed against them. Koora had pointed the smudge out, suspicious, at first, that the drow had been so careless in their passage. Sorrell would otherwise have completely missed it. He peered at the ceiling, wondering if Nairen had somehow found a way to hide himself there.

Nairen? he called again. *Where are you?*

A hand touched his shoulder. Sorrell whirled and saw that the hand had emerged from solid stone. Nairen stepped out of the wall, his skin warming from deep blue to red as the stone released him. He shivered, then pointed at a crack in the wall near the cave mouth.

You'll have to hide yourself the conventional way, he said. *Unless you have magic?*

The latter was phrased as a question, but the tone suggested a challenge. Sorrell did have some magic—his voice. With his singing, he'd been able to captivate even the most unruly audience. His songs could calm quarrelsome drunks before they came to blows, could make his listeners laugh so hard their eyes streamed with tears, and could soothe to sleep the most restless babe. Many were the nights he'd used the latter, back when Remmie was small . . .

The lump of ice was back in his throat. He blinked away the sudden sting in his eyes, and shook his head. *A little bardic magic*, he replied. *Nothing useful.*

Nairen gave the mental equivalent of a grunt. *Keep*

your eyes open, he warned. *Don't assume that just because we already came this way, the cavern isn't worth watching.*

Koora's voice: *Is he in position?*

Sorrell squeezed his body into the crack in the rock.

Nairen: *He is. I'm coming in.*

The moon elf crept silently away. Sorrell watched, fascinated, as Nairen's dull blue boot prints slowly faded from the floor of the passageway, then remembered his duty. He turned his head, keeping watch on the empty cavern.

There was a brief flurry of mental conversation as Koora reported to the group that she had replaced Adair, and as the half-elf hooked up with Nairen and Pendaran, back at the place where they'd halted. Then silence, as the three not on watch settled into Reverie.

Time passed.

Sorrell found himself wondering if dawn had broken in the World Above. While they'd been on the move, it had been easy to distract himself with the necessity of constantly surveying the terrain around them—searching for handholds and places to put his feet. Easy to focus on their objective: catching up to, and killing, the drow who had broached Cormanthor's defenses.

Now that he was simply standing, he was all too aware of the depth to which they'd descended, of the weight of the stone above his head. He stared at the cold dark purple walls, wondering if he'd ever see daylight again.

Lonely, isn't it?

Koora's voice. It sounded as though she was standing right next to him. Sorrell startled, wondering if the ring had been broadcasting his thoughts. It was only supposed to relay intentional messages—and only to the intended recipient.

I felt the same way on my first hunt, the wild elf continued. *An outsider. I had nothing when I came to Shevarash. The Silent Slayers became my clan—in time, you will feel the same. You earned yourself a place among us by finding the crawl-chests—something I should have spotted. Nairen and Adair will come around, eventually.*

And Pendaran has already trusted you with a watch. Her silent voice developed a chuckle. *Though a safe one. Had we passed a side passage, it might have been different.*

Sorrell kept a watchful eye on the tunnel as he listened, determined not to let his attention waver a second time. Koora's accent reminded him of someone—a centaur he'd once met.

Where are you from? he thought back.

For several heartbeats there was only silence. Then, *The Satyrwood.*

Sorrell knew it well. The forest—called the Chondalwood by humans—lay south of Arrabar, a city he and Dalmara had performed in more than twenty years ago. Dalmara, intent upon collecting more folk songs, had insisted on making a trek to a wild elf camp deep in the Satyrwood. The centaur had been their guide. Sorrell searched his memory, looking for the name of the harpist they'd met there.

Do you know a woman named Bronwynn, of the Redleaf Clan?

Koora's mental voice, when she answered, was small and tight. *There is no Redleaf Clan. Not any more.* A pause, then, *I was deep in the forest, hunting, when it happened. Now I hunt drow.*

Sorrell blinked in surprise, but said nothing. What could be said? He remembered the murmured kindnesses, the polite words that had been spoken after his own loss. He knew that nothing he said could banish the grief he heard, loud as a tolling bell, in Koora's silence. His fists were clenched around his club; glancing down, he saw that his fingers had faded to a dull red.

Did you . . . He had to blink furiously before he was able to continue. *Was there a child?*

I was not yet a mother, thank Angharradh for small mercies. But my sister was. Three daughters, all dead.

Sorrell felt a tear furrow its way through the dirt on his cheek. It dripped, a bead of dark blue, onto the stone at his feet and faded to purple. He didn't want to hear any more.

Thankfully, Koora was silent.

Sorrell raised a hand to wipe his cheek—and paused as he heard a noise in the passage behind him. A faint thudding, like footsteps on stone. He started to turn to see which of the others was approaching, then remembered their magical boots.

He whirled just in time to see a monstrous shape scuttling across the ceiling of the cavern, tearing a scuff of darkness in the lichen as it ran. It looked like a cross between drow and spider—dark elf from the waist up, but with a spider's bulbous thorax and abdomen, and eight legs.

Sorrell's heart pounded as he stepped out of the crack and raised his club to meet the monster's charge. He needed room to swing his club; he'd have to count on his invisibility to hide him. Knocking the monster down into the crimson spitters would be his best chance.

Sorrell! What's happening? Pendaran's voice. Alert. Tense.

Monster attacking! Sorrell shouted back. *Half spider, half drow.*

The creature's eyes locked on his.

Sorrell felt a sudden chill. *It must have magic! It can see—*

A ray of indigo light flashed from one of the creature's hands. It caught Sorrell square in the chest. Dots of blackness swam before his eyes. His legs wobbled and nearly buckled. His club—suddenly too heavy—sagged in his hands. The monster whipped its abdomen forward and a line of dull brown web shot from fingerlike spinnerets at its tip. The sticky strands nearly smothered Sorrell, fouling his hair and clothing, gumming his face and eyes. He tried to pull free, but the web was stuck fast to the stone wall behind him. The more he tore at it, the more his hands became entangled. The monster, meanwhile, jammed itself into the passageway and plucked Sorrell away from the wall, then began turning him around and around. More web surged from its spinnerets, winding around his legs, binding them tightly together.

Don't let it get away! Pendaran's voice, excited. *Keep it busy until we can get there.*

Sorrell groaned.

As if it had heard the silent message, the monster laughed. Its voice was disturbingly elflike. Its face, however, was not. Curved fangs sprang out of its cheeks like a pair of scissors opening. Each was beaded with poison at its tip.

Sorrell's hands were trapped by the web; it would be impossible to reach the anti-venom vial on his belt. All he could do was close his eyes and pray. At first, instinctively, to Corellon Larethian, then to Shevarash. He begged the Hunter to hear his plea.

Not yet! he cried. *I haven't had a chance to kill—*

The god's reply came like a clap of thunder. A deep male voice, grim as a dirge. *Day is Done.*

Sorrell's eyes sprang open. He knew immediately what the god wanted, and understood what the result would be. In a quavering voice, he began the lullaby he'd composed for his son: "Birds have flown home to their nests. I know we all could use some rest . . . "

A flicker of what looked like white flame sprang to life around the monster's head.

"Close your eyes now, day is done . . . "

The flame brightened. The monster shook its head and gnashed its fangs.

"Sleep now till the morning comes . . . "

The monster squeezed its eyes tight against the glare and shook its head.

Tears tumbled from Sorrell's eyes as he continued to sing. The lullaby brought back memories of his son's soft cheek against his own, the smell of Remmie's milk-sweet breath and tiny arms hugged tight around Sorrell's neck, a smaller head on the pillow next to his own.

Gone now. Dead.

Sorrell had vowed, in that dark cellar, never to sing

that lullaby again—never to *sing* again. But what was a vow, compared to a god's command?

"Go to bed, now don't you cry . . . "

Sorrell's voice broke then, but it had been enough. The monster collapsed on the floor of the tunnel, its eight legs jerking reflexively, claws scraping on stone. Sorrell felt hands touching him, and realized that Nairen and Adair had reached him. He fought to pull himself together as they sliced the webs from him. Distantly, he heard Pendaran's *Well done,* and felt a calloused hand squeeze his shoulder.

Pendaran turned away, murmuring. His hands made a gesture over the monster. Suddenly released, it sprang to its feet, revived by Pendaran's magic.

Shocked out of his grief, Sorrell snatched up his club. Before he could attack, however, Adair lowered his spear, blocking the way.

Wait, he urged. *Pendaran's charming it.*

Pendaran said something to the monster in a chittering voice. It grinned back at him and its body bobbed up and down. Then it turned and clambered up onto the ceiling of the cavern, motioning with one of its elflike arms for them to follow. Pendaran's lips twitched—a suppressed smile.

It captured one of the drow, he announced.

He ordered Koora to maintain her position, and Adair, Nairen, and Sorrell to follow him back across the cavern. They did, Sorrell keeping a wary eye on the monster above.

What is that thing? he asked the group.

It was Nairen who answered, as they carefully picked their way between the crimson spitters, *A drider. A reject of Lolth, their goddess. Driders hate the drow as much as we do, even though they used to be drow themselves.*

Sorrell shuddered. He'd heard that Lolth was a cruel and uncaring goddess, utterly without mercy; that she deformed those who displeased her. He couldn't conceive of worshiping such a deity.

If it's a drow, why aren't we killing it?

Nairen winked. *Be patient.*

On the far side of the cavern, the drider reached into a shoulder-deep crevice in the rock and pulled out what looked like the top of a broken staff, set with a fist-sized emerald. Chittering at Pendaran, the drider crawled around a bend in the passageway, then touched the gem to the wall. The emerald glowed, and a hole silently sprang into being in the rock. The drider scrambled through it, still holding the broken staff. A putrid smell wafted out of the opening.

Nairen? Pendaran's voice. *What can you detect*?

Sorrell heard a quick, whispered prayer.

It's a dead-end cavern. There's no sign of a mate. Even so, he held his sword in one hand. Ready.

Adair, keep watch fifty paces on.

The half-elf nodded at his leader, and trotted away.

Pendaran, Sorrell, and Nairen followed the drider into a cavern that was dimly illuminated by more of the phosphorescent lichen. A pool of water filled one end of it. Hanging from a web that spanned the ceiling, twisting slowly in a cocoon of sticky web, was a drow. Only a portion of face showed, the skin black against the dull white of the web. Even though no more than a day could have passed since the drow had been captured, it smelled as though the body was already decomposing. Rancid liquid dripped from it onto the floor.

There's one of them, Nairen said. *We'll soon have some questions answered.*

But he's dead, Sorrell protested. *How—?*

On three, Pendaran said, cutting Sorrell off as he met Nairen's eye.

The moon elf's fingers tightened on his sword.

One, two . . .

Realizing what they were up to, Sorrell started to raise his club. *No! Let me—*

The drider whirled to face him, fangs flashing.

Three!

Despite the haste dweomer on Sorrell's weapon, Nairen was quicker. With a single stroke, he severed the drider's neck. Blood fountained as the monster collapsed to the floor. Splatters landed on Sorrell's shoulder and arm.

Thanks for the distraction, Nairen said.

Sorrell fumed. "That should have been my kill," he said, forgetting Pendaran's strict orders to maintain silence.

Your time will come, Pendaran said, *when Shevarash wills it*. Then, to Nairen, *Cut the body down*.

Nairen levitated and sawed through the web with his sword. He lowered the cocoon carefully to the floor. Pendaran squatted beside it and cleared the web away from the lower portion of the drow's face.

Sorrell stared down at the drow—the first one he'd seen up close. A female. The dead scout had the narrow face and pointed ears of a surface elf, but her skin was as black as a starless sky, her hair, bone-white. Even in death, her face had a cruel cast. Sorrell clenched his fists. Nairen caught his arm, as if sensing Sorrell's urge to smash the body, over and over again, with his club. Steadying himself, Sorrell spat on the body instead.

A waste of good spit, if you ask me, Nairen said.

Pendaran tore away more of the webbing from the drow's shoulder, revealing a bandage, dark with dried blood. One arm was swollen to twice its normal size, and bore puncture marks.

Their leader, he observed. *The remaining three will be running scared*.

They'll also be running faster, now that they're no longer encumbered by her, Nairen observed.

Sorrell shook his head. He'd heard that the drow noble Houses were all matriarchies, but somehow, it hadn't sunk home. The drow who had killed his son might have been a woman. He thought of Dalmara, of her tenderness. How could a woman have been so cruel as to murder a three-year-old boy?

Pendaran was praying over the corpse. To what end, Sorrell couldn't guess—until, with a creaking yawn, its jaws sprang open. Breath hissed from dead lungs.

"Asssk," it whispered, its lips glowing with Shevarash's holy light.

"Your *thalakz*—what city sent it?" Pendaran asked.

"Brundag," the corpse answered. Bile bubbled at the back of its throat and trickled down its chin as it spoke.

Sickened, Sorrell turned away. He walked over to the pool and dipped his arm in it, trying to wash the blood from his sleeve.

Good idea, Nairen said as he squatted beside Sorrell. *Just remember to renew your armor paint; it washes off.*

He dipped his sword in the water, cleaning it. By the light of the lichen, Sorrell saw the inscription on his blade, done in black filigree: "Bane of the Depths." He dried the sword and sheathed it, then dipped his hands in the pool. As he splashed water on his face, his sleeves fell back, revealing forearms mottled with patches of pale white—the healed scars of what must have once been terrible burns.

The polite thing to do would have been to pretend not to have noticed, but Sorrell couldn't contain his curiosity.

What happened?

It was many years ago, Nairen said. *We lived in the High Forest. Not in Nordahaeril itself, but on the outskirts, because of Adair. The night the drow came, the townfolk drew up their rope ladders, too frightened to help us. Even when our tree began to burn.* He stared at the wall with eyes as green and restless as a storm-tossed sea. *Even when our mother started screaming.*

Sorrell took a deep breath. *My son—*

Nairen held up a hand. *Don't try to play the "my grief is greater than yours" game*, he warned. *I've heard it all before.*

He stood abruptly and walked to the exit. Slowly, Sorrell rose to his feet and walked back to where Pendaran crouched beside the corpse.

Pendaran glanced up at him. *Have you ever been to Amrutlar*?

Sorrell frowned at the odd question. *Yes. Years ago.*

How far would you say it is from the Yuirwood, by surface travel?

Sorrell shrugged. *A tenday. Or maybe a tenday and a hand, depending on the weather. Why?*

Pendaran gestured at the corpse. *The city she named—Brundag—lies roughly under Amrutlar. A journey through the Underdark would take twice as long. Interconnected passageways stretching for such a distance are hardly likely.*

Sorrell could see where the sun elf's thoughts were leading. *A portal*?

Pendaran nodded. He turned back to the corpse. "Where is the portal that the scouts will use to reach Brundag?"

"In the *maglustarn sarg zhaunil*."

Sorrell leaned closer. *What did she just say*?

Nothing that will help, Pendaran answered. *"Place-apart of battle-might learning"—a drow term for a warriors' academy that isn't within a city. It could be anywhere. We need something more specific in order for Koora to find it with her magic.*

As the sun elf stared at him, Sorrell realized that Pendaran expected him to have the answer. All Sorrell knew about the Blackened Fist was that he wanted them dead.

Sorrell wet his lips. *The academy doesn't have a name*?

What do you mean?

They always do, in the ballads. Have a name. Palaces, temples . . .

Pendaran's eyes brightened. *Let's find out*. Then, to the corpse. "What is the name of your academy?"

"Maglustarn Jainna'hil Krish."

Monastery of the Black Fist, Pendaran repeated. *Got that, Koora?*

Got it!

Pendaran stood. *Close up on me, and get ready to move out.*

The others acknowledged his order and began making their way to the cave. When Koora entered, her face was even grimmer than usual. After a brief, private exchange with her, Pendaran turned to the group.

The academy is inside a faerzress, he told them.

The others glanced at each other, uneasy.

What . . . does that mean? Sorrell blurted.

A faerzress distorts magic, Pendaran explained. *If we try to teleport into it, we'll wind up inside solid stone.*

Should we split up? Adair asked. *That will guarantee that some of us will live to carry on the hunt.*

Pendaran shook his head. *No use. The thalakz has too good a lead. If we don't teleport, we won't catch them. But—this could be it. Short of a miracle, we're not going to make it.*

May Shevarash grant one, Koora whispered.

And if we do make it, I'll need every one of you, Pendaran continued.

There was silence for a moment.

I'm ready, Koora said.

So are—

—we, the brothers answered, nearly as one.

Sorrell took a deep breath, and met the leader's eye. *"To continue on, until our own deaths should come." I'm in.*

Pendaran nodded, as if he'd expected no less. *Good. Let's go.*

Sorrell gripped his club. "Vengeance," he whispered.

And he remembered . . .

He and Dalmara had been passing through Shadowdale, on their way to Tilverton, and had stopped for the night at the Old Skull, an inn named after a nearby, dome-shaped hill of white granite. The place had a cozy feel, with a low, smoke-stained ceiling of hardwood beams and a warm fire crackling in the hearth to ward off the night's chill. They had earned their supper through song; he playing his lute, and she, her dulcimer. Taking turns, one sang while the other kept an eye on Remmie.

They had been hoping that Remmie would fall asleep, but the boy was, as usual, basking in the attention the inn's patrons were giving him. Sorrell had made a tiny lute for his son, and Remmie had been "playing" it furiously that night, strumming away—still with no idea of how to finger a chord—and making up a song of his own, to the delight of the patrons.

"Daddy is happy; Daddy play his loo," he cooed. "Mama is sing; Mama play dull-er." The patrons roared their laughter as Remmie took a bow, beaming. "Clap!" he told them. "Clap-clap!"

There had been ale that night, and laughter, and more song. Sorrell had thought that Dalmara had ushered Remmie up to bed in their room; Dalamara thought Sorrell had taken him. Sorrell still remembered the horrified look on his wife's face, and the hollow that opened at the pit of his stomach when they realized their son had wandered off on his own.

"He can't have gone far," Sorrell reassured her, praying that it was true.

"We'll find him," she said, her own eyes worried.

Sorrell set his lute aside, stood. "Has anyone seen our son?"

Shoulders were shrugged, heads shook.

That was when the scream had come from the inn's cellar, followed by a shout and the clash of steel on steel.

Sorrell had to fight his way through the crush of people who blocked his way to the cellar door. He could only vaguely remember the white-faced barmaid who passed him on her way up the stairs, and the ranger who stood, sword in hand, staring at the crossbow bolt lodged in his leg. He could no longer remember exactly what the ranger looked like—tall or short, fair-haired or dark, human or elf. His eyes would take in nothing that night but the dagger that lay on the floor—and the body of his son lying next to it.

He remembered scooping his son's body up in his arms, howling, "No, no, no, no . . . " as the tiny head fell back on a limp neck. The head he'd cradled, oh so carefully, when his son was still too young to hold it upright on his own. He remembered Dalmara appearing at his side, screaming, "He's going cold!" as she shook Remmie's arm, trying desperately to make him wake up. Remembered the wound: a terrible bloody puncture in his son's hand—a hand that should have been holding a child-sized lute, lay trampled on the floor beside them. Imagined his son, terrified, trying to fend off the dagger. He remembered the ranger saying, "It's no use. The blade was poisoned," each word a cold stone laid on Sorrell's heart. Remembered someone, upstairs, shouting for a cleric.

None came.

That was when Dalmara, her face white as bone and her eyes already red with tears, had spoken the awful truth. "Remmie is unpledged. No god will claim him. He will enter the Fugue Plain alone." Her eye fell on the poisoned dagger. Her expression turned steely. "I will not . . . let the demons . . . have my son."

She picked up the dagger.

Sorrell grabbed her wrist. "No! I won't let you!"

Dalmara's eyes became ice. She turned the dagger hilt toward him. "Then you do it."

Sorrell's felt his eyes widen. He released her wrist. "I love you," was all he'd been able to manage.

Dalmara hugged him fiercely—and carefully, as if Remmie was still alive and she was afraid of crushing him. "Until Arvandor," she whispered.

Then she pricked her palm with the dagger.

That had been two years ago. Since then, Sorrell had learned that the Old Skull Inn concealed an entrance to the Underdark, and that the drow who had killed his son that night were most likely assassins who had tried—and failed—to kill a famous wizard who had been visiting Shadowdale that evening. Sorrell pieced together what had happened: Remmie had wandered down to the cellar and surprised the drow as they emerged from their secret hole. He'd been "silenced"—even though he was barely three years old, still full of baby talk and babble that probably wouldn't have been understood by anyone but his parents, two elf bards ignorant of the secret doings of the Dales. And his death had been pointless; a moment later, the serving girl and the ranger, intent upon a liaison, had descended to the cellar and also surprised the drow. Despite taking a crossbow bolt in the leg, the ranger had managed to raise the alarm and drive the drow back below. And he'd knocked the poisoned dagger out of the last drow's hand.

A hand which, the ranger's keen eyes had noted, had been coated in a layer of pitch.

Sorrell had learned everything he could about the Blackened Fist in the months since then—though what he'd learned had been precious little. But Shevarash had rewarded his persistence. In just a few moments, Sorrell was either going to avenge his family, or die trying.

Sorrell gripped his club tightly in one hand. His other hand was on Pendaran's shoulder as the leader whispered the prayer that would send them either into the drow stronghold—or, more likely, into solid rock, spilling their spirits into the Fugue Plain. Sorrell wondered which god would claim him and carry him to Arvandor. Would Corellon Larethian summon him to sing at his side? Or would Shevarash claim Sorrell to join him in his grim wanderings? Perhaps both would find him wanting, and Sorrell's spirit would linger on the Fugue Plain for all eternity.

Nairen kissed the blade of his sword, then locked eyes with his half-brother. Adair took a deep breath, nodded. Koora raised her right hand above her head, sling trailing from her fist, in Shevarash's defiant salute. She caught Sorrell's eye. A rush of exultation filled his heart. Soon, he told himself, Shevarash willing, he might be killing the very drow who had murdered his son.

Pendaran completed his prayer.

Adair's voice: *Here we—*

The tearing sensation came. Sorrell closed his eyes.

—go!

The world went white with Shevarash's holy fire.

Sorrell's body was yanked through space . . .

Dalmara, he thought, panicked, I'm coming. I'll find you.

His feet touched solid ground.

He gasped. Glanced down, saw the dull purple of cold stone. He wasn't dead!

Flash! Pendaran shouted. The leader's hand swept down, releasing a flash gem.

Sorrell had only a heartbeat in which to register the room they had teleported to. A large, circular hall, with eight arched exits leading to corridors. The statue of a spider, carved from glossy black obsidian, stood at the center of the room on fragile-looking legs. On the far side of it were three drow: two males, kneeling before a larger female. As the flash gem clattered toward them between the legs of the statue the males sprang to their feet and yanked daggers from sheaths on their belts. The female leaped into the air, levitating.

The gem . . .

Sorrell screwed his eyes shut just as a silent flash of white filled the room. The instant it was dark again he ran forward, club swinging.

The two males stood blinking, their pupils mere pinpricks. The one that Nairen and Adair rushed had the presence of mind to cock his head sideways, listening, and to slash with his dagger. He died with Adair's spear through his chest as Nairen's sword lopped off his arm at the elbow.

The other male turned and bolted for a corridor. Sorrell heard a sling stone whistle past his ear. It slammed into the back of the drow's head, staggering him. Sorrell swung his club in a sweeping arc. It connected with the head of the reeling drow, shattering it like a gnarlwood nut. Chunks of brain, glowing a bright red to Sorrell's magically enhanced vision, slid from the ruined head as the body fell.

Sorrell stood, panting. His first drow kill! He should have been exulting, but instead he felt only a sick revulsion.

He heard a sob above him. He glanced up and saw the female drow, still levitating, shudder with grief. Tears poured from her eyes. For a moment, he thought she was mourning the two males. They looked young enough to be her sons. Then he realized that Pendaran was casting a spell at her. The sun elf pointed at the drow, his lips moving in silent prayer.

With a violent shake of her head, the drow shook the spell off.

Pendaran cursed.

Koora whipped her arm forward. Another sling stone whistled past, shattering on the wall just behind the female drow's head. The drow—not blinded, she must have realized what the flash gem was and closed her eyes in time—whirled in mid-air to stare at the spot the stone had come from and shouted something in the drow language. A spider the size of a large dog appeared in mid-air, and fell onto Koora's shoulders.

Soul spider! Koora gasped. Suddenly the wild elf was fighting for her life.

Sorrell took a step toward her.

The priestess! Pendaran shouted, nocking an arrow in his bow. *Attack her!*

The drow dropped to the floor behind Sorrell. He whirled, swinging his club. The drow dodged the blow without effort, as though she could see him. Adair hurled his spear at her, but she sidestepped it. She leaped toward Adair, one foot extended in a kick. He ducked, and she missed, spinning gracefully on her other foot directly into the path of Nairen, who held his sword ready to deliver a killing slash. The blade swept down—but then the drow seemed to blur. As Nairen's weapon slashed through empty air, throwing him off balance, the drow crashed into him, chest to chest, and sank her teeth into his cheek.

The cheek Nairen had washed clean, back in the drider's cavern.

The moon elf stiffened. Adair scrambled to get one of the potion vials out of his belt.

"Nairen!" he gasped aloud.

Pendaran's bow *twanged.* One of his black-shafted arrows plunged into the drow's back and found her heart. Twitching like a crushed spider, she fell.

So did Nairen, his face already paling to a dull purple. His half-brother rushed to his side, ripped the cork out of the vial he held with his teeth, and fought to pull Nairen's mouth open. Locked in a death grimace, the jaw wouldn't budge.

Sorrell heard a cracking noise behind him. He turned, saw Koora with her arms wrapped around the spider. As she slowly squeezed it, her body glowed with Shevarash's fire. A final crunch, and the spider was dead. Koora, however, staggered as she let its body fall. Despite her armor paint, her arms had several deep, bloody puncture marks. As Pendaran turned toward her, a look of concern on his face, she swayed, steadied herself with a hand against the wall.

I'm good, she said. *Just a little drained.*

Are the corridors clear?

Koora held out a palm, swept it in a circle while she prayed. *Nothing.*

Pendaran nodded and turned his attention to the brothers. Adair had peeled back Nairen's lower lip and was pouring the potion onto his brother's clenched teeth. Most of the liquid dribbled down Nairen's chin, a grim echo of the corpse in the drider cavern.

Pendaran lowered his bow. *He's gone, Adair*, he said quietly. *Gone to Shevarash.*

The half-elf turned, his eyes dangerous. *No.*

Pendaran's voice was steely. *Yes.* He pointed at Adair's spear. *Now on your feet, warrior, and grab that weapon. Don't let his sacrifice be for nothing.*

Adair hesitated.

Move!

Adair snapped erect. He strode across the cavern and picked up his spear.

Pendaran, behind him, closed his eyes and sighed. His mental voice, however, retained its steely control. *We've got to move quickly. Sorrell, keep watch. Koora, conceal the bodies. And Adair . . . collect your brother. I'll find out where the portal is.* He squatted beside the dead female and whispered a prayer. Her lips began to glow with Shevarash's light.

Holding his club at the ready, Sorrell glanced back and forth, trying to keep an eye on all eight of the chamber's exits at once. His eye kept straying, however, to the dark elf he had killed. Now that the fight was over, he noticed the drow's age. Judging by what remained of his face, he looked like a boy in his teens.

As Pendaran questioned the dead priestess, asking where the portal was, Koora walked, slowly and unsteadily, to the body Sorrell had been staring at and prayed over it. The dull glow of warmth that remained in the body winked out as it was rendered invisible. She crossed the chamber, and did the same to the other male corpse. Adair, meanwhile, straightened his brother's body, picking up Nairen's sword and laying it across his chest. Then he pulled from a pouch at his belt a large bag of a thin, glossy material that was as thin and slippery as silk. Opening it, he tucked Nairen's feet inside. It seemed only large enough to accommodate Nairen's lower legs, but it kept going, swallowing Nairen whole. As Adair pulled the drawstring shut, the bag collapsed, seemingly empty once more. Adair folded it, and tucked it back into his pouch. Then he picked up his spear.

He glanced at Sorrell and touched the pouch.

Sorrell nodded. Necessary sacrifices.

Sorrell heard a faint noise. Out of the corner of his eye, he saw something in one of the corridors. He whirled . . .

And saw a tiny figure. A drow child, not even as tall as Remmie. A child whose mouth was open in an O of surprise, whose eyes were wide and fixed on the dead woman whose creaking voice filled the chamber as she answered Pendaran's questions.

"Ma?" the boy whispered, tears starting to spill from his eyes.

The word was the same, in any language.

Sorrell leaped forward and grabbed the boy. He clapped a hand over the boy's mouth. The boy went rigid with fear. Then he began to struggle. And to wail, behind Sorrell's muffling hand.

Shut him up! Adair shouted.

Sorrell glanced up. The half-elf had his spear raised. Sorrell would have to work quickly. Clutching the little boy against his chest, he started to sing. "Birds have flown home—"

Pendaran scrambled to his feet. *I've got it! The portal's close by!*

The boy twisted like an eel, nearly slipping free.

Do it! Koora raged. *The spider kissers' brat will give us away.*

I'm trying! Sorrell kept singing: "—to their nests. I know we all could use some rest."

Pendaran nocked an arrow. *Kill him now, or get out of the way.*

I'm putting him to sleep.

He's a drow! Adair gritted.

Sorrell continued his song. A moment more, and the child would be asleep. *He's a child.*

Koora's swift fingers loaded a stone into her sling. *He's a spider kisser,* she hissed. *Vermin.*

Sorrell halted his song, glanced from one face to the next. He saw the same emotion on each: hatred. And an utter lack of pity. Had their skin been black, they could have been drow.

The fist of ice that was Sorrell's heart finally cracked. "No!" he shouted, turning his back on the others, still holding the struggling boy in his arms. "The boy's not going to give us away. He isn't even old enough to talk ye—"

Koora's sling stone slammed into the back of his head, filling Sorrell's vision with sparks of white light almost as bright as Shevarash's cold white fire.

Almost.

Sorrell shook his head. He rose to his feet, and staggered away with the child in his arms. One step, two . . . But the pain in his head was too much. He sagged to his knees, still hugging the small boy against his chest. The boy's hair smelled like Remmie's had, brought back a flood of memories. Sorrell stared back over his shoulder at the Silent Slayers, tears stinging his own eyes.

"Please," he begged. "Don't—"

Pendaran's bow thrummed. Sorrell grunted as the arrow tore a sharp line of pain through his body.

He felt a soft, startled breath against his hand as it found the boy's heart.

Two figures stood together on a gray, featureless plain, under a sky filled with flat gray clouds. An elf with coppery skin and reddish brown hair, the hand that once held a club empty at his side—and a child with skin the color of midnight, bone-white hair, and wide, bewildered eyes. The man glanced up at the sky, as if searching for something. The sky remained flat and empty. The man nodded, as if that was what he'd expected. He squatted next to the boy, extending his arms, and said something in a soft voice. After a moment's hesitation, the boy allowed himself to be embraced. A tear trickled down the man's cheek as he hugged the boy tightly. Then he smiled.

The man stood, cradling the boy in strong arms, and began the long, slow walk to the horizon, singing softly as he went.

THE GREATER TREASURE

Erik Scott de Bie

Eleasias, the Year of the Helm (1362 DR)

Flames rose into the morning air, the sounds of clashing blades projected far and wide, and merchant wagons shied away from the gates. Even from a distance, it was clear that the city of Elversult rocked in dire turmoil.

"This is it?" the cloaked maid asked in her native tongue. Her harsh tone carried not a little disgust—something that sounded discordant and almost ugly in Elvish. *"You believe those bearing the relic are here?"*

The bronze-skinned elflord beside her did not bother to reply. Instead, he spurred his horse toward the city, intent on arriving in time to aid.

She followed, albeit much more slowly.

As they rode closer, it was clear that only one building burned in Elversult—the great central tower. Battle raged in the air over the city, where a handful of black-robed mages wheeled, hurling spells at a flying lass in leathers, who swatted them like gnats, one by one, with bolts of lightning and flame. On the ground, a band of adventurers fought a dozen men-at-arms, gradually triumphing over impossible odds the way only adventurers can.

As the sun elves rode up to the gate, a great cheer sounded from within the walls. The last of the black robes dived to avoid a storm of animated blades but caught an amber ray full in the chest. He fell to earth, burning.

It was fortunate for the sages who predicted the weather that he had not been *above* the blade barrier, or it might have been raining that day in Elversult.

And so it was the Scarred Eagles adventuring band defeated the Cowled Skull dynasty of Elversult and Yanseldara—the flying lady with the slaying spells—was crowned in the Skulls' place. Some merchants cheered, some scowled, but by and large the people of Elversult took note of the radical change in government, shrugged, and went about business as usual.

It was, after all, the Dragon Coast.

And so it was that Yldar Nathalan, the disgraced, exiled son of a great Evermeetian family, was too late to participate in the glory—again.

As soon as the two elves had dispensed with their fine steeds at a not-so-fine bank of stables, Yldar stomped over to the fountain in the center of town and crossed his arms.

He looked around at the myriad faces, people going about their business. To all, he felt a sense of detachment, even more so than he felt with any of the foolish humans he had met in his travels. Life in Elversult had shifted so radically, so quickly, leaving his—a visitor's—head spinning, but no native seem to notice much.

"Humans," Yldar cursed in Elvish.

"Do not act thus," Cythara said, putting a gentle hand on his shoulder. Her full red robe hid her golden mane. *"This was not your day."*

"No day is my day," replied Yldar. He possessed a melodious voice, but one hardened by discontent and years of disappointment. *"First the Tower, then the bladesingers, even the border guards. . . How long have we been traveling, sister, yet you do not know this?"*

Similarly sharp of feature and lean of body, Cythara was Yldar's double in many ways, but one could never say that she suffered from his excess of pride—the flaw that ran through the Nathalan family like blood. Rather, her faults were subtler, more insidious, and altogether beyond her younger brother's ken.

"Yldar," she said. *"What would Father say?"*

"I might as well not exist." The elflord shrugged. *"The feeling is mutual."*

Cythara felt her hand tense, but thought better of striking the stubborn, almost petulant Yldar. It would only hurt her hand.

"Brother," she said. *"Have you forgotten the relic?"*

His eyes bright, Yldar jumped to his feet. *"Yes!"* he said. *"I mean—no!"*

Cythara smiled a little, but it was an irritated smile. *"Let us search, then,"* she prompted.

Yldar was already off and away.

Sunlight streamed through the window, mingled with a fair amount of flame, it seemed. With a mild oath, she rolled out from under the bedclothes.

She had *slept* again.

The Reverie came so infrequently to the moon elf these days. Perhaps she dealt with humans too much, or perhaps the elf gods truly had cursed her. The trick smacked greatly of the whims of her fickle patron.

While she considered that, a growling sound from her stomach convinced her that it was time to head down. She even managed clothes before obeying its command.

As she padded downstairs in her doeskin boots, the moon elf was pleased to see the gruff and stocky men who frequented the Splitskull stepping aside, giving her space. That was polite. Trying to weasel their way into her good graces, mayhap—and eventually her bed, likely. Then again, she thought with a smile, they might simply be justly wary.

She sat down at the bar, eschewing the tables that miraculously opened up when she entered and waved to the owner. "Keep," she called. She realized that she had never bothered to learn his name, but he seemed content with the moniker. Or perhaps that *was* his name, in which case it was irrelevant.

"What'll it be, 'Light, ye heartbreaker?"

"You're such a flatterer," she said, brushing a raven lock out of her pale eyes. "A morning meal? And drink?"

"On your tab, I s'pose."

Twilight inclined her head. Keep shouted a few words back to the kitchen, then pulled her an ale from a tapped keg.

"News o' the day? The Skulls're out." Keep's voice was nonplussed.

Dragon Coast indeed.

"Truly?" Twilight took an unladylike swig.

"Aye, indeed. Yanseldara an' her lover, Vaerana, done ousted the lot o' 'em."

Twilight shook her head. Little in the realms took her by surprise these days. "Costs will rise, eh?"

Keep shrugged. "Goods'll be safer, and competitors driven mostly underground." He wiped a tankard and grinned. "Better atmosphere, ye might say."

Twilight raised her ale to that.

Then the door to the dark tavern opened, letting in heinous light, and Twilight blinked in surprise. Faces of such hue were not to be seen everyday in Elversult—

especially not one so handsome as the elflord who entered.

Delicious, she thought with a wry smile.

A gentle hush came over the Splitskull when the tall sun elf entered. His skin of polished bronze and the fine elven blade that hung from his belt seemed out of place in a smoky tavern filled with grizzled, dirty men. No one felt like taking the challenge in Yldar's eye.

When the delicate maiden in the red cloak followed him, even more eyebrows rose. She wore her cowl low, but the tip of her angular, bronze chin could be seen beneath a pair of thin lips. Cythara inflamed more than a few bodies that day, striding by, oblivious to all and above it.

Yldar guided Cythara to a table in the corner, where she sat haltingly. She did not possess the robust vitality of her brother.

"Are you sure this is the right place?" she asked in Elvish.

"We could have stayed at the Axe and Hammer, but dwarves staff the place," said Yldar with a scowl. *"Nor did I like the price at the Wyvern's Pipe. I shall see to refreshments."*

"Remember why we are here. No duels."

Yldar gave his sister a roguish smile. *"I would not think of it."*

They both knew the truth of that assertion.

Yldar left to get tea and mead. Cythara leaned back against the wood paneling and blew out a long sigh.

She did not resent her brother, but neither did she enjoy having to rely upon his strength. In body, Cythara was sickly and weak, but in mind and will. . . One look in her cold, strangely red eyes told anyone to think twice before crossing her.

Anyone, that is, except the burly Marthul, who apparently wasn't looking quite high enough to meet her gaze.

Marthul was an impressive man in the way a wild boar is impressive. Few would guess it, but a shrewd-enough mind lay behind his scarred and craggy visage, one that should have seen the danger inherent in his chosen course. But done in by rotgut as he was—Marthul being possessed of a strong consititution, but not a dwarf's stomach—the big man saw only a lithe body in desperate need of his brand of companionship. He flopped into the seat beside her.

All the while, a pair of glittery pale eyes watched from the smoky end of the bar, and it was this searching gaze that drew Cythara's attention. She could not make out the face.

"Well met, me pretty lass," Marthul slurred. "Ye here alone?"

"Six heartbeats," Cythara said without looking.

"Wha—?"

"Six heartbeats to retract your offer and be gone." Dark magic flared behind her haunting eyes. "Four now."

"Ay, is that any—"

"Two." Under the table, her fingers twitched in a spell.

"Now hold—"

"One."

He felt a chilling jolt as an unseen black ray struck his knee. "Ye little . . ."

Marthul's words trailed off and he grasped at his throat. His dusky skin turned gray and his eyes rolled up in their sockets. All eyes in the inn turned toward them, most looking out of faces rapt in horror.

Unable to breathe, Marthul waved vainly at the elf beside him. The life was slowly ebbing out of him as though some creature of the night leeched away his soul.

With her bronze hair and face, however, Cythara looked more like a creature of the day.

"*This was your choice,*" she said, speaking in Elvish once more. Her voice was soft, as though the spell drained a bit of her vitality as well. She looked at Marthul for the first time, coldly. *"I hope 'tis all you expected."*

Had Marthul been left in the grip of Cythara's slow, draining spell, he might well have stopped breathing and collapsed. However, to Cythara's chagrin—but not to her surprise—Yldar was there, seizing Marthul by the collar.

"Away from my sister, you damned, dirty ape-spawn," he growled.

Marthul wasn't about to argue. Neither did he resist—if indeed he could have—as Yldar twisted him over his shoulder and sent him tumbling into a game of cards at the next table. Marthul's bulk splintered the table and sent cards, coins, and players scattering.

Angry glares fell upon the sun elf then, but when Yldar drew his long sword with a flourish and sneered, those gazes passed by. Satisfied, the sun elf turned back to his sister.

As soon as his back was turned, a dozen blades snickered quietly out of well-oiled belt, boot, wrist, chest, neck, back, and even bodice and codpiece sheaths. There was a reason the inn was called the Splitskull. Oblivious, Yldar smiled fondly at his sister. Cythara saw the attackers coming and sucked in a breath.

Then a lithe figure stepped between Yldar and the throng of attackers. All eyes snapped to the newcomer, and just as quickly the blades slid away. Before Yldar even sensed something happening behind him, the Splitskull had gone back to a comfortable tranquility.

It was, after all, the Dragon Coast.

"Quite the throw," the newcomer said.

The sun elf turned, hand on his sword hilt, to find a mischievous smile waiting. Despite his touted inability to be impressed, Yldar stood blinking.

Shifting her weight from one foot to the other sensuously, the moon elf was easily the most beautiful maid he had ever seen—on par with the high nobles of Evermeet, even.

Her laughing eyes were pale, of indeterminate color

that seemed to shift with the light. Standing against her pale skin, the raven hair falling to her waist in a loose cascade gleamed like the sky at midnight. She wore tight black breeches, a white tunic, and a gray vest with a half cape of dark scarlet silk that covered her left arm. Only one hand—the right, in a scarlet glove—was visible, perched on a slim hip.

Most significantly, though, she wore certainty and strength of will about her like a cloak. Her gaze unnerved Yldar even as it sent thrills down his spine, and her body . . . *Well.*

"Aye?" she said again. Yldar realized he had been staring. "See something that pleases?"

The sun elf flushed with indignation. "*My thanks, lady,*" he said, speaking Elvish without thinking. "*For the—*"

At that moment, Marthul—who had recovered in the pause and drawn a twisted knife—roared and leaped at the pair. Yldar cursed and reached for his blade, but the maid did not blink. Her left hand shot out from beneath the cape.

There was a click, and Marthul roared. His wavy dagger clattered to the ground as he clutched at his hand—and the quarrel sticking through it.

Only then, in the midst of Marthul's curses, did the maid look back, along the line of her previously concealed hand crossbow, and flashed a wry smile. Marthul's face went ashen and he dashed out the door of the Splitskull, cursing.

Yldar blinked. She had moved too fast for him to see, much less react. He was starting to see reason behind her self-assured carriage.

If only he knew.

"*My thanks again, and well met,*" he said in Elvish. "*I am Yldar Nathalan and this is my sister, Cythara, of the House of the Crescent Bow.*"

Cythara hissed at Yldar, but he was too absorbed in the maid to pay attention.

"Impressive—really," the moon elf said in Common, shrugging. "I am called Fox-at-Twilight." She held out her left, ungloved hand. As he disdained human customs, Yldar did not take it. "You can call me 'Light, if you wish."

"I do not," Yldar said. *"You insult us with the tongue of animals?"*

"So that's how you're playing it," Twilight muttered under her breath.

"You give us disrespect?" Yldar sniffed superciliously. His hand went to his sword hilt.

Twilight raised one brow. *"Quite the temper,"* she observed. A short rapier engraved with a weathered, asymmetrical star hung at her waist. *"A duel? That's one way to catch a maid's eye."*

Cythara reached out and caught Yldar's arm, but her eyes never left Twilight. *"Your help was neither solicited nor desired,"* she said. *"Begone."*

"Well met to you as well, your Highnesses," came the reply in the common tongue, perking every ear in the room. Twilight smiled as Yldar and Cythara's eyes nearly popped. She added in Elvish, *"And unless you'd like every cutpurse and cutthroat in the Splitskull visiting your table, I suggest you ease the censure."*

Yldar balked. Cythara's eyes glittered dangerously.

"You know who we are?" Cythara hissed.

"The House of Nathalan is known to me," said Twilight. Her accent was odd—almost human in its sound, though Yldar heard a trace of Evermeet there. *"Known for its wealth and prestige—enough to rival most dynasties of Faerûn, and to draw the attention of most of her sellswords—though I doubt anyone in Elversult has heard of you. Thus, 'Highness' it shall be*—If it please you, Highness." Her last words were loud enough to carry through the room.

Cythara scowled and hunched down, shutting her mouth.

"What do you want?" Yldar asked.

Twilight grinned. "Just a friendly chat—in Common,"

she said. "And if it becomes something more, well then. May I?" She gestured to Yldar's seat, and the sun elf winced. Twilight sat heavily. "Both hands on the table, your Highness."

Cythara, suppressing a frown, drummed her fingers on the wooden surface to show that she was casting no spells.

Satisfied, Twilight turned to Yldar. "Buying a lass a drink? My lord, you're too kind."

Fuming, Yldar waved over the barmaid, who approached the table hesitantly.

"Your best feywine," Twilight said. They sat in silence until the drink came. Twilight downed it in one go and waved for another.

"What shall we talk about?" Yldar asked.

"Tell me why you're here," she said. "I don't see many of the People in the Splitskull, after all—*Well, few enough cousins of Queen Amlauril, anyway.*"

"Yldar. . . ." Cythara warned.

"*No choice, Cyth.*" He turned back to Twilight. "We are looking for something."

Twilight accepted her second glass from the barmaid and teased the liquid close to her rosy lips. "We're most of us looking for something, and for those of us who aren't, it's some*one*," the rogue said. "Anything in particular? Any*one*, mayhap?"

Yldar bit his lip, and Twilight rolled her eyes.

"Come now, Lord Nathalan—don't be coy. It's not like you suns."

"Very well," Yldar said. "What if I were to tell you we were searching for a certain powerful elven artifact, which we've traced from the ruins of Ascalhorn southeast along trade routes, through the hands of adventurers, and is now somewhere, we believe, along the Dragon Coast, if not in Elversult itself?"

Twilight shrugged in a "so-it-goes" way. "Why, is it something you're likely to say any time soon?"

Yldar bit his lip. "We seek . . . Ynloeth's Bracer."

Silence. Twilight's eyes flickered, like the glinting of coins. There it was.

Ynloeth was not a name known to many in Faerun, but most elf children knew the ancient story of Coronal Ynloeth of Shantel Othreier, a hero of the Crown Wars that had split the elf race asunder. And all who knew his name remembered the legend of his shattering swords, upon which he had called to slay a thousand foes in a heartbeat of destructive fury. Legendary, too, was that the power of the blades destroyed its wielder—unless he had the Bracer's protection.

"I see," Twilight finally said. From her blank expression, one would assume she cared little for legend or history—one would *assume*.

"*The Bracer is a priceless relic of antiquity, just as are Ynloeth's shattering swords,*" Cythara said with a scowl, stubbornly holding to Elvish.

"I've always been intrigued by the concept of 'priceless'," Twilight said. "Well, mayhap we can be of some use to one another."

"What possible use can you serve?" Yldar scoffed. He wished his arrogant words held more of the heat he intended. They were more of a defense, a front for uncertainty. "A nameless, landless rogue, who speaks with the tongue of apes? Ha!"

If his pride rankled Twilight, she made no sign. "Two uses," she said, brushing a raven lock out of her eyes. "For the first, I'm good at acquiring things."

"*You are a thief,*" Cythara whispered.

"In a word, and not that of men, it seems." Twilight inclined her head. "Though I am more a thief in the Common sense, my lady, than in the Elvish."

"No," said Cythara, finally relenting. "You have taken my bracelet."

"Oh, yes." Twilight grinned sheepishly and put a gold bracelet with twin rubies on the table. Cythara snatched it back.

"My apologies," Twilight said. " 'Tis a poor practice to steal from one's associates."

"Associates?" Yldar asked.

"Oh, aye—number two," Twilight said. "You're looking for the Bracer. I know who has it." She met his gaze demurely, but her eyes flickered with something more. "You and I are meant for each other, Prince."

Yldar wasn't certain whether he should be outraged or excited, indignant or accepting, but one thing was sure: his heart had definitely started beating faster.

"Now, if your Highnesses will excuse me," Twilight said.

She rose, and Yldar's heart leaped. "Wherefore do you go?" he asked.

Twilight gave him a little sly smile. "Why, to talk to the shadowy, mysterious man sitting in the corner, who will either harm or help," she said. "Meet me here for evening meal. I shall have a plan for you then."

"How do you know there is such a man," asked Cythara, "without looking?"

"In a place like this? There always is." And with that, she was gone, leaving Cythara and Yldar to stare at one another, then after her, wordless.

And sure enough, there was a man skulking in the shadows they had not noticed before—one who saw Twilight coming, stifled a curse, and rose to flee. Not to be deterred, Twilight angled to follow him into a backroom hidden behind a tapestry of a boar hunt.

None of the three elves realized that a certain scowling, pained face—this man not so shadowy or mysterious, merely prudent—was listening at the window and had heard every word.

Cursing and clutching his hand, Marthul left the window of the Splitskull and made his way up Temple Hill. His spying mission complete, even if it had suffered a setback, he extricated himself from the elves' proximity as quickly as possible, elbowing his way through the streets, heedless of anyone who might be trailing him.

He would get his revenge, and he knew right where to go.

Upon arriving at the gates of the struggling House of Coins—the temple of Waukeen, Lady of Merchants—Marthul detoured down a dark alley and paused beside a pile of refuse. Services had ended within—turnout was low with the goddess's strange absence, which had lasted since the Godswar—and the place seemed empty.

Marthul knew better. He felt along the wall until he found it—a small hole, something that would seem little more than a nick to a curious street urchin.

He took off his gold coin necklace and twisted the ornament in two, revealing a jagged key. This he inserted in the hole, and a door appeared in the wall, surrounded by black light that only his initiated eyes could see. Marthul smiled and went through the yawning portal, which closed behind him like a mouth.

Appropriate that the missing goddess's ailing temple hid a thriving temple devoted to her captor.

As he descended the long tunnel, Marthul let delicious darkness enfold him and breathed deeply. The lingering scent of blood, sweat, incense, spoiled meat, and the rituals of their demon lord tainted the air. The steps led to an anteroom outside the altar chamber, where a ritual was being prepared for that very night.

In order to heighten his experience, Marthul had meant to consume quite a few drinks during his spying mission, but the gods had frowned. Perhaps he would enjoy it anyway—he hoped the victim would be a pretty lass again. Criminal, streetwalker, or barmaid, it mattered little to the cultists, but Marthul always preferred the innocent ones.

"Slaveling Marthul," came a chilling, feminine voice in the anteroom shadows.

A chill ran down his spine and he turned to see a voluptuous woman in a black cloak—and, clearly, nothing else—searching him with a pair of red eyes.

"Chosen Leis'anna," he murmured, bowing. "Blessings of our Prince be upon—"

"They already are," the woman said, flashing her long, daggerlike teeth. As always when he met her gaze, Marthul's head pounded and everything went blurry. "You are late."

"Trouble at the Splitskull," he said.

Something about his tone gave it away—or mayhap the feral-faced Chosen could indeed read minds. Leis'anna frowned, her face that of a displeased lioness. "I sent you to spy upon the seekers of the Bracer, not to spark a duel with them," she said.

"Well, me apologies," he spat.

Marthul moved to stomp off, but she seized his arm. Her great strength belied her soft frame, startling him. More surprising, though, her touch felt soft, comforting.

"There is more," she said. "Speak." The words carried a subtle compulsion.

Marthul realized he should have refused, but her touch . . . The seductive magic there, reaching into his soul and laying claim to it, made such a thing impossible. Her face seemed strangely feline then, and her eyes swam with black. He fell deep into those pools and sank as a man who does not realize he is drowning until darkness surrounds him.

Marthul could no longer control himself. He told her everything—about the elves who had come to town, about the black-haired elf, and about the Bracer of Ynloeth.

Leis'anna's eyes flashed at that, and she smiled. Marthul felt himself freed, though the muddiness in his head was still there.

"The Fox has once more involved herself," she said. "Interesting." She traced soft fingers down Marthul's cheek. "Our agreement with her still stands, I believe."

She fixed Marthul with her discerning stare again. He realized that a crowd of cultists had formed around them—faceless figures in black cloaks.

Leis'anna seemed to tower over him. "We are, though, displeased you introduced them all. Steps must be taken."

"That . . . that wasn't what I . . . I didn't mean . . . " He began feeling sleepy.

"Oh, I realize that, child," Leis'anna said. "I simply do not care. Nor does Lord Graz'zt, for that matter."

As darkness claimed him, Marthul grew aware of a noise issuing from deep within her throat—something like purring.

And when he woke again, he was on the altar of the demon lord.

The Splitskull kept a room hidden behind a tapestry for private meetings, business or pleasure—the kind of encounters the watch just didn't need to know about. At the moment, there were perhaps a dozen appropriately secluded individuals sitting around half as many tables, taking part in just those sorts of consultations.

The cloaked man ducked into the chamber, and shed his cloak, tossing it in a corner. Underneath, he was unwashed, pot-bellied, and anything but mysterious. A dozen eyes shifted his way, and moved away just as quickly.

The retreat had been prepared for him, with a tankard of small beer, a bowl of mutton stew, and a chunk of hard bread awaiting at a table. He slid into the chair across from the wall and fell to eating as though he had long been there.

"Well met," Twilight said out of the shadows.

When he looked up, she was sitting there, leaning against the wall, one leg up on the bench. A dozen gazes turned to her, a touch more unsettled, but a tiny shrug turned them away.

"Gods," the man growled in a mixture of shock and disgust. "What are ye about—giving me heartstop?"

"And be deprived of such witty repartee with so handsome a swain?" asked Twilight. "Surely you jest."

With the scar that twisted his lip and the deep pockmarks across his forehead and cheeks, he was more of a handsome *swine*. Looks deceived, though, as they usually do, for this was Macognac Whisperweb, expert fence, dealer in controlled substances and fleshmonger, and the best informed spy in Elversult—in the Dragon Coast entire, he said. He was, of course, wrong, as they both knew, but that didn't get his ego down any.

"Muck, I need a favor," said Twilight.

Macognac winced. "I wish you wouldn't call me that," he groaned. He was undoubtedly recalling their long and uncomfortable—mostly on his end—history.

"Very well." Twilight shrugged. "Mucky, I need information for some people I'm . . . doing business with."

"No."

"I'll pay."

"No."

"You need the coin."

"No—I mean, yes, but no. I won't do it."

Twilight gave him a petulant pout. "Oh, Mucky," she said sweetly. "You know what they say. The friend you feed is a friend in—"

"I don't want to have anything to do with your deeds, 'Light," Macognac said. "This isn't Westgate."

"What about the robbery of Arfiel's a tenday past?"

"Mucky" couldn't stop a flicker of recognition. "Don't know nothing about that."

"What about usury with the dwarves of Steel Hollow?" pressed Twilight.

Another wince. "Didn't have nothin' to do with—"

"How about those necklaces back in Mirtul? I heard the countess lost a pretty—"

"All right, all right," Macognac spat. "What do ye want to know?"

Twilight gave him a little wry smile of victory. "A group of cultists—I need to know where their temple is."

"Which cultists? They're a silver a dozen in Elversult."

"The Deep Coven."

Macognac blinked and his face went pale. "Ay, lass, ye don't want to be dealin' with that pack. Devil worshipers, they be."

"*Demon* worshipers, actually," said Twilight. "Speaking of which, I seem to remember something about you and the coven—what was it? Lotus shipments, perhaps?"

Macognac grimaced. " 'Gainst me better judgment, but aye, I'll do it." He eyed her with suspicion. "Ye'll be taking something from 'em. How do ye know they 'ave it?"

Twilight's eyes flickered. "Call it feminine intuition," she said. "The thiefly kind."

It was his turn to light up. "Ye're playing both sides," he said. "Again."

Twilight flashed him a winsome smile. "Always a pleasure doing business with you, Mucky." She got up to leave, but he caught her by one loose white sleeve.

"Now, what's say ye and me go up to my room and play some Lafat together," Macognac offered, citing a strategy card game where players set down cards like units of soldiers. "I'll go easy on yer flanks this time—just charge up the middle." As he spoke, his hand drifted from her arm to her side and over to her firm belly.

Twilight gave the hint of a smile. "Now my dear Goodman Macognac, what would your blushing wife say if she heard this kind of talk?"

"She's a modern sort of woman," he reassured her, drawing Twilight into his lap. "She'd join us, I think."

"And if she heard about the Sunite celebrants on Midsummer?"

"Very open minded, me wife be," Muck said. His fingers played with the fringe of her vest and moved upward.

"And the Loviatans later that night? With the whips?"

The color drained from Macognac's face. "How did ye know . . . about the . . ." Then anger flared. "Ye saucy wench!"

Standing, Twilight glided out of reach.

"That's me," she said with a smile.

"I suggest you get a good night's rest before tomorrow," said Twilight that evening over wine in the common room of the Splitskull. She had played more gently with Yldar's coin pouch this eve, insisting on a glass of the house's second best feywine, rather than the first.

"You know where we must go?" Yldar said.

Cythara cast her brother a dangerous glance. "We do not go at night?" she asked. "You mean to steal the Bracer, yes? Is such a thing not done best at night—*thief?*"

"Not with these clients," Twilight said to Yldar.

"Clients?" asked Yldar.

"Our unwilling business associates," said Twilight. "Who until the very near future, have been in possession of a certain relic, of which they shall, in that very same near future, find themselves bereft." She grinned. "And they are the kind who live for the night hours—day shall be much to their dislike and our advantage."

"As you say," said Yldar. Cythara looked askance at him, shocked that he would so readily trust this rogue, but the treasure hunter did not return her gaze.

Twilight continued, "We leave at dawn, when Selûne sets and the sun first warms the horizon. Be ready." Finally she glanced at Cythara. "And prepare your spells. They may prove useful."

Cythara glared.

"I find it very convenient," Cythara was saying in imperious Elvish, *"that she seems to know exactly who has the Bracer and where to go. Neither did she question us as to the Bracer's nature."*

She did not shout, but Yldar knew her fury knew no bounds.

They spoke in the room they shared, Cythara poring

over her grimoire and Yldar pacing back and forth, looking up as though carrying on a conversation with the ceiling.

"Mayhap her contact told her where to look," said Yldar. *"And as to knowing of the Bracer, she is an elf, is she not? Coronal Ynloeth's fame is legendary. I would look with suspicion upon a mere human who knows the name, but is it so surprising that an elf would?"*

Cythara grimaced and chanted the words to a spell.

He looked up again. "Flower of the starless night, or dusk's perfect lily?" he asked. "Which is more fitting?"

The rafters did not deign to show a preference.

"What are you doing, anyway?" Yldar asked his sister.

Ignoring him, the gold-skinned wizardess completed the chant and stared sightlessly into the air for a breath. Then she blinked, scowled, and fell back to reading.

"Attempting to scry your thiefly friend," Cythara said. *"And failing, as though she does not exist."*

"She is a ghost, then?"

"No, dwarf-beard. She cloaks her movements in magic, or something else does so."

She flung away the lingering scrying magic and turned another rasping page in her grimoire, giving up. *"I swear on Corellon's blade, something is amiss here."* Another page creaked. *"She manipulates us to her advantage, and you—fool that you are—allow her."*

"Don't be ridiculous, sister. She's one of the People—surely she wouldn't—"

"Now you speak *like her."* Cythara went pale with fury, and Yldar realized that he had lapsed into the common tongue without realizing it. *"Seldarine, brother! Ever an idiot for a pretty maid."*

"So you think she's pretty," Yldar said.

Cythara slammed the spellbook closed. *"Good rest, brother,"* she said as she rose.

"But where do you go? I thought we were making plans for the morrow."

"I see you are not in the necessary state," said Cythara. *"And so I go—I shall see if this hovel has another room to offer. Sweet water and light laughter."*

And with that, she slammed the door shut.

"Thank the Maid, I thought she'd *never* go," said a dark figure, stepping from the shadows behind the door.

Yldar whirled, sword out, but it was only the beautiful Twilight.

"Aillesel seldarie," he gasped. "Do you always startle folk this way?"

"Only those who amuse me so," she said.

Yldar did not know why he felt so stung. "Upon whom do you swear? Is 'the Maid' our Lady Moonbow, or Hanali Celanil, mayhap?"

"The Maid of Misfortune." When Yldar stared, she smiled crookedly. "Beshaba and I have an understanding." Then her ears perked up, like a feline's might.

"Besh . . . ?" Yldar let it trail off. He knew better than to try to decipher this strange and confusing maid. He would discern her business and insist she leave him in peace.

"Why, ah—" he started, but then Twilight leaped across the room and kissed him.

Yldar was so shocked, he did not even protest for a breath. Then confusion took over.

"What?" asked Yldar as he fought off her mouth—her *sweet* mouth. "What?"

"We're about to be rudely interrupted," Twilight informed him. She kissed him again, hard. "Just hold me, eh?" She positioned his hands on her backside. "Like this."

Yldar stammered, shocked, but didn't resist. It provided Twilight an easy target for her lips.

As they kissed and ran their hands over each other—or, rather, as Twilight did so and Yldar stood rather woodenly—portals of crackling darkness opened behind them. There was an awkward silence as the two elves simply stood, exploring one another's mouths rather fully, and the intruders looked at one another, trying to decide what to do.

"Oh, put your back into it, golden boy," Twilight said between kisses.

Yldar stiffened uncomfortably. "*Truly maid, you—*"

"Ahem," said one of the intruders.

Twilight smiled. "That shall do."

Without turning, she sent a crossbow bolt streaking for the head of the cougher.

There were three of them—two men in dark mail with wavy, zigzagging blades held in both hands, and one in tattered, black robes who stood behind, staff in hand. One of the former leaped into the path of the quarrel—or, rather, was forced there by magic—and caught it with his face. The staff wielder scowled.

"You!" he barked at Twilight. He pointed. *"Zsa'kai!"* Yldar didn't understand the foul tongue, but the meaning was clear enough, as the remaining swordsman ran at them.

"Goldie," snapped Twilight, "get the mage!"

Twilight drew her rapier just in time to block the advancing swordsman. Her dusky blade sparked as it struck his fiendishly serrated sword and turned it low. Out of the corner of his eye, Yldar thought he saw flames lick down Twilight's blade and electricity crackle down its length.

He had other concerns, though.

"Get the mage?" he asked, confused.

Then the gnarled, darkwood staff glowed with abyssal power, and Yldar gulped. He desperately wove a spellshield.

The next thing he knew, he was pulling himself out of the shattered wall, batting at the black flames that licked at his tunic. His defense had not been enough, it seemed.

"Yldar!" Twilight hissed. "What did I say?"

"You sa—" he began, but he saw the necromancer looming over him, chanting darkly.

"In Graz'zt's name," the man hissed, and laid a burning black hand upon Yldar's chest.

Vile magic ripped its way into the sun elf, burning through his blood and seeking his heart. He sensed its purpose—to still that beating organ forever—and fought it with every bit of his strength, every fiber of his vitality. He willed his heart to pump on, resisting the foul magic.

And resist it he did, for the corrupting spell faltered, undone by his robust body. Yldar fell back to the ground, coughing and retching the foul magic out.

"What's this?" the necromancer growled. "Not a mage?"

Yldar smiled despite himself. Without the physical training in his swordsmanship classes—if he had studied only magic, say—he would never have fought off that spell.

"Wrong sun," came a voice from above.

Drawn by the magic thrown about, Cythara floated through the ceiling as though it were mist. The necromancer whirled, calmly intoning the words to a spell, but Cythara was the faster. She threw a beam of shimmering gold at his chest, meaning to reduce the necromancer to dust.

Her power struck a shield of shimmering black and dissipated as though it had never been.

"Imposs—" she managed just before the necromancer's dark bolt struck her. Searing, profane blackness scourged her body and her soul, and while her will kept her life-force intact, her body was weak. She fell and slumped to the ground, still burning with freezing, black flames.

"Such power," Cythara whispered. A glaze that was not unlike lust passed over her eyes, and she succumbed to the demonist's spell.

The necromancer grinned and turned back to Yldar—who promptly stabbed his sword into the man's guts. The mage screamed and twisted, black eating away at the blade as though his blood were acid. Yldar let go in disgust and hurried to his sister, who groaned.

"In Graz'zt's name, I shall slay—!"

The necromancer never finished the threat, for Twilight leaped across the room and plunged her rapier through his side. The man's acid blood didn't harm the ancient steel, however, and he died without protest.

The door slammed open and the burly innkeeper shoved his way into the room, stout club in hand, along with two equally wide bouncers, one holding a thick length of chain and the other a long knife. They looked at the battlefield with a mixture of confusion and disbelief. Then Keep found Twilight, spattered with blood, and rolled his eyes.

"Better clear out my room, Keep," Twilight said brightly. "I shall be on my way in the morning."

The burly innkeeper turned the stout club in his hands. "And what about thy tab, pretty lady? I am owed a fair amount of gold."

Twilight shrugged, stood up on her toes, and planted a quick kiss on his cheek. "Oh, Keep," she said. "You know better than to doubt me, don't you?"

"Ahem," said Keep. "Something like that."

Fox-at-Twilight gave him a smile and danced past him, out into the corridor.

The innkeeper and the two sun elves were left in the room then, where silence reigned for a long breath. Then Keep shrugged.

"Quite the fox, that 'Light," he said.

"Indeed," said Yldar, thinking Keep meant her name.

From his slightly raised brow, it was clear he hadn't.

Over "fresh" bread—only two days old!—cheese, and hen's eggs the following dawn, Twilight's face seemed tired, the lines deepened and stretched in a way that did not diminish her beauty but only caught Yldar's notice and concern.

"Are you well this morn, maid?" he asked.

"As well as to be expected," she said, "with so little rest."

Yldar furrowed his brow. "Four bells rang in Elversult's square since the attack. Cythara and I found it to be more than enough time for Reverie. Did you not rest well?"

She offered a crooked smile and said, "Something like that."

Twilight spent much of the rest of the meal trading wry repartee with Yldar, even making some lewd comments that made the treasure hunter blush and Cythara scowl. She never declined an opportunity to cast a mistrusting glance in Twilight's direction.

After a particularly witty exchange that left Twilight smiling sensuously and Yldar absolutely confused, the wizardess threw up her hands.

"*Can we not simply get to business?*" she asked in Elvish. "*I grow weary of your child's games.*"

Twilight rolled her eyes and shrugged. "*Very well, Highness,*" she replied in kind. "You're probably wondering where you have to go to find the Bracer."

" 'Tis the theme," Cythara muttered.

Yldar gave his sister a scolding look and said, "Go on."

"Well—it's in the hands of the Deep Coven."

"Who?" Yldar asked.

"A cult of a demon lord named Graz'zt," said Twilight. "Our friends from yestereve."

There was silence, because it was time for Cythara's angry interjection, which didn't happen. Yldar glanced at her. The sun elf wizardess had leaned back in her seat, eyes far away. Yldar wasn't about to guess what she might have been thinking, but he was glad of the respite from her tongue. He liked hearing Twilight's voice rather more, for some reason.

Speaking of Twilight speaking, she did so, explaining a fair amount about the Deep Coven over tea. It seemed they operated from beneath the House of Coins, which wouldn't be holding services this day. From her calm reassurance, it was almost as though she had already planned to steal the Bracer before she'd ever met the sun elves.

"Are you sure about going there by day?" Yldar asked, reiterating Cythara's concern of the previous day. He looked out the window, and there wasn't a cloud in the sky.

"The cultists are probably sleeping off a ritual as we speak," Twilight said. "Light's always on your side, as a rule, when dealing with demons."

Yldar recognized that she could mean herself by " 'Light," but kept his witticism to himself. He looked at his sister. "Cyth, you've been rather quiet. Are you well?"

Cythara stared straight ahead, as though she had not heard him. When he touched her arm, she flinched. Yldar felt far from her.

"*Oh yes,*" she said in Elvish. She concealed her smile. "*Yes. I was merely . . . thinking.*" She looked at Twilight. "When do we begin?"

"Right now," Twilight said. She took another sip of her tea and smiled through the steam. "Well, soon enough."

When they had finished their meal, paid, and left, Twilight and Yldar's flirtation only continued, much to Cythara's extreme consternation and Yldar's frustrated enjoyment. The moon elf had led them on a twisting route through the streets—to avoid any trails, she had explained—that seemed hopelessly complex and time consuming. From her glower, Cythara suspected that it was only for the sake of continuing her repartee with Yldar, which the latter found himself hoping was indeed the case.

As the midday sun rose overhead, Twilight led them down a dark alleyway beside the House of Coins on

Temple Hill. As Yldar shifted uncomfortably and Cythara flitted about in an unusual surplus of energy, Twilight examined the wall closely.

"Are you *sure* this is it?" Yldar asked for the eleventh time in about as many breaths.

"Silence, Shiny," Twilight hissed. "Let a lass work."

With a little growl, the treasure hunter fidgeted, unhappy to be standing in such a filthy place, doing nothing. It made him terribly self-conscious.

Yldar had never liked standing still—he had a fundamental lack of patience that had interfered with his myriad studies. According to his masters on Evermeet, he lacked the attention and focus wizardry demands, and could learn only paltry spells. For someone who—in his own mind, at least—had been destined to wield high magic, it had been quite a blow. Then, when he hadn't been admitted to the bladesinger order for the same reason, Yldar had abandoned his elf teachers. Not that humans—or any other race, for that matter—were any better, he had found.

Cythara was no help. She paced back and forth, cast spells—divinations, he guessed—and Yldar had the presence of mind to realize that she only did so when it was least likely Twilight would notice.

After a moment, he asked again. "Are you *sure—?*"

"Yes, Brother," Cythara said softly. She spoke in Common, which Yldar marked as unusual. "Magic abounds from that wall. There is almost assuredly a door."

Twilight narrowed her eyes at Cythara distrustfully. Then she shrugged. "My thanks, Your Highness. Almost there . . ." Her fingers found a groove, then an indentation, and she clicked her tongue in victory. "Got it." Her right hand dipped down to her belt and obtained a pair of wire lockpicks from a hidden pocket. "Now . . ."

In a breath or three, the door gave a shudder and the stones began to shift. Twilight leaned back, admiring her handiwork. The bricks rippled and spun and a portal yawned in the wall, like a demonic maw lit from within by strange, dull flames—torches, Ylar hoped. The scent of rotting flesh and congealed blood came from below.

How appropriate, Yldar thought, fighting the nausea.

"Now remember," Twilight warned. "These cultists worship a demon who stands for seduction, betrayal, and perversion for the sake of dark power. Quite the vilest people you can conceive. If they catch you, it'll be worse than death—much worse, I would imagine."

The hairs on the back of Yldar's neck rose. "Cheerful. What precautions do we take?"

Twilight shrugged. "Don't get caught."

They descended into the darkness, Twilight leading the way and searching for pitfalls and guards, then Cythara with her spells of detection, followed by Yldar with a hand on his sword hilt.

The temperature slowly increased as they descended, so much that, even with the elves' resistance to extremes of temperature, a thin sheen of sweat broke out on their foreheads. Twilight made her way down the steps slowly, cautiously, searching the walls with sensitive eyes and the tips of her fingers.

Several times, she motioned to Cythara and Yldar to avoid a certain step, or move away from the wall at a certain point. Sometimes she fiddled with a mechanism Yldar hadn't noticed, disarming a trap or removing a ward he could hardly sense even with seven decades of magical training. She had a remarkable facility with magical traps, which often eluded his largely self-taught thieving skills. He made a mental note to ask about her technique later.

After fifty steps, the stairs ended in a rounded anteroom with half a dozen identical sets of reinforced oak double doors. Yldar immediately began the overwhelming task of deciding which one to investigate first, but Twilight did not hesitate.

"No lead on these doors," she murmured. "Unlocked, too. I should lodge a complaint."

She went immediately to the door that was second from the right and listened at it. After a breath, she nodded and motioned Cythara and Yldar forward.

"How do you know where to go?" Yldar arched an eyebrow.

Cythara studied Twilight silently.

"I . . . well . . . it would take some explaining. Suffice to say—I can sense this Bracer. Call it a gift. Shows me exactly where to go. Like magic." She snapped her fingers. When the others did not join in her smile, she laughed nervously. "Only not."

"I'm familiar with that spell," Cythara said. "As is my brother. In order to find something unique, as Ynloeth's Bracer is, you must know it firsthand. Is this not true?"

"I didn't know *you* knew any Art," Twilight said shortly to Yldar, ignoring his sister.

"We're elves," he said quickly, trying to deflect her accusatory tone. "It comes second nature to us."

"Well, not to me," said Twilight coldly. "Never been comfortable around mages."

Yldar's face flushed and he cursed his sister for including him in those ranks, which lowered him in Twilight's eyes. He didn't know why that upset him so, but it did.

"So, answer my question," Cythara said. "How do you know where the Bracer is?"

"I'll explain later," said Twilight. "Let's make haste. I don't know if you find this place comfortable, but I really don't. Reminds me of the Abyss—but I guess that's appropriate, since it is Graz'zt's temple . . ."

"Agreed," Yldar said. He glanced at Cythara, who bit her lip, and let the matter go for the moment. He stepped to the door and opened it slowly.

Within was the altar chamber of Graz'zt. Torches smoldered in wall sconces about the place and put off a hazy purplish light, producing a strange, surreal atmosphere. Musk and blood mingled in the air. Crude murals defaced the walls, depicting disgusting, horrifying demons and acts of violence and lust. A huge obsidian altar dominated the room, piled all around with skulls and bones. Something metallic glinted from it, and Yldar's eyes lit up.

"The Bracer!" he exclaimed despite himself. He would have continued had not Twilight slapped a hand over his mouth to silence him.

"Easy there, Goldie," she said, gesturing around the room with her sharp nose.

Indeed, though they had not seen them before in the dim haze, black-robed bodies lay scattered about the chamber, all breathing shallowly. Most of them were half-unclad and entwined with one another. Cowls and shadows obscured the faces, but the elves were certain they were sleeping. Yldar could only imagine what their ritual had involved, and his gorge rose.

"Let's just get it and go," Yldar whispered.

They moved slowly into the room, ever alert. Cythara cast a spell to make their movements silent, and they picked their way carefully over sleeping bodies.

It was not until they were halfway into the room that Twilight perked up and furrowed her brow. She stopped and reached for Yldar's shoulder, but he was already a step out of reach. She caught Cythara instead.

"What, *thief?*" Cythara asked.

"That's not it," Twilight replied.

Yldar had not paused. He had just reached the dais and gazed upon the silver Bracer, plain of ornamentation but engraved through with delicate strands of three pointed leaves. It was, without a doubt, one of the most beautiful works of craftsmanship he had ever seen.

He traced his fingers through a detection spell, searching for traps or wards. There seemed to be none, but he detected an aura about the Bracer—one of illusion. Perhaps that was its own magic, meant to shield the wearer. Just to be sure, he decided to dispel it; he doubted his minor talent with the Art would permanently damage such a powerful relic. Yldar began the spell.

"The Bracer," Twilight said. "That's not—Yldar! Stop!"

She was about to leap forward, but it was Cythara's turn to catch *her* by the arm.

"Oh, let him." There was newfound self-confidence in her voice. "Have you not done enough?"

"But—but it's not real," Twilight said, confused.

Cythara leaned in close and whispered something in Twilight's ear. The moon elf's eyes widened and she drew her rapier.

"Yldar!" Twilight shouted the same instant Cythara cried, "It's a trap!" and began a spell.

As one, all the cultists in the room surged to their feet, wavy daggers or swords in their hands. The elves were surrounded.

In the same breath, Yldar's dispelling did more than suppress the Bracer's magic: it twisted and warped the false relic. The silver armguard dimmed, shriveled, and became a disembodied human hand, one that leaped up and clamped down on his wrist as though alive. Yldar shouted and shook his arm furiously to dislodge the fiendish claw, but it was in vain. The blackened, filthy nails drove into his flesh, through the mail hauberk he wore.

He chanted through clenched teeth a spell that would wrench it free, and barely managed to draw in time to defend himself against two burly cultists who hacked at him with flambergé swords. Letting his spell fizzle, Yldar sidestepped one slash and parried the other, but the strength of the blow sent him staggering. Combined with the lingering pain in his left arm, the ringing feeling in his right made Yldar dizzy.

Meanwhile, a cultist stepped out of the horde, pointing a zigzagging long sword in the direction of the two elf maids. "Surrender or die!" he rasped.

That one got Twilight's crossbow bolt between his cowled eyes. At the same time, the moon elf thrust at Cythara, but the mage's ruby-studded bracelet flashed and the dusky-bladed rapier sparked off a shield of golden magic that surrounded her.

Cythara countered with a spell, bringing her hands—blurring with energy, bolts of electricity arcing between them—together and lashing them apart. Twilight's eyes widened and she dived aside, twisting in ways that seemed impossible.

Crimson lightning erupted from Cythara's hands and lashed over and around Twilight, cutting down three hapless cultists. The bolts sprang from the smoking bodies back toward the moon elf, but she dodged again with seemingly unnatural grace. As though it gave up, the lightning went for another of the demonists, who screamed and blackened.

Twilight landed and rolled over the fallen cultists, coming up just in time to parry a swinging axe and dance away. Cythara's lightning ripped and flew freely around the chamber until a spell from one of the chanting cultists caught it harmlessly in a patch of icy darkness.

Meanwhile, Yldar had managed to elude one attacker by skirting the other. With only one sword to face, his fencing lessons came back in a flash, and he shuffled back, varying the distance. When the two-handed sword whipped out, predictably short, Yldar leaped in with a thrust and slash that cut deeply into the cultist's black cloak. The man went down with a grunt. Apparently, the cultists wore little in the way of armor under those robes.

He had a breath before the second swordsman came lumbering over his fallen comrade, and he dared a glance around the chamber. What he saw widened his eyes.

There Cythara stood, surrounded by hacking blades that bounced off her magical shields, weaving and lashing out with the fearsome powers at her disposal. Yldar knew it would not be enough—not with a quarter of the cultists chanting counter spells. The chain lightning had been one of her most powerful spells, and that had failed to fell the primary target: Twilight.

Twilight, who even then dipped and dodged cultists' slow strikes and parried their quick ones. Her bladework was excellent, her slim sword circling around blocks and parries as though the point had a life of its own, but her dancing footwork was nothing short of amazing. Yldar did not envy her opponents the chore of landing a blow upon her.

In that breath, Yldar watched as Twilight spun her blade in circles around a wild, jerking parry, leaped to the side even as she feinted, and ran the cultist through.

Then Yldar had to turn back to his foe, sidestepped, and barely avoided having his head chopped in two like a cabbage.

"Yldar!" Twilight shouted as she parried and leaped away from a cultist with a short, jagged sword. "We have to get out of here!"

"No!" Cythara shouted, beads of sweat running down her bronze skin. "Don't listen to her, Yldar!" She cast another spell, and five spheres of energy burst into existence around her, each with a different color, like rainbow marbles. They whirled around her head like tiny orbiting worlds. "She's a traitor!"

Twilight growled and parried a blow high and sent in a low riposte that had her opponent scurrying back. "*She*'s the traitor, Yldar! Don't—" She might have said more, but the clashing of steel cut off her words.

Yldar's head spun. Who did he believe? His sister, who had stayed with him loyally through all his adventures since Evermeet, or Twilight, a mysterious, caustic, and deceptive woman—a thief by her own admission?

On the surface, the choice seemed perfectly obvious, but something in Yldar rebelled against it. What was this feeling that surfaced within him?

Then Twilight made the choice for him. Near the exit a feral-faced acolyte raised a hand to call down a slaying spell upon Cythara's faltering shield, thus revealing the glint of silver on a very feminine arm.

"The Bracer!" Twilight shouted.

A sudden leaping lunge drove her opponent from his feet, but Twilight made no move to follow with a strike.

Instead, she broke away and made a mad dash for the lady acolyte. As she ran, the shadows coalesced around her like a gathering cloak.

"Stop her, Yldar!" Cythara shouted between spells. A wand she had drawn from her hip flashed, sending an ochre beam streaking at Twilight, but it struck a demon thrall instead, dropping him, melting, to the floor. "She's getting away. Stop her!"

A cultist loomed in her path, but Twilight didn't slow. She leaped into the shadows a pace before him and reappeared, a heartbeat later and ten paces distant, near the exit.

A shadowdancer, Yldar thought. *This maid is full of surprises.*

Yldar parried his opponent into a stone pillar and ran after Twilight, heedless of any attack. He bore down on the demonist mage at the exit and a hulking cultist with a wicked spear.

Twilight leaped upon the lady acolyte like a pouncing fox, bearing her to the ground and going straight for the Bracer on the hooded woman's wrist. The acolyte's guard brought his spear back.

"No!" Yldar shouted as he charged, drawing a shocked glance from Cythara.

Then reality flickered, and Yldar thought he heard light laughter from somewhere, like that of an elf child who was entirely too amused by his own joke.

Twilight rose and caught the spear solidly beneath the left breast. Her eyes opened wide as the shaft carried her back and pinned her against the wall. Twilight convulsed and blood trickled from her mouth.

His eyes bleary, the world gone red, Yldar threw himself at the spear wielder with his sword slashing. His furious rush sent the bodyguard staggering down, and a great blow to the right shoulder made the arm flop uselessly at his side. The brute roared and spat at Yldar, but the sun elf did him one better. He rammed his sword through the hulking man's chest.

Yldar turned from the slumping body. The thief seemed dead upon the wall, her face even paler than normal, but Yldar clutched at the spear to pull it free anyway.

Twilight's eyes snapped open and she gave a cry of more discomfort than pain. "Careful with that!" she chided. "Hurts, you know."

Yldar was stunned. He had expected the moon elf to be dying, if she wasn't dead already, but talking? And calm?

He yanked the spear out of Twilight and she grunted. Blood trickled out. Somehow, it must have missed all her vital organs. Yldar wondered how such a thing was possible.

"Come!" she snapped. "Let's—"

"Traitors!" Cythara shouted. Deep in another spell, she sent her five orbiting spheres streaking after them with a flicker of will.

Yldar shouted a warning and shielded Twilight with his body. The spheres burst against his back, scorching him with fire, splashing him with acid, jolting him with electricity, and stunning him with a burst of discordant sound. One got through—the blue sphere, which exploded with chilling energy against Twilight's shoulder. But a ring on the thief's hand flashed and the deadly cold faded away. Teeth clenched, Yldar sagged.

"Come!" Twilight shouted again. Slinging the limp Yldar's arm over her shoulders, she made a break for the stairs. "Put your head down!"

They ran toward the door.

"Stop!" Cythara shouted.

She snapped off another spell and a sheet of flame fell across the exit, ringing the room, but Twilight and Yldar were already through, crashing through the oak doors.

"Yldar!" was Cythara's last, lingering shout.

The two elves lay stunned on the anteroom floor outside a wall of flame, struggling to think. It took a breath to recover the skill. Yldar looked back at the burning curtain that separated them from the cultists and mouthed a single word: "Cythara."

For Twilight, it was a different word.

"Up," she said, hauling him that direction. Yldar's injuries flared, and he staggered. He would have fallen had she not caught him.

"What happened back there?" Yldar asked. "I thought I'd lost you!"

"Erevan won't let me go that easily." Twilight gritted her teeth and hauled Yldar up the steps. She was obviously in pain, but at least she could walk—he could not make the same claim.

"Erevan . . ." Yldar gaped. "Erevan Ilesere? The Fey Jester?"

"By the black bow, goldie," Twilight cursed as she struggled to haul him away. "How much do you eat, anyway?"

Through the pain, Yldar managed to cast a strengthening spell on Twilight, such that she could lift him like a sack of feathers.

The sudden might caught her off guard, though, and when she kept pulling, she slammed him against the low ceiling. The world went dark, and Yldar knew no more.

Cythara dropped her hands with a look of anguish. As though it no longer mattered, she let her defenses fall, all except the wards that kept anyone from approaching within five paces. Standing in the center of the altar chamber, she felt very weak, very frail, and very alone.

But the cultists did not regard her thus. Instead, they eyed her warily and kept their weapons out. The instant any saw an opportunity, Cythara knew her blood would spill.

Then there was a strange sound, one that started off

weak but grew in intensity until it echoed around the chamber: Cythara's laughter.

It only lasted for a breath, but it was quite enough to send a visible chill through every demonist present. There was nothing uncertain or mocking about the laugh—it was quite mad.

Then, stifling her giggle, Cythara assumed an imperious stance and lifted her chin. "Your leader," she said. "Who gives the orders in this coven?"

A thickly muscled man stepped forward. "I do," he said. "And who might you . . ."

A ray of amber light shot from Cythara's fingers and struck him in the chest. A hole appeared through the cultist, which spread in a flash. He twisted in agony as more and more of his flesh melted and disintegrated before their eyes. In a heartbeat, only dust remained.

"Who *truly* leads?" Cythara asked.

The woman from near the exit, the one who had worn the Bracer, stepped forward then. She pulled back her hood, revealing sharp, almost feline features and a mop of burning red hair. Voluptuous and sensual in her movements, she was lovely, in a cruel way.

"I am Leis'anna, Chosen of Graz'zt. Who are you who so disturbs our peace?"

"One born to command, not to follow," Cythara replied. "Do you yield?"

Leis'anna laughed.

The sun elf launched a spell at her—a black, enervating ray—but Leis'anna batted it aside with defensive magic conjured from the amulet she wore.

"You wish to do battle, elf?"

Cythara just smiled.

"Very well," the demonist said. "Submit to me."

She felt Leis'anna's compulsion magic beat upon her mind. The words cut through her consciousness like a suggestion from a bandit who held his knife at her throat.

Cythara felt a tiny flicker of Leis'anna's mind, and she knew what she faced: the chosen servant of a powerful demon prince—a master of manipulation, who read and controlled minds with the blessing of the mightiest of dark powers.

Mighty dark powers. Cythara smiled.

Then Leis'anna gasped as she felt her own power turned back upon her. Not only had Cythara defeated the Chosen's will, but the sun elf had answered with a compulsion spell of her own.

Leis'anna writhed on the floor, snarling and scraping her claws across the stone as she shattered her own illusions. The alluring female body swelled into the powerful torso and legs of a great lion, and her hands became mighty paws. Her face grew darker, furry, and distinctly feline. Her illusions ruined, the lamia stared at Cythara in horror.

"Who truly leads?" Cythara asked again.

The lamia rose, but only to her knees. Around the room, the cultists dropped into obeisance. Cythara heard the whispers of Leis'anna's demon lord, and saw how badly Graz'zt wanted her darkening soul. She shivered at the power she felt through that mindlink.

How cleverly evil disguised itself, in the flesh of the brightest and most radiant.

"You do," Leis'anna said with a little curl of her lip.

When the sun elf awoke, it was to a sensation of lightness and warmth. He slowly realized that he lay nude in a wide, soft bed. A warm hand caressed his brow, and he looked up a pale arm to see a dark-haloed lady with pale eyes smiling down at him.

Yldar wondered if it had all been a dream, and whether he was not back in Evermeet.

Then he remembered the cultists, the lair, and Cythara's agonized scream, and he gasped. He realized that the elf maid was Twilight, clad in a simple white shift.

"Worry not," she said. "You're safe. I've taken a room

at the Axe and Hammer. You're surrounded by a veritable army of battle-hardened dwarves even Elminster'd think twice about. No one shall find us here."

Yldar half-rose, wincing at the effort, and reached for his tunic on the edge of the bed. Twilight intercepted his arm, leaning between elf and garment. She held his hand between them for a long, quiet breath. Then she pushed him back to the pillows and kicked up out of his reach.

"Stand aside! I have to—"

"Shiny, really. In your delicate condition, you're in no shape to face stairs, much less a cabal of demon-cultists." Twilight's tone was almost chiding.

"But—"

"I didn't go to all that work to save that gleaming body of yours just to have you get it torn up again." She looked him up and down and smiled, that wry upturn of the edge of her lips that set Yldar's hairs standing on end with anticipation. "It's too pretty."

He elbowed the feeling aside. "Away from me, traitor!" he snapped. "You left Cythara to her death!"

"Don't be ridiculous," Twilight said. "She's the traitor. She told me enough in the temple: I said, 'The Bracer's not real,' and she leaned in to say, 'I know.' "

"Lies."

"Naturally, you don't believe me," said Twilight. "Fine. Ask me anything—I promise the truth. Nothing less. My word."

"The word of a thief?" Yldar's voice was sarcastic.

"It will have to do."

"Very well, then," he replied. "For a beginning: what's your name?"

"Fox-at-Twilight, like I told—"

"Your real name," Yldar corrected.

Twilight bit her lip. "Ask me anything *else*."

Yldar scowled. "Very well. Is it true?"

"Is what true?"

"That you work with the demonists. That's why you

knew they had the Bracer and where to go. Why you knew everything."

Twilight rolled her eyes. "I could tell you, but who would you believe? Me, a thief, or your precious sister, who you still think, despite all evidence to the contrary, is a friend?"

"Speak, and we'll see what I think," Yldar said.

"Fine," Twilight said. "Do I work with them? No—perish the thought! Too hung up on power, darkness, and manipulation—not a sense of humor among the whole lot. Bor-*ing*. Demons. Ever heard a demon lord tell a joke? No? Well, of course, you've never met one, but take my word for it. Graz'zt, Orcus—thoroughly unfunny. The only ones who're worse are the archfiends, Mephistopheles in particular—"

"You're babbling," Yldar said.

"What? Right," Twilight said. "No, I don't work for them. Hardly done anything for them." She shrugged dismissively. "Just a little minor work here and there . . . a theft—nothing serious . . . maybe something like . . . I don't know . . . this." She revealed the silver Bracer on her right arm. "Nothing big."

"You stole Coronal Ynloeth's Bracer in the first place?" Yldar asked. "From who?"

"Whom," Twilight corrected. "No one important . . . Coronal Ynloeth. Vaporized himself with his swords, you know. Wasn't *that* a surprise—'Whoop: no Bracer, no protection. Damnation.' "

Yldar's face went ashen and his mouth gaped open.

"I jest, I jest," Twilight said. "Should've seen your face, though—priceless." She laughed. "If such a thing is possible."

The sun elf swallowed. He sat again and pulled the covers back so he could rise. "But, but—" He scowled. "Doing the right thing has no price—your spirit has no price, or did you sell it so long ago for wit and beauty?"

In a flash of motion that would have made any duelist

proud, Twilight slapped him. So much for worrying about his delicate condition.

"Easy for you to make judgments," she said. "Your black and white morality is a luxury that those of us who didn't grow up in the lap of Evermeet serenity can't quite afford."

Yldar was about to retort, but she kept on.

"The Realms aren't as simple as you suns think. Your precious Retreat—ha! *Escape* is more like it. You simply could not bear to see a race that lived more passionately, more fully than yourselves. And so you ran—in fear of the world."

"B-b-but—" said Yldar, but there was no stopping her.

"Life doesn't fit into your haughty, academic . . . arithmetic! Humans see farther than you elves, in ways you never imagined. Elves fear the humans because the humans are what elves fear to become—alive, vibrant! They see more to life than just good and evil, honor and duty. They know passion and beauty, real love—spontaneity. I bet you suns don't even—"

This time Yldar was the one to interrupt, and that with a kiss that shocked both of them. Uncharacteristically, Twilight hesitated—she was stunned.

Yldar broke the kiss. "Sorry," he said. "I . . . I didn't know what I was . . . "

Pouncing like a tigress, Twilight cut off his next words by locking his lips in a fierce, passionate kiss that left Yldar breathless even as she knocked him tumbling back. He didn't even think of protesting as she crushed him into the feather mattress. The pain of cuts and bruises faded into nothing, overcome by the heat that pulsed through him.

It was like nothing he had ever felt. Yldar had known the love of women before, but never had one pressed against him so hard, so fiercely . . .

Twilight pulled back, tugging on his lip as she did, and appraised him with lustful eyes. "After yestereve, I was wondering what it might feel like to do that when you weren't complaining," she said in that ironic way of hers. "And I was right." She untied her bodice with a flick of the wrist and a single pull of the string.

Then Yldar blinked as rationality tried to return, and whispered half-heartedly, "But I thought I was in no shape—"

"Shape enough for this," she said. With a snap, she undid her raven hair, and it tumbled over bare shoulders.

Words failed him.

Cythara awoke into a place of darkness.

Even her keen elf eyes could not penetrate a thumb's breadth in front of her face. From the rich, muggy air beating on her skin, she knew she was nude. Though she should have been cold, instead all was sweltering and heavy, bringing out a thick sweat that soaked every inch of her skin. She moved to brush her brow, but her hand would not move. She must be chained down, spread-eagled.

Cythara tried to call out, but she realized, with a start, where she was. Blood coursed through her like fire and her lungs pulsed rapidly, tearing air in and out of her body.

She lay upon the altar of Graz'zt.

She had thought all was silent but for the buzzing in her head, but she became aware of a dull beat that was not her heart pounding. It was the beat of a drum, and though she could not see it, somehow she knew the covering was the skin of a sentient creature. Her pulse quickened.

Through sheer will, she calmed herself. This was not a surprise—she had chosen this path, and now she had to walk it.

Then the chanting began.

Deep, low, and haunting, she could hear voices all around her, intoning words of darkness. The language was Abyssal, she knew, but twisted somehow, as though passing through the jet blackness distorted the words.

As though on an unspoken cue, the chant rose in volume, and she could discern the words. Horrible, depraved acts that defy names fell upon her ears like candied daggers. Despite herself, Cythara felt her stomach knot and her fingers shake.

"Sa'Graz'zt, sa'za, sa'za," was the chant. *"Graz'zt, sa'za, rzal'za! Sa'lza, rzal'za!"*

Lord Graz'zt, come, come, Cythara translated silently. Graz'zt come and slay us . . . Come into us, slay us . . .

Then there was a hush. Gradually, the darkness deepened and beat down harder upon her, heavier and denser, burning and sweltering. She became aware, with a start, of two glowing green-white eyes that peered down out of the darkness.

That was when Cythara's certainty faltered. She who had met no equal in a mageduel, she who had never suffered a genuine threat, she who had never known real fear—she recognized true terror in that moment.

If she had been afraid before, this sensation completely destroyed her resolve. It bore down upon her as relentlessly and as mercilessly as the headsman's axe fell upon the neck of the condemned. Her skin crawled, and her body inched away as far as it could. She could not think—all her power, all her security, all her will vanished from her in that moment.

Then she saw him, and breath left as well.

An ebony, muscular chest loomed over her, balanced on powerful, double-jointed goat legs. Powerful arms branched out, the hands spread wide, as though summoning forces of darkness to do the demon lord's will. And his face; it was beautiful, in the way that a perfect murder is beautiful, with strong, angular features like an elflord's might be. But this creature was so much more than an elf—any mortal—could ever be. Her mind roiled in horror even as her body twitched with desire—Cythara who had never known a lover, nor considered one.

Then he smiled, and her spirit melted away.

One six-fingered hand hovered up her body, and

Cythara shrank from its touch even as she longed for it. Graz'zt bent over her, and Cythara's body strained toward him.

One of his fingers found her forehead and traced its way down her face, lingering over the lips and dipping into her mouth—he tasted of honey, blood, and ashes—then down. The finger made its way down the hollow of her throat, down her chest, and over her belly.

Then the dark lord paused. And grinned.

He snapped two of his twelve fingers, and Cythara's restraints fell away.

She tingled to throw herself into his arms. Either that, or scurry away in terror. But no, she could not move, could not think beyond the burning desire in her body and spirit.

The demon lord waved his hand, and Cythara felt a hundred hands grasp her. Before Cythara knew what was happening, the thralls turned her onto her belly.

The dark lord renewed tracing his finger along her skin, flesh that tingled for him. His finger glided over her buttocks and came to the hollow at the base of her spine. He touched her there, and she felt with unholy ecstasy a mark burn itself into her skin. She gasped and rolled over to face him, eye to eye, but it was done and could not be undone.

"*Now I claim you, Cythara Nathalan,*" said Graz'zt. "*Wear my mark, and know that you are mine.*"

He pressed his lips to hers. Cythara could not think, could not react, could not flee. She had lost all control, and she loved it.

"Yes!" she gasped.

And Cythara knew an ecstasy she had never imagined: the ecstasy of darkness.

As he laced his hauberk of elven mail, the morning after taking in Reverie with Twilight, Yldar chanced a look at the rogue as she slipped into a pair of sleek black breeches. He marveled at her back and the gentle curves that defined her hips. Had he dreamed last night, or had it really occurred?

Then Yldar's eye caught a twinkle of gold against her creamy skin, at the base of her spine, as of a mark. He took a step closer, looked, and blinked. It had not been a trick of the light—truly, there was a star with eight asymmetrical rays snaking out like blades seemingly etched with gold into her back.

With the kind of boldness only a lover can know, Yldar moved to Twilight and embraced her from behind. The rogue smiled mischievously and swayed in his grasp, reaching around to his rump.

He would not let her change the subject, though. Yldar ran his hand down her spine and paused at the star.

"What's this?" he asked, placing his palm on the mark. Yldar felt a ripple of power like a jolt of electricity run through him, and he was stunned.

Twilight recoiled and spun away, sliding out of his arms as out of loose manacles. She turned on him with dangerous eyes and reached to her hip as though to draw steel.

When Yldar only stared, Twilight shivered and straightened once more.

"The mark of Erevan Ilesere," she said. "Borne by all his maidens."

"A birthmark?"

That same wry smile. "A gift," she said. "When his whim moved from me, Erevan sent me on my way, but he was not ungrateful for the nights we spent together."

Yldar blinked. "Y-you mean," he stammered. "You have lain with . . . with a *god?*"

"He always called me his little Moonbow," she said. "A fantasy, mayhap?"

Yldar gave a little strangled cry. "You can't—you can't be serious!"

Twilight smiled, walked up, and kissed him on the cheek.

"Make you feel special?" She patted him on the shoulder and glided on. "Oh." She turned back. "More skilled than you, of course."

Yldar blushed a fierce golden red. "Well, perhaps with practice," he said.

Her eyes smoldered. "I rather doubt that."

The elves made their way back to the stairs that led to the temple again that afternoon. Twilight had argued against it, but Yldar had insisted. They owed his sister at least an attempt.

The door they found open and the passage yawning. The darkness, reeking of the sacrifice of sentient beings, felt lighter, somehow empty. Yldar allowed himself a sudden flare of hope.

Had Cythara slain the cultists? Perhaps she had escaped!

They found no one in the lower levels. The acolytes' doors all hung open, the cells empty. The double doors to the altar chamber, charred and splintered from the events of the previous day, stood closed. Though Twilight tried to stay him, the determined Yldar crossed to the doors and shoved them open.

The altar chamber was empty, all its vileness cleaned away, all traces of sacrifices expunged. All except one figure who stood, facing them, in a robe of purest black. She pulled back her hood, revealing a familiar golden face.

"Sister!" Yldar shouted, moving to rush forward.

A gesture from Cythara stopped him, as surely as if he had run into an invisible wall. Yldar dropped a hand to the hilt of his sword.

"Brother," Cythara said. She spoke Common, he noted. "You still do not understand. All these years, and you have learned nothing."

She turned and let her sheer gown slip down her back.

There, nestled at the base of her spine: a demonic rune—a six-fingered hand. The mark of her new master.

"You—" Yldar breathed. "You've become one of them!"

"Be silent, and let me speak," Cythara said. Her voice stabbed him like a knife. Dark charisma dripped from her like sweat and passion. "Too long I have dwelt in your shadow, aiding in *your* quests, helping you reclaim *your* honor. I have tolerated enough, brother. I have chosen my path—that of darkness and power. Now you must choose."

"Choose?"

"The Bracer or me," Cythara said. She pointed at Twilight's wrist, where the silver armguard gleamed. "Which is the greater treasure? The dust of Ynloeth's legacy or Cythara's beating heart? That treacherous thief or your once-loved sister? Your duty and honor or your kin and blood. Choose."

Perhaps it was his pride. Perhaps it was his inability to change. Or perhaps it was Twilight.

Regardless, Yldar hesitated.

Cythara nodded and gave an almost imperceptible sigh. "You have chosen," she said. "There is no love in the hearts of brothers."

"But—"

"Farewell, Yldar," Cythara said. "You have your path, and I have mine. I bear you no ill will, but I swear that if you follow me, I will forget that we were once siblings." With those words, she vanished into black smoke and heat.

"No!" Yldar cried, but Cythara was gone.

He searched the spot where she had stood, but there was no trace of the mage. He looked back at Twilight, but all she could do was shrug. Yldar slammed his fist against the empty altar and screamed once, a pained cry from the depths of his soul.

Yldar righted himself slowly, angrily. He lifted his chin and his eyes went cold. "What now?" he asked, once more the haughty elf prince.

There was a long silence.

Then Twilight threw her arms around him and kissed him passionately. "Come with me," she said. "We'll sell the Bracer—it's worth a fortune in coin. I could use a partner." Yldar looked away, and Twilight laid her head against his shoulder. "Let your sister go. She made her choice—you owe her nothing now."

"No," Yldar said. "No, I cannot."

Twilight opened her mouth to speak, but Yldar stopped her with a kiss.

"Come with me," Yldar asked. "I must go, but you can help me—help me save her."

Twilight did not answer for a long moment. When she finally spoke, her voice was soft, like the whisper of a breeze. "You do not have the right to ask this of me."

"But I love you," Yldar said. "Does that mean nothing?"

Twilight smiled, but her eyes seemed far away.

They lay together again that night, clinging to each other as though they would never see each other again, as if the dawn would never come.

But come it did, and when the sun kissed the eastern horizon, Yldar withdrew from Reverie and Twilight was gone.

Yldar lay alone, and despite the hollow feeling in his heart, he could not claim to be surprised. He rose and dressed, hardly interested in the rising sun, casting its rays down over another lonely road and an empty bed.

For Yldar, the next centuries looked lonely and empty indeed.

A sparkle of silver caught his attention from the floor. It was something under his mail shirt. He pushed the armor aside and his breath caught. It was the Bracer of Ynloeth, a marvelous fragment of a long-forgotten age.

There was a note. Three words, written on parchment.

Just three little words in Common, but for Yldar they carried a sea of meaning.

"Farewell," it said, "and remember."

Yldar shut his eyes, but he could not stop the tears.

COMRADES AT ODDS

R.A. SALVATORE

Winter, the Year of the Unstrung Harp
(1371 DR)

He looked out at the night sky with an expression of complete derision, for the rogue drow, Tos'un Armgo, had hoped he would never again look upon the vast ceiling of the overworld. Years ago, during the drow raid on Mithral Hall, Tos'un had lost his companions and his House, preferring desertion to the continued insanity and deadly war that had gripped Menzoberranzan.

He had found friends, a group of similar dark elf renegades, and together the four had forged a fine life along the upper tunnels of the Underdark, and even among the surface dwellers—notably King Obould of the orcs. The four had played a major role in spurring the invasion that had taken Obould's army to the gates of Mithral Hall. The drow instigators had covertly formed an alliance between Obould and the frost giants of the northern mountains, and they had goaded the orc king with visions of glory.

But Tos'un's three drow companions were dead. The last to fall, the priestess Kaer'lic, had been slain before Tos'un's eyes by King Obould himself. Only his speed and sheer luck had saved Tos'un from a similar fate.

So he was alone. No, not alone, he corrected himself as he dropped a hand onto the crafted hilt of Khazid'hea, a sentient sword he had found beneath the devastated site where Obould had battled Drizzt Do'Urden.

Wandering the trails of Obould's newfound kingdom, with smelly, stupid orcs encamped all around him, Tos'un had come to the conclusion that the time had come for him to leave the World Above behind, to go back to the deep tunnels of the Underdark, perhaps even to find his way back to Menzoberranzan and his kin. A deep cave had brought him to a tunnel complex, and trails through the upper Underdark led him to familiar ground, back to the old abode he had shared with his three drow compatriots. From there, Tos'un knew his way to the deeper tunnels.

And so he walked, but with every step his doubts grew. Tos'un was no stranger to the Underdark; he had lived the first century of his life as a noble soldier in the ranks of House Barrison del'Armgo of Menzoberranzan. He had led drow scouting parties out into the tunnels, and had even guarded caravans bound for the trade city of Ched Nasad.

He knew the Underdark.

He knew, in his heart, that he could not survive those tunnels alone.

Each step came more slowly and deliberately than the previous. Doubts clouded his thoughts, and even the small voice in his head that he knew to be Khazid'hea's empathetic communication urged him to turn back.

Out of the tunnel, the stars above him, the cold wind blowing in his face, Tos'un stood alone and confused.

We will find our place, Khazid'hea telepathically

assured him. *We are stronger than our enemies. We are more clever than our enemies.*

Tos'un Armgo couldn't help but wonder if the sentient sword had included Drizzt Do'Urden and King Obould in those estimations.

A campfire flared to life off in the distance, or a cooking fire, and the site of it reminded the drow that he hadn't eaten in more than a day.

"Let us go and find some well-supplied orcs," he said to his growling stomach. "I am hungry."

Khazid'hea agreed.

Khazid'hea was always hungry.

Sunlight glistened off the white-feathered wings of the equine creature as Drizzt Do'Urden brought the pegasus in a steep bank and turn. Astride her own pegasus to the north of the drow, the elf Innovindil caught the view in dramatic fashion, contrasted as it was by the great dark clouds hovering over the Trollmoors to the south. The pair had set out from Mithral Hall three days before, confident that the standoff between the dwarves of Clan Battlehammer and the invading orc army would hold throughout the brutal winter months. Drizzt and Innovindil had to go far to the west, all the way to the Sword Coast, to retrieve the body of Ellifain, a fallen moon elf and kin to Innovindil, slain at the hands of Drizzt in a tragic misunderstanding.

They had started out traveling south and southwest, thinking to pass the city of Nesmé on the northern banks of the dreaded Trollmoors to see how the rebuilding was commencing after the carnage of the previous summer. They had thought to cross over Nesmé, skirting the Trollmoors so that they could catch a more southerly route to the west and the distant city of Luskan.

It was bitterly cold up in the sky with winter beginning to blow. Sunrise and Sunset, their pegasi mounts, didn't complain, but Innovindil and Drizzt could only remain in the air for short periods of time, so cold was the wind on their faces. Bruenor had given both of them fine seal coats and cloaks, thick mittens and hoods, but the wind bit too hard at any and all exposed skin for the pair to remain aloft.

As Drizzt came around in his lazy turn, Innovindil began to motion for him to put down on a plateau directly west of his position. But the drow beat her to the movement, motioning west and a bit to the north instead—and not for her to descend, but only to look.

Her expression soured as soon as she turned that way, for she didn't miss the drow's target: a line of black specks—orcs, she knew—moving south along a narrow trail.

Sunrise flew under her mount as Drizzt began a slow, circling descent. He put a hand to one of his scimitars and drew it a bit from its sheath then nodded, silently asking the elf if she was up for a fight.

Innovindil smiled back at him as she guided Sunset into Sunrise's wake, following Drizzt's descent.

"They will cross just to the west of us," Drizzt said as she put down on a wide, flat rock a few feet to the side of him.

She couldn't see the drow's white smile for he had pulled his scarf up over the bottom half of his face, but his intense lavender eyes surely smiled at her.

Innovindil loosened her collar and pulled her hood back. She shook free her long golden hair, returned Drizzt's look, and said, "We have hundreds of miles before us, and winter fast approaching. Would you delay us that we might kill a few orcs?"

Drizzt shrugged, but as he pulled his scarf down, he still grinned with eagerness.

Innovindil could hardly argue against that.

"We should see what they're about," the drow explained. "I'm surprised to see any of the orcs moving this far to the south now."

"With their king dead, you mean?"

"I would have thought that most of the orcs would be turning back to the north and the security of their mountain holes. Do they mean to press forward with their attacks absent the unifying force that was Obould?"

Innovindil glanced to the west, though they had lost sight of the orcs during their descent. "Perhaps some, at least, have grown overconfident. So much of the land came so easily to their overwhelming numbers, perhaps they've forgotten the mighty resistance aligned against them."

"We should remind them," said Drizzt. He lifted one leg over the pegasus so that he sat sideways on the beast, facing Innovindil, then threw himself backward in a roll over the mount's back, flipping as he went to land lightly on his feet on the other side. He moved around under Sunrise's neck, patting the muscled creature as he went. "Let us see what they're about," he said to the elf, "then send them running."

"Those we do not kill outright," Innovindil agreed. She slid down from her saddle and unfastened her great bow from the straps behind the seat.

Trusting that the intelligent pegasi would remain calm and safe, the pair moved off with all speed, stealthy and nimble across the uneven stones. They headed northwest, thinking to approach the long ravine a bit ahead of the orcs, but the sound of metal against stone stopped them and turned them back to the southwest.

A short while later, Drizzt crawled out onto a high outcropping of stone, and while he understood then the source of the hammering, he grew even more confused. For there below him, at a bottleneck along the trail, he saw a group of orcs hard at work building a wall of cut stones.

"A gate," Innovindil remarked, creeping up beside him.

The pair watched as several orcs came up the trail from the south, carrying rocks.

"We need a better look," Innovindil said.

"The sun is fast setting," said Drizzt, pulling himself up and starting back to the east and the pegasi.

They had less than half an hour of daylight remaining, but in that time they found much more than they had anticipated. Just a few hundred yards from the as yet unfinished gate sat a blockade of piled stones, and a second had been thrown together a hundred yards ahead of that one. Sentries manned both posts, while workers disassembled the one closest to the gate, carrying the stones for cutting and placement on the more formidable wall.

The coordination and tactics could not be denied.

"The fall of Obould has not yet corroded their unity and precision," Innovindil remarked.

"They wear uniforms," Drizzt said. It seemed as if he could hardly draw breath—and from more than the cold wind, Innovindil could plainly see.

His words rang true enough to the elf, for the sentries at all three points wore similar skull-shaped helms of white bone and nearly identical black tabards.

"Their tactics are perfect," the drow went on, for he had seen many similar scenes during his time in Menzoberranzan among his warrior people. "They hastily set blockades to slow down any attackers so that they won't be caught vulnerable at their more permanent construction site."

"Orcs have always been clever, if not cohesive," the elf reminded him.

"It would seem that Obould has remedied the weakness of the latter point more completely than we had thought." The drow looked around, his gaze drifting in the direction of Mithral Hall. "We have to investigate this more fully and go back to Bruenor," he said as he looked back at his elf companion.

Innovindil held his stare for a short while then shook her head. "We have already decided our course."

"We could not know."

"We still do not know," the elf replied. "These southern orc scouts and laborers may not even yet know of Obould's demise. We cannot measure what we see here as what we can expect a month from now, or after the winter season. In any case, the stalemate will hold with the coming snow and cold, and nothing we can tell King Bruenor now will alter his preparations for the winter."

"You would still recover the body of Ellifain," said Drizzt.

Innovindil nodded and replied, "It is important—for my People, and for our acceptance of you."

"Is this a journey to recover a lost soul? Or is it to determine the veracity of a potential friend?"

"It is both."

Drizzt leaned back as if stung. Innovindil reached out for him.

"Not for me," she assured him. "You have nothing to prove to Innovindil, Drizzt Do'Urden. Our friendship is sincere. But I would have no doubts lingering among my sorely wounded and angry people. The People of the Moonwood are not many in number. Forgive us our caution."

"They bade you do this?"

"There was no need. I understand the importance of it, and do not doubt that I, that all of my people, owe this to the lost one. Ellifain's fall marks a great failing in the Moonwood, that we could not convince her of the error of her ways. Her heart was scarred beyond reason, but in offering her no remedy, we of the Moonwood can only see Ellifain's fall as our failing."

"How will retrieving her body remedy that?"

Innovindil shrugged and said, "Let us learn."

Drizzt had no answer for that, nor did he think it was his place to question further. He had agreed to fly beside Innovindil to the Sword Coast and so he would. He owed her that, at least. But more importantly, he owed it to Ellifain, the lost elf he had slain.

They returned to their mounts and moved higher up on the trails as darkness fell and the cold closed in, accepting the less accommodating climate so that they could try to get a better understanding of what the orcs around them were up to. They found an overhang to block the biting northeastern wind and huddled close.

As they had expected, campfires came up. A line of lights ran off from the gate construction to the north. More curiously, every few minutes a flaming arrow soared into the night sky. For more than an hour, Drizzt measured the signal flares against the movements of the moon and the small star that chased it, and it wasn't long before he was nodding in admiration.

"Not random," he informed Innovindil. "They have devised a coded system of signaling."

For a long while, the elf didn't respond. Then she asked, "Is this how kingdoms are born?"

The next day dawned warmer and with less of a wind, so Drizzt and Innovindil wasted no time in getting their flying horses up into the air. They set down soon after, moving into position on the bluffs above the gate construction, and soon realized that their suppositions were right on the mark. The orcs continued to coordinate the deconstruction of the protective barriers to the south with the construction of the more sophisticated gate. The caravan they'd first spotted arrived soon after, laden with supplies for the workers, and that, too, seemed quite extraordinary to the two onlookers.

No typically orc squabbling came from below regarding the food and drink; it was passed out in an orderly fashion, with enough set aside to feed those orcs still working in the south upon their return.

Even more curiously, the guards rotated, with several caravan guards replacing those at the wall, who set out on the return journey to the north. The new guards, too, were dressed in the skull helmets and black tabards that seemed to be the uniform of Obould's minions.

Intrigued by the surprising orderliness of the orcs, the two elves, moon and drow, moved back from the ledges and put their mounts to the sky once again. They veered along a more northerly route, wanting to more fully explore the continuing organization of the orc army. They noted wooden pyres set on many hilltops—signal fires. They saw other well-guarded caravans moving out along the various trails like the tentacles of a gigantic octopus. The center of that creature, a huge encampment, was not hard to find.

They flew beyond it, continuing more north than west, and found new construction everywhere. Clusters of stone houses and incomplete walls showed across every snow-covered lea, and every other hilltop, it seemed, was set with the base stones of a new, fortified keep.

"Word does not spread quickly among the orcs, it would seem," Innovindil said when they landed in a secluded vale.

Drizzt didn't reply, but his doubting expression spoke volumes. All those orcs couldn't still be ignorant of an event as momentous as the fall of Obould Many-Arrows. Could it be that the cohesion Obould had spawned among his people would outlast him?

That possibility rattled Drizzt to his bones. The decapitation of the orc army, the death of Obould, was supposed to work like a cancer on the stupid beasts. Surely infighting and selfishness would destroy the integrity of their enemies. The nature of orcs would accomplish what Bruenor's army had not been able to.

"The tale is early in the telling," Innovindil said, and Drizzt realized that his fears played out on his face.

"Not so early."

"Our enemies have not been tested since Obould's fall," Innovindil said. "Neither by sword nor winter's fury."

"They are preparing for both, it would seem."

Innovindil touched her hand to the drow's shoulder, and he looked into her blue eyes. "Do not abandon hope," she reminded him. "Nor make judgments on things we cannot yet know. How will these remainders of the orc army fare when winter comes on in full? How will they manage when some tribe or another decides that it is time to return to the safety of its mountain hole? Will the others try to stop the retreat, and if they do, if orcs begin to battle orcs, how long will it take for the entire mass to feed upon itself?"

Drizzt glanced back to the distant trails and the working orcs and let his gaze linger there for some time. "It is too early to make a judgment," he finally agreed. "Let us go to the west and finish our task. Perhaps the day will shine brighter upon our return."

Innovindil took his hand and walked him back to the waiting pegasi, and soon they were on their way again, flying due west, the miles to Luskan rolling out below them. They set their course and held it true, and they each tried to hold on to their reasoning that the events around them were not likely indicative of what they would find upon their return.

But they each glanced to the sides, and watched the continuing progress and cohesion of an orc force that was supposed to be disintegrating.

The sights of that day, the signal fires and coordinated flares of that night, and the sights of the next day, until they broke clear of the orcs in the Haunted Pass to the west, did not bolster their confidence.

As a minor noble in a major House of Menzoberranzan, Tos'un Armgo had done many years of battle training at Melee-Magthere, the school of warriors. He had served under the brutal and legendary weapons master, Uthegental, who had distinguished himself among drow warriors with his fearsome, offensive style of battle. Never known for his subtlety, what Uthegental lacked in finesse he made up for in sheer strength and ferocity, and the Barrison del'Armgo warriors he commanded learned to strike hard and strike fast.

Tos'un was no exception. So when he descended upon a caravan of orcs, Khazid'hea in his right hand and a second sword in his left, he did not hesitate. He came down from on high in a great leap, stabbed out with his left as he landed beside the lead orc, then spun across with Khazid'hea and cut the foolish creature shoulder to hip. A sudden reversal and backhand sent Khazid'hea slashing at the next orc in line, who lifted a sack of supplies to block.

The blade, with an edge as fine as any in all the world, slid in and out of the bag, through the orc's raised arm, and into its surprised face with such ease Tos'un wasn't even sure he had hit the creature.

Until, that is, it fell in a blood-spraying heap.

Tos'un planted his foot on the fallen orc as he leaped forward, scoring another kill by stabbing Khazid'hea through the planks of the caravan's lead cart and into the chest of the orc that had leaped behind it for cover.

More! the sentient sword screamed in his head. It sent waves of rage at the drow, telepathic impartations that agitated him and drove him on with fury.

A pair of orcs moved to intercept, their swords out level to hinder him.

Out went Tos'un's second sword, tapping across left to right under the blade of the orc on his right. He rolled it under and tapped the underside of the other orc blade, then back again to the right and back to the left in a series of light parries. The orcs didn't resist, for the hits were not strong, but neither did they realize that the drow was walking their blades up ever so slightly.

Tos'un stopped in mid-swing and tossed his second sword into the air to fly between the surprised orcs. In the same fluid movement, the drow dropped low and spun, slipping forward to one knee and ducking under the orcs' blades. Khazid'hea ripped across, shearing thick belts and leather tabards as if they were made of parchment.

Both orcs howled and fell away, grabbing at their spilling entrails.

Khazid'hea howled, too, but in pleasure—in Tos'un's head.

Another pair of guards came at the drow, each circling to the side and prodding at him with metal-tipped spears. He analyzed their movements and ran through an internal debate about how to proceed, where to parry and which counter to follow through.

When the thrust came, Tos'un proved more than ready. With his superior agility and speed, he slipped his foot back and half-turned, dodging the stab that passed behind him and slapping aside the one in front.

One step forward had him in range, and Khazid'hea tasted more orc blood.

The other foolish orc pursued the drow from behind, and Tos'un executed a brilliant backhand, behind-the-back deflection with his more mundane blade, spun following his own blade as he continued to force the spear aside, and bore in to put Khazid'hea through the orc's heart.

The sword flooded Tos'un with appreciation.

The drow saw an opening to the left, where an orc began scrambling away. He started that way but then cut back having seen a pair of orcs running right, abandoning the wagon to save their lives. He took a few steps in pursuit, but his delay had cost him any chance of catching them quickly, so he sheathed his swords and went to the carts instead to realize the spoils.

Khazid'hea went silent, but the sword was more intrigued than pleased. Tos'un was a fine wielder, a solid drow warrior, certainly superior to the human woman who had wielded the sword for several years before, a female warrior who too often favored her bow—a coward's weapon—over Khazid'hea's magnificent blade.

We have much to learn from each other, the sword related in Tos'un's thoughts.

The drow glanced down at Khazid'hea's hilt, and the sword could sense his trepidation.

You do not trust your instinctive warrior self, the sword explained.

Tos'un put down the food he had found and drew Khazid'hea from its sheath, holding the gleaming blade up before his red eyes.

You think too much, the sword imparted.

Tos'un paused for a bit, then re-sheathed the blade and went back to his food.

That was good enough for the time being, Khazid'hea believed. The drow had not dismissed the suggestion. The sword would be more prepared in their next fight to help the dark elf achieve a state of more fluid concentration, of heightened awareness, in which he could trust in his abilities, and fully understand his limitations.

Not long before, Khazid'hea had been wielded by Drizzt Do'Urden, a champion among drow. That dark elf had easily dismissed any of the sentient weapon's intrusions because he had achieved a perfect warrior state of mind, an instantaneous recognition of his enemies and evaluation of their abilities. Drizzt moved without conscious consideration, moved in a manner that perfectly blended his thoughts and actions.

Khazid'hea had felt that warrior instinct, the concentration that elevated Drizzt above even a superbly trained warrior such as Tos'un Armgo. The sentient sword had studied its wielder intently in the fight between Drizzt and Obould, and Khazid'hea had learned from the master.

And the sword meant to teach that technique to Tos'un. Though this drow would never be as powerful in heart and will as Drizzt Do'Urden, that was a good thing. For without that inner determination and overblown moral compass even as he gained in physical prowess, Tos'un would not be able to deny Khazid'hea, as had Drizzt. The sword could make Tos'un as physically formidable, but without the dead weight of free will.

Khazid'hea could not settle for second best.

⊕ ⊕ ⊕ ⊕ ⊕

"You have been very quiet these last days," Innovindil remarked to Drizzt when they pulled up to set their camp for the night.

The smell of brine filled their nostrils and the sunset that night shone at them across the great expanse of dark waters rolling in toward the Sword Coast. The weather had held and they put hundreds of miles behind them much more quickly than they'd anticipated. The two elves even dared to hope that, if good fortune held, they could be back in Mithral Hall before winter came on in full, before the deep snows filled Keeper's Dale and the icy winds forced them to travel exclusively on the ground. In the air, the pegasi could cover thirty miles in a single day with ease, and those thirty miles were in a direct line to their goal, not winding around hillocks or following rivers for hours and hours until a ford could be found. On the ground, along the winding trails and empty terrain of the wilderness, where they had to beware of monsters and wild beasts, they would be lucky to travel ten miles in any given day, and luckier still if more than a third of those were actually in the direction of their goal.

"Our progress has been amazing," Innovindil went on when Drizzt, standing on a bluff and staring out at the sea, made no move to reply. "Rillifain is with us," she said, referring to an elf forest god, one of the deities of her Moonwood clan. "His calming breath is keeping the wintry blows at bay, that we might recover Ellifain and return with all speed."

She continued on, speaking of the god Rillifain Rallathil and the various tales associated with him. The sun's lower rim seemed to touch the distant water and still she talked. The sky turned a rich blue as the fiery orb disappeared behind the waves, and she realized that Drizzt was not listening, that he had not been listening to her at all.

"What is it?" she said, moving up beside him. She asked again a moment later, and forced him to look at her.

"Are you all right, my friend?" Innovindil asked.

"What did Obould know that we do not?" Drizzt asked in reply.

Innovindil took a step back, her fair elf face scrunching up, for he had caught her off guard.

"Are there good orcs and bad orcs, do you suppose?" Drizzt went on.

"Good orcs?"

"You are surprised that a goodly dark elf would ask such a question?"

Innovindil's eyes snapped open wide at that, and she stuttered over a reply until Drizzt let her off the hook with a disarming grin.

"Good orcs," he said.

"Well I am sure that I do not know. I have never met one of goodly disposition."

"How would you know if you had?"

"Well then perhaps there are such creatures as goodly orcs," an obviously flustered Innovindil conceded. "I'm sure I wouldn't know, but I'm also sure that if such beasts exist, they are not the norm for that race. Perhaps a few, but which are more predominant, your mythical goodly orc or those bent on evil?"

"It does not matter."

"Your friend King Bruenor would not likely agree with you this time."

"No, no," Drizzt said, shaking his head. "If there are goodly orcs, even a few, would that not imply that there are varying degrees of conscience within the orc heart and mind? If there are goodly orcs, even a few, does that not foster hope that the race itself will move toward civilization, as did the elves and the dwarves . . . the halflings, gnomes, and humans?"

Innovindil stared at him as if she didn't understand.

"What did Obould know that we do not?" Drizzt asked again.

"Are you suggesting some goodness within King Obould Many-Arrows?" Innovindil asked with an unmistakably sharp edge to her voice.

Drizzt took a deep breath and held his next thoughts in check as he considered the feelings of his friend Innovindil, who had watched her lover cleaved in half by Obould.

"The orcs are holding their discipline and creating the boundaries of their kingdom even without him," Drizzt said, and he looked back out to sea. "Were they ready to forge their own kingdom? Is that the singular longing Obould tapped into to rouse them from their holes?"

"They will fall to fighting each other, tribe against tribe," Innovindil replied, and her voice still held a grating edge to it. "They will feed upon each other until they are no more than a crawling mass of hopeless fools. Many will run back to their dark holes, and those that do not will wish that they had when King Bruenor comes forth, and when my people from the Moonwood join in the slaughter."

"What if they don't?"

"You doubt the elves?"

"Not them," Drizzt clarified, "the orcs. What if the orcs do not fall to fighting amongst themselves? Suppose a new Obould rises among them, holding their discipline and continuing the fortification of this new kingdom?"

"You can't believe that."

"I offer a possibility, and if so, a question that all of us—from Silverymoon to Sundabar, Nesmé to Mithral Hall, the Moonwood to Citadels Felbarr and Adbar—would be wise to answer carefully."

Innovindil considered that for a moment then said, "Very well then, I grant you your possibility. If the orcs do not retreat, what do we do?"

"A question we must answer."

"The answer seems obvious."

"Kill them, of course."

"They are orcs," Innovindil replied.

"Would it truly be wiser for us to wage war upon them to drive them back?" Drizzt asked. "Or might allowing them their realm help foster any goodness that is within them? Allow it to blossom, for if they are to hold a kingdom, must they not necessarily find some measure of civilization? And would not the needs of such a civilization favor the wise over the strong?"

Innovindil's expression showed that she wasn't taking him very seriously, and truthfully, as he heard the words leaving his own mouth, Drizzt Do'Urden couldn't help but think himself a bit mad. Still, he knew he had to finish the thought, felt that he needed to speak it out clearly so that the notion might help him to sort things out in his own jumbled mind.

"If we are to believe in the general goodness of elf society—or dwarf, or human—it is because we believe that these peoples are able to progress toward goodness. Surely there are ample atrocities in all our respective histories, and still occurring today. How many wars have the humans waged upon each other?"

"One," Innovindil answered, "without end."

Drizzt smiled at the unexpected support and said, "But we believe that each of our respective people move toward goodness, yes? The humans, elves, dwarves—"

"And drow?"

Drizzt could only shrug at that notable exception and continue, "Our optimism is based on a general principle that things get better, that *we* get better. Are we wrong—shortsighted and foolish—to view the orcs as incapable of such growth?"

Innovindil stared at him.

"To our own loss?" Drizzt asked.

The elf still could not answer.

"Are we limiting our own understanding of these creatures we view as our enemies by thinking of them as no more than a product of their history?" Drizzt pressed. "Do we err, to our own loss, in thinking them incapable of creating their own civilization?"

"You presume that the civilization they have created over the eons is somehow contrary to their nature," Innovindil finally managed to say.

Drizzt shrugged and allowed, "You could be correct."

"Would you unfasten your sword belt and walk into an orc enclave in the hopes that they will be 'enlightened orcs' and therefore will not slaughter you?"

"Of course not," Drizzt admitted. "But again, what did Obould know that we do not? If the orcs do not cannibalize themselves, then by the admission of the council that convened in Mithral Hall, we have little hope of driving them back from the lands they have claimed."

"But neither will they move forward," Innovindil vowed.

"So they are left with this kingdom they claim as their own," said Drizzt. "And that realm will only thrive with trade and exchange with those other kingdoms around them."

Innovindil flashed him that incredulous look yet again.

"It is mere musing," Drizzt replied with a quiet grin. "I do that often."

"You are suggesting—"

"Nothing," Drizzt was quick to interrupt. "I am only wondering if a century hence—or two, or three—Obould's legacy might prove one that none of us has yet considered."

"Orcs living in harmony with elves, humans, dwarves, and halflings?"

"Is there not a city to the east, in the wilds of Vaasa, comprised entirely of half-orcs?" Drizzt asked. "A city that swears allegiance to the paladin king of the Bloodstone Lands?"

"Palishchuk, yes," the elf admitted.

"They are descendants, one and all, of creatures akin to Obould."

"Yours are words of hope, and yet they do not echo pleasingly in my thoughts."

"Tarathiel's death is too raw."

Innovindil shrugged.

"I only wonder if it is possible that there is more to these orcs than we allow," Drizzt said. "I only wonder if our view of one aspect of the orcs, dominant though it may be, clouds our vision of other possibilities."

Drizzt let it go at that, and turned back to stare out to sea.

Innovindil surprised him, though, when she added, "Was this not the same error that Ellifain made concerning Drizzt Do'Urden?"

A stream of empty white noise filled Tos'un's thoughts as he worked his spinning way through the orc encampment. He slashed and he stabbed, and orcs fell away. He darted one way and cut back the other, never falling into a predictable routine. Everything was pure reaction for the dark elf, as if some rousing music carried him along, shifting his feet, moving his hands. What he heard and what he saw blended into a singular sensation, a complete awareness of his surroundings. Not at a conscious level, though, for at that moment of perfect clarity, Tos'un, paradoxically, was conscious of nothing and everything all at once.

His left-hand blade, a drow made sword, constantly turned, Tos'un altering its angle accordingly to defeat any attacks that might come his way. At one point as he leaped to the side of a stone then sprang away, that sword darted out to his left and deflected a thrown spear, then came back in to slap a second missile, turning the spear sidelong so that it rolled harmlessly past him as he continued on his murderous way.

As defensive as that blade was, his other, Khazid'hea, struck out hungrily. Five orcs lay dead in the dark elf's wake, with two others badly wounded and staggering, and Khazid'hea had been the instrument of doom for all seven.

The sentient sword would not suffer its companion blade the pleasure of a kill.

The ambush of the orc camp had come fast and furious, with three of the orcs going down before the others had even known of the assault. None in the camp of a dozen orcs had been able to formulate any type of coordinated defense against Tos'un's blistering pace, and the last two kills had come in pursuit of fleeing orcs.

Still, despite the lack of true opposition, Khazid'hea felt that Tos'un was fighting much better this day, much more efficiently and more reflexively. He wasn't near the equal of Drizzt Do'Urden yet, Khazid'hea knew, but the sword's continual work—blanketing the drow's thoughts with disruptive noise, forcing him to react to his senses with muscular memory and not conscious decisions—had him moving more quickly and more precisely.

Do not think.

That was the message Drizzt Do'Urden had taught to Khazid'hea, and the one that the sentient sword subtly imparted to Tos'un Armgo.

Do not think.

His reflexes and instincts would carry him through.

Breathing hard from the whirlwind of fury, Tos'un paused beside the wooden tripod the orcs had used to suspend a kettle above a cooking fire. No spears came at him, and no enemies showed themselves. The drow surveyed his handiwork, the line of dead orcs and the pair still struggling, squirming, and groaning. Enjoying the sounds of their agony, Tos'un did not move to finish them.

He replayed his movements in his mind, mentally retracing his steps, his leaps and his attacks. He had to look over by the boulder to confirm that he had indeed picked a pair of spears from mid-air.

There they lay in the dirt by the stone.

Tos'un shook his head, not quite understanding what had just happened. He had given in to his rage and hunger.

He thought back to Melee-Magthere. He had been a rather unremarkable student, and as such a disappointment to mighty Uthegental. At the school, one of the primary lessons was to let go of conscious thought and let the body react as it was trained to do.

Never before had Tos'un truly appreciated those lessons.

Standing amidst the carnage, Tos'un came to recognize the difference between ordinary drow warriors—still potent by the standards of any race—and the weapons masters.

He understood that he had fought that one battle as one such as Uthegental might have: a perfect harmony of instinct and swords, with every movement just a bit quicker than normal for him.

Though Tos'un didn't know how he had achieved that level of battle prowess, and wondered if he could do it again, he could tell without doubt that Khazid'hea was pleased.

Sinnafain moved from cover to cover amidst the ruined orc encampment. She paused behind a boulder then darted to the side of a lean-to where a pair of orcs lay dead. That vantage point also afforded her a wide view of the trails to the west, the direction in which the dark elf had fled.

She scanned for a few seconds, her keen elf eyes picking out any movement, no matter how slight. A chipmunk scurried along some stones about thirty feet from her. To the side, a bit farther along, a breeze kicked up some dried leaves and sent them twirling above the snowy blanket. The drow was nowhere to be seen.

Sinnafain scampered to the next spot, the overturned cooking tripod. She crouched low behind the meager cover it offered and again paused.

The breeze brought wisps of flame from the dying embers beside her, but that was the only life in the camp. Nodding, the elf held up her fist, the signal to her companions.

Like a coven of ghosts the moon elves appeared from all around the dead camp, drifting in silently, as if floating, their white and dark brown cloaks blurring their forms against the wintry background.

"Seven kills and the rest sent running," remarked Albondiel, the leader of the patrol. "This drow is cunning and fast."

"As is his sword," another of the group of five added. When the others looked at him, he showed them one of the dead orcs, its arm severed, its heavy wooden shield cleanly cut in half.

"A mighty warrior, no doubt," Sinnafain said. "Is it possible that we've found a second Drizzt Do'Urden?"

"Obould had drow in his ranks as well," Albondiel reminded her.

"This one is killing orcs," she replied. "With abandon."

"Have drow ever been selective in their victims?" one of the others asked.

"I know of at least one who seems to be," Sinnafain was quick to remind. "I will not make the same errors as did my cousin Ellifain. I will not prejudge and be blinded by the whispers of reputation."

"Many victims have likely uttered similar statements," Albondiel said to her, but when she snapped her disapproving glare at him, she was calmed by his grin.

"Another Drizzt?" he asked rhetorically, and he shrugged. ""If he is, then good for us. If not. . . ."

"Then ill for him," Sinnafain finished for him, and Albondiel nodded and assured her, "We will know soon enough."

⊙ ⊙ ⊙ ⊙ ⊙

Drizzt brushed the last of the cold dirt away, fully revealing the blanket. Beneath it lay the curled form of Ellifain, the misguided elf who had posed as the male Le'Lorinel, and who had tried to kill him in her rage.

Drizzt stood and stared down at the hole and the wrapped body. She lay on her side, her legs tucked to her chest. She seemed very small to Drizzt, like a baby.

If he could take back one strike in all his life. . . .

He glanced over his shoulder to see Innovindil fiddling with one of the saddlebags on Sunset. The elf produced a silver censer set on a triangle of thin, strong chains. Next came a sprinkler, silver handled, green-jeweled, and with a bulbous head set with a grid of small holes.

Innovindil went back to the saddlebag for the oil and the incense, and Drizzt looked at Ellifain. He replayed again the last moments of the poor elf's life, which would have been the last moments of his own life as well had not Bruenor and the others come barging in to his rescue, healing potion in hand.

His reputation had been her undoing, he knew. She could not stand to suffer his growing fame as a drow of goodly heart, because in her warped memories of that brutal evening those decades before, she saw Drizzt as just another of the vile dark elves who had slaughtered her parents and so many of their friends. Drizzt had saved Ellifain on that long-ago night by covering her with the blood and body of her slain mother, but the poor elf girl, too young on that night to remember, had never accepted that story.

Her anger had consumed her, and in a cruel twist of fate, Drizzt had been forced to inadvertently destroy that which he had once saved.

So intent was he as he looked down upon her and considering the winding roads that had so tragically brought them crashing together, Drizzt didn't even notice Innovindil's quiet song as she paced around the grave, sprinkling magical oil of preservation and swaying the censer out over the hole so that its scent would mask the smell of death.

Innovindil prayed to the elf gods with her song, bidding them to rescue Ellifain from her rage and confusion.

When Drizzt heard his own name he listened more intently to the elf's song. Innovindil bade the gods to let Ellifain look down upon the dark elf Drizzt, and see and learn the truth of his heart.

She finished her song so melodiously and quietly that her voice seemed to merge with, to become one with, the night-time breeze. The notes of that wind-driven song carried Innovindil's tune long afterward.

She bade Drizzt to help her then gracefully slipped into the hole beside Ellifain. Together they brought the corpse out and placed a clean second blanket around her, wrapping her tightly and tying it off.

"Do you believe that she is at peace?" Drizzt asked when they were done, both standing back from the body, hand-in-hand.

"In her infirmity, she remained worthy of Corellon's gentle hand."

After a moment, she looked at Drizzt and saw the uncertainty clear upon his handsome features.

"You do not doubt that," she said. "You doubt Corellon himself."

Still Drizzt did not answer.

"Is it Corellon specifically?" Innovindil asked. "Or does Drizzt Do'Urden doubt the very existence of an afterlife?"

The question settled uncomfortably on Drizzt's shoulders, for it took him to places he rarely allowed his pragmatic views to go.

"I do not know," he replied somberly. "Do any of us really know?"

"Ghosts have been seen, and conversed with. The dead have walked the world again, have they not? With tales to tell of their time in the worlds beyond."

"We presume ghosts to be . . . ghosts," Drizzt replied. "And those returned from the dead are vague, at best, from all that I have heard. Such practices were not unknown among the noble Houses of Menzoberranzan, though it was said that to pull a soul from the embrace of Lolth was to invoke her wrath. Still, are their tales anything more than cloudy dreams?"

Innovindil squeezed his hand and paused for a long while, conceding his point. "Perhaps we believe because to do otherwise is self-defeating, the road to despair. But surely there are things we cannot explain, like the crackling magic about us. If this life is finite, even the long years an elf might know then . . . "

"Then it is a cruel joke?" Drizzt asked.

"It would seem."

Drizzt was shaking his head before she finished. "If this moment of self-awareness is short," he said, "a flicker in the vastness of all that is, all that has been, and all that will be then it can still have a purpose, still have pleasure and meaning."

"There is more, Drizzt Do'Urden," Innovindil said.

"You know, or you pray?"

"Or I pray because I know."

"Belief is not knowledge."

"As perception is not reality?"

Drizzt considered the sarcasm of that question for a long while then offered a smile of defeat and of thanks all at once.

"I believe that she is at peace," Innovindil said.

"I have heard of priests resurrecting the dead," Drizzt said, a remark borne of his uncertainty and frustration. "Surely the life and death of Ellifain is not the ordinary case."

His hopeful tone faded as he turned to regard his frowning companion.

"I only mean—"

"That your own guilt weighs heavily on you," Innovindil finished for him.

"No."

"Do you inquire about the possibility of resurrection for the sake of Ellifain, or for the sake of Drizzt Do'Urden?" Innovindil pressed. "Would you have the priests undo that which Drizzt Do'Urden did, that about which Drizzt Do'Urden cannot forgive himself?"

Drizzt rocked back on his heels, his gaze going back to the small form in the blankets.

"She is at peace," Innovindil said again, moving around to stand in front of him, forcing him to look her in the eye. "There are spells through which the priests—or wizards, even—can speak with the dead. Perhaps we can impose on the priests of the Moonwood to hold court with the spirit of Ellifain."

"For the sake of Drizzt Do'Urden?"

"A worthy reason."

They let it go at that, and set their last camp before they would turn for home. Beyond the mountain ridge to the west, the endless waves crashed against the timeless stones, mocking mortality.

Innovindil used the backdrop of that rhythm to sing her prayers yet again, and Drizzt joined in as he assimilated the words, and it occurred to him that whether or not the prayers drifted to the physical form of a true god, there was in them power, peace, and calm.

In the morning, with Ellifain secured across the wide rump of Sunset, the pair turned for home. The journey would be a longer one, they knew, for winter grew thicker and they would have to walk their mounts more than fly them.

The orc overbalanced as Tos'un knew it would, throwing its cumbersome broadsword out too wildly across its chest. It stumbled to the side and staggered ahead, and Tos'un reversed his retreat to begin a sudden, finishing thrust.

But the drow stopped short as the orc jerked unexpectedly. Tos'un fell back into a defensive crouch, concerned that his opponent, the last of a small group he had ambushed, had feigned the stumble.

The orc jerked again then came forward. Tos'un started to move to block, but recognized that it was no attack. He stepped aside as the orc fell face down, a pair of long arrows protruding from its back. Tos'un looked past the dead brute, across the small encampment, to see a pale-skinned, black-haired elf woman standing calmly, bow in hand.

With no arrow set.

Kill her! Khazid'hea screamed in his head.

Indeed, Tos'un's first thought heartily concurred. His eyes flashed and he almost leaped ahead. He could get to her and cut her down before she ever readied that bow, he knew, or before she could draw out the small sword on her hip and ready a proper defense.

The drow didn't move.

Kill her!

The look on her face helped the drow resist both the sword's call and his own murderous instincts. Before he even glanced left and right he knew. He might get one step before a barrage of arrows felled him. Perhaps two, if he was quick enough and lucky enough. Either way, he'd never get close to the elf.

He lowered Khazid'hea and turned back its stream of curses by filling his mind with fear and wariness. The sword quickly caught on and went silent in his thoughts.

The elf said something to him, but he did not understand. He knew a bit of the Elvish tongue, but couldn't decipher her particular dialect. A sound from the side finally turned him, to see a trio of elf archers slipping out of the shadows, bows drawn and ready. On the other side, three others made a similar appearance.

And more were still under cover, the drow suspected. He did his best to silently inform Khazid'hea.

The sword replied with a sensation of frustrated growling.

The elf spoke again, but in the common tongue of the surface. Tos'un recognized the language, but he understood only a few of her words. He could tell she wasn't threatening him, and that alone showed the drow where he stood.

He offered a smile and slid Khazid'hea into its scabbard. He held his hands up, then moved them out and shrugged. To either side of him, the archers relaxed, but only a bit.

Another moon elf moved out from the shadows, this one wearing the ceremonial robes of a priest. Tos'un bit back his initial revulsion at the site of the heretic, and forced himself to calm down as the cleric went through a series of gyrations and soft chanting.

He is casting a spell of languages, to better communicate with you, Khazid'hea silently informed the drow.

And a spell to discern truth from lies, if his powers are anything akin to the priestesses of Menzoberranzan, Tos'un replied.

As he completed the thought, the drow felt a strange calm emanating from the sentient sword.

I can aid you in that, Khazid'hea explained, sensing his confusion and anticipating his question. *True deception is a state of mind—even in the face of magical detection.*

"I will know your intent and your purpose," the elf cleric said to Tos'un in words the drow understood perfectly, jarring him from his private conversation with the sword.

But that connection had not been fully severed, Tos'un realized. A continuing sense of pervading calm filtered through his thoughts and altered the timbre of his vocal reply.

And so he passed through the priest's line of questioning, answering sincerely though he knew well that he was not being honest.

Without Khazid'hea's help, he would have felt the bite of a dozen elven arrows that day, he knew.

⊙ ⊙ ⊙ ⊙ ⊙

And where am I to run? Tos'un asked Khazid'hea much later. *What is there for me beyond the perimeter of this camp? You would have me hunting orcs for their rotten foodstuffs, or venturing back into the wilds of the Underdark where I cannot survive?*

You are drow, the sword answered. *You have stated before your hated of elves, the oppressors of your people. They are unsuspecting and off their guard, because of my help to you.*

Tos'un wasn't so sure of that. Certainly those elves nearest to him seemed at ease. He might get through a few them. But what others lurked in the shadows? he wondered, and so the sword felt his question.

Khazid'hea had no answer.

Tos'un watched the elves moving around their camp. Despite their proximity to enemies, for they were across the Surbrin and in Obould's claimed territory, laughter rang out almost constantly. One took up a song in Elvish, and the rhythm and melody, though he could not know the words, carried Tos'un's thoughts back to Menzoberranzan.

Would you have me choose between these people and Obould's ugly kin? the drow asked.

Still the sword remained quiet in his thoughts.

The drow sat back, closed his eyes, and let the sounds of the elves' camp filter around him. He considered the roads before him, and truly none seemed promising. He didn't want to continue on his own. He knew the limitations and mortality of that route. Eventually, King Obould would catch up to him.

He shuddered as he considered the brutal death of his lost drow friend, the priestess Kaer'lic. Obould had bitten out her throat.

We can defeat him, Khazid'hea interrupted. *You can slay Obould and take his armies as your own. His kingdom will be yours!*

Tos'un had to work hard to stop himself from laughing out loud, and his incredulity served as a calming blanket over the excited sword. With or without Khazid'hea, there was no way Tos'un Armgo would willingly do battle with the powerful orc king.

The drow considered the road to the Underdark again. He remembered the way, but would it be possible for him to battle back to Menzoberranzan? The mere thought of the journey had him shuddering yet again.

That left him with the elves. The hated surface elves, the traditional enemies of his people—might he really find a place among them? He wanted to kill them, every one, almost as badly as did his always-hungry sword, but he knew that acting on such an impulse would leave him without any options at all.

Is it possible that I will find my place among them? he asked the sword. *Might Tos'un become the next Drizzt Do'Urden, a rogue from the Underdark living in peace among the surface races?*

The sword didn't reply, but the drow sensed that it was not amused. So Tos'un let his own thoughts follow that unlikely course. What might his life be like if he played along with the surface elves? He eyed a female as he wondered, and thought that bedding her might not be a bad thing. And after all, among the surface elves, unlike in his own matriarchal society, he would not be limited by his gender.

But would he always be limited by his ebon skin?

Drizzt wasn't, he reminded himself. From everything he had learned over the past days, Tos'un knew that Drizzt lived quite well not only with the surface elves but with dwarves as well.

Could it be that Drizzt Do'Urden has created a path that I might similarly follow?

You hate these elves, Khazid'hea replied. *I can taste your venom.*

But that does not mean that I cannot accept their hospitality, for my own sake and not for theirs.

Will you stop fighting?

Again Tos'un nearly laughed out loud, for he understood that the only thing Khazid'hea cared about was wetting its magnificent blade with fresh blood.

With them, I will slaughter Obould's ugly kin, he promised, and the sword seemed to calm.

And if I hunger for an elf's blood?

In time, Tos'un replied. *When I grow tired of them, or when I find another more promising road . . . .*

It was all new, of course, and all speculative. The drow couldn't be certain of anything just then, nor was he working from any position of power that offered him true choices. But the inner dialogue and the possibilities he saw before him were not unpleasant. For the time being, that was enough.

Drizzt stood, hands on hips, staring in disbelief at the signpost:

BEWARE! HALT!
The Kingdom of Many-Arrows
Enter on word of King Obould
Or enter and die!

It was written in many languages, including Elvish and Common, and its seemingly simple message conveyed so much more to Drizzt and Innovindil. They had spent a month or more traversing the wintry terrain to return to that spot, the same trail on which they had seen the orcs constructing a formidable gate. That gate, which they had already carefully observed some fifty feet farther along the path to the north, showed design and integrity that would make a dwarf engineer proud.

"They have not left. Their cohesion remains," Drizzt stated.

"And they proclaim their king as Obould, and their

kingdom takes his surname," Innovindil added. "It would seem that the unusual orc's vision outlasted his breath."

Drizzt shook his head, though he had no practical answers against her obvious observation. Still, it didn't make sense to him, for it was not the way of the orcs.

After a long while, Innovindil said, "Come, the night will be colder and a storm is brewing. Let us be on our way."

Drizzt glanced back at her and nodded, though his thoughts were still focused on that sign and its implications.

"We can make Mithral Hall long before sunset," he asked.

"I wish to cross the Surbrin," Innovindil replied, and as she spoke she led Drizzt's gaze to the form of Ellifain strapped over Sunset's back, "to the Moonwood first, if you would agree."

With the weather holding and the sun still bright, though black clouds gathered in the northeast, they flew through Keeper's Dale and past the western door of King Bruenor's domain. Both of them took comfort in seeing that the gates remained solid and closed.

They crossed around the southern side of the main mountain of the dwarven homeland, then past the wall and bridge that had been built east of the complex. Several dwarf sentries spotted them and recognized them after a moment of apparent panic. Drizzt returned their waves and heard his name shouted from below.

Over the great river, partially covered in ice and its steel gray waters flowing swiftly and angrily, they set down, their shadows long before them.

The land was secure. Obould's minions had not pressed their attack, and predictably, as their campfire flared in the dark of night, the snow beginning to fall, they were visited by a patrol of elves, Innovindil's own people scouting the southern reaches of their domain.

There was much rejoicing and welcoming. The elves joined in song and dance, and Drizzt went along with it all, his smile genuine.

The storm grew stronger, the wind howling, but the troupe, nestled in the embrace of a thick stand of pines, were not deterred in their celebration, their joy at the return of Innovindil, and their somber satisfaction that poor Ellifain had come home.

Soon after, Innovindil recounted the journey to her kin, telling them of her disappointment and surprise to see that the orcs had not gone home to their dark holes after the fall of King Obould.

"But Obould is not dead," one of the elves replied, and Innovindil and her drow companion sat intrigued and quiet.

Another elf stepped forward to explain, "We have found a kin of yours, Drizzt Do'Urden, striking at the orcs much as you once did. His name is Tos'un."

Drizzt felt as if the wind, diminished as it was through the thick boughs of the pines, might just blow him over. He had killed two other dark elves in the fight with Obould's invading army, and had seen at least two more in his personal battle. In fact, one of those drow, a priestess, had brought forth a magical earthquake that had sent both Drizzt and the orc king tumbling, Drizzt, with good fortune, to a ledge not far below, and Obould, so Drizzt had thought, into a deep ravine where he surely would have met his demise. Might this Tos'un be one of those who had watched Drizzt's battle with the orc king?

"Obould is alive," the elf said again. "He walked from the carnage of the landslide."

Drizzt didn't think it possible, but given what he had seen of the orc army, could he truly deny the claim?

"Where is this Tos'un?" he asked, his voice no more than a whisper.

"Across the Surbrin to the north, far from here," the elf explained. "He fights beside Albondiel and his patrol, and fights well by all reports."

"You have become accepting," Drizzt remarked.

"We have been given good reason."

Drizzt was hardly convinced.

⊕ ⊕ ⊕ ⊕ ⊕

He is in the Moonwood, Khazid'hea reminded Tos'un one brilliant and brutally cold morning.

They were still out across the Surbrin, in the northern stretches of the newly-proclaimed Kingdom of Many-Arrows, just south of the towering easternmost peaks of the Spine of the World. The drow tried not to respond, but his thoughts flickered back to Sinnafain's announcement to him that Drizzt Do'Urden had returned from the west and stopped in the Moonwood.

He saw you on that day he battled Obould, Khazid'hea warned. *He knows you were in league with the orcs.*

He saw two drow, Tos'un corrected. *And from afar. He cannot know for certain that it was me.*

And if he does? His eyes are much more attuned to the glare of the sun than are yours. Do not underestimate his understanding. He did battle with two of your companions, as well. You cannot know what Drizzt might have learned from them before he slew them.

Tos'un slid the sword away and glanced around the ring of boulders fronting the shallow cave that he and the elves had taken for their camp the previous night. He had suspected that Drizzt had been involved in the fall of Donnia Soldue and Adnon Khareese, but the sword's confirmation jarred him.

You will exact vengeance for your dead friends? Khazid'hea asked, and there was something in the sword's telepathy that led him to understand the folly of that course. In truth, Tos'un wanted no battle with the legendary rogue that had so upset the great city of Menzoberranzan. Kaer'lic had feared that Drizzt was actually in Lolth's favor, as chaos seemed to widen in his destructive wake, but even if that were not the case, the rogue's reputation still brought shudders up Tos'un's spine.

Could he bluff his way past Drizzt's doubts or would the rogue just cut him down?

Good, Khazid'hea purred in his thoughts. *You understand that this is not a battle you are ready to fight.* The sword led his gaze to Sinnafain, sitting on a rock not far away and staring out at the wide valley beyond.

Kill her quickly and let us be gone, Khazid'hea offered. *The others are out or deep in Reverie—they will not arrive in time to stop you.*

Despite his reservations, Tos'un's hand closed on the sword's hilt. But he let go almost immediately.

Drizzt will not strike me down. I can dissuade him. He will accept me.

At the very least, he will demand my return, Khazid'hea protested, *so that he can give me back to that human woman.*

I will not allow that.

How will you prevent it? And how will Tos'un answer the calls of the priests when Khazid'hea is not helping him to defeat their truth-seeking spells?

We are beyond that point, the drow replied.

Not if I betray you, the sword warned.

Tos'un sucked in his breath and knew he was caught. The thought of going back out alone in the winter cold did not sit well with him, but he had no answer for the wretched sword.

Nor was he willing to surrender Khazid'hea, to Drizzt or to anyone. Tos'un understood that his fighting skills were improving because of the tutoring of the blade, and few weapons in the world possessed a finer edge. Still, he did not doubt Khazid'hea's estimation that he was not ready to do battle with the likes of Drizzt Do'Urden.

Hardly aware of the movements, the drow walked up behind Sinnafain.

"It is a beautiful day, but the wind will keep us about the cave," she said, and Tos'un caught most of the words and her meaning. He was a quick student, and the Elvish language was not so different from that of the drow, with many similar words and word roots, and an identical structure.

She turned on the rock to face him just as he struck.

The world must have seemed to spin for Sinnafain. She lay on the ground, the drow standing above her, his deadly sword's tip at her chin, forcing her to arch her neck.

Kill her! Khazid'hea demanded.

Tos'un's mind raced. He wanted to plunge his sword into her throat and head. Or maybe he should take her hostage. She would be a valuable bargaining chip, and one that would afford him many pleasures before it was spent, to be sure.

But to what end?

Kill her! Khazid'hea screamed in his mind.

Tos'un eased the blade back and Sinnafain tilted her chin down and looked at him. The terror in her blue eyes felt good to him, and he almost pulled the sword back, just to give her some hope, before reversing and cutting out her throat.

But to what end?

Kill her!

"I am not your enemy, but Drizzt will not understand," Tos'un heard himself saying, though his command of the language was so poor that Sinnafain's face screwed up in confusion.

"Not your enemy," he said slowly, focusing on the words. "Drizzt will not understand."

He shook his head in frustration, reached down, and removed the helpless elf's weapons, tossing them far aside. He jerked Sinnafain to her feet and shoved her away, Khazid'hea at her back. He glanced back at the cave a few times, but soon was far enough away to understand that no pursuit would be forthcoming.

He spun Sinnafain around and forced her to the ground. "I am not your enemy," he said yet again.

Then, to Khazid'hea's supreme outrage, Tos'un Armgo ran away.

"It is Catti-brie's sword," Drizzt said when Sinnafain told him the tale of Tos'un a few days later, when she and her troupe returned to the Moonwood. "He was one of the pair I saw when I did battle with Obould."

"Our spells of truth-seeking did not detect his lie, or any malice," Sinnafain argued.

"He is drow," Innovindil put in. "They are a race full of tricks."

But Sinnafain's simple response, "He did not kill me," mitigated much of the weight of that argument.

"He was with Obould," Drizzt said again. "I know that several drow aided the orc king, even prompted his attack." He looked over at Innovindil, who nodded her agreement.

"I will find him," Drizzt promised.

"And kill him?" Sinnafain asked.

Drizzt didn't answer, but only because he managed to bite back the word, "Yes," before it escaped his lips.

"You understand the concept?" Priest Jallinal asked Innovindil. "The revenant?"

"A spirit with unfinished business, yes," Innovindil replied, and she couldn't keep the tremor out of her voice. The priests would not undertake such a ritual lightly. Normally revenants were thankfully rare, restless spirits of those who had died in great tumult, unable to resolve central questions of their very being. But Ellifain was not a revenant—not yet. In their communion with their gods, the elf priests had come to believe that it would be for the best to *create* a revenant of Ellifain, something altogether unheard of. They were convinced of their course, though, and with their confidence, and given all that was at stake, Innovindil was hardly about to decline. She, after all, was the obvious choice.

"Possession is not painful," Jallinal assured her. "Not physically. But it is unsettling to the highest degree. You are certain that you can do this?"

Innovindil sat back and glanced out the left side of the wooden structure, to the hut where she knew Drizzt to be. She found herself nodding as she considered Drizzt, the drow she had come to love as a cherished friend. He needed it to happen as much as Ellifain did.

"Be done with it, and let us all rest more comfortably," Innovindil said.

Jallinal and the other clerics began their ritual casting, and Innovindil reclined on the floor pillows and closed her eyes. The magic filtered through her gently, softly, opening the conduit to the spirit the priests called forth. Her consciousness dulled, but was not expelled. Rather, her thoughts seemed as if filtered through those of her former friend, as if she was seeing and hearing everything reflected off the consciousness of Ellifain.

For Ellifain was there with her, she knew, and when her body sat up, it was through Ellifain's control and not Innovindil's.

There was something else, Innovindil recognized, for though it was Ellifain within her body along with her own spirit, her friend was different. She was calm and serene, at peace for the first time. Innovindil's thoughts instinctively questioned the change, and Ellifain answered with memories—memories of a distant past recently brought forth into her consciousness.

The view was cloudy and blocked—by the crook of an arm. Screams of agony and terror rent the air.

She felt warmth, wet warmth, and knew it to be blood.

The sky spun above her. She felt herself falling then landing atop the body of the woman who held her.

Ellifain's mother, of course!

Innovindil's mind whirled through the images and sounds—confused, overwhelmed. But then they focused clearly on a single image that dominated her vision: lavender eyes.

Innovindil knew those eyes. She had stared into those same eyes for months.

The world grew darker, warmer, and wetter.

The image faded, and Innovindil understood what Ellifain had been shown in the afterlife: the truth of Drizzt Do'Urden's actions on that horrible night. Ellifain had been shown her error in her single-minded hatred of that dark elf, her mistake in refusing to believe his reported actions in the deadly attack.

Innovindil's body stood up and walked out of the hut, moving with purpose across the way to the hut wherein Drizzt rested. She went through the door without as much as a knock, and there sat Drizzt, looking at her curiously, recognizing, no doubt, that something was amiss.

She moved up and knelt before him. She stared closely into those lavender eyes, those same eyes she, Ellifain, had seen so intimately on the night of her mother's murder. She brought a hand up against Drizzt's cheek, then brought her other hand up so that she held his face, staring at her.

"Innovindil?" he asked, and his voice sounded uncertain. He drew in his breath.

"Ellifain, Drizzt Do'Urden," Innovindil heard her voice reply. "Who you knew as Le'lorinel."

Drizzt labored to catch his breath.

Ellifain pulled his head low and kissed him on the forehead, holding him there for a long, long while.

Then she pulled him back to arms length. Innovindil felt the warm wetness of tears rolling down her cheeks.

"I know now," Ellifain whispered.

Drizzt reached up and clasped her wrists. He moved his lips as if to respond, but no words came forth.

"I know now," Ellifain said again. She nodded and rose, then walked out of the hut.

Innovindil felt it all so keenly. Her friend was at last at peace.

The smile that was stamped upon Drizzt's face was as genuine as any he had ever worn. The tears on his cheeks were wrought of joy and contentment.

He knew that a troubled road lay ahead for him and for his friends. The orcs remained, and he had to deal with a dark elf wielding the ever-deadly Khazid'hea.

But those obstacles seemed far less imposing to Drizzt Do'Urden that morning, and when Innovindil—the whole and unpossessed Innovindil—came to him and wrapped him in a hug, he felt as if nothing in all the world was amiss.

For Drizzt Do'Urden trusted his friends, and with the forgiveness and serenity of Ellifain, Drizzt Do'Urden again trusted himself.

TEARS SO WHITE

Ed Greenwood

12 Alturiak, the Year of Lightning Storms (1374 DR)

Firelight played a gentle dance across the old, faded map of Faerûn painted on Storm Silverhand's kitchen ceiling. Rathan Thentraver lowered his gaze from idle study of familiar coastlines and forests to growl happily, "Ahhh, that was *wonderful!* The sauce . . ."

The burp that erupted through Rathan's rhapsodizing just then was as violently sudden as it was unintended. Wherefore it left him momentarily speechless.

His best friend Torm sat at his elbow—and Torm, by far the most sly of the Knights of Myth Drannor, was a man who'd never needed more than half a moment to launch anything in all his life.

"Certainly had a certain something to it, Storm," he grinned, finishing the sputtering priest's sentence. "Care to share just this one cauldron-secret?"

Their hostess gave him a smile over her shoulder, not turning from the sink. "Boiled serpents' eyes—two heaping handfuls, and they must be fresh. Vipers only, mind."

All around the gleaming table, full-bellied Knights, lounging contentedly over mugs of hot greenleaf tea, chuckled good-naturedly. All except Dove and Merith, who arched eloquent eyebrows at each other, knowing the Bard of Shadowdale told the plain truth.

Torm was also a man who missed little. He saw their traded glances, and his grin faded a little. "You're not jesting, are you?"

Storm turned around, long silver tresses playing about her shoulders like so many restless snakes, and said, "No."

Florin winced, Rathan gaped in open-mouthed astonishment, and Jhessail sighed and regarded the ceiling.

Rathan's next belch, arriving in the moment of silence that followed, was rather less contented.

"And fair even to *ye*, Master Thentraver," an old and gruff voice made reply to it, adding a hearty belch—almost before its owner faded into visibility. The Knights around the table blinked, but no one swore or snatched for weapons. The speaker was all too familiar.

The wizard Elminster, as beak-nosed and bright-eyed as ever, stood just inside the west door of Storm's kitchen—a stout old oval of crossbraces, eye-windows, and entwined berry-vines that had been closed all evening against the icy Alturiak chill, and even then remained quiet and closed behind him.

The Old Mage of Shadowdale wore his preferred garb: robes, breeches, and boots of worn, soft leather, as weather-torn as those of any vagabond. He was clad like a lack-coin wayfarer—but dominated the room like a king.

The six Knights who'd feasted under Silverhand's roof

all stared at him. Not one of them—Florin, Dove, Jhessail, Merith, Torm, nor Rathan—had ever seen the Old Mage look quite so grim before. Moreover, one of his eyes glimmered as if it held liquid fire, or a twinkling star restless to spill forth. Grim, indeed.

So were his next words: "I need ye. Now. With whate'er weapons ye've ready. Spells matter not."

Torm sighed and set down his empty tallglass. "Care to tell us what particular corner of Faerûn we're rushing off to save *this* time, Oldbeard, or are you playing Mage Most Mysterious, as usual?"

Elminster raised a hand. Two of its long, bony fingers pointed at Torm and Rathan.

"Not ye two. Thy sort of mischief is best worked here—keeping Fzoul at bay, trouncing any daemonfey foolish enough to come skulking hereabouts; that sort of thing. *Ye* know."

Then the great archmage strode forward, tiny stars winking out of the empty air around him as he went. Everyone watched them drift into the shapes of two long sword blades in his hands.

Elminster rounded the table, followed by curious stares, to nod at Storm and add gruffly, "Bide ye safe here, lass. Someone has to protect the dale against yon prize pair of fools." He inclined his head in the direction of Torm and Rathan, walked right up to the great trunk of the shadowtop tree that grew in the heart of Storm's kitchen, and stepped into it as if it was made of mere shadow.

Dove was on her feet in an instant, murmuring, "Hurry. 'Ere yon way closes again. Just pluck up and carry your boots."

The Knights hastened, plunging into the dark nothingness of the tree after Elminster in a few swift moments, leaving Torm and Rathan staring rather crossly at each other.

"Now what was all *that* about?"

"Aye, tell us nothing, as usual. We happy dancing fools never need to know anything important."

With one accord, they turned to Storm Silverhand—and fell silent, jaws dropping open in unison.

Storm Silverhand stared in dismay at the tree five friends had just vanished through, and her face was as white as the fresh-fallen snow outside her kitchen windows.

The world was white. Not the cold, wet heavy white of Shadowdale snow, but drifting mists amid an endless web of smooth strands, some large, some small, all curving . . . and all thrumming with tireless force that made teeth ache and skin itch. All white, and nothing else—no sky, no horizon, no keeps nor trees, nor anything else to make for.

"Is it permitted," Florin asked quietly beside Elminster's ear, as the Knights hauled their boots on, "to ask where we are?"

The ranger was startled by his lady Dove taking his head in both her hands and kissing him deeply. Through the faint lace of the firewine she'd been drinking in Storm's kitchen, her mouth seemed hot, her tongue like fire against his own.

Before Florin had time to feel real surprise, she drew back to look longingly into his eyes, their noses almost touching, and murmur, "Remember me always."

And she was gone, stepping back from him to stand with her back pressed against the nearest large strand—one of countless thousands within his view that rose like leafless trees in the misty, endless web. Spreading her arms and legs wide into a great **X**, Dove slapped them against the thrumming whiteness, her eyes steady on his.

Florin made a small sound of bewilderment and stepped forward, raising a hand toward her—even as she gasped, shivered, arched her back, and . . . went white all over, her curves thrumming like the strand she had become part of. The ranger watched his wife's face . . . and the rest of her

. . . melt into smooth featurelessness, in utter silence and within mere moments becoming no more than a suggestive prow on the strand.

And as quietly and easily as that, a Chosen of Mystra was gone.

Florin turned to Elminster, shaken. "My lady spoke as if she did not expect to see me again. So one or both of us will likely die here?"

"We all die, lad," the Old Mage said, peering into the distance with his two swords of twinkling stars raised and ready. "More than that, I cannot say."

Jhessail's sigh of exasperation was sharper than usual. "Where *are* we?"

"The Tshaddarna. What some call the 'Worlds of the Weave.' "

"Oh, *well*," Merith said, "that explains *everything*." The raven-haired moon elf drew his slender sword. Its silvery blade went sapphire-blue and started to thrum.

He gave it a look of disgust and set his jaw, marched up to Elminster, and stepped right in front of him, drawing himself erect to try to block the Old Mage's view with his own slender, leather-clad bulk. "Now just what, by Mystra's whispered secrets, is or are the Tshaddarna, and what does our being here *mean?* Straight answers for once, wizard."

"So the gentle and charming Strongbow has fangs, after all," Elminster observed, something that might have been a twinkle shining in his normal eye. The other one rippled like restless silver flame. "Lore useful to know."

"Something you have in plenty, Old Mage, and the rest of us lack," Merith snapped. "I'm tired and beyond tired of following you hither and yon, to places only the gods know or have forgotten, to do sweat-work while you smile and nod and *tell us nothing*. So speak, Elminster. What is this place, and why are we here?"

"The 'why' seldom changes, young Merith. Faerûn needs saving so often these days."

The elf waited, but Elminster merely stepped back, saying no more.

Merith strode forward, after him and demanded, "Saving from what or whom this time? Plain truth, Elminster!"

"Trust not in magic," the wizard replied. "You've finally become wise folk, you Knights. You will know who to trust, and what to do."

He threw up his hands, his sparkling swords touching a great strand rising behind him and melting into it. In utter silence, sudden whiteness fell over Elminster like a curtain.

A moment later, the wizard was no more than a craggy bulge in the strand. Florin, Jhessail, and Merith stared at him—or what he'd become—and frowned at each other. Around them, everything seemed a brighter white, and the thrumming rose swifter and stronger.

With Elminster's dominance hidden, Florin's ruggedly handsome frame and kingly manner shone once more. The tall ranger drew his sword. "I hope," he said to Merith, "you weren't really expecting any answers."

"I never do," the dark-clad elf replied, with a grin as mirthless as that of any fox. "Not this last century, at least."

His wife rolled her eyes, but held her tongue.

The three Knights looked in all directions. The same drifting mist and endless forest of strands met their eyes everywhere.

After they tired of the view, the man and the elf turned to the woman between them. Their silent looks were requests for advice.

Merith's wife stared back at them both with her usually merry face twisted in thought, hands on hips and slender fingers stroking the pommel of her belt-dagger. Despite her elfin beauty and small stature, she'd become something of a stern mother to her fellow Knights over the years. Her large, gray-green eyes looked from one sword-companion to the other, and back again. They knew her well enough to let her think in silence.

She kicked one boot-heel against the smooth, flat white ground; an action that made no sound at all. Florin turned to survey the mists, so Merith watched his wife, enjoy the view. Above knee-high boots, her shapely legs were sheathed in tight, well-worn leather breeches. A broad leather belt gathered her tunic at her slender waist so its flying-free lower end flared like a short skirt around her thighs. Above the belt, a leather vest hid her chest behind a wall of mage-pouches, leather loops for hanging tools, and pockets. Jhess had gathered her long, unbound flame-brown hair into a mare's tail with a leather sleeve, and had left her staff behind in Storm's kitchen.

She reached a decision with an imperious flourish of her hand. "I'm reluctant to leave them," she told her fellow Knights, waving at the misshapen strands that held—or had been—Dove and Elminster. "If we leave this spot, we might never find it again . . . and whatever's happened to them, are they not our most likely road home?"

Florin nodded and said, "One spot, in all this, seems no better than any other. I'm glad we'll know what to do—because as of right now, I haven't the flying faintest."

He went to one knee to put a cautious hand on the perfectly smooth, flat whiteness that served as the ground beneath their feet—so flat that his mind insisted it must be a "floor"—and waited for any change in its cool hardness.

None came. After a time Florin shrugged and sat down, setting his sword across his lap. "So we wait. Am I turning white?"

Merith shook his head. "Not even a little. But then, you're not a Chosen."

"Look!" Jhessail hissed, pointing.

The two male Knights snapped their heads around in time to see it: a tall, dark figure of a woman, standing motionless in the distance with her back to them. She looked both human and—by her hair and the shape of her hips and shoulders—female, but there was something odd about her. Something . . . gaunt.

And she was gone, and there was nothing where she'd been standing but humming white strands and lazily-rolling mists.

"You didn't see her walk to that spot, did you?" Florin asked, hefting his sword.

"No," Jhessail told him. "I did happen to be looking thereabouts, and I tell you plain and true: She was not there—then she was there. As you saw her, standing still. Facing away from us. No walking, and as far as I saw, she never looked this way."

"Is this some sort of magical place," Merith mused, "that spellhurlers wink through when teleporting? Or casting some other sort of spell?"

"Your guess is as grand as any," Florin replied. "We'd best keep alert for more . . . visitors."

As if his words had been a cue, a large, dark figure towered over him, come out of nowhere. No gaunt woman, but half a man, its upper half floated in the air with nothing at all below its belt.

The helm that regarded Florin hung dark and empty, above great black-armored shoulders that shifted in menacing silence as long, mighty-thewed arms swung a black greatsword back—then down at the ranger.

Florin sprang aside into a roll that brought him to his feet, brushing through strands that wavered aside like breeze-plucked leaves, and whirled, blade rising—

In time to see Merith Strongbow's blade bite into the apparition's right vambrace with a curiously dull, muffled clang. No blood flew, but armor plate shattered and tumbled, and hacked flesh could be seen beneath. Gray skin over flesh, neither withered nor shriveled but dry, with no hint of blood.

The sinister thing whirled to face its new foe, snake-swift and showing no signs of pain. Merith raised long sword and dagger, wearing the gentle smile battle always brought onto his face—and Jhessail sprang at it from behind with her dagger raised.

"No!" Merith snapped, measuring his wife's meager leather vest against the fell length of that black greatsword, even as the floating thing spun around again to hew her down.

Florin, leaping high, put all of his weight behind a two-handed slash aimed at its gauntlets, but angled so he could hook his blade up its arms and into that empty helm where the face and throat should be.

His steel bit into what felt like leather with flesh and bone beneath, every whit as solid and heavy as the last living man—a Zhentilar spy—he'd carved. An armored finger flew, tumbling, the greatsword rang and shivered and spun after it, and his own blade sliced—

Empty air. There was nothing solid in that dark, staring helm, and nothing corporeal between it and the armored shoulders beneath. Nothing but Merith's long sword, striking a spark off Florin's blade as it came darting up through the empty armor from below.

So the thing was hollow, save for its arms. Merith's blade sliced viciously sideways inside the dark armor—and in uncanny silence one of those burly arms fell off the floating thing, plunging to the smooth whiteness underfoot. It bounced once, Jhessail dodging aside, and . . . faded away—presumably to the same place the severed finger and the greatsword had gone.

Florin had no time to do more than glance around at his footing and see not a trace of them—the sinister thing's remaining arm came at him like a flying lance. Dark and terrible, its black-gauntleted fingers reached as if to grab.

As it loomed and he fought to bring his blade up before him and back in time to hew it aside, Florin saw tiny mouths open in the tips of its fingers, maws ringed with little fangs like those of blood-bats, opening to snap at his eyes.

Jhessail hissed in disgust and worked a spell. Whatever

she tried to hurl turned into rippling silver flames in the air just beyond her fingertips, fire that snarled vainly toward the armored thing, but dwindled and faded before Florin could even draw breath.

Merith's blade bit into the silent thing's helm, but seemed not to bother it in the slightest. Old steel, it must be, and soft. Very old steel.

Old steel that still reached for Florin with chill patience, swooping around to his other flank, that chorus of tiny fangs gnashing and clattering. Merith pursued it, whipping his blade around sidearm like a flail, hacking until fingertips flew. Florin Falconhand leaned into the heart of that singing steel and slid his own stout sword home, deep between the fingers and up the arm behind, armor plates rippling.

Still no blood, but unseen force shoved against him until his hilt fetched up against spasming fingers. Merith grinned as he pruned fingers—and winced back from the sudden flood of sparks that marked Jhessail's dagger-thrust through the open front of the helm into the baleful nothingness there.

The dark armor tumbled away, falling and fading at once. With a faint clank and rattle it was gone, leaving three panting Knights facing each other across unmarked, smooth whiteness, ringed by apparently curious mists.

"What was it?" Jhessail asked, a little wild-eyed. She worked her fingers as if she could still feel something, around the hilt of a dagger that was clouded as if with frost.

Merith shrugged. "Now, do I look like Elminster?" he teased.

Florin, who was darting glances in all directions, took time enough to eye the white semi-statue he knew to be the Old Mage, and frowned. "You will know who to trust, and what to do," he murmured. "I think *not*."

Suddenly he was staring into the glittering eyes of a skull-faced man in robes who'd just winked into visibility among the strands off to his right.

" 'Ware!" he snapped, hefting his sword, but before the word had quite left his lips the lich—if that's what it had truly been—was gone.

Jhessail tossed her head, nodding to tell Florin she'd seen it too, and backed her hips toward his even before the ranger commanded, "Back to back! That thing could reappear any—"

"Naeth," Merith cursed, as quite a different undead man—one wearing a crown askew on its yellowed skull, and an armored tabard of arcane design—blinked into existence not ten paces away. It gave them a cold stare 'ere it vanished again, just as suddenly.

"Knights!" Jhessail cried, and in response two swords whistled past her shoulders to bite where her dagger couldn't reach.

The lich that had just appeared—a female with blackened teeth dropping like shed pearls from sagging jaws as she reared back from clawing at Jhessail to avoid the two points of thrumming steel—tried to smile, her head twisted to one side and wobbling sickeningly, before she winked out of existence again.

"D'you think our presence here is drawing them?" Merith asked, swinging back to his former position, to peer again into mists all around, his blade up and ready.

"I wouldn't doubt it," Florin replied. "Things seem . . . *whiter*, somehow, just here."

"And spreading out from here," Merith added.

"Spreading from Dove and Elminster," Jhessail murmured. "I'd like to know why they did—whatever they did, bonding with these strands."

"I think they're . . . *powering* this place, somehow, or augmenting its forces . . . or something," Merith muttered.

"*Thank* you, sage most learned," Florin chuckled. "Yet I find I must agree. That musing feels right, somehow. That thing we fought, and the liches, are probably drawn to El and my lady-love, not we three."

"But why?" Jhessail hissed, almost weary. "What *is* this place?"

Something arose out of a drift of mists at her feet and soared steadily upright. She almost stabbed at it 'ere she saw sapphire-blue hair, elfin features, and a smile that she could only term "tender."

"This is a place only the Weave can reach, now," a musical voice replied. "Well met, Knights of Myth Drannor. Be welcome. You are needed. You see, there are liches—and there are liches."

This apparition was certainly easier on the eyes than the others. The three Knights beheld an elf of dainty stature, curvaceous and yet so slender as to be wasp-waisted, with a glorious fall of rich sapphire-blue hair, eyes like beaten gold, and that gentle smile. She wore a turquoise-and-moonstone girdle around her hips, leggings of turquoise shimmerweave, and a matching breastplate trimmed with golden teardrops. Her skin was a pale tan, and her tiny hands were empty and . . . fading, going swiftly translucent and . . . she was gone again, leaving only mists behind.

Jhessail sighed. "So 'there are liches—and there are liches.' As my life unfolds, I increasingly find that I *hate* cryptic utterances and mysterious puzzles. Would it not be easier and more efficient for all if folk simply spoke plainly?"

She turned to her mate, only to find Merith staring past her at Florin, his eyes wide with wonder. "Was that—?"

Florin nodded once. "You think so, too?"

Whatever else any of the Knights might have gone on to say then was dashed into forgetfulness forever by another looming apparition, appearing out of a sudden swirl of mists between Florin and Jhessail.

They found themselves close enough to smell its whiff of herbs and faint decay, and brought their blades up.

It was an elf taller than Florin, retreating swiftly even before their warsteel menaced it, gliding back from between the ranger and the mage as it cast glances of silent alarm at all three Knights, out of eyes that were two glowing white motes in deep, hollow sockets.

It looked . . . dead, its skin faint blue and shriveled. In clawlike hands it clutched a fell scepter, nigh as long as one of its legs, that whispered of stored magic. It wore an ornate tabard of archaic design over robes of white silk that age had darkened to black in every crease and curl. The Knights of Myth Drannor had met baelnorn before, and knew it for what it was.

Merith bowed and spoke to it in the tongue of elves, adding the lilts and flourishes he'd heard the eldest of his kin use: *"Revered Guardian, we are well met, for there is no quarrel between us. We stray and are lost, and would fain know: What is this place, and what guard you here?"*

Any elf who has a right eye of blue and a left one of green, as Merith did, was used to sharp and appraising glances from other elves, but he was sure it was his speech that earned him the hard stare, and the muttered reply, *"I guard the Weaving of Raulauve, and you should not be here,* thaes. *Yet I begin to think I should not be here, for I feel the Weaving but faintly. What is this place?"*

"In truth, we know not," Merith replied.

The glowing eyes flickered at that, and blazed with sudden fire. "So you intrude, and must be slain!"

The scepter flashed up, Jhessail hissed in exasperation and ducked aside—and Florin's long sword stabbed low and swift over her shapely back and through a bony blue wrist before that scepter could be aimed precisely.

The baelnorn struggled to move its hand as it desired, to bring the scepter down, but Florin's transfixing steel and strength prevented it—and Merith's blade struck its other hand aside.

There was a flash from somewhere behind the undead elf, in the curling mists, and Jhessail and Merith shot glances that way in time to see a second baelnorn, some distance off. The elf-lich stared in astonishment at them over the winking, smoking end of another scepter that had just unleashed magic that had obviously done something its wielder had not expected.

The baelnorn facing the Knights chose that moment to voice its own frustration with a hiss very like that Jhessail had made. Still wrestling against Florin's brawn, it triggered its own scepter.

There was a flash, a flood of drifting sparks, and . . . nothing but empty air, the mist shrinking back as if afraid or revolted. The baelnorn gaped at the widening drift of fading, winking-out sparks in shocked dismay, its face a mask of bewilderment. It vanished—scepter, astonishment, and all—half a breath before the distant baelnorn winked out of existence too.

Their disappearance left Florin wincing and shaking his numbed hand, the sword it held frosted over and thrumming no longer.

Jhessail was already looking around, rather wildly, in all directions—at nothing but mist, mist, and more curling mist. "I'd give a lot to know why Elminster brought us here, where and *what* 'here' is, and just what we're supposed to do. If we're going to be facing one foe after another, translocating in under our noses out of nowhere, it's only a matter of time before—"

" 'Ware!" Florin snapped, whirling around.

It was another lich, shorter and more withered and gaunt than the previous ones. Florin's blade sliced into the hand it was raising, and bit through a staring eye that had just opened in its withered palm. The lich vanished in a burst of blue flame and acrid smoke, taking the tip of Florin's sword with it.

The ranger studied the clean, squared-off end of his shortened blade just long enough to be sure the metal wasn't melting away further or trying to turn into something else.

Then he turned to Merith, who looked ashen, and asked, "What befalls?"

The elf Knight sighed. "Did you see the sigil in that lichnee's palm? Around the eye that was trying to get a look at us?"

"Not well enough to draw it properly, no, but I'd probably recognize it again," Florin replied. "What of it?"

"It's one of the signs of Larloch," Merith said grimly. "That lich was his, and he was probably looking through that eye."

Jhessail winced. "Did we blind him? Or just cut off his view through that lich?"

"Just cut off his view, most likely."

Merith delivered that judgement as if it comforted him not at all. Reaching a long arm around Jhessail's shoulders, he drew her close, hugged her tight, and kissed her fiercely and swiftly—'ere whirling away, sword up, to glare all around, as if expecting an onrushing foe in the next breath.

He didn't have to say a word to tell her: *I want to do this, because for one or both of us, this kiss may be our last.*

His lady sighed. "So there are liches, and then there are liches. Baelnorns don't seem pleased to find us here, but don't know where 'here' is, and their magic fails them in this place. And then there are Larloch's liches. *Marvellous.* That brings us not a stride closer to knowing what's going on, or what we're supposed to be doing."

"Ride easy, Jhess," Florin said as they returned to standing back to back, looking outward with weapons ready. "There are worse fates than not knowing what's going on. After all, that's the life most folk in Faerûn live, almost all their days."

"Your words are both clever and utter failures as reassurance," Jhessail told him, but her voice was more amused than angry. "At least that baelnorn stood in the same boots as we do: not knowing what was going on."

"Yet it should not have attacked so swiftly," Merith mused. "And its eyes seemed to *change* then."

"Aye, I saw that too," Florin agreed. "Could something—or someone—be controlling it?" He peered into the mists for a few moments then added, "I understood its speech well, old stylings, flutings and all, save for one word. What means 'thaes'?"

Merith's head turned far enough that the ranger could see one end of his frown. "An exact translation is difficult, but . . . 'young stranger-elf?' 'Tis a neutral word, but wary, combining 'I know you not' with something of 'there is no hostility between us—yet.' However, the Revered said something far more interesting than one old, little-used word. It spoke of its duty to guard the Weaving of Raulauve. Now, Raulauve is the name of an elf, not a place—but by 'Weaving', I tell you true, he meant a mythal."

"So the baelnorn was a mythal-guard," Jhessail murmured. "And surprised to find itself away from its mythal. Wherefore it did or experienced nothing unusual to bring itself here." She stared into the endless mists. "I wonder if someone else fetched it here, and tried to turn it against us?"

"Larloch, you're thinking," Florin said.

Jhessail spread her hands. "Does it not seem more than merely possible? Yet its master could be a thousand-thousand other beings, or a chain of old spells, or other causes entirely, I grant. To be certain, we'll have to see if all the liches bear some mark of Larloch, or proclaim allegiance to him. If other baelnorns—or anyone or anything *else*—appear, we must try to learn by sign or speech if anyone is compelling them."

Merith nodded. "Baelnorns do not usually behave thus; that much is certain."

Florin gave him a sudden sidelong grin. "Oh? You've met many?"

The darkly handsome moon elf did not smile back. "Ask me not. Please."

"I'd give a lot to know why my spells turn to harmless flames," Jhessail muttered, "but all manner of creatures seem able to translocate here freely—and at least one creature is able to farscry through a lich, *and* at least one creature can magically or mentally control a baelnorn." She looked from Merith to Florin and back, and added, "And spare me the clever comments about every mortal desiring to know the whys and wherefores of their life, but only the gods being cursed to understand such things."

Obligingly, the other two Knights gave her silence—in which they shared a wink.

Jhessail rolled her eyes at that, and observed, "As I started to say earlier, it's going to be but a matter of time before one of these sudden arrivals manages to slay or wound one of us—and if we all stand wary with weapons ready, we'll eventually grow too tired to defend ourselves, and—"

"My, you're in a dark mood this even, my love," Merith said, stroking her cheek in the manner he knew she liked. "Stand easy, whilst Florin and I think awhile. Our wits move more slowly than yours, mi—"

A drift of mist not far from them turned golden, a warm glimmering that became firelight. The Knights found themselves peering, as if through a window in thickly-swirling mists that seemed for a moment like the falling snows of Shadowdale in deep winter, into a firelit study. There an elf with skin like silver metal, wearing a strange upswept tabard, sat upon a floating-on-air couch, intently studying a tome bound in dragonhide.

Jhessail leaned forward in quickening interest, angling her head to try to catch a glimpse of what was written on those pages. The elf seemed to sense he was being watched, and lifted his head to glare at her—or past her, not quite seeing her—with rose-red eyes that were sharp with anger.

He waved a long-fingered hand in an intricate spell-weaving none of the Knights recognized. They hastily scattered, out of long habit, only to watch whatever it was flare up golden . . . and turn to rippling silver flames that faded away in an instant, a mere handspan away from the hand that had birthed them.

The elf sprang from his crouch, anger turning to real alarm at what his spell had become, and flung his spellbook away. It grew fins or spines that looked swordblade-sharp, and flew away, swooping in a tight arc like a swallow, to vanish from view beyond the edges of the window in the mist.

The elf mage snatched up a staff that crackled with power. The staff grew blades, glittering with moon-runes, from both ends. He brandished it, silently shouting something at the adventurers he could not see.

The window drifted closed again, leaving the Knights blinking at white mist, and at each other.

"Hey-hah," Jhessail muttered. "Wondrous strange. Was this scene sent to us as some sort of message, or are we just standing in a place that touches many other places, often, and—" She shrugged in bewilderment.

"Your guess," said Florin, "is as grand as mine own. That elf mage was familiar to none of us, right?"

Merith and Jhessail both started to shake their heads—and the light changed behind Merith. He whirled around to face the flare, and flung up a hand in warning.

In the distance, roiling mists flickered ruby-red, and shone green for a moment longer. In that moment, two silent, dark-robed figures strode out of the emerald rift. The next moment the mists were white again, but the two newcomers were still there, striding toward the Knights.

"More liches," Merith said with disgust, seeing noseless faces that were half withered flesh and half yellowed bone. The two tall once-men loomed up and long, gaunt arms reached for him.

The elf hacked aside one arm with his thrumming long sword, and struck aside the clawlike reaching fingers of the other with his dagger. As the second lich leaned in to rake at his face, Florin's humming blade thrust over Merith's shoulder. Jhessail ducked down and out from between them, to shear off fingers and send their owner reeling away.

"They're not even trying to work spells," Jhess murmured,

hefting her dagger and peering into the mists all around for signs of other attackers.

The two liches reached for Merith again with the dogged mindlessness the Knights usually saw in shuffling tomb-zombies. Baleful eyes glared out of their palms.

Jhessail drew a long stabbing-bodkin from its sheath down the back seam of one of her boots and put it through one of those eyes as Florin tangled the fingers of that lich's hand in his blade.

The eye of the other spat something at her that turned into flickering, short-lived silver flames.

She gave those wriggling tongues a brittle smile and said, "Well, at least it's not just *me*."

"Useful lore," Florin agreed, as his blade slashed one way and Merith's sliced another—and the head of a lich toppled and rolled through scudding mists.

The decapitated undead bent to retrieve its lost part—and Merith sprang into the air and kicked its bent-over shoulders with all his might, hurling it back into the other lich. They fell in a softly-thudding tangle together, and he and Florin pounced on them, hacking like butchers in a frantic hurry. Glancing only fleetingly at their viciousness, Jhessail stayed between the thickened strands that were Dove and Elminster, casting glances into the mist.

Almost immediately there came another bright red flash in the mists right behind Florin. Jhessail cried a warning, and the ranger whirled and drove his long sword into another lich, just as it stepped out of an emerald rent in the drifting mists.

It clawed the air, flung up a hand in which an eye was opening, and Florin's backswing cut that hand into ruin. Shards of dry flesh, dust, and tumbling fingers sprayed back into the lich's silently-snarling face.

Merith whirled from his completed butchery to chop Florin's lich down, muttering, "No spells, and not a word do they speak! This seems . . . unsubtle for Larloch. Too stumble-headed."

Florin nodded. They dismembered their silent foe, turned its remains over with their swordpoints to peer in vain for items of interest, and hastened back to Jhessail.

"Far more fumbling than Larloch's reputation suggests," Florin agreed, as they turned back-to-back once more. "And why offer themselves to our steel so? Without their spells, we can destroy them readily enough. Why attack us? If they're compelled, whoever commands them must be slow-witted indeed!"

There was another red flash to Jhessail's left, and another to her right—and two more liches strode forward. The more distant one winked out of sight again, even as another two appeared, not far from Merith.

"Huh," the elf grunted, "*this* is more what I'd been expecting. Perhaps he's just been testing us."

"Costly way to test a foe," Florin commented, lunging out from the cluster of Knights to hack at a startled lich's arm, and drawing smoothly back before it could even start to reel.

Jhessail frowned. "Perhaps that's just it. Impress our livers out of us, as we gasp at how many liches the foe sending them can afford to lose."

"That's minstrels' thinking," Merith said, holding off a glaring lich with his sword and kicking it hard in the belly—if it still had a belly—to send it stumbling away. "Taunt and gloat time. Why impress someone you're going to slay?"

More liches stepped out of rifts all around the Knights—a dozen or more—and they were joined by a baelnorn, tall, gaunt, and bewildered. It stared all around in seeming anger, and stumbled toward the Knights, shuffling reluctantly. As it came, it grimaced, convulsed, and trembled, murmuring something inaudible and visibly struggling.

"At war with itself," Jhessail murmured.

"Fighting Larloch or whoever's bidding it, you mean," Florin murmured. He raised his thrumming-anew blade and took a step to one side so he and Merith—who stayed right where he was—could flank the guardian.

The baelnorn halted and gazed at them sadly, well aware of the peril prepared for it. Then, with a sigh, it reached over its shoulder and from an unseen baldric reluctantly drew forth some sort of long, very slender, black-bladed sword that bent readily—and flickered, but did not start to hum. Runes flashed up and down the sable length of that strange sword as the guardian swung the supple steel around itself at shoulder-height, as if limbering up for a fray.

As it stepped forward, blade still whirling, four liches were flanking it, bearing long knives in their hands.

Florin thrust his sword up high to parry that black blade—and ducked his body low, hurling himself into a forward roll even as sparks showered him. His arm went numb, and his sword shrieked in protest overhead.

A moment later he was slamming into the baelnorn's shins, and it was toppling, black blade whipping wildly—into the nearest lich. Florin rode it to the ground, twisting himself to bring what was left of his own sword around in a slash at the closest lich that had stood on the baelnorn's other flank.

He caught a momentary glimpse of a malevolent eye glaring out of one of its palms. Then he bounced atop two struggling bodies and the twisted stub of his sword could no longer reach the lich he'd swung at—and it bent forward.

Jhessail hurled herself through the air like a thrusting sword, feet first. The lich folded up around her with a startled crunch, and fell, leaving the lich beyond them both to stare down in what would have been bewilderment if there'd been enough flesh left on its skull to express any emotion.

Jhessail bounced to her feet out of the writhing limbs of the lich she'd felled, slashed the throat of the staring undead with speed and savagery enough to send its skull whipping around on its shoulders in an unsteady, bobbing wobble, and hissed at it, "Shall we dance? If 'tis my death you seek, care to try again?"

It glared at her and brought its hands up, its fingers lengthening like talons, so she sliced each of them off, wondering how soon her blade would grow dull—or one of them would loom out of the mists and serve her the same way.

Behind her, Merith finished dismembering the lich she'd first taken down, and murmured, "Ladylove mine, would the flames your spells become burn lich-flesh, d'you think?"

Florin hacked at liches' shoulders, thighs, and necks, ignoring the baelnorn. He was aware of Merith doing the same, off to his left, and . . . the last lich left standing faded away. The baelnorn sank into nothingness with its black blade writhing like a lashing-tailed snake, and there was *another* gods-blasting disturbance in the white mist. A rift of dark, raging red laced about with flickering green radiance spilled down for all Faerûn as if it was a glowing green waterfall.

In its wake was a bright green gulf—out of which strode yet another pair of liches. These stalked purposefully, menacing, their hands up to cradle glimmering eyes that glared out of their palms as they came.

The moment Florin met the gaze of one of those palm-eyes, he felt a sudden deep iciness stab through him as if driven like a thrusting sword blade.

He staggered, and found himself shuddering—an uncontrollable shiver that wrenched at him more and more slowly, his spasms becoming slow driftings, his limbs heavy, his . . .

They strode toward him, dark and terrible, and beside him Jhessail sobbed with effort, struggling against the same fell cold.

Florin heard Merith curse, close by on the side his head was turned away from. He could not hope to turn his head to see before the liches reached him, their hands raised like claws to rend and tear.

⊛ ⊛ ⊛ ⊛ ⊛

Sister?

The mind-voice snapped into Storm Silverhand's mind with such savage force that she gasped and almost spilled the herb-brew she was dipping her fingertips into, to gentle into a sick child's mouth.

The little lad's mother drew back in alarm, whirling her ailing son behind her. All Shadowdale knew that when the Bard did something sudden or unexpected, magic was apt to come roaring forth from her—and people died.

"Yes?" Storm answered, speaking aloud to try to reassure the farmwife. "What troubles the Queen of Aglarond this fair night?"

Ethena Astorma, HAVE DONE! Where is my Elminster, and why can I not reach him, or feel his presence anywhere?

Storm drew in a deep breath, beckoning to the farmwife to put the sick infant into her arms, and thought back: *Alassra, back in Alturiak, El led Dove and three of the Knights—*

So frightened and furious was the Simbul that she broke all courtesy and sent her mind racing along the link between them, flooding unbidden into Storm's own consciousness in her impatience to see all the Bard of Shadowdale knew.

Memories and mind-pictures flashed and crashed, washing over the farmwife and the child alike. Storm barely heard their startled cries in the swirling tumult that ended abruptly. She was left trembling and drenched with sweat in the lamplit room, alone in her own head again, all contact with the Simbul gone.

The farmwife stared at her in terror, too frightened to do more than mew softly. Her baby, however, blinked, and said the first coherent words he'd ever uttered—in the fierce, feminine tones of the Witch-Queen of Aglarond:

"And when I find them—!"

The two women stared at him, but his face was once more full of wonder, as he stared back at them, and his next word was: *"Glaaooo?"*

Steel flashed into Florin's view: Merith's daggers, spinning smoothly end-over-end, heading for the eyes glaring out of liches' palms—forlorn strikes, doomed to miss those swiftly-moving targets.

The liches thrust their arms forward to keep the eyes glaring at Florin and Jhessail as they twisted around to head away from Merith's hurled daggers.

Something else flashed past Florin's shoulder—two somethings that sang and shimmered, whisker-thin and silvery-white. Bright beams of force stabbed out to strike the tumbling daggers in a spinning, whirling cage of silver-white stabbings, and turn them—yes, *turn* them—guiding them toward the liches.

Florin overbalanced, trapped in a shudder that held his body captive. Jhessail fell too, toppling over him.

She'd come down on his arm, the war-leader of the Knights thought calmly, as his spasms spun his turned-to-the-side head helplessly around to regard the place where they'd all been standing before the baelnorn came.

As he came down softly into unbroken whiteness where the baelnorn should have been lying—but seemed to have entirely faded away—Florin saw that those singing lines of force stabbed out from the thickenings in two strands that marked where Elminster and Dove had melded into the whiteness.

He didn't actually have to see those beams aim the daggers, curving their flights into arcs that bit into glaring eyes in lich-palms, he knew they'd done so. The chill that clawed him was gone, he could move again, and Jhessail thudded into him, trailing startled curses.

Florin cradled her and hurled her back upright, watching his oldest friend sway, seeking her balance in a swirl of flame-hued hair. He fought his own way back to his feet in time to see the liches grimace, their palms pierced with Merith's daggers—daggers that blazed like little torches, burning away to nothing but inky wisps of smoke. Beyond them, the mist flickered red and green in a dozen places or more, and liches stalked forth in scores, a walking wall of silent undeath.

Jhessail shook her head. "Sweet Mystra," she murmured, "if they could work their spells. . . . "

Her husband chuckled, shrugged, and replied almost merrily, "If magic served us here, I'd be able to keep us alive—I think. As it is . . . "

Merith shrugged again, and hefted his humming sword in one hand, and the long knife he so rarely drew in the other. Catching Florin's look, he murmured, "Wanted to use it one last time, if we're going to—"

And the menacing ranks of liches were swept aside as if by a giant hand, as the white mists erupted into blue-white fire.

Out of the heart of those blue-white rifts strode upright warriors of metal, stiffly stalking things that moved in a series of jerks and swiveling movements, all gleaming battle-limbs and keening, whirling blades. They had no faces, but moved as if they could see. No two of them were the same. Some had arms ending in great axes, and others sported heads that looked like gigantic kettles with spouts that stuck out straight rather than angling upward. Gears and cogs whirred and clattered in chorus within their shining hides.

All three Knights stared in disbelief, and just a little wearily lifted their weapons and prepared to die by sharp, slicing steel rather than chilling lich-claws.

"Delight me," Jhessail whispered bitterly. "Show me new and exciting sights, take me far from the boringly familiar—and there slay me!"

"Steady, love," Merith murmured, beside her. "We'll be together."

The clockwork automatons whirred and clanked

right up to the Knights—and turned aside, to stab and stalk liches.

Dark robes and cloaks swirled as undead limbs drew back in alarm, long-fingered hands became talons, and—

A kettle-head gouted fire that made a lich blaze up like a torch, and before Merith could begin to chuckle, half a dozen of the gaunt undead collapsed in the flashing flurry of a dozen dicing clockwork blades.

The three adventurers watched, open-mouthed, and became aware that the blue-white fire was fading, revealing in its darkening remnants the beautiful elf they'd seen earlier, standing smiling at them. Her sapphire-blue hair gently quested through the air around her, as if possessing a restless, curious life of its own.

"Well met again, Knights. Valiantly fought—too valiant to fall, if this or any world knew fairness. Fight on!" A tiny tan hand waved at them—and faded again, along with the last of the blue-white fire.

Crimson and bright green flashes flared in a score or more places in the mist, rolling across the whiteness as if angered or goaded by the blue-white rift. Baelnorns winked into being here, there, and everywhere to stare in bewilderment then—one after another—turn their heads to glare at the Knights, and thrust out withered blue arms straight, pointing.

They pointed not at the Knights, but at the largest red-and-green rift yet, which split the mists vertically like a giant, reluctant clam parting its shell. The high, eerie keening that the Knights knew to be mythal-song trilled forth along those arms, ringing through the air in almost visible echoes as it met and roiled along the edges of the widening rift.

"Ah, yes," Merith murmured. "This would be the traditional time for me to announce that I have a bad feeling about this, would it not?"

Florin grinned. "It would."

Jhessail rolled her eyes.

With clanks and gleamings, the marching automatons turned in unison from the last smoking remnants of liches to face the widening rift—and started walking toward it.

"As I recall," Jhessail observed with an edge to her gentle voice, "I was just going to ask Storm for some more tea, when Old Weirdbeard stepped out of thin air and volunteered us for this little jaunt. Someone remind me why I ever agree to go along on these—"

A lone figure stepped out of the green flare of the rift. Tall, dark, and terrible, it stood motionless in the heart of the rising trilling of mythal force that seemed to enshroud it in gilded, half-seen, writhing curves and fantastic curlicues of force that shaped and reshaped themselves constantly around it.

Within that writhing of mythal magic, the lich grew visibly darker and taller, looking at the Knights in silent menace. It was more intact and muscled than any they'd yet seen, looking more like a mighty, black-cloaked archmage with a sickly pallor than an undead.

"Mystra forfend," Jhessail muttered, "is this Larloch?"

"No," Merith replied. "Or at least, if it is, he looks much different than he did when I saw him."

Both of the other two Knights gave the elf sharp glances.

"When this is done, friend Merith," Florin said, "if the gods grant that both of us can still speak together, I'll be wanting to hear some answers from your lips, believe you me."

Merith's grin was as bright as ever. "I find myself unastonished."

Bereft of liches to dice and scorch, the clockwork automations clanked toward the lich, passing in front of the Knights to converge on the lone figure that stood a head taller than the largest of the clanking things.

"Stop the baelnorn," Merith said. "Whatever they're doing, it's feeding yon Bad Sir Blackcloak with power, and fairly soon he's going to—"

Silver fire snarled out in a cone of torn and shrieking mists. Jhessail's grim smile of satisfaction fell into a soft curse as the flames died away and the lich's spell took effect—blasting an automaton into shards of flying metal.

"Its spells are *working*, blast it!" she snarled. "Mother Mystra's tears!"

The Knights flung themselves hastily down as another two clockwork things exploded in twin shattering roars.

Deadly metal whirred in all directions. Jhessail saw a cog bounce once in the mist, and soundlessly sink out of sight as if into a bog.

The next spell bore no silver flames at all, and seared away the mist, as four streaking spheres shot into the heart of the marching automatons and burst with an ear-shattering roar and a flash of blinding, blistering-hot flame.

"Well," Florin said, "at least we're already lying down, and can die reclining at ease."

A second meteor swarm smote their ears, and the mists rained shrapnel and the twisted toothed arcs of gears and cogs that would turn no more.

Merith peered into smoke-darkened, shifting mists and muttered, "That's pretty well taken care of the clock—"

Another four spheres spun out of the mists, trailing sparks as they came, right at the Knights.

"Farewell, friends," Florin said, "we've had a good ride togeth—"

Right above their heads, the spheres flickered as they always did in the instant before they exploded—and froze, spinning vainly in the grips of four vibrating silver spheres that had formed out of nowhere.

The spheres had spark-trails of their own, leading back to the thickened strands that were, or had been, Elminster and Dove.

The humming strands faded, the spheres tightened like crushing fists, and the lich's four meteors winked once and were gone as if they'd never been.

More lines of thrumming force raced out from the two strands, flaring out into a great web as they raced toward the Knights. There was a sudden flare of crimson beneath their glow, and the lich stood beside the strands, leaning toward them malevolently.

"Will someone please tell me what's going on?" Jhessail snarled, clambering to her feet again.

The lich turned its head to glare at her, another spell roaring from between its fingers—and the silver strands flashed blinding-bright before it, blocking the speeding magic.

From behind that sudden wall came a larger flash and roar. White strands bent outward and writhed. The dark figure of the lich reeled back, crashing against the strand that was Dove.

The strand grew arms—Dove's arms—that wrapped around the lich from behind, embracing it fiercely. Her face emerged from the whiteness, contorted in pain, her eyes closed and cords stood out like curved blades on her neck as she clung to the struggling lich.

The Knights were all on their feet, sprinting toward the struggle. The lich dwindled in Dove's grip, melting and shuddering even as it tried vainly to turn and claw her, its fingers lengthening into cruel, curved talons each as long as Jhessail's forearm.

Dove's arms tightened around the lich as it sank and sagged, crumbling. Ash fell in streams from it as she slid down the strand, bringing her arms in tightly and her knees up, curling around the undead as it crumbled entirely away, leaving her shuddering and gasping.

"Dove!" Florin cried, rushing up to her. "Love, I—"

She shook her head at him, fighting to speak, and managed only to gasp, "I'll call—" 'ere her violent shudderings overwhelmed her. Waving him away, she sank back into the strand, melting into smooth whiteness once more beneath Florin's reaching fingertips.

His fiercely-hissed curses were interrupted by Merith. "She's back," the elf snapped, pointing.

By which he meant that the tiny, beautiful, blue-haired elf had returned, stepping out of a rift with one arm raised to point at the baelnorn.

It vanished. She pointed again, and the next one winked out. And the next.

She'd banished over a dozen baelnorn, and their singing mythal-force with them, before the mists erupted in dozens of crimson-and-green mouths. Whereupon she vanished in an instant, even before more liches with glaring eyes in their open palms came striding through the new rifts and looked hurriedly in all directions.

They ignored the Knights as if the three humans were mere mist, to peer at the few remaining baelnorn. Then the liches hissed various curses, exchanged dark glances with each other, and started to cast spells—or rather, the same spell.

It was a magic unfamiliar to the warily-watching Knights, that made drifts of mist flee from the liches in all directions, laying bare the endless webwork of white strands—and the glittering web of silver threads around and above the Knights.

Several liches peered at that web with narrow, unfriendly eyes, and stood sentinel, watching it from right where they were in the distant mists. Others worked spells that sent seeking radiances bobbing among the strands like agitated will-o-wisps, searching behind every strand.

"So few," one lich snarled in disbelief. "What happened to them all?" It waved at the three Knights. "Those worms could not have slain more than a handful at most."

Even Merith, whose ears were far keener than those of his two human companions, could not hear the reply that the lich standing nearest made to that angry cry.

Nor could he properly hear what the loud-voiced lich said next, because a soft, melodious whisper sounded between his own ears. The voice was that of the she-elf who'd welcomed them there, the one he was almost certain was the—

Knights of Myth Drannor, the warm whisper said to them, and Merith knew they were all three hearing it; he could *feel* the mind of Florin, like a bright sharp sword, and his beloved Jhess, like her warm arms around him, moving against his own thoughts. *I need you to strike at these creatures of Larloch. Please. Without their spells, they are but striding undead.*

"Larloch? We can't prevail against Larloch!" Jhessail's voice held a sob of horror amid her incredulity. "Nor against so many liches!"

Oh, but you can, the whisper came, confident, *with my aid and with what Elminster is sending you.*

"And Larloch? What will you do to shield us when he appears?"

He won't. He plays a long game, and this is but one ploy among a thousand thousands for him. He's too coldly calculating to ever come to consider it worth risking his own existence. Long before that fate would be faced, he'll judge the cost in lost liches too high.

"Again," Jhessail snarled, "I'd like to know what by all the gods is going on."

There was silence in their heads; the mind-voice was gone.

"Sing, minstrels, of my total lack of surprise," Jhessail snapped. "I thought I took up adventuring to escape being marched through life under the commands of others—but then, to be an adventurer is to be a fool."

Florin said that last quotation along with her, grinning. She gave him a black look and said savagely, "Care to join me in blasting a lich or two?"

"Your spells won't work, remember?"

"Then I'll just have to scratch them to shreds with my bare hands, won't I?" she growled, striding toward the nearest lich. As she went, she dipped a hand into one of her boots to draw her largest dagger.

Merith and Florin exchanged glances, and watched silver tendrils drift after the purposeful mage known to many—behind her back—as "the Mother of the Knights."

They sighed and trotted after her, hefting their thrumming blades as they went.

The liches ignored them. Larloch's undead came together in small groups, forming circles around every baelnorn and working strange, elaborate castings. Mythal force flowed golden once more.

Jhessail paid it no heed, just as the liches ignored the three Knights. When she overtook her chosen victim and stabbed him viciously, the liches walking just ahead of him—heading to join the nearest baelnorn cluster—kept right on walking, even after the three Knights hacked that lich apart and watched its limbs fade away into the whiteness around their ankles.

Jhessail shook her head, and started striding toward the next lich.

Merith and Florin rolled their eyes at each other and trotted after her.

At the heart of every circle, spell-glows rose, ghostly rings of emerald light forming and rotating at various inclinations around the motionless baelnorn. Gold mythal-force spun out to join those rings, and long, spider-fingered lich hands worked intricate spells that made the green and gold rings rise around their heads. Rise, and spin, and brighten. . . .

"What're they up to now?" Jhessail wondered aloud.

Trotting at her shoulder, Merith grinned and shrugged. "You're the spell-hurler here, love."

Jhessail's answer wasn't long in coming. She was still a dozen hurrying strides away from the lich she was running down—and it was barely half that distance from joining a ring of undead around a baelnorn—when a familiar crimson radiance burst into being within the emerald rings above that circle of liches, and widened into a bright green.

And in that glow was another baelnorn, blinking in surprise as it floated down into the circle. Mythal-force tugged at its raised arms until golden curlicues flowed from its fingers, and it lost its look of alarm.

Merith frowned. "They're fetching more baelnorn hither!"

"Soon there won't be a mythal left unguarded in all Faerûn," Florin commented, watching other rifts open above circles.

Jhessail slowed as her quarry joined a circle. "Should I strike at yon?" she asked. "Or will I just be dooming us for no good reason?"

Dooming yourselves, I'd say.

The voice in their heads was back.

The mage of the Knights sighed. "Are you going to tell us who you are? And what we're doing here? And what *they* are up to?" Jhessail kept her voice to a low mutter, but her gesture at the backs of the nearest liches was so violent it seemed a shout.

Of course. As soon as I work a particular spell. Larloch's creatures have obligingly prepared the perfect conditions for me.

The Knights looked all around, but saw no swirl of sapphire-blue hair, nor the tiny tan elf who should have been beneath it.

"Let's get back to Elminster and my lady," Florin suggested. "I'm thinking standing near liches might not be the wisest stratagem, just now."

In silent unison, the three Knights turned and hastened back together, glancing often over their shoulders.

They were about halfway back to the strands that sourced the silver web when it began.

A low ripple in the blood, an uneasy swell and surge. The Knights might have thought it mere indigestion if every white strand in sight wasn't bending in time to the slow, inexorable rhythm.

"I'm still not being told what's happening," Jhessail whispered, but she sounded more amused than exasperated.

Then something swept through the mist and strands, broke over them, and rolled on. Something vast and heavy and nigh-soundless, that plucked up and hurled away liches in velvet silence, and spun mythal-gold and emerald rings alike up into great spheres of white strands, englobing each and every baelnorn. The spheres fell softly from their heights, to bounce and roll gently among the strands, and halt here and there.

Something like a rag doll fell less gently out of the white misty nothingness overhead, and would have smashed Florin flat had he not cast aside his blade, stepped back, and cradled his hands to catch it.

The force of her fall drove him to his knees, and over onto his shoulders. Sapphire-blue hair blinded him, and soft limbs tumbled across his chest as their owner gasped, groaned, ducked under Jhessail's wary dagger, and plucked up Florin's sword.

On hands and knees, the elf grinned up at the lady mage. "Worry not, I won't be using this steel on you or anyone. 'Twould be poor reward for rescuing me from harm to lose one's blade." She turned her head to look at Florin. "My thanks, man."

The ranger rolled up to his knees, barely winded. The elf had been little heavier than a child. He gave her a polite smile, and she took hold of his sword by the blade and held it out to him.

As she did so, Merith went to his knees with the full flourishes, as if to a coronal or great lady.

She smiled at him. "I'm done with such things, young gallant. I hope. Yet I'll not entirely abandon the courtesies. Well met in a strange glade, blood of Meirynth. I see the blood runs strong."

Merith blushed, but the sapphire-haired elf turned her head to include the other two Knights as she continued, "Have my thanks, all of you." Then she turned fully to Jhessail, golden eyes twinkling. "And my explanations."

From up close, her beauty was even more breathtaking. Perfect skin of that tan, almost golden hue, long arms and longer legs for one so tiny . . . even Jhessail found herself staring.

A delicate hand waved dismissal. "I've seen far fairer; there's no need to be staring at these old bones."

"Ah, Lady . . . " Florin began, unable to take his eyes off that gorgeous sapphire-blue hair.

She sighed—and Florin found himself looking at a feminine version of Merith, with that glorious fall of hair turned jet black, and her skin a soft white.

"There. Does that set you more at ease?"

"Only if I could know I was seeing your true shape, Lady," Florin said. "We've fought so many fair-seeming foes who were scaled serpents—or worse—beneath the beauty they lured us with."

She shrugged, and became once more tan-skinned and blue-haired. "This is the one I've grown used to. In truth, I can't recall how far it is from what I looked like before I mastered my first spells."

She drew her feet under her and sat, hands planted on the misty whiteness that served as "ground" in the Tshaddarna. "Forgive me," she murmured. "I'm still weary after that mythal-twisting." She waved a hand at the nearest strand-spheres.

"You're the Srinshee," Merith said.

She turned to look at him, lost her smile, and nodded. "I am."

He regarded her cautiously, and murmured, "Forgive me, lady, but—are you of my sort . . . among elves, that is, or . . . ?"

A slender shoulder lifted in a shrug. "Moon elf, sun elf," the Srinshee murmured. "I have moved so far beyond that."

Eyes fixed on his, she sat still and silent—as her skin turned a faint blue, her hair went silver-white, and her eyes deepened into bottomless pools of green. Then they went blue, along with her hair, as her skin turned bronze, her hair shifted again to a coppery hue and to a blaze of gold.

Florin made a wordless murmuring sound deep in his throat, at the striking beauty of one of her combinations—but the Srinshee went on changing. Her skin became deep brown, her hair shifted to match, her skin slid to copper tinged with green, her eyes went hazel and lilac—and obsidian black, and Merith drew in his breath with a hiss.

The Srinshee looked at him with blood-red eyes, lifted her lip in a mirthless smile that was more sneer than anything else, and fell back into tan skin, gold eyes, that sapphire blue hair, and a nice smile again.

"Enough games," she said. "I'll be happy to chat at ease with you later—if we can carve out a later for us all—but for now I need you still, valiant Knights. The sooner we prevail, the better, for know this: Time passes far more slowly here than in Faerûn. Back in the Realms, days are racing by like scudding storm clouds."

Three pairs of eyebrows rose in silence, and her smile broadened. "Later."

"Lady," Jhessail said, "I'm content to wait for some lore, but please—why us, and what should we be doing next?"

"You, because Elminster thought you were the best to bring. We're here to foil Larloch's latest scheme. He's hit upon the idea of subverting baelnorn to act on his behalf. They'll eventually become his slaves, and he'll be able to draw on the magical energies of their mythals."

Florin blinked, and waved his hands at the mist all around. "Is this his . . . private play-yard?"

"No. I managed to lure the baelnorn into the Tshaddarna, so as to bring Larloch's liches here, too. Larloch will remain elsewhere, working only through his servitor liches. 'Tis his way."

Jhessail frowned. "What *is* this place?"

"The Tshaddarna—there are others—are extra-dimensional spaces created by spells, long ago."

Jhessail made a circular motion with her hand, an "out with it" prompting that made Merith grimace—and the Srinshee grin.

"The spells were cast by certain Imaskari, Netherese, and even by the Blood of Malaug, before they departed for their Place of Shadows that's much larger and better suits them."

The Srinshee waved her hand at the white mists and strands. "As I said, these are places only the Weave can reach, now. Their 'Faerûn ends,' if you will, have been destroyed, but—obviously—the places themselves aren't swept away with them."

Florin looked at her rather grimly. "And how many armies are hiding in these hidden places? For that matter, how many Tshaddarna are there?"

"No armed hosts—there's nothing to eat in a shaddarn but each other, and nothing to drink but your own blood and leakings. More than that: gather an army in one, and months have passed in that brief mustering—where's your foe gone, in all that time, and what's he done? As for how many, no one knows. At least ten-and-four I know of. They're caught in the Weave like flies in a spider's web. It's finding and reaching them that's well-nigh impossible, unless one can ride the Weave."

"You can," Jhessail said, ducking her head so it wouldn't sound entirely like an accusation.

The Srinshee nodded. "Some few can. Larloch is one. He uses them to store magic and treasure. I can take you to a shaddarn that's waist-high with gold coins, as far as the eye can see."

"*Don't* tell Torm about that," Merith said to his fellow Knights, "whatever you do."

"Manshoon of the Zhentarim is another. He's left echoes of himself in various Tshaddarna, most of them in spell-stasis."

Florin crooked an eyebrow, his sword rising. "Should we expect to meet up with him here?"

The Srinshee smiled like a grandmother fondly guarding a secret, but said merely, "No."

Florin pounced on her momentary hesitation. "Just 'no'?"

The Srinshee's smile went wry. "One of the early Manshoons, still active and powerful in the Realms, retreats to a particular shaddarn like a snake seeking its burrow whenever danger gets too close to him in Faerûn. Another shaddarn than this one."

Jhessail nodded. "You've been hiding in Tshaddarna too, haven't you?"

The Srinshee's smile never changed. "Of course."

"Why?"

"To let elfkind grow again, turning aside from decadence and the mind-death of shunning other beings—a shunning that could only grow into mutual hatred and slaying. So long as I and certain other elders were present, with the most powerful magic of the People in our hands, elves everywhere could trust in their matchless superiority, and exalt themselves over others. Even those who dwelt with humans could cling to inward beliefs that they were wiser, better . . . purer. And no race finds the condescension of others pretty—or its own condescension healthy."

"Mielikki have mercy, the patience you must have," Florin whispered.

The Srinshee's smile turned a little crooked. "I'm not the paragon you believe me to be, Lord Falconhand. In some ways, I'm what certain humans like to call a 'witch' or 'bitch.' Vindictive and childlike, in my way. I *do* consider myself superior to certain humans, you see."

"And so you are," Florin replied. "From outlaws to fell Zhentarim, Faerûn holds no shortage of—"

"Villains? Indeed. I've amused myself—I cannot dignify my actions by any more noble description—by pruning the ranks of some of the more ambitious and magically-gifted among them."

Jhessail's eyes narrowed. "Oh? How, exactly?"

The Srinshee waggled her eyebrows and leered in a wild parody of maniacal villainy, until Jhessail couldn't help but smirk and both of the male Knights chuckled.

"Attempts to magically reach Tshaddarna can rob the seeker of their wits—that is, some spells, abilities, and memories—if I lure a prying one into a shaddarn that holds allips, chaos beasts, devourers, nishruu, or other beings who steal memories or cause insanity. When I find a Red Wizard, or a Zhentarim mage, I . . . give in to the temptation to cleanse your race, just a little."

"And thereby confirm yourself as no better . . . " Merith whispered, face falling.

"Exactly, Lord Strongbow. *Precisely.*" The Srinshee's murmur went icy for a moment, and she added, "So if I'm slain by such a foe, 'tis no better than I deserve. Yet I'll not seek death by challenge or carelessness, nor take my life with my own hands, because so many foes all Faerûn must be defended against remain. I am needed."

"So long as there are Larlochs," Florin observed.

"So long as there are Larlochs," the Srinshee echoed, and gave them a wide smile. "Ah, I've missed this. Not since I dwelt with Elminster in Myth Drannor have I tested wits and tongues like this. Swords crossed with respect."

"I . . . Lady, we are so unsuited to this, so unworthy," Merith began, groping for words—and stiffened as her hand touched his wrist. Her fingers were warm and alive with magic, and yet somehow icy, too.

"The Art's unreliable here," she told the Knights, "especially for undead. The magic that sustains them begin to fail. Wherefore you oh-so-unworthy Knights can be effective foes to the liches—and, if need be, to the baelnorn."

The Srinshee leaned forward, and sudden sparks swirled around them all, blotting out all sight of surrounding white mists and strands.

"My intent," she added, her shieldings vibrating around them, "is not just to defeat the liches, but to deceive Larloch as to how they were defeated."

"So?"

"So, Lady Strongbow, he'll believe his scheme with the baelnorn can never work—and won't keep trying. We all need those mythals to stand strong for years upon years to come."

"What if Larloch perceives you as the barrier to his plots, and comes here to destroy you?" Florin asked.

The Srinshee smiled. "I was fading away, lord, well on my way to becoming little more than a beckoning phantom and a half-remembered name—then Mystra died. Much of her essence came here, stealing into me in my loneliness, restoring me, and more than that, making me wiser than I ever was before. I had the pride all along, but she gave me the power."

Jhessail winced. "Those are words that probably fit many mages all too closely."

Even as the Srinshee nodded, her shieldings crackled and darkened around them.

"Up, friends," she said. "I believe Larloch's grown tired of being unable to listen in, and brought battle back to us."

The tiny elf waved a hand, and her shielding melted into glistening translucence. They could see white mist overhead, whiteness under their feet, and a dark, solid wall of maliciously-smiling liches all around, scores deep.

The Srinshee's face went grim. "He has more liches than I knew. This may mean doom for us all."

There was a flash of silver behind that dark wall of undead for a moment. It thrust unwilling liches aside for an instant, like a fire-crack in the blazing darkness of a log turning to ash, to show the Knights the strand that was Elminster ablaze with furious silver fire.

Then it darkened, and the wall of liches was whole once more.

There came another flash, dragging the liches asunder at a slightly different spot. They saw the strand that was Dove pulsing silver, more gently—or more feebly?—than Elminster's had blazed. Then it, too, darkened, and the liches came together again.

Grinning coldly, they closed in around the Knights, who raised their weapons and waited to die.

"Stout hearts, heroes," the Srinshee urged from behind their backs. "I've a trick or two yet—"

The world exploded in roaring silver fire.

Hurled down and tumbled in whirling helplessness like leaves dashed and rolled in a gale, the Knights beheld the Srinshee's startled eyes burst into leaping silver flames. More flames exploded from her mouth, and her body leaped at them, hurled like a helpless ragdoll.

Those tiny arms and legs overtook the rolling Knights and smashed them flat, silver fire rolled over them in a tingling, terrifying snarling that left them numbed and gasping.

A furious female voice snarled, "*Stay down!*"

Jhessail had ended up panting on her back, with one of the Srinshee's shapely legs across her throat, so she saw who spat out that angry command.

Silver hair lashing and whirling snakelike above a torn and tattered black gown, a woman whose eyes were two smoldering silver stars glared around at ranks of cowering, hissing liches. She curled her body back like a snake rearing to strike then lashed out with both arms flung forward, like a whip cracking, to send silver fire forth in an all-consuming flood.

The Witch-Queen of Aglarond had come calling.

All the liches in front of her were gone. Where they'd stood, the mists had given way to scores of tiny wisps of smoke streaming from lumps of ash that had been feet.

The liches behind the Simbul fled, dwindling into the mist like so many large and ungainly black bats, trying to escape before she—

Turned and let fly once more, hurling forth another destroying flood of silver fire to sear strands and running liches alike.

It was impressive, and went on for a long time. Severed white strands slumped in the dim, misty white distance. The barefoot woman in the black tatters reeled, her eyes going dark and her arms falling to her sides like boneless things, and fell on her face.

The few liches left nearby swarmed up from where they'd been cowering, flat amid the last curling sighs of mist, and raced desperately toward the fallen Chosen, hands raised into claws.

The Srinshee sped to the Simbul even faster, springing up from the Knights in a racing flight powered by vitality snatched from the three adventurers. Her life-leeching magic left the Knights sick and shuddering.

"Sorry, friends," she called back, as she flung out a hand toward the strands that had swallowed Elminster and Dove, and did something that called forth more silver fire from them.

The liches recoiled as it came racing to her in two thin, snarling beams, outlined her briefly in a halo of silver flames, and sank down into her. The Srinshee went to her knees atop the sprawled Queen of Aglarond and kissed her slack mouth—a kiss that leaked silver fire.

By then Florin was on his feet, swaying, leaning on his sword as if it was a walking-stick. He managed two unsteady steps toward the Srinshee before she was flung back into him by the Simbul's eruption back upright. Tumbling together, they rolled over a weakly-cursing Jhessail, and beheld the Queen of Aglarond once more hurling silver fire.

The radiance came not in great floods, but in tiny bursts that streaked from her pointing finger at this lone lich—who burst into flames, like a screaming torch—then that one, who burned even more violently.

One by one the liches fell to the Simbul's stabbing silver fire, as the whiteness all around the shuddering, struggling-to-their-feet Knights seemed to pulse with silver, and surge beneath their boots. It began to fold up around them, the whiteness slashed with rifts, countless spiderweb cracks, and great tumbling vistas of spreading darkness. Strands collapsed into glowing white soup;

mist, blazing liches, and all whirled around them wildly; a great roaring rose from bone-shaking depths into ear-clawing heights; and—

Out of the deafening chaos, the Srinshee plucked at Merith and shouted, "The shaddarn is collapsing!"

He twisted, trying to reach his wife, but Jhessail was beyond the tips of his straining fingers, and falling away from him—into the waiting grip of a long-fingered hand that looked familiar.

Merith had just time to conclude it must belong to Elminster, and that the elbow streaking past his nose must be Dove's, grabbing Florin, before everything whirled up into shrieking darkness and he was falling . . .

Falling . . .

⊚ ⊚ ⊚ ⊚ ⊚

Falling through sunlight into soft, dark earth with a crash and clatter of beanpoles, as familiar tripods of silver-with-age spars of wood toppled over, trailing tendrils and dancing leaves.

Lush green leaves? *Roseberry* leaves? Warmth and sun and no snow? Just when had high summer come to Storm's kitchen garden?

Just how long had they been away in the shaddarn?

Merith bounced as someone heavy landed on him and was as suddenly gone again, more leaves dancing past his gaze. He felt someone else's boot strike his and flop down on him and roll aside . . . and he was blinking up at the amused face of Storm Silverhand, reaching a sun-browned hand down to him.

"Things went well, I see," she commented, "unless one happens to be a bean plant. Sister, must you always crush the same sort? 'Tis not as if you ever actually eat them . . ."

The Simbul, sprawled face-down under most of the Knights amid a welter of poles and crushed greenery, neither moved nor responded.

“We must go,” the Srinshee said, “right now. The minds of the baelnorn Larloch affected must be restored.”

At her elbow, Elminster merely nodded—’ere they winked out, together.

Dove and Storm looked at each other, sighed, and reached down for the Simbul. “She sent forth a *lot* of power,” Dove said. “One of these days, she’s going to spend too much, and—”

Jhessail caught her breath then, so sharply that the sound she made was almost a sob.

Florin and Storm looked up sharply—and froze, letting silence fall and deepen like an unrolling cloak.

The cloaked figure standing on air a few strides away across Storm’s garden was tall, terrible, and a-crawl with chill power. A ring of floating, faintly-glowing gemstones that fairly throbbed with power drifted in a slow, patient circuit in the air above the apparition’s gray head. Eyes like twinkling pits of white fire regarded the three sisters and the trio of Knights on their knees around them, and a hand that was little more than withered gray flesh over bones tightened around a staff that crackled with power.

Merith hefted his sword, strangely thrilled that it was no longer humming, and opened his mouth to spit words of defiance.

“Larloch,” Storm said in greeting, as calmly as if she’d been identifying the sort of tree a leaf blowing by had fallen from.

“Who never risks himself,” Jhessail whispered. “So why . . . ?”

The lich-king kept his eyes on the Bard of Shadowdale. His withered hands spread slightly, as if in entreaty, nothing about the gesture suggesting fragility or enfeeblement.

“This was . . . not my doing,” Larloch said, his voice dry and deep. “From time to time I . . . test the lichnee who serve me by showing them a measure of freedom, and observing what they do with it. This time, they did foolishness.”

"This is no sending," Florin murmured. " 'Tis truly him."

Merith nodded. "His want—or need—must be very important."

Swords ready, the two rose slowly to their feet, each out of long habit stepping to one side to spread out and so offer this new foe more widely-spread targets, and a broader field of menace.

Larloch ignored them. Those chilling eyes regarded Dove and Storm as they stepped forward in slow unison, hands empty of weapons and hair rising to swirl around them restlessly.

"And now?" Storm asked, her words a clear challenge.

Silver fire danced in her eyes, and those of her sister.

The Shadow King made no reply, and Storm did something wordless that made a tear of silver fire drop from her eye to her breast—where it became a thin line of silver flame that raced up to her shoulder and down her arm, consuming and darkening nothing, to fill her palm and rise there in restless hunger, flickering and blazing.

Even stronger hunger rose in Larloch's eyes as he gazed at what danced in Storm's palm. "And now," he replied, lifting his gaze only reluctantly from silver flames to Storm Silverhand's eyes, "I tender my apologies and depart. I seek greater Art, always. I do not seek battle with you, or any who serve the Lady."

"No?" Dove asked, lifting her empty hand as if to hurl something.

"No," Larloch said, bowing to her. Emerald fires crackled from nowhere to trail across withered gray flesh. "I am not a fool. No matter how powerful one becomes, there are always those who are stronger."

"Yet you tarry," Storm reminded him, as politely as a lady of minor nobility conversing with a king.

"Lady, I go," the undead lord replied. "I confess I . . . " He sighed, and announced in a near-whisper, "Looking upon the silver fire is precious to me."

Storm regarded him wordlessly for what seemed a long time then slowly stepped forward, her face solemn. In breath-held silence the Knights watched her walk to him.

The Shadow King took a step back in the face of her calm, lilting advance. Then another.

Where he held his ground, an errant breeze stirred the long, stringy white hair that clung to the tight-stretched gray flesh on his skull. His eyes seemed to burn with rising white fire, and green lightning leaped out of his skin to race restlessly across him at Storm's approach. They heard him murmur, "I know my peril."

The Bard of Shadowdale came to a stop almost touching Larloch, and lifted her hand slowly between them. He held his staff hastily aside, out of the way, and stared down.

Storm let silver fire leap and dance in her palm, and Larloch bent to peer at it until his nose was almost touching the tallest licking silver tongues. He trembled with desire, his hands rising almost involuntarily.

Dove seemed to rise with them, gathering herself to do something, and Jhessail licked her lips and lifted her hands to be ready to work what would almost certainly be an utterly futile spell.

And Larloch straightened up, looked at Storm eye to eye, and said, "Thank you. It has been a very long time since someone has shown me kindness."

He stepped back, bowed deeply, and said, "Fear me no more. Inspired, I return to my Art."

The Shadow King turned, whipped his cloak around himself—and it fell to the ground, empty, fading to nothingness as it touched the earth of Storm's freshly-turned roseberry bed. There was a faint chord of chimings, like a flourish on the highest strings of a harp strung with metal, in the wake of the departing stones that had floated above Larloch.

Storm stood watching, twirling her fingers in a swift spell . . . and turned, visibly relaxing, to announce, "He's gone. Quite gone, with no spying magic nor lurking peril left behind."

"What?" The whisper was raw and horrible, but the fire in the Simbul's eyes, as she lifted her chin from the ground, was as fierce as ever. "Without even giving me a chance at him?"

"Alassra," Dove said with sincere tenderness, " 'Twould have been no chance at all."

The Queen of Aglarond whirled and stiffened in an instant, like an aggrieved cat. "Sister, are you implying—?"

"No," Dove said, effortlessly plucking the Simbul up by the shoulders and holding her upright, "I'm saying it straight out. No matter how broken or weary you may be, you can turn yourself into leaping lightning—I've seen it often enough, Mother Mystra knows—and nothing Larloch can muster can stand as a barrier against silver fire. As sheer silver fire, you couldn't help but reach him, and at a touch destroy him."

Storm nodded as she rejoined them all in the trampled beans. "That's what he meant when he spoke of knowing his peril. You saw the green fire crawling all over him? That's the spell he's crafted to maintain his unlife, quickening as Mystra's fire came close."

"He dares not have silver fire, but desires its power so much," Jhessail said. "He knows 'twill bring him oblivion—and longs for that, too—yet cannot bring himself, after so fierce and long a struggle to cling to life, to let it all go in an instant."

The three sisters all nodded, in their own ways.

"While mere young, vigorous brutes watch," Florin added. "Seeing through his dignity."

Merith gave his friend a sidelong look. "Not so much of the 'vigorous,' there. I'm feeling a touch weary, myself. Perhaps 'tis all this listening to high-tongued jabber."

"Perhaps," Storm agreed, a familiar twinkle in her eyes. "Tea, anyone?"

"Tea?" The Queen of Aglarond twisted that word into a dripping symphony of disgust. "Is that all you can offer?

After I destroyed nigh on a hundred liches, the replacement of which should keep Old Shadow-wits busy for a few decades at least?"

"I can manage wine if Merith and Florin yet have strength enough to stagger down to my cellar, and soup if you've patience to wait till 'tis ready," Storm chuckled. "But as to something more substantial, I fear Torm and Rathan have taken to dining here every evening in your absence, on the pretext of being ready-to-hand upon your return, and there's not a joint of meat nor a barrel of fish left in my larder."

The Simbul frowned, sighed, and frowned a little harder. And an entire roast boar—spit and all—sizzled and dripped onto the beans, floating in midair right in front of her.

She smiled in triumph, spread her hands in a flourish, and reeled. The boar sank, and Dove flung an arm around her shoulders to steady her. The Simbul winced and shuddered, white-faced.

Storm's hair stirred around her shoulders like a whirlwind, and the boar's descent halted. "I suppose you'd be offended if I asked where you thieved this from?"

Leaning into Dove's shoulder, the Simbul gave her sister a dirty look and muttered, " 'Tis mine. From my kitchens, I mean, and taken with a spell that tells my cooks whose hand removed it."

Dove examined her own fingernails, and said to them, "My, working in your palace must be fun."

The Simbul rolled her eyes. "Don't bother fighting to win a throne, and defend it by slaughtering Red Wizards year in and year out," she told Florin, straightening and stepping away from Dove's arm with a determined effort. "See the respect it wins you?"

"Lady Queen," the ranger replied, offering her his arm like a grave courtier, " 'twas not foremost in my personal plans, no."

With a smile, the Simbul leaned on him. She was surprisingly heavy, but Florin saw no safety in commenting on that or even betraying his realization of it. With stately tread he led her along one of the garden paths in Storm Silverhand's wake.

Behind him, Jhessail shook her head. "Sunrise, sunfall, and as inevitably, here we go again!"

"What," Merith chuckled into her ear, "there're more liches? Where?"

"Oho ha hearty ha," she replied. "*I* want tea, if no one else does. I'll stay for that soup, too. Right now, I could eat a—"

"Boar?" Merith suggested.

"The problem with elves," the Witch-Queen of Aglarond observed from behind him, "is how easily their clever senses of humor rule them."

Storm Silverhand turned in her kitchen doorway, eyes dark and twinkling, and said, "Ah, no, sister, there you have matters wrong. That's not the *problem* with elves. That's their *glory.*"

THE BLADESINGER'S LESSON

RICHARD BAKER

Flamerule, the Year of Lightning Storms (1374 DR)

Daried Selsherryn prowled through the warm green shadows of the ruined palace. Cold hate gleamed in his perfect eyes. He was attired for battle in a long shirt of golden mail so fine that it might have been made of snakeskin, and in his hand he carried a deadly elven thinblade imbued with potent magic. He was strikingly handsome, even by the high standards of the sun elves, but in his wrath his fine features darkened into the image of an angel wronged.

He measured the damage he could see—the black scars of an old fire, the ruined courtyard, the broken windows and holed roof—and slammed his sword back into his sheath without a flourish. He simply could not see the reason for it, and that angered him until his head swam with bright rage.

"They have made a ruin of my home!" he snarled, then he took a deep breath to compose himself.

Seventy summers ago he had left the old manor of his mother's family warded by strong spells against weather, time, and thieves. But it seemed that his careful labor had been for nothing. His spells had been broken, and strong young trees stood in the overgrown courts and halls amid thick undergrowth and the damp smell of rotten wood.

Root and rain had wreaked their damage on the old manor, but that was the way of growing things and fleeting seasons. What was the point of finding fault with nature's work? No, he would be wiser to save his anger for the plunderers and looters who had battered down the ancient doors his grandfather had made, dispelling the enchantments woven to preserve the Morvaeril palace for the day when once again an elf's foot might tread its marble-floored halls.

Daried turned in a slow circle, studying the manor's empty rooms. Nothing to do now but learn the extent of the damage and try to piece together what happened in the long years the house had stood silent and empty in the forest. The tale of the front hall was easy enough to descry. The strong old doors had been battered down. The beautiful carvings of his grandfather's hand had been bludgeoned and dented by the impact of a rough-hewn timber that still lay just outside the entranceway. Nothing remained of the improvised battering-ram except for a ten-foot long outline of rotted wood, but the splintered doors were just inside the hall.

"How long for a fresh-hewn tree to molder so?" he wondered aloud. "Forty years? Fifty?"

Evidently, the thieves had come not very long after he and his family had Retreated, abandoning Cormanthor for the green haven of Evermeet. He would have hoped that a few generations might pass before the humans set about despoiling the old places of the People. But patience had never been a human virtue, had it?

Daried followed the old signs into the house. The front hall itself had been turned into someone's stable, at least for a time. Low heaps of rich black compost showed where straw bedding and animal dung had been allowed to fall. Thick greasy soot streaked the wall above a haphazard circle of fist-sized stones, telling of campfires long ago. Daried poked around in the old ashes, and found charred bits of bone, the remains of a leather jack, a wooden spoon carelessly discarded. Human work, all of it.

He straightened and brushed off his hands. Then he followed the trail of damage deeper into the house. Each room showed more of the same. Not a single furnishing remained in the old elven manor; everything had been carried away.

He came to the steep stone stair that led to the vaults below the house, and there Daried smiled for the first time in an hour. One of the old invaders had fallen afoul of the house's magical guardians. The chamber had been warded by a living statue, a warrior of stone animated by elven spells. The statue itself lay broken into pieces nearby, but against one wall a human skeleton slumped, blank eye-sockets gazing up at the holed roof overhead. One side of the skull had been staved in—the work of the stone guardian, Daried supposed.

"At least one of you paid for your greed," he told the yellowing bones. "But it seems your comrades didn't think enough of you to bury or burn you. You had poor luck in choosing your friends, didn't you?"

He knelt beside the skeleton and examined it closely. A rusty shirt of mail hung loosely over the bones. Beneath the mail a glint of metal caught his eye, and he carefully drew out a small pendant of tarnished silver from the dead man's tunic. A running horse of dark, tarnished silver raced across the faded green enamel of the charm.

I've seen that emblem before, Daried realized. Some of the Riders of Mistledale wore such a device. In the fly-speck human village not far off from the Morvaeril manor, there stood a rough and grimy taphouse with that symbol hanging above its door.

"Dalesfolk pillaged my house?" he muttered. He tore the pendant from the skeleton's neck and stood with the tarnished charm clenched in his fist.

The sheer ingratitude of the thing simply stunned him. Daried Selsherryn had returned to the forests of Cormanthor with the army of Seiveril Miritar, in order to destroy the daemonfey who had attacked Evermeet. The wretched hellspawn hid themselves in ruined Myth Drannor, threatening all the surrounding human lands with their conjured demons and fell sorceries. Daried and all who marched in the Crusade hazarded their lives to oppose that evil. Elf blood and valor stood as the only shield between those same Dalesfolk and a nightmare of hellfire and ancient wrath. Not five miles from where he stood twenty more elf warriors in the service of Lord Miritar's Crusade guarded that miserable human village. Yet he could see all around him how the wretched human thieves and squatters who'd inherited stewardship over Cormanthor had treated the things Daried's People had left behind.

Did they forget us in less than a hundred years? he fumed silently. Why should a single elf warrior risk harm in order to protect such creatures? What sort of fool was Seiveril Miritar, to waste even one hour in seeking out the goodwill and aid of the Dalesfolk, or any humans for that matter?

Grimacing in distaste, Daried wrapped the dead thief's pendant in a small cloth and dropped it into a pouch at his belt. He meant to ask hard questions about that emblem, and soon. Then he ducked his head beneath the low stone lintel of the stairs leading below the manor-house, and descended into the chambers below.

The air grew cool and musty, a striking change from the humid warmth of the summer woodland above. He didn't bother to strike a light; enough of the bright midday sun above glimmered down the stair for his elf eyes to make out the state of the vault below.

It, too, had been despoiled.

Jagged pock-marks of bubbled stone showed where some fierce and crude battle-magic had been unleashed. The old summoning-traps that would have confronted the intruders with noble celestial beasts, loyal and true, had been scoured from the walls.

Five pointed archways led away from the room at the foot of the stair, and the adamantine doors that had sealed each one were simply gone. Destroyed by acid, disintegrated by magic, perhaps carried away as loot—it didn't matter, did it? What mattered was that the old vaults stood open, unguarded.

Daried's clan had not left any secret hoards of treasure behind in a manor they abandoned, of course. But they had certainly thought that the long-buried dead of the family would be safe behind walls of powerful magic and elven stonework. One by one Daried glanced into each vault, and found dozens of his mother's ancestors and kin stripped of any funereal jewelry they might once have possessed. Their bones lay strewn about in thoughtless disorder, rummaged through and discarded like trash.

Hot tears gathered in Daried's eyes, but he did not allow himself to avert his gaze. Having come this far, he would not allow himself to turn away until he had seen all that there was to be seen.

It was not the elven way to send the dead to Arvandor with roomfuls of precious jewels or wealth for use in the next life. Sun elves were not humans, so frightened of death that they hoped such rites and treasures promised dominion in ages to come. Most sun elves of high family were interred in their finest clothes, wearing the jewels and diadems that went with such formal dress, as a simple matter of reverence. But that did not mean that the remains of the honored dead were to be picked over by whatever scavenger happened along.

He came to the last vault, and there the loss was bitter indeed. It was the resting place of his mother's cousin Alvanir, last of the Morvaerils. He had been interred with the ancient moonblade of House Morvaeril, since with the passing of the last of the line the sword of the Morvaeril clan had itself faded into powerlessness and slumber. Each moonblade was meant for one elven House, and if the House failed, the moonblade was of use to no other.

The ancient sword had been taken too, of course.

Even though the blade was dormant or extinguished outright, it was still a treasure of House Morvaeril, and through Daried's mother, House Selsherryn as well. All else Daried could bear, bitter as it was, but the theft of a dead moonblade left a deep, hot ache in the center of his chest.

"What good is it to you?" he asked the long-vanished plunderers of the tomb. "Is there nothing you hold sacred?"

He drifted back to the central chamber, and wept silently in the gloom and shadows. He'd been born in this house, seventeen decades ago. He remembered the soft lanterns swaying in the chill evening breezes of the spring, the green and lush canopy of leaf and vine that had roofed the courtyard in summer, the tall windows of the library gleaming orange and gold on a frosty autumn morning. Nothing else was left to him of his youth, so many years ago.

The soft click of a taloned claw on the steps behind him saved his life.

Daried roused himself from his sorrow just in time to leap aside, as the foul hellborn monster threw itself on him from the stairs. In a dark rush the thing bounded past him, its hooked talons hissing through the air where the elf's face and throat had been an instant earlier. A hot sharp claw grazed Daried's cheek, and the thing's powerful rush sent him spinning to one side as the creature missed its chance to bear him to the ground and rip out his throat.

Daried grunted once in surprise and backstepped, gaining a double arm's-reach of space to get his bearings and sweep out his sword. His adversary had a shape not unlike that of a man, but a long, thick tail twisted behind it like a hungry serpent, and from head to toe it was studded with barbs of steel-hard horn as long as daggers.

Its skin was crimson and hot, and its eyes glowed like balls of green flame in the shadows of the crypt.

"You weep for the dead, elf?" it hissed. "Be at ease. I will leave your bones here with the rest of this dry old wreckage."

"You mock my ancestors at your peril, hellspawn," Daried growled, keeping his swordpoint between the monster and himself.

The creature grinned with a mouthful of sharp, carious fangs, and leaped at the elf with a flurry of jabbing barbs and slashing talons. But Daried was ready for the monster; he allowed himself to slide easily into the bladesinger's waking trance, a timeless state of mind and body in which each movement became a choreographed dance. With calm deliberation Daried moved his sword to guide the monster's talons away from his flesh, parry the stabbing tail, disguise delicate ripostes and counters.

The thinblade's razorlike point darted between barbs and spikes to pierce infernal flesh, then again and again. Hot spatters of black blood fell to the dusty floor, but the creature gave no sign that it had been hurt. It snapped and flailed wildly, claws and fangs and stabbing spikes whistling past Daried. Elf and devil fought in grim silence, with no sound other than the dull click and scrape of talons against steel. Sharp barbs gouged Daried's limbs and talons raked his shining mail, but he battled on, refusing to allow pain or fatigue a foothold in his concentration.

The devil managed to seize Daried's sleeve in one taloned hand, and it hurled itself on him, trying to impale him like a living bed of nails. But Daried twisted away, turning the creature's hand over as he spun. At the same instant he barked out syllables of a deadly spell, and with his free hand grasped the monster's arm. Golden lightning exploded from the bladesinger's touch, charring his adversary's arm into useless black ruin.

With a low hiss the devil recoiled, its grip on Daried failing. It crouched low and whirled, bringing its fiercely spiked tail whistling around in a blow powerful enough to crush stone. But Daried leaped over the devil's strike, and with one smooth motion he sank a foot of his thinblade into the hollow of the monster's throat.

The devil drove him back with a frenzy of slashes and jabbing barbs. But black blood fumed in its mouth and ran between its yellow fangs. It took two more steps toward Daried, the green flame in its eyes dimming, and it stumbled to the floor in a pool of its own foul ichor.

Daried took careful aim and transfixed its head with one more thrust. Then he backed away, waiting for the corpse to vanish. Summoned monsters always did. But nothing happened; the hellspawn's body remained where it had fallen.

"It wasn't summoned?" he muttered in dismay. It hadn't been called to Faerûn by a conjuring spell, it had traversed some sort of gate between the planes of its own volition. It was as real in this world as he was.

An ill omen indeed. Was the creature's presence in the world the work of the daemonfey, or did some other peril confront Daried and the elves who followed him?

Whatever the answer, it did not seem likely that he would find out more in the ruins of the Morvaeril manor. Nor, for that matter, would he learn anything about who had taken the ancient moonblade and what the Dalesfolk had had to do with the theft.

Battered and heartsick, Daried shook the foul blood from his sword and climbed back up the stairs to the summer warmth above.

Daried returned to the encampment an hour before sunset. It was a pleasant spot, a well-shaded forest glade a stone's throw from the gravel-voiced Ashaba, where a score of elf warriors under Daried's command kept watch. It was their task to make sure that the Sembian mercenaries in Battledale—allies or dupes of the daemonfey,

Daried did not know or care which—did not reach the west bank of the river by crossing unopposed in the green depths of the forest. Should the Sembians get across the Ashaba here, they would outflank the elf legions that stood ready to defend the main crossing at the town of Ashabenford fifteen miles farther north.

It struck Daried as a fool's errand. No one considered it very likely that the Sembians would search for a path through the trackless depths of the forest in order to try a river crossing where no easy fording-point existed. That was why Vesilde Gaerth, the knight-commander who captained the Crusade forces in Mistledale, had detached only two dozen warriors to guard against the possibility. If, by some amazing feat of endurance, the Sembians succeeded in the forest march and river crossing, Vesilde Gaerth needed a few hours' warning so that he could abandon his defenses at Ashabenford and retreat out of the trap.

Gaerth had also told Daried that he was to capture, drive off, or kill any Sembian scouts who tried to spy out the elven defenses in the southern verge of the dale. And for that matter, he was supposed to do what he could to deal with any demons, devils, or similar monsters who appeared to harry the human villagers and farmers who lived nearby. In fact, that was why Daried had been given this task. As a bladesinger, he at least had a chance of dealing with such monsters using his skill and magic. Most of the other elves in his small company would have been overwhelmed by a hellspawn of any real strength.

"Lord Selsherryn returns!" called a clear voice. Daried glanced up; the moon elf Andariel stood atop a large boulder-fall overlooking the camp, raising his bow in welcome. Young and impetuous, Andariel regarded Daried's high family and personal accomplishment with such seriousness that Daried sometimes suspected secret mockery in his manner. But he had never found a trace of sarcasm behind the younger elf's earnestness.

Daried returned Andariel's salute with a curt wave, and made his way to the temporary shelter that served as his resting-place and command post. Two more elves awaited him there—Hycellyn, another moon elf, and the sun elf mage Teriandyln, who might have been the closest Daried had to a true friend in all the Crusade. Very unusually for an elf, Teriandyln possessed a thin, pointed goatee of fine golden whiskers. Along with his grim manner and brilliant green eyes, the trace of beard lent him an acutely sinister, almost feral, appearance.

The mage glanced up at Daried and frowned. "What in the world happened to you?"

"I met a devil in the wreckage of the Morvaeril manor."

"A devil?" Hycellyn asked sharply. She set down the arrow she was fletching. "Are you hurt, Lord Selsherryn?"

"Nothing serious," Daried answered. He directed his attention to Teriandyln. "I slew it, but its body did not vanish. It was not summoned."

"The daemonfey must control a gate of some kind. Or perhaps the creature was one of the devils trapped in Myth Drannor. I have heard that many such monsters have roamed the ruins for years." Teriandyln frowned deeper. "What sort of creature was it? Do you know?"

"A half-foot taller than a tall elf, with a heavier build. It had no wings, but it was covered in great jutting spikes or barbs."

"A hamatula, then—a barbed devil, as they are sometimes known." The sharp-faced sun elf looked at Daried more closely. "You are fortunate to have walked away from that fight, Daried."

Daried shrugged and said nothing. But Hycellyn retrieved a slender wand of white ashwood from her belt and knelt beside him, murmuring the words of a healing prayer. The bladesinger winced as punctures, gouges, and bruises announced themselves again, but the pain of each injury faded at once, soothed away by the moon elf's magic. He took a deeper breath, and gave her a nod of gratitude.

"So what was a devil doing in the Morvaeril manor?" she asked as she put away the wand.

"The house lies in ruins now," Daried said. "It has been plundered, its warding spells broken. Even the vaults underneath have been despoiled. My mother's kin were robbed in their eternal sleep and left to lie wherever they fell. The thieves even stole the Morvaeril moonblade, dead for a hundred years now. Nothing is left.

"I grew up in that house. It's only been seventy summers since I left it. To see it now you might think our People's absence from this place had been counted in centuries, not decades."

"Who would do such a thing?" Hycellyn wondered aloud.

"Someone who wore this emblem." Daried held out his hand, showing the others the pendant with its image of the running horse. "I found it on the skeleton of a human lying in the house."

"I know that sign," Teriandyln said. "It hangs above the inn that stands in the human village called Glen."

Daried closed his fist around the pendant, and slipped it back into his tunic. "I know."

Hycellyn sighed and shook her head. "Lord Selsherryn—Daried—how long has that skeleton been there? How long ago was your family's house broken into? Ten years? Twenty? Fifty? The humans who live in Glen now may have had nothing to do with it."

"For their sake, I hope that is true." Daried stood, and glanced at the sun sinking in the west. "Have our scouts seen anything worth reporting this afternoon?"

"No, it has been quiet," said Teriandyln. "But Ilidyrr and Sarran are not due to report for a couple of hours yet, and they are the farthest east of any of our folk."

"If nothing is happening, then I will leave you in charge for a while longer," Daried told him. "I am going to Glen. Someone there has much to answer for."

An hour later, Daried Selsherryn stood under a battered green tavern-sign in the human village of Glen. The emblem of a running horse graced the signboard, but the bright silver-white paint was threadbare and peeling. Insects buzzed in the summer twilight, filling the air with chirps and rasping calls. Thousands of tiny midges fluttered around the bright lanterns hanging from lightposts scattered through the hamlet.

Human farmers and townsfolk stood in pairs here and there throughout the village, dressed in ill-fitting leather jerkins and gripping rusty pikes or old bows. Since the daemonfey had begun stirring up old evils in Myth Drannor's ruins, the Dalesfolk had been subjected to deadly raids and rampages by all sorts of monsters and demons. They'd been posting a village watch for two or three tendays—not that some untried farmer had much of a chance against the sorts of infernal creatures Sarya Dlardrageth might send to harry Mistledale. Daried had heard from other elves that there was often more to the Dalesfolk than met the eye, and not a few of those who stood guard were seasoned veterans or onetime sellswords who still remembered how to swing a sword. But he hadn't seen any human watchmen in Glen that he'd trust with a sharp fork, let alone a spear or a sword.

The muted sounds of thick human voices and the clumsy strumming of a crude stringed instrument spilled out of the door. Setting his face in a scowl, Daried pushed open the door and entered the taproom.

It was a smoke-filled, low-ceilinged room with heavy black timbers for beams and posts. The sight made him wince. Could they have killed any more trees when they raised up this oversized kennel? he wondered. He shook his head and turned his attention to the people in the room.

A half-dozen humans sat staring at him, their conversations faltering in mid-word. Between the smoke and the humid warmth of the night, the taproom was quite warm, and sweat flowed freely over hairy faces and around thick homespun tunics. One tall, lanky fellow with long hands and a lanternlike jaw stood behind a weathered bar—the innkeeper, or so Daried assumed.

The tall man managed an awkward bow, and addressed Daried in the common speech the humans used. "Good evening, sir. We heard that some of the Fair Folk were camped in the forest nearby. What can I get for you?"

"Answers," Daried grated. He dropped the tarnished emblem on the rough countertop before the innkeeper. "This pendant was left in an elf manor five miles east of here. The human who wore it has lain dead in that house for some time, but I know he visited that manor no more than seventy years ago. Who among you would know anything about what happened there?"

The innkeeper frowned and shuffled his feet. Daried's vehemence had taken him by surprise, and he finally turned away to wipe his hands on his apron and back a couple of steps away from the bladesinger.

"Are you speaking of the House of Pale Stone?" he asked over his shoulder. "An old unwalled villa of white stone, over on the east bank of the river, its walls covered with green growing vines?"

The House of Pale Stone? Daried had never heard the Morvaeril palace called any such thing, but it seemed apt enough. "The doors to the house lie battered down outside. They are carved in the image of a crescent moon rising above a forest glade, with seven seven-pointed stars at the top."

"Yes, that's the place," the innkeeper said. "I visited the place once when I was a young lad. I remember the sign on the old doors. I didn't dare go in, though. Everyone knows that deadly magic and restless spirits lurk in the ruins." He looked down at the pendant again. "You mean to tell me that you found this in the House of Pale Stone?"

"If you did not enter the house, who did?"

The innkeeper wrung his hands in his apron again, drying them anxiously. "I did not break down those doors, sir elf. Nor did anyone I know. The place has been like that since my father's time, maybe my grandfather's time. It's haunted. Sometimes bold young lads of the town go and have a look, like I did when I was a boy. But we've all heard stories of the dangers of that old manor. Sellswords and freebooters have died in that house."

"Red Harvald did not fear that old dusty tomb!"

Daried turned his head, surprised. By the cold fireplace an old townsman sat smoking a long-stemmed pipe, grinning at him. He hadn't realized that all the folk in the taproom were watching his interrogation of the innkeeper. Deliberately, he put his back to the wall and shifted so that he had a better view of the room.

"Vada, you mean to say that Red Harvald dared the House of Pale Stone?" the innkeeper asked the old man.

"Aye, and a dozen tombs, crypts, and palaces more. The woods are full of places the Fair Folk left empty. Red Harvald had a look in every one within forty miles." The old man—Vada—nodded at his own musty memories. "I remember the day that Red Harvald and his bold fellows sat right at that table over there and recounted the harrowing traps and fearsome dangers they met in the House of Pale Stone. Half the folk of Glen crowded into this very room to hear the tale."

"How long ago was this?" Daried demanded.

The old man drew his pipe from his mouth and frowned in thought. He tapped out the ashes on the stones of the hearth, and blew the bowl clean with an expert puff of breath. "It was a few days before midsummer, in the Year of the Striking Falcon. Forty years, good sir. Not much time as you reckon it, I suppose, but long enough for a human. Why, Earek there—" he nodded at the tall innkeeper—"was only a toddler then."

The bladesinger motioned the man to silence with a curt gesture. "Where is this Red Harvald now?"

Vada blinked, taken aback. After a moment he smiled again. "Why, he is dead, sir elf. Twenty-five years, it must be."

Daried glowered at him. "I suppose the thieving dog

finally met a just end in one of the houses he plundered."

"You misunderstand, sir. Red Harvald was a hero, not a thief. He was the most courageous man I've ever met, and generous too. Oh, he had a quick temper sometimes, but he never remained angry for long. He hunted down highwaymen, scattered brigands and bandits, warded Glen from more orc and ogre-raids than I could care to count, and even faced stranger and more deadly monsters when they emerged from the depths of the forest to harrow our town. And when true tomb-plunderers and over-eager freebooters drifted through the Dale and risked stirring up real trouble, well, he'd run them off with nothing but a hard look and a few quiet words. I owed him my life at least twice over. Many Glen-folk did."

Daried stared hard at the garrulous old fellow, weighing the truthfulness of his words and manner. Vada's bland smile seemed less warm than it had been before, but the elf could sense no duplicity in it. He scowled and turned back to the innkeeper, searching for a sly grin or insincere smirk that might give the lie to the old man's story, but Earek merely nodded in agreement.

"He was always kind to me when I was a lad," the innkeeper said. "A good man, a hero who never treated others like they were somehow less than he was. Red Harvald was a leader of this town for many years. He was no thief."

It's only to be expected that they would band together to defend their own, Daried told himself. Likely this Harvald fellow bought himself a town full of friends and admirers with the fine things he stole from the honored dead. Even so, the sun elf could see that he was not going to get far by lashing out with more accusations. The townsfolk remembered the man as a hero, and in Daried's experience, no one liked to learn about their hero's failings.

Besides, if Vada and Earek were telling the truth, then this Harvald fellow had spent his plunder well for many years. By now the funerary wealth of the Morvaeril dead must be scattered across half of Faerûn, traded and sold a dozen times over.

The humans in the taproom watched him warily. Daried resigned himself to a more patient approach, and let the doubt and hostility fall from his face.

"As you must have guessed, the ruin that you name the House of Pale Stone was once my family's home," he began. "I have but lately returned from Evermeet, and I was appalled to discover that the palace had been broken into and the crypts defiled. I hope that you can see why I was upset."

Earek the innkeeper nodded cautiously. "Anyone would be," he agreed. He waited for Daried to continue.

"Perhaps the man you call Red Harvald was the one who opened our vaults, or perhaps someone else pillaged the place before he ever set foot in it. The gems and jewelry removed from our dead are not that important to me. I wish that my ancestors' sleep had not been disturbed, but it is done, and I will speak no more of it.

"But there is one thing I ask of you, only one heirloom of my mother's family that I would wish to recover. It was a sword of fine elven steel, with three pearls set in its crossguard and a hilt shaped like a sea serpent. A design like a row of breaking waves graced its blade. Once it was enchanted, but its magic faded away centuries ago. It is nothing more or less than a beautiful old sword now, but it would please me greatly to find it." Daried felt his temper rising again at the idea of the Morvaeril moonblade in the hands of some human brigand, but he checked his anger with a deep breath. "I will, of course, pay a very handsome finder's fee to the current owner. I pass no judgment on anyone who happens to own it now. I will be satisfied with its return."

The innkeeper's eyes narrowed as Daried described the blade. When he finished, Earek glanced past the bladesinger's shoulder at Vada, seated by the hearth. Daried turned slowly, but Vada made no secret of his assent.

"I believe him," the old man told Earek. "He and his people have come a long way to shield us from terrible foes. It would be ungrateful—and stupid—of us to ignore his grievances."

The innkeeper nodded, and returned his attention to Daried. "I've seen that sword," he told the bladesinger. "It hung in a scabbard of red dragon-leather above the fireplace of a man named Andar, the son of Harvald. He lived in the house Harvald built."

"Very good," said Daried. "I will—"

Earek stopped him with a raised hand. "Andar was killed two days ago, sir. He led some of our folk against a large warband of Chondathan marauders. But after he drove them away, some of the mercenaries decided to follow him back to his manor. They killed him, looted the place, and burned much of it to the ground. I don't know if your sword is still there or not."

Daried grimaced. He remembered his scouts telling him of a skirmish near the town a couple of days past, but he had given it little thought. Gangs of desperate men and bands of reavers roamed the dale; he and his elves drove off or slew the ones they caught, but some eluded them. After all, they were watching the forests to the southeast, not the open lands to the west.

"Chondathans? I thought your enemies were Sembians."

The innkeeper snorted. "The Sembians don't do much of their own fighting, sir. They hire companies of mercenaries from all over Faerûn to serve as their army. Hard, cruel men, all too eager to add some plunder to their Sembian gold."

"Where can I find the manor?"

"You'll find the place a little less than two miles southwest of the town," the innkeeper said. "It's a strong fieldstone farmhouse on the top of a small hill, with a big apple-orchard all around it. Just look for the smoke."

The bladesinger nodded and turned to go, but paused. Two or three violent deaths in a village the size of Glen was a hard thing to bear, even for humans. The Glen-folk hadn't despoiled his family's palace or stripped elven dead of their funerary attire, even if it was likely that their fathers had. They didn't deserve the brunt of his anger. He looked back to Earek and Vada from the door. "Do any of the family survive?" he asked.

"Andar's sons and their families live here in the town; they weren't there," Vada said. "Nilsa lived with her father, but she went up to Ashabenford earlier that day. She didn't return until the morning after." The old man fixed his watery gaze on Daried, and pointed the stem of his pipe at the elf. "If you should meet them at Harvald's house, remember that they've lost enough in the last few days. Speak less harshly to them than you did to us, if you have a dram of compassion in your heart."

Daried nodded once and left, shrugging off the weight of the human gazes on his back.

The warmth of the day did not diminish noticeably when the sun set. The long, hot afternoon simply faded into a humid, clinging night. The moon was only a thin crescent in the southeast, and the stars were faint and few. If there had been no moonlight at all, it might have been difficult for Daried, but as it was, he could easily follow the trail left by the marauders who had pillaged and burned Harvald's old house. They were driving most of the farmstead's livestock with them and moving slowly, as one might expect of a band of raiders burdened with loot.

They think that no one dares to chase them, Daried decided. They are that stupid, or that arrogant. Perhaps they figured that no village in this empty corner of the Dale would be able to muster enough skilled warriors to challenge thirty-five or forty seasoned mercenaries. That was Daried's guess as to the size of the warband. It could be larger, if there were other bands who had split off to roam in different directions before he had picked up their trail.

He'd found the farmstead half-burned, as Earek had

told him. The walls of the old fieldstone house survived, but the roof was mostly gone, and the various outbuildings were all burned. An astonishing array of mundane possessions—pots and kettles, stools and chairs, chests and cabinets—had been dragged out of the house and strewn around. Three fresh-dug graves lay a short distance from the house. He didn't know who else beside Harvald's son had died there, but there had been no one at the burned manor to ask.

A quick divination spell had confirmed his suspicion: the Morvaeril moonblade was no longer there, carried off by the marauders who had pillaged the place. Without a moment's hesitation, Daried had set off in pursuit.

Humans were unlikely to travel all night long, and the raiders were not moving quickly in any event. Elves, on the other hand, traveled swiftly indeed by night or day and could go for days with minimal rest. Even with their head start, he thought he might be able to overtake the marauders before they reached the Sembian encampment in Battledale. It was his only chance to regain the Morvaeril moonblade.

Besides, dealing with murderous scum such as the marauders he pursued was one of the reasons Vesilde Gaerth had posted Daried and his small company to Glen in the first place. Corellon only knew what other acts of violence and robbery they had already committed elsewhere in the Dale, or would commit given the chance.

Daried trotted southward throughout the night, following the swath the mercenaries left behind. Instead of making straight for Battledale, the mercenaries seemed to have veered west for a few miles, skirting the forest border as they made their way south. No doubt they hadn't yet had their fill of blood and loot, and hoped for more opportunities for mayhem before turning homeward. On two occasions he passed lonely farmsteads, sacked by the marauders he followed. Whatever the reason, each detour the murderers took gave Daried more time to catch them before they rejoined the Sembian army.

At daybreak he allowed himself an hour of rest, eating a little bread and dried fruit he carried in a pouch by his belt. Then he roused himself and pushed on. In the mid-morning the marauders' trail finally turned eastward and disappeared into the shadows of Cormanthor.

Beneath the trees the day was still quite warm; not a breath of wind stirred the branches. The raiders' path followed an old track in the woods—not an elfroad, for it would have taken elven woodcraft to find and follow one of Cormanthyr's hidden highways. This was a woodcutter's foot-track, for Daried passed a number of old stumps, trees cut down years ago. He paused to examine the first few he found, and discovered that the old woodcutter had gone out of his way to take only dead or dying trees. At least some humans took elven teachings to heart, though elves wouldn't have scarred the forest so much with their harvesting of wood.

A little more than ten miles from the place where the marauder's trail entered the forest, Daried came to the Ashaba. And there, in the middle of the forest, he found a bridge.

It was not a human-built bridge, of course. Instead, it was one of the old elven crossings, a set of submerged and semi-submerged boulders that had been surreptitiously arranged to form an easy path across the river. The riverbed itself was arranged to accommodate flooding by spreading the water out across a wide, shallow gravel bank instead of drowning the crossing altogether. Long ago spells of illusion had concealed parts of the span, so that anyone who came across it without knowing its secret would have seen no crossing there. But those spells had failed with time, and the whole pathway was there for anyone to see. Even forest-blind humans couldn't miss it—and in fact they hadn't, because the marauders' trail led over the old crossing.

The bladesinger halted in amazement. There were supposed to be no easy crossings of the great forest river between Ashabenford and the Pool of Yeven. His company was keeping watch twelve miles upstream, ignorant of a perfectly serviceable crossing that at least some of the Sembian sellswords knew about and made use of. The Sembian army hardly needed to improvise a crossing near Glen, when this one would serve almost as well. It was farther from Ashabenford, of course, but it also had a fine path leading right into the western portions of Mistledale.

Daried thought for a moment. He and his archers could hold the bridge against a small company of human sellswords, but if a few hundred human warriors went that way, they could do little more than slow the attack. But there was a chance at least that the leaders of the Sembian army did not know of the crossing. The mercenaries in Sembia's service might not have reported the crossing to their employers—not before they had an opportunity to do some pillaging first.

After all, if the Sembians *had* known about the crossing, why would they not have attacked already?

"That is tenuous reasoning, Daried," he told himself.

But if there was even the slightest chance that he could keep knowledge of the crossing from finding its way back to the Sembian commanders, he had to try. And it also meant that he could continue his pursuit of the marauders, didn't it?

Striding easily from boulder to boulder, he hurried across the hidden bridge and picked up the path on the east bank of the Ashaba. He redoubled his pace and ran through the long, warm hours of the afternoon, gliding through the tree-gloom and brush like a silent green shadow. Sweat glistened on his brow, and his eyes ached from lack of rest, but he refused to slack his pace. Only the soft thudding of his footfalls on the forest loam and the light creaking of his armor betrayed his haste.

He slowed only when he heard the sounds of human voices ahead of him on the trail.

Carefully, Daried raised the hood of his cloak and drew it closer around his shoulders despite the heat of the day.

Its dappled gray-green hue and concealing enchantments would make him much more difficult to see. Then he closed in on his quarry.

The mercenaries had halted near a dark, still forest pool, setting their camp for the night. They were big, dirty men, dressed in hauberks of heavy mail and leather. Sweat soaked their brows and dripped from their faces, staining their arming coats and tunics. They were crude, callous, and slovenly, but Daried did not miss the care with which they set their sentries or the alertness of those who remained on watch. They might have been mercenaries of the lowest sort, but that also meant that they were professional fighters, and they knew enough to be careful of Cormanthor's watchful silence.

In an hour of watching, he counted thirty-one of them. He also earmarked the leader of the rough band, a tall, thin fellow with a badly pocked face and a scalp shaven down to short stubble. Most of the mercenaries satisfied themselves with arranging simple lean-tos or rigging open-sided awnings of canvas to keep off any rain, but the leader had a tent, in which he kept most of the band's loot. Several fierce war-hounds prowled about the camp, and in a small hollow nearby the mercenaries created a small corral for the cows, pigs, and horses they'd carried off from the Dalesfolk. The air reeked of dung, sweat, and woodsmoke.

After a time, Daried withdrew a few hundred yards and found himself a good spot to lie out of sight and rest. He ate a light meal, and permitted himself several hours of Reverie in order to refresh himself and regain his strength. The humans would be there all night; he could afford a few hours' rest.

Three hours after dusk, he arose from his hiding place. The night was even warmer than the previous one, and the air felt heavy and still—there would be a thunderstorm before long. Avoiding the path, Daried returned to the mercenaries' camp through the trackless forest. He spotted a pair of sentries watching over the path leading back toward Mistledale, and two more keeping an eye on the forest nearby. After watching for a time, he decided that two more sentries guarded the other side of the camp.

And he found someone else watching the camp, too.

A short distance ahead of him, a young woman crouched behind a tree, a powerful bow in her hands. She wore a tunic of homespun linen, breeches rather than a skirt, and a green cloak with its hood drawn. She was dressed like one of the Dalesfolk, but it seemed unlikely that one girl would have tracked a whole band of mercenaries into the forest. Of course, Daried himself had done just that, but he was a highly skilled bladesinger and a seasoned warrior; he knew what he was about.

The girl drew a deep breath, and raised her bow, sighting on the nearest sentry, a shot of twenty yards or so from where she crouched. Daried scowled—if she started shooting mercenaries, she'd rouse the whole camp and likely get herself killed. It certainly would not aid his efforts at all.

He glided closer and whispered, "Do not shoot. You'll wake them all."

The girl whirled in surprise, bringing her bow around to aim at him, but Daried had been careful enough to place a tree between them. He made a small motion of his hand: "Wait."

Slowly, the girl lowered her bow. She studied Daried with suspicion. She was unusually fine-featured for a human, with delicate eyes, a narrow face, and ears that showed just the subtlest of points.

She has elf blood! Daried realized. Of course. The humans plundered everything else of ours. Why not take what they wanted from our women as well?

He considered leaving, and allowing the girl to simply get herself killed. She was born in violence and robbery; why should he intervene to spare her from the consequences of human rashness? But before he decided to abandon her, she spoke.

"Who are you?" she hissed at him. "Why are you interfering with me?"

"I am Daried Selsherryn, of Evermeet," he answered, keeping his voice low. "Those sellswords have something that belongs to my family, and I mean to get it back."

"Fine, you are welcome to search their belongings when I am done with them." She turned her back on him and raised her bow again.

Daried had certainly not expected to be ignored. He was so nonplussed that he almost let her begin her fight without another word. But he took two soft steps closer and shook his head. "I can't have you put them on their guard yet. Now, who are you? And why is one human girl seeking her own death by attacking a camp full of hardened sellswords?"

"I am Nilsa Harvalmeer. These murderers killed my father and burned my home. I am going to see them pay for what they have done."

Daried looked at her more closely. "Nilsa, the daughter of Andar?"

"Yes. How do you know me?"

"I followed this band of mercenaries from your father's house."

The girl studied him. "You're the elf captain whose archers are near Glen, aren't you?"

"I am." He hadn't realized that any of the Glen-folk knew who he was.

"Are the rest of your warriors nearby? Can you wipe out this whole band?"

Daried shook his head. "I am the only one here," he said.

Nilsa frowned. "Why are you here by yourself?"

Do I explain myself? he wondered. She might regard the Morvaeril moonblade as a heirloom of her House, not mine. Still, in his experience, it was always better to be truthful, even when the words would be hard to hear.

"I came for the sword your grandfather took from my family's ancestral home," he said. "I only learned two days ago that it was missing. The townspeople told me that it was in your family's keeping. When I found that your house had been plundered, I decided to follow the marauders and take it back."

She stared at him in disbelief. "You came here to take back a sword?"

"Yes, but now that I am here, I think I'll discourage these brigands from raiding your Dale again. It would be unconscionable to leave them free to murder and rob anybody else."

"You have a high opinion of your ability to discourage them."

"I know what I can do," he said. He looked at the bow in her hands. "Are you skilled with that weapon?"

"I know what I can do," Nilsa answered him. "At this range, I'll kill a man each time I shoot."

Reading her face, Daried decided that she believed she was speaking the truth. That was no more or less than he would expect from an elf archer, after all. Whether or not her opinion of her own archery was founded on truth, he could not say. Most likely, she'd manage a couple of good shots, but she'd lose her nerve and her aim when the surprise of her attack faded. But still, he could use a couple of good arrows at the right moment.

"All right," he said. "I will take care of the sentries on this side of the camp, then slip in and slay their captain. Then I will call out for you in Elvish. You will shoot any man you see in the middle of the camp. Fire five arrows, and withdraw. Accurate fire is more important than rapid fire. I'd rather have one man dead or wounded than five men missed. I will trust that you do not shoot me.

"After I have caused a little more havoc, I will also withdraw. I will meet you a half-mile back down the trail, and we will set an ambush in case we are pursued."

Nilsa scowled in the shadows. "Who decided that you were in charge of this?"

"I did. Do you have a better plan?"

The girl remained silent, evidently considering the

question. Finally she nodded. "All right, we'll try it your way. I'll wait for you to call out before I start shooting."

Daried nodded once and slipped away into the forest-shadow. He circled away from Nilsa's position, moving slowly and carefully. He did not know whether the girl's shooting would help him at all, so he determined to dismiss it from his plan. If she managed to injure or kill some of his foes, well, good. If not, even wild arrows fired into the fight would add to the chaos he intended to create in the Chondathans' camp.

When he reached a good position, he paused and whispered the words of a few spells to aid him in the fight—a spell of supernatural agility and quickness, and another that would ward him from enemy blades. A bladesinger's training combined the study of magic with the study of swordplay, and Daried was a competent wizard as well as an accomplished swordsman. He would need both arts for the task ahead of him.

Guarded by his enchantments, Daried stole closer to the camp and approached the first two sentries. They stood in the trees, well away from the firelight, about twenty feet apart. Again, he found that he had to give the mercenaries marks for experience. A single sentry would have been easy to neutralize in silence, but two close enough to see each other but disciplined enough to remain apart were much harder to deal with. For this, he would need magic.

Thunder rumbled in the distance.

Daried waited for the next faint flicker of light in the distance, silently counting for the thunderclap. Then, as the low rumble washed over the forest, he quickly spoke the words of another spell, using the thunder to drown out the sounds of the arcane syllables. The nearer sentry heard something anyway and started to turn toward him, but then his chin drooped to his chest and he folded to the ground, fast asleep. The other sentry simply sank down, his back to a tree.

He probably could have left them, since it was not likely they would wake on their own for a time, but the approaching storm concerned him. A loud thunderclap might rouse the sentries again, and he did not want to have to elude them when he left the camp. So Daried bound and gagged both men thoroughly before moving on to the next two sentries. Killing men in their sleep was a hard thing to do, even men such as these.

The next two sentries were a little less wary then their fellows. A thick stand of trees stood between them, so that it was hard to keep each other in view. Daried simply distracted the one on the left with a magic word and a flick of his hand, creating a rustle in the underbrush near the guard's feet. While that man looked down and backed up a step, Daried glided close behind the second and killed him with a sword-thrust through the throat. It was not a nobly struck blow, but he reminded himself that these Chondathans were murderers and robbers. He'd seen what they had left behind in the farmsteads they'd plundered south of Glen. The man at his feet died far better and more swiftly than many of the mercenaries' victims.

"Roldo?" called the first man. "Did you hear something?"

The remaining sentry took two steps toward the place where his fellow had fallen, and Daried stepped out of the shadows and whispered another spell.

"*Swift and silent,*" he hissed, "*run back to the Ashaba and keep watch over the crossing there.*"

The big human stared at him slack-jawed for three heartbeats, caught in the power of Daried's spell. Then he nodded vigorously and hurried off into the night, vanishing into the forest. The Ashaba was better than ten miles off in that direction. Daried wondered whether the man would reach the river before the enchantment wore off, or if he would come to his senses somewhere in the middle of the forest.

Four sentries dealt with; the two on the other side of the camp would not be relevant to Daried's efforts. A few fat, warm raindrops began to patter down in the branches overhead. It seemed likely that there would be a downpour within a matter of minutes, but the bladesinger decided that heavy rain would only help him. He ignored the raindrops and glided toward the firelight.

A couple of the Chondathans still sat up, talking with each other near the fire. Better than a score of their fellows lay scattered about the clearing, lying on top of their bedrolls since it was a warm night. Among the sleeping men were three big war-hounds with iron-spiked collars, drowsing with their masters.

The hounds were dangerous . . . but if things went as he planned, they would not trouble him much.

He took a deep breath, and waited for another rumble of thunder. It was not long in coming, and as the treetops sighed and shook in the warm night wind, he whispered the words of an invisibility spell. Then he advanced into the camp, picking his way past the sleeping men all around his feet. The captain slept in a tent apart from his men. It was a surprisingly large and well-made pavilion that must have weighed hundreds of pounds. No elf leader would have burdened himself with such an ostentatious shelter, but Daried supposed that the mercenary captain had likely taken it from some pillaged enemy camp long ago, and had his men carry it along to put on airs of nobility.

Daried slipped into the tent, steel in his hand. He could not help disturbing the flap that served as the tent's entrance, but he did it in silence. Heaps of plunder filled the inside of the tent, the wreckage of dozens of lives ground out in the last few days by the mercenary band. The bladesinger moved past the sacks and bundles. A small partition separated the sleeping area. Grimly, he used the point of his sword to edge the drape out of his way.

The mercenary captain sat facing him behind a small camp desk, his bared sword leaning against the table. He glanced up at the motion of the drapery and frowned, perhaps puzzled by the strange motion of the partition. His eyes gleamed oddly in the faint light of an oil lamp.

On the folding cot, the Morvaeril moonblade sat in its human-made scabbard of red leather. Rain began to patter more heavily against the heavy canvas of the tent, and the air smelled of distant lightning.

Daried smiled coldly and returned his attention to the mercenary leader. The fellow glanced over at the ancient sword lying on the cot, and glanced back in Daried's direction. A tiny motion of his eyebrow betrayed a hint of surprise.

He sees me, Daried realized. He *sees* me!

Whether the captain knew some magic of his own, or possessed some enchanted token that allowed him to discern magical invisibility, Daried did not know. But now he had to strike and strike quickly, because his advantage was gone. In the space of a heartbeat he leaped forward, his swordpoint aimed at the lean man's heart.

But the human captain reached the same conclusion Daried did, and just as quickly. He seized his own sword and with one powerful shove flung the light camp desk into Daried's path. Daried tried to jump over the desk but failed, and found himself sprawling at the feet of the man he'd intended to kill. And his invisibility-spell faded, spoiled by the attack he'd just launched against his foe.

"To arms! To arms!" the captain shouted to his men outside. "We are attacked!" Then he stabbed viciously at Daried, his sword darting and striking like a silver shadow in the darkened tent.

Daried's magical agility saved his life. He threw himself aside, fetching up against the foot of the cot.

"Damn it all to Lolth's black hells!" he growled in Elvish. Then he rolled back in the other direction and threw out a hand to lever himself to his feet, only to snatch it back a moment later as a small viper with jade-green scales struck at his outflung arm. The little serpent's eyes glittered with unnatural intelligence, and it hissed at him maliciously.

A wizard's familiar, the elf realized. That explained much. The leader of the mercenaries was more than he seemed, and Daried would have to live with the consequences of his unfounded assumptions.

"I do not know what your quarrel with me is, elf, but you won't have long to regret your mistake," the human snarled.

He pressed close and slashed at Daried's legs, but Daried finished his roll and got to his knees and one hand. The bladesinger snapped out the words of a spell of his own, a burst of eldritch fire that seared everything around him. The viper recoiled and slithered into the pile of loot it had been hiding in, and the captain roared in rage and staggered back.

Finally free to stand, Daried took a deep breath and threw himself into the state of perfect clarity, of action without thought, that marked the bladesinger's dance. He moved his swordpoint through the familiar passes, and arcane symbols formed in his mind. He retreated out of the mercenary's tent, since he fought best with plenty of clear space, and he would not want to be trapped in the tent between the captain and his warriors.

He emerged into a scene of complete chaos. All around him men struggled to their feet and groped for weapons, shouting to each other. More than a few simply stared in astonishment as he appeared from their captain's tent, an elflord in golden mail whose sword whirled about in a dizzying weave of bright steel.

Only three steps in front of him a scar-faced swordsman with rotten teeth glared at Daried in dull fury. "What in the Nine screaming Hells is going on here?" he roared, sweeping a curved tulwar from his belt.

"The elf tried to kill Lord Sarthos!" someone cried.

The scarred swordsman grunted and threw himself forward. But Daried barked out another spell and shrouded himself in a brilliant aura of blue flame. He reached out to take the scarred man with a thrust to the throat. Like a zephyr of white steel and deadly magic, he danced across the clearing. Lost in the bladesong he hardly knew what he was doing. He slipped into the space between eyeblinks, sharpening his perceptions until it seemed that raindrops sank slowly through the night and lightning-swift swordstrokes were languid and slow.

He cut the legs out from another man and turned to find a war-hound bounding at him. He crouched and readied himself to let the animal have his forearm instead of his throat, but the animal shied away from the magical flame wreathing his body. It growled savagely, filling the night with its barking, but it dared not come any closer. A mercenary nearby was not so lucky. He managed to land a shallow cut across Daried's shoulderblade, but Daried's flame-aura returned the blow with searing heat. Wrapped in blue flame, the man stumbled screaming into the night.

This might work after all, Daried thought. Then the captain—Lord Sarthos, he guessed—came out of his tent. Snarling his own dire invocation, Sarthos threw out his hand and scoured Daried with a bolt of crawling black power. Even in his trance Daried cried out in pain as his side sizzled and smoked, and the strength drained away from his limbs. He stumbled into the path of a grizzled old sergeant with a poleaxe, who nearly took his arm with a powerful overhead chop, and a small wiry man with a pair of curved daggers got close enough to slash him badly across the midsection before the flame-shield drove him back, blinded and screaming.

I have to deal with the wizard, he decided. With the right spell the mercenary lord might immobilize or cripple Daried outright, and he would be cut down in a heartbeat.

Fighting through his exhaustion, Daried threw himself toward the enemy lord. He thrust at the wizard's midsection, but the man easily beat his blade aside with his own.

"Don't use your swords, lads!" Sarthos called to his men. "The elf's guarded by a fire-shield. You'll need spears or arrows for this work."

Stepping back from Daried, the mercenary lord snatched a wand from his belt and riddled Daried with a barrage of magical bolts that burned finger-sized holes in the armor over his heart. Daried stumbled and went to one knee, his bladesinger's trance finally broken by the pain and fatigue. Only his fire-shield served to protect him, and as he looked up, he saw a half-dozen mercenaries approaching with long spears to transfix him where he kneeled.

I underestimated them, he realized. I thought my skill and magic would be enough.

He looked back to the Chondathan lord, who watched him with his teeth bared in a bloodthirsty grin. "You're not as good as you thought, are you?" Sarthos sneered. He gestured to the spearmen.

An arrow flashed in the firelight and struck the pock-faced lord on the right side of his chest, spinning him to the ground. Then another one took a spearman approaching Daried in the eye, dropping the warrior like a puppet with its strings cut. A third arrow lodged in the small of the sergeant's back, driving him to the ground with a strangled cry.

"Archers!" shouted one of the men. "Archers!"

"She shoots as well as she said," Daried murmured in surprise.

He glanced at Lord Sarthos, who sat up on one elbow, grimly wrestling with the arrow in his chest as blood streamed from his wound. The man's breastplate had taken much of the blow, but he gasped with pain and paid no attention to the bladesinger. Other men thrashed into the woods, seeking to flush out their attackers and get out of the firelight.

The Morvaeril moonblade was only fifteen feet away. But it would cost him his life to try for it. With a snarl of frustration, Daried wove a spell of darkness over the camp, plunging the clearing into utter blackness. Then, allowing his fire-shield to gutter out, he staggered to his feet and groped his way out of the mercenaries' camp.

The ill effects of the mercenary lord's black ray seemed to wear off with time. By the time Daried reached a good spot half a mile north of the Chondathan camp, he no longer shook with complete exhaustion. His wounds troubled him, of course, but in a few moments of work he bound the worst of them and decided that he could fight again if he had to. Moving a few yards off the trail, he settled in to wait and watch, wrapped up in his gray-green cloak with little more than his eyes showing in the darkness.

The thunderstorm slowly moved off, leaving the forest dripping wet but noticeably cooler in its wake. It was past midnight, and the moon was sinking quickly toward the west. Another elf might have replayed the skirmish in the camp in his head while he waited, but Daried was not given to regret or wishful thinking. What was done was done; there was no point in wishing otherwise. He would not underestimate his adversaries again.

He more than half-expected the whole band of human sellswords to come crashing down the path at any time, but to his surprise, they did not pursue him. Perhaps they thought there were more elf archers roaming around in the night. With the failing moonlight and the overcast skies, he found it dark indeed under the trees. To human eyes it was likely pitch-black, and even the most blood-thirsty mercenary would think twice about blundering around blindly in the dark.

An hour passed before he began to worry about Nilsa.

At first, he told himself that she was simply circling away from the trail, swinging wide of the camp so as to throw off pursuit. That could easily turn a ten-minute trot into the work of a long, slow hour. But as one hour stretched toward two, he found it harder to remain patient. Did she simply become lost in the darkness? he wondered. Her woodcraft seemed better than that, but in the confusion of the fight at the camp, who knew? Or had she fallen into the hands of the mercenaries? If that was the case . . . Daried sincerely hoped that she'd forced them to kill her instead of taking her captive. He had an idea of what men such as the Chondathans were capable of, and death would have been preferable.

He was wrestling with the question of whether to head back to the camp when she finally appeared, picking her way down the trail. Every few steps she paused and spent three heartbeats listening and peering into the woods.

When she drew closer he stood and called softly, "Here, Nilsa."

The girl started. "You scared me half to death, elf," she muttered. She hurried off the trail and joined him in the shadows.

"Where have you been? What happened?" he demanded.

"I was going to ask you the same thing. You were supposed to run off the whole camp. That was your plan, I seem to recall."

"I did not expect to meet with a competent wizard. Things would have gone differently otherwise."

"If you say so." She snorted softly in the darkness. "After you cast that darkness spell, I tried to lay low and wait out the Chondathans. But they turned loose their hounds, and I realized I couldn't stay hidden for long. So I shot the two dogs that were left, and evaded the men by circling way to the south before doubling back in this direction."

Daried stared at her in the shadows. He knew more than one skilled elf warrior who wouldn't have had the nerve to lie still that close to so many enemies, or the cold calculation to kill the hounds in order to stymie pursuit.

"I misjudged you," he murmured aloud. "I am sorry that I did not think better of you. Or our adversaries, for that matter."

"You don't know the half of it," Nilsa answered. "When I circled to the south, I came across a very large camp, a little less than a mile farther down toward Battledale. Chondathans, just like the others, but I'd guess their numbers at three hundred, perhaps more."

"Three hundred?" Daried repeated. His heart grew cold. "Are you certain?"

"I didn't count heads, but I know what I saw. Does the exact number matter?"

Daried shook his head. A couple of hours ago he would have dismissed the girl's claim as wild exaggeration, but he was coming to learn that he could take her at her word.

"If you are right, they must be on their way north to invade the western portions of the dale, behind our defenses along the Ashaba. The marauders that came to Glen were scouting the route for the main force."

"That's what I make of it, too," Nilsa said. She sighed and looked away. "Naturally, they indulged themselves in any murder or mayhem they liked while they were at it. Glen just happened to be in their way."

Daried quickly gathered his belongings. "Come. We have not a moment to lose," he said. "By daybreak these woods will be swarming with the Sembians' mercenaries."

He hurried back to the trail, Nilsa a couple of steps behind him, and set off at once. By his reckoning they had twenty-five miles, perhaps a little more, back to the human village. The bladesinger was tired and his wounds felt stiff, but with luck he thought he might be able to reach his warriors sometime in the late afternoon. The question was how much the half-human girl would slow him down. If she couldn't keep up, he didn't see any alternative to leaving her behind and making the best speed he could alone.

He took a quick glance over his shoulder to see how Nilsa was faring. She jogged along a short distance behind him, a sheen of sweat over her brow, but her breathing was easy and even.

They ran together through the summer night, slowing only a little when the moon finally faded altogether. He noticed that Nilsa managed better in the darkness than a full-blooded human would have—one small gift of her unfortunate elf ancestor, whoever he or she had been. Perhaps it also meant that she'd tire less easily, too.

Nilsa caught him looking back at her. Between strides she asked, "Can you stop them, elf?"

"If they are as strong as you say, then they are too many for us."

"Then what will you do?"

"This attack will turn the flank of our army at Ashabenford. I have to get word to Lord Gaerth and warn him."

Daried returned his attention to the trail at his feet. The last thing he needed was to turn an ankle on an unseen root.

"Will he be able to fight them off?" Nilsa asked.

"He could, but it would be a mistake. We can't risk getting trapped between the Sembian army east of the Ashaba and these mercenaries coming up from the south." He trotted on a few steps, gathering his breath. "Gaerth will abandon the Ashaba defenses and pull back before we are trapped and destroyed along the river."

Nilsa kept up in silence for a time before she spoke again. "That won't do much to help the folk in Glen or Ashabenford."

"There is no help for it," he told her. "Enemies on this side of the Ashaba makes the defense of Ashabenford pointless. There is nothing to be served by allowing our warriors to be destroyed here."

"While your elf warriors are abandoning the dale, mercenary bands will ravage my home!" Nilsa snapped. She stumbled in the darkness and swore to herself. Daried turned back and offered her a hand, but the girl waved him off angrily.

"I do not know what you think I can do," Daried said. "I have scarcely twenty warriors under my command. We do not suffice to stop a warband of hundreds. As matters stand, flight is our only option."

"We can muster close to a hundred bows in our own defense. If you aid us, we might be able to drive off the attack."

Farmers and merchants, fighting against hardened sellswords three times their number? Daried shook his head. There was no sense in it. If he had fifty or sixty skilled elf warriors, he could whittle down their strength with a strategy of ambush-and-retreat, keeping ahead of the slow-footed humans and avoiding a stand-up fight. But the folk of Glen would get themselves slaughtered if they tried any such thing—especially since the Chondathans evidently had at least one capable wizard leading their troops. It would be a slaughter.

They reached the old elven crossing about an hour before daybreak, and paused to splash cold water over their faces and brows. Daried's legs burned with fatigue and his wounds ached abominably, but he knew his own endurance. He'd be exhausted when he reached the town, but he would reach it.

Nilsa's hair was plastered to her head by sweat and the morning damp, and she looked pale in the gray glimmers of daybreak. She was careful not to sit down while they rested, walking in slow circles by the riverbank as she studied the old river-crossing. The river's song filled the air, murmuring of gravel and worn stone.

"I don't suppose you have any magic to make this place unusable, do you?" she asked Daried.

He shook his head. "I have no illusions suitable for concealing it, and much of my battle magic is exhausted. Given a few hours of work with my hands, I could do something. But I do not think we have the time." He glanced up at the gray streaks brightening the sky in the east. "I expect the Chondathans are already marching. They know they've been found out. That means speed is their best weapon now."

"Lathander preserve us, you're right," Nilsa muttered. She turned away from the coming dawn, and hugged her arms to her chest. "Could I have been any more stupid? The whole warband will be on our heels. I thought I was going to kill my father's murderers, but all I've done is lead the rest of them back to Glen."

Daried grimaced. In truth, he had no answers for her. He had little gift for meaningless words of comfort, and he simply couldn't lie about what he saw coming for the tiny village of Glen and its folk in the next few days. He'd seen the marauder's handiwork at the home of Nilsa's father and the homesteads along their bloodstained trail. Still, he tried.

"They were marching against Glen anyway, Nilsa," he said. "If you hadn't pursued the marauders, you would not have discovered the danger that approaches your village. And you would not have been close at hand to rescue me from the consequences of my own foolishness."

She looked over her shoulder at him. "My father's death is only the beginning, isn't it?"

The bladesinger studied the girl. In the growing half-light he could see the elf traces in her features more clearly. Her eyes were as green as spring, and yet she had a sprinkling of freckles across the bridge of her nose. Whatever else she was, she was hardly unfortunate in her heritage. In her face an elf's timelessness met a human's youth, a human's passion, and was transformed into something new again. He could read the despair, the exhaustion, the grief in her features, and yet fire and determination still flickered in her eyes. She was the daughter of heroes, after all. And a daughter of the People, too.

He met her eyes evenly. "It will be hard on you and your people, Nilsa. But nothing is written yet. This is what we have won with our foolish chase—a few hours to make our choices. Perhaps we will choose more wisely today than we did yesterday."

The girl shivered in the cool damp air. She glanced to the north, perhaps imagining the long miles still ahead of them. Then she looked down at her feet and said, "Daried, I am sorry you weren't able to get your family's sword back. My grandfather shouldn't have taken it. I don't think he meant to hurt you or your folk, but that doesn't make it right."

He shrugged awkwardly. "I should have held my temper in check," he said. "Besides, I am not sure that I have lost my chance to get the Morvaeril moonblade back. I think I am not done yet with Lord Sarthos. Our paths will cross soon enough."

Nilsa gave him a sharp look. "You are going to help us fight the sellswords?"

Daried nodded. "Yes . . . I owe you that much for saving my life in the marauders' camp." He shouldered his pack again, and gestured at the river-crossing. "Come, we have a hard day's travel ahead of us still."

An hour before sunset, Daried and Nilsa parted ways at the smoking ruin of her father's farm. The girl hurried back to the town to carry warning of the Sembian column marching up from the south, while Daried sped back to his warriors' encampment by the banks of the Ashaba.

He stumbled into camp covered with road dust, his legs hollow and weak, his wounds throbbing and blazing like lines of fire drawn across his limbs and body. Distantly he noted the high clear call of welcome from the sentry, and the rustle of activity as elves emerged from shelters or came running from work in the woods nearby to hail his return. "It seems I've been missed," he muttered to no one in particular. Grimacing in pain, he allowed himself to fall to the ground by the shelter he used as his own. He seized a waterskin close at hand and drank long and deep, then upended the rest of its contents over his head.

"By Corellon's sword, Daried, what happened to you?" The mage Teriandyln appeared and knelt by his side. His face was sharp with anxiety. "Where have you been?"

"Summon Andariel," Daried said. "I must have him carry a message to Lord Gaerth right away."

Teriandyln frowned, but he motioned to a warrior standing nearby. The fellow nodded and hurried off to find the young moon elf. Daried forestalled the wizard's questions with a raised hand, fighting against his exhaustion and organizing his thoughts. "Have our scouts found any sign of the Sembians in the area?"

"No, we have seen no signs that the Sembians are nearby. Another demon appeared yesterday, though. We spent the day tracking the monster." The wizard paused, then added, "Your sword was missed, Daried. Rollael and Feldyrr were badly wounded fighting the hellspawn."

"I am sorry for that," Daried said. He looked away. "I should not have been so quick to set aside my responsibilities here. But it may have been for the best that I did."

The moon elf Andariel ran up to the shelter and sketched a hasty bow. "You sent for me, Lord Selsherryn?"

"I did. You must ride to Ashabenford at once, and take this message to Vesilde Gaerth—or whomever you find in command, if Gaerth is not there. Tell him that a strong force of Chondathan mercenaries is marching north through the forest. They've found an old trail through Cormanthor that opens into the western verge of the dale. It seems that there is an old elven crossing of the Ashaba there that we did not know about."

The warriors around him exchanged grim looks at that. They understood the peril that threatened the elf army in Ashabenford.

"They are at least three hundred strong," Daried continued, "but there may be more following. As of moonset last night, they were about five miles south of the river, and twenty miles west of Glen. I think they will reach us here around sunset tomorrow, and Ashabenford late in the day after.

"It is my intention to oppose their march for as long as possible, and help the Glen-folk to defend their town."

The other elves did not manage to conceal their surprise at that, either. They knew that he had had no plan to skirmish against such a large force or to let the elf company be tied down in the defense of a nameless human village. If he were not so tired, Daried would have found their guarded glances more than a little amusing. As it was, he pretended that he simply didn't notice. He looked up at Andariel, and said, "Repeat what I have just told you."

Andariel repeated his message, almost word for word. Daried judged it good enough. With a weary nod, he clasped Andariel's shoulder. "You are our swiftest rider. Ride quickly, but ride safe. It is more important for the message to get to Gaerth than it is for you to astonish us with your speed."

"I will not fail you, Lord Selsherryn," the serious young moon elf replied. He bowed again and hurried off.

"That's taken care of," Daried sighed. Wearily he pulled his dusty gauntlets from his hands, and began to unbuckle his fine golden mail. After three days of constant wear the armor, light and well-fitted as it was, felt like a lead shroud.

Teriandyln seated himself on the ground nearby. "I don't recall that you had any intention of fighting such a strong force," he said, speaking to Daried alone. "Are you sure this is wise, my friend?"

"We need to give Lord Gaerth time to slip away from Ashabenford. Every hour we delay the Sembians' mercenaries gives our warriors a better chance to withdraw without a fight. And we will provide the folk who live in the eastern portion of this dale with a chance to escape the armies converging here."

"If you are right, they are ten times our number, Daried. Perhaps twenty times."

"We do not have to face them alone. The Glen-folk can muster a hundred bows in their own defense."

The wizard looked at Daried thoughtfully. "You did not give much account to that when we first took up our watch here."

"I hadn't seen any of them shoot then. Now I have." Daried laid his armor on the ground, and stretched himself out on the blankets, loosening his tunic. He could already feel Reverie stealing over him, but he resisted long enough to add, "Make sure you set watchers along the track leading southwest out of Glen. That's the road the mercenaries will follow. We need to find the mercenaries and shadow them until they get here."

"It will be as you say," Teriandyln answered. "Get some rest, Daried. We will rouse you when we need you."

The bladesinger nodded once, and sank into silence.

Late the following afternoon, scouts sighted the mercenary warband marching on Glen. They had moved faster than Daried expected, but many of the mercenaries were mounted. A few of the Chondathans rode big warhorses draped in leather barding, while most of the other riders made do with a saddle and blanket. The men who weren't riding simply walked alongside the column, with dust caking their faces and sweat staining their dirty leather jerkins.

They must have brought most of the horses with them, Daried decided. It seemed unlikely that the marauders could have appropriated so many horses from the farmsteads dotting the countryside south of Glen. And that meant they faced even more enemies than he'd feared—Nilsa would certainly have noticed any horses corralled near the camp she had found. Given that, Daried couldn't avoid concluding that some of them at least were mercenaries they had not yet encountered.

"I did not expect so many riders," Teriandyln said softly.

"Nor did I," Daried admitted.

He brushed the hair out of his eyes. It was another hot day. Insects hummed and chirped in the still air. They stood in the apple orchards of Andar's manor, warm and fragrant in the late afternoon sun. The blossoms had fallen long ago, and small, tart golden fruit clustered in the branches. In a tenday or so they'd be ready to pick, but Daried wondered if anyone would be left to tend to that work by the time the apples ripened.

The Chondathans approached slowly, following the dusty cart track through broad grainfields that shone golden in the sun. A few hundred yards farther, and their road would lead them past the orchard where Daried and his warriors waited.

The sharp-featured mage frowned. "The cavalry ruin your battle plan, Daried. Perhaps it would be wiser to just let them pass. Most of the Glen-folk have taken shelter across the Ashaba in Cormanthor. These marauders will find nothing but an empty village."

The bladesinger studied the approaching warriors, taking their measure for a long moment. Then he shook his head. "No, we will continue. I suspect that many of those fellows won't handle their horses well in a fight."

"Do not underestimate them, my friend."

"Trust me, Teriandyln, I am through with making that mistake. I would have liked fewer riders or more bows, but this is the fight we have, and we will do our best." Daried did not take his eyes away from the approaching band. "Pass word to our warriors to aim first at any man riding a barded horse—those will be the men who have skill in fighting on horseback."

He waited for a short time, as the mercenaries came closer. The air was heavy and humid, as it always was in this wide green land in summer. The scent of vanished apple blossoms lingered in his memory. Evermeet had no season like it; the fair island of the west was kissed by ocean breezes throughout the year. He hadn't realized how much he had missed the lush richness of Cormanthor's summers in the decades he'd been away.

"Now?" Teriandyln asked.

The bladesinger drew in one deep breath. "Yes," he answered, and made a single curt gesture with his hand.

Twenty elves hidden among the apple trees bent their white bows and loosed arrows at the hundreds of mercenaries marching north toward Glen.

In the space of three heartbeats, chaos erupted in the mercenary ranks. Silver death sleeted into the horsemen. Men slumped from their saddles, arrows feathering throat or chest. Others roared in sudden pain and anguish, pinioned by elven shafts that did not kill in a single stroke. Horses screamed and reared, footmen scattered, and another round of arrows struck, moving farther back into the human ranks.

Despite their surprise, the Chondathans were not easily broken. Shouting and swearing, the human mercenaries began moving while the third flight was still in the air. Footmen shrugged large diamond-shaped shields off their shoulders and hurried to kneel shoulder-to-shoulder, interlocking their shields to form a wall of wood and leather against the elven arrows. Crossbowmen closed up behind the shield wall and began to fire blindly back into the trees. Quarrels hissed and whirred through the air over Daried's head.

Sweeping his sword from its sheath, a captain near the head of the mercenaries avoided several arrows whistling past him. "Come on, you dogs!" he roared. Shouting defiance at the unseen archers, he led a score of the riders straight into the orchard.

Farther down the Chondathan column, large bands of cavalry swept out into the open grainfields on either side of the track and rode hard, circling wide around the covered ground.

"Watch the flanks!" Teriandyln warned. "They're trying to trap us here."

"I see them," Daried replied. But first they had to deal with the Chondathans storming the orchard. He pointed at the captain and riders thundering toward the elves' hiding places. "Take that one first!"

The mage nodded once. Deftly he retrieved a pinch of silvery dust from a pouch at his side. With a weaving motion of his hand he cast the dust into the air, then snapped out the words of a deadly spell and gestured at the approaching riders. Each mote of dust hanging in the air above his fingertips grew into a long needle of silver-white ice, and flew swifter than an arrow at the charging horsemen. The brilliant shards punched through steel breastplates and mail shirts like paper, only to explode an instant later in a white flash of deadly frost. The first impulsive rush of the Chondathan horsemen disintegrated in the lethal hail of frost-needles, man and beast alike pierced through or seared by cold so intense that flesh whitened and blood froze.

Glistening frost and dark blood blighted the apple trees. Daried winced, but he clapped the mage on the shoulder and ordered, "Now move! They may have mages of their own."

The two elves dashed back thirty yards, darting between the trees. Behind them a great blast of fire erupted in the orchard, just where they had been standing. A wave of sulfurous hot air flapped Daried's cloak around his shoulders and singed the hair on the back of his head. Daried went another ten yards or so, crouched behind a tree, and quickly surveyed the skirmish.

Arrows still hissed into the ranks of the Chondathans on the road, but they were far fewer. The elf archers moved between shots, trying to avoid being spotted. And Daried could see at a glance that the riders sweeping through the fields around the orchard were drawing the fire of the archers on his flanks. In a matter of moments he and his warriors would be trapped in the grove, and that would be all for them.

He clutched a silver medallion hanging above his heart, and whispered the words of a spell. The magic carried his words to all the elves in the grove, whether close by or a hundred yards away.

"Fall back now!" he commanded them. *"To the second line, quickly!"*

Together, the bladesinger and the wizard turned and sprinted toward the north, heading for the far side of the great orchard. Daried glimpsed more of his warriors, appearing and disappearing as they ran through the trees alongside them. He could hear the distant shouts of the humans behind him—it had not taken the Chondathans long at all to realize that their ambushers were in flight.

They know what they're doing, he decided. After meeting the wizard-warrior Sarthos two nights ago he hadn't really expected that the mercenary leaders would prove incompetent, but he'd still hoped to surprise them with his show of resistance.

They reached the edge of the orchard and broke into the open fields beyond. Daried lengthened his stride and ran at his best pace, all too aware of the lack of cover around him and his warriors. At a glance it seemed that most of his warriors were still with him—more than a dozen elves silently dashed across the field at his heels. But sweeping up from the west, only a couple of hundred yards away, threescore cavalrymen appeared, galloping furiously around the great orchard.

"Daried!" called Teriandyln.

"I see them!" he replied. "Keep on!"

Across the fields a long, low ridge covered by a dense thicket lay like a green wall across their path. Daried risked another glance over his shoulder, and altered his course to the right, veering away from the oncoming horsemen so that they would take just a little longer to overtake his warriors. The hot sun beat down on him, and the golden wheat weaving around his waist forced him to take high, plunging strides, wading more than running. He kept his eyes fixed on the dark thicket ahead and did not allow himself to slow down, even though sweat streamed down his face and the humid air seemed as thick as molasses in his lungs.

Behind him, he could hear the drumming hooves of the riders following. The shouts and cries of the mercenaries took on a savage, triumphal tone—and the elf warriors were still fifty yards short of the copse ahead.

A single horn-call sounded from somewhere in the woods ahead. Instantly Daried shouted to his warriors, "Down!" He threw himself into the tall grain and rolled, wheat stalks whipping his face and arms.

Over his head better than eighty bows thrummed at

once. In the shelter of the trees ahead, just about every man of Glen who could pull a bow—and some of the women, as well—rose up and fired at the cavalrymen intent on riding down the withdrawing elves. They did not all shoot as well as elf warriors would have, but some did, and the rest certainly shot well enough. Horses screamed and reared, riders toppled from saddles, and others wheeled in panic beneath the withering fire. After three quick volleys the Chondathan mercenaries spun around and spurred away from the green thicket, leaving half their number dead or dying at the feet of the elves they'd intended to ride down.

Daried and his warriors leaped back to their feet, and trotted into the shelter of the thickets. The bladesinger found Nilsa waiting for him, alongside Earek, the tall innkeeper from the White Horse. More villagers and farmers stood nearby, grim looks of satisfaction on their faces. They were dressed in a ragged collection of armor ranging from none at all to old mail shirts or jerkins of rivet-studded leather, but all carried well-cared for bows, and many wore swords or axes at their belts, too.

There's more to these Dalesfolk than meets the eye, Daried decided. "That was well done, Nilsa. We would have been ridden down if you and your folk had not shot so well."

"I waited as long as I could before sounding the signal," Nilsa said. She shrugged awkwardly. "I didn't think they would be after you so quickly. It's a good thing you are fleet of foot, or you never would have gotten away from them."

"So?" Earek asked Daried. He served as the town's militia captain, since the death of Nilsa's father. The easy-going innkeeper became a different man in the field. His bland smile and easy laugh were gone, replaced by determination and worry. "How many do we face?"

Daried took a quick tally of the elf warriors who remained with him. Of the twenty he had had in the orchard, sixteen stood with him. Two were wounded, and Hycellyn, who had waited with the Dalesfolk, tended to them with her healing spells. There was a small chance that his missing warriors might still be hiding in the orchard, unable to rejoin him, but it was more likely that they had been caught before they could make their escape.

He sighed and turned back to his human allies. "We counted about two hundred on foot and the same number mounted. We shot many riders, but not enough to even the odds. I think you should consider abandoning your plan, and withdraw while you still can."

Earek watched the mercenary riders, hovering out of bowshot near the apple orchard. The riders milled about, glaring fiercely at the treeline in which the elves and the Mistledalefolk waited.

He shook his head. "You did your part, now we will do ours. They won't get across those fields without losing a lot of men, and they can see that already. Remember, they're mercenaries—they're paid to fight, not to die. If we can wound or kill a good number, the rest might decide it isn't worth it to press the attack."

"I hope he is right," Teriandyln murmured in Elvish. *"Many of these folk will die if the mercenaries decide that dead comrades make for bigger shares of the plunder."*

Daried studied the land carefully. It was a good place to stand, and the densely wooded ridge offered a covered retreat, at least for a couple hundred yards. But behind the hill lay open farmland around the Harvalmeer manor. If enemy horsemen broke through the woods into the fields behind them, few of the defenders would escape from their line.

"Nilsa, can men on horseback get around this ridge?" he asked.

"Not easily. It runs for several miles like this. To the east it gets higher and rockier until it meets the forest and the Ashaba. To the west, it runs out into a wide stretch of difficult woods."

"You've barricaded the cut where the road passes through?"

"As best we could," Earek answered for her. "We felled several trees across the road, and made a thornbrake a good ten feet thick. I've got more archers covering the cut."

Nothing to do but wait, the bladesinger decided. "I'll keep four of my warriors with me, and intersperse the rest in pairs along the line," he told the Glen-folk. "If we have to give ground, we'll withdraw to the west, staying in the woods along the ridge."

"That would place the Chondathans between us and our families," one of the men nearby grumbled.

"Yes, but if we fell back toward the east, I am afraid that we could get trapped with the river at our back. Or, worse yet, we might lead the battle to the refuge where the rest of your people are hiding." Daried knew that his warriors could escape across the Ashaba even if the mercenaries were on their heels, but he did not think that the villagers could manage it.

"If we hold them here, we won't have to make that choice," Nilsa said.

Daried quickly counted off his warriors and sent them to their places in the villagers' ranks. Then, just in case, he sent a pair of scouts to the back side of the ridge to provide warning in case the Chondathans surprised them by finding a way to get around or through the ridge unseen. Then he settled in to watch and wait.

The Chondathan riders gathered at the far side of the field, under the shade of the orchard. Men rode back and forth, carrying messages and orders. Standard-bearers unfurled their scarlet flags and took up positions. Then rank after rank of footmen emerged from the orchard, arranging themselves behind the standards. Men buckled on heavier armor and unslung their shields, making ready for battle. The elves watched while the Dalesfolk fidgeted and muttered nervously to one another.

"Something is happening," Nilsa said.

Daried followed her gaze. Beneath the main standard a number of sellswords arrayed in fine armor with plumed helmets arranged themselves in ranks. Even from a distance, he could see the difference in arms and armor between the men by the standard and the rest of the mercenaries. Then he caught a glimpse of a tall, lean man standing behind the others, weaving his arms in the sinuous motions of a spellcaster.

"That's Sarthos," he said. "The wizard-captain from the camp."

"What is he doing?" Nilsa asked.

"Working magic," the bladesinger answered. He glanced at Teriandyln. "I can't make it out at this distance. Can you?"

The sun elf wizard shook his head. "No, it's too far. But I think he is not the only wizard among the Chondathans. I've seen a couple of others casting spells."

Horns sounded somewhere in the mass of the Chondathan fighters. Raggedly the footsoldiers started forward, marching across the yellow field behind their banners. Rows of interlocked shields guarded the front ranks, while the men in the second and third ranks kept their shields raised overhead. Bands of horsemen pranced and waited back in the orchard.

"They're coming!" cried voices all up and down the line.

"Steady!" Earek called.

"The horsemen are waiting to ride us down after we rout," Teriandyln observed quietly to Daried.

"Possibly," Daried answered. He wasn't certain of that yet. Sarthos and his Chondathans were up to something sinister; he could feel it. He thought again of calling for the retreat, but it would be hard to get the Glen-folk away at this point . . . even if they would agree to go. They were not likely to flee until they had seen whether the Chondathans could hurt them or not.

"Let them get closer, lads!" Earek called to the villagers. "Don't waste arrows on those shields yet. Wait until you can choose your marks and make your arrows count!"

The footmen slogged closer, crouching behind their

shields. The line began to drift to their right, as each man in the line consciously or unconsciously closed up under the shield of the man beside him. Steel and leather rasped with each step, and a chorus of challenges, catcalls, and foul oaths rose up from those sellswords who were inclined to shout or snarl defiance at the archers waiting for them.

"Fire!" Earek shouted.

The bows of the Dalesfolk thrummed, and arrows streaked out from the thicket, buzzing like angry wasps. Many glanced from shields or breastplates, but the Dalesfolk had waited for such a short range that their powerful bows were perfectly capable of driving a yard-long shaft through armor, given a clean hit. For their part, the elf archers did not try to power their missiles through a foe's armor. Instead, elven arrows found throats, eyes, or underarms, places where a swordsman's cuirass did not guard him. Mercenaries shrieked, swore, or stumbled to the ground, wounded or dying. With each man that fell, gaps appeared in the shield wall, and more arrows sleeted into the mass of soldiers.

The Chondathans let out a roar of rage and surged forward, charging to bring the archers to sword's reach. Despite the weight of their steel, they covered the last few yards of the open field faster than Daried could have imagined. Men dropped and died with every step, but still they came on—and now Daried saw their plan. Across the field, the waiting horsemen spurred their mounts forward, charging in the wake of the armored footsoldiers. With the Dalesfolk and elves occupied in shooting the men right in front of them, the riders covered the open space unmolested.

"Teriandyln! Stop the cavalry!" Daried cried.

The wizard barked out the words of a spell, and hurled a scathing blast of fire at the oncoming riders. A tremendous detonation left a dozen men and horses dead in the field, and a black pall of smoke rose over the field. At once Teriandyln turned and threw another spell at a different group of riders. "There are too many!" he shouted back at Daried.

While the wizard wove his deadly spells and arrows continued to scythe through the Chondathan ranks, Daried drew a slender wand from his belt and turned his attention to the line of swordsmen swarming into the trees. The wand was Teriandyln's, but Daried could use it well enough. He leveled it at the first group of Chondathans and snapped out its activating word. A brilliant blue stroke of lightning blasted five men from their feet. Recklessly Daried triggered the wand again and again, trying to stop the attack in its tracks.

For a moment, he thought they might succeed. Scoured by arrows and lightning, the footsoldiers faltered at the very edge of the woods, and the wheeling bands of horsemen beyond shied away from Teriandyln's fiery blasts. But then a wave of dull thuds or booms like distant thunder rippled through the woods behind Daried and his warriors, filling the shadows beneath the trees with a sulfurlike stench.

"Devils! Devils!" came the cry.

Daried wheeled in sudden horror, and found a gang of hamatulas—barbed devils—materializing in the middle of the defender's ranks. Eyes aglow with emerald hate, the fearsome creatures immediately tore into any villager or elf hapless enough to be within talon's reach. Blasts of hellfire blackened the trees and seared flesh.

Without a moment's thought, Daried slid easily into the bladesinger's trance and glided forward to meet the hellborn fiends. The furious battle around him faded into a strange, dull silence. Distantly he noted the skirmish of Chondathan swordsmen and Dalesfolk archers around him, the desperate cut and parry of men and women fighting for their lives, but he simply avoided the fray and moved to the first of the monsters.

The creature grinned maliciously and hurled a great orb of green fire at Daried, but the bladesinger whispered the word of a spell and caught the whirling ball of flame on his swordpoint. He flicked it over his shoulder at a Chondathan swordsman behind him, immolating the man with the devil's fire. Then there was a sudden clash of talons and barbs against elven steel, and the creature recoiled, bleeding from several deep cuts. Daried spun from a high guard to a low crouch, and used the lightning wand in his left hand to strike down another three swordsmen before returning to his duel against the hamatula.

"Now you die, elf!" the hamatula hissed.

It sprang at him, arms spread wide, seeking to impale the bladesinger on the forest of spikes covering its body. Daried folded to the ground and ran it through the belly, rolling under its feet as it crashed to the ground behind him. Jagged spines caught him at the shoulder and the top of his back, but he simply set the pain aside and rolled up onto his feet, continuing his blade-dance.

More battle magic crashed and thundered in the thicket, blasts of fire and stabbing forks of lightning. He glimpsed Nilsa, moving gracefully among the trees as she drew and shot, taking a man with every arrow. Then he spotted another barbed devil, crouching over the torn body of Feldyrr, a moon elf. The monster leered at the dying elf as it clenched its talons in his chest.

Daried knocked the devil away from his warrior with darting daggers of magic. The devil staggered to its feet with a hiss of rage. It hurled its fearsome will against the bladesinger, trying to paralyze him with its terrible magic, but in his trance Daried was hardly conscious of such things. While the devil glared at him, he spun close and sliced its throat open with a long draw cut, leaving it to crumple to the ground beside Feldyrr's body.

He danced through a knot of mercenary swordsmen next, leaving one man blinded with his magic and another dying from a thrust through the belly. But then he was driven out of his trance by the staggering impact of a barbed devil hurling itself into his back like a battering ram of red-hot steel. Agonizing hooks and spikes pierced

Daried's flesh in a dozen places, but his golden mail held just enough to keep him from being killed at once.

The devil on his back hissed and spat fire, burning Daried as it tried to clamp its foul black fangs in the back of the bladesinger's neck. He struggled in the dirt and underbrush to get his feet under him or get an arm free so that he could get away, but the devil's strength was terrible. It tore a bloody gobbet of flesh from his shoulder, and despite himself Daried screamed.

"Get off me!" he snarled.

"You did not like that?" the creature hissed in his ear. "Ah, how you will sing before I am through with you, delicious elfling!"

Daried reversed his grip on his thinblade and tried to stab at the monster, but the devil swatted the blade out of his hand. Desperately Daried rolled back in the other direction, and found the lightning wand with his groping fingers. Quick as a cat he jammed the end of the wand over his shoulder into the devil's face, and blew its head apart with a stroke of lightning that picked him up and flung him down a dozen feet away.

His mail charred and smoking, Daried climbed unsteadily to his feet. The arming-coat under his mail was sopping wet with his own blood. Ignoring the clamor of battle all around, he staggered over to the devil's twitching corpse and retrieved his thinblade. Then he straightened up as much as he could, and tried to make sense of what was going on around him. It seemed that the battle still continued, though scores of dead or dying humans—and some elves, too—littered the ground.

"Aillesil Seldarie," he breathed.

The Dalesfolk hadn't been overcome yet, but it didn't seem possible that they could keep fighting against such odds. At least no more barbed devils remained in the fight.

"I had a feeling we would meet again, elf."

Daried wheeled and found himself facing the wizard Sarthos. The Chondathan lord wore a breastplate worked in the image of a snarling dragon, and wore an ornate helm over his stubbled scalp. The human smiled cruelly.

"A shame you are wounded already," he said. "I hoped to try you at your best. That would have been a contest to remember."

He carried the Morvaeril moonblade bared in his hand.

"You should take care with your wishes, Chondathan," the bladesinger rasped. "You might get exactly what you want."

Ignoring the hollow unsteadiness of his legs and the stabbing aches that crisscrossed his back, he raised his thinblade in challenge. Slowly he circled Sarthos, taking the measure of his opponent while the battle raged all around them.

The mercenary struck first. Snarling the words of a sinister spell, he threw out his arm and launched a black bolt of crackling power at the bladesinger. But Daried was still warded by the parrying spell he'd used to deflect the fireball the first barbed devil had thrown at him. He managed to interpose his thinblade and bat the ebon ray back at Sarthos. The ray caught the mercenary wizard on his side and spun him half around, its frigid darkness draining away strength and vitality.

Sarthos struggled to fight off the effects of his own spell, and Daried saw his chance. He stumbled in close to the Chondathan and managed to cut the man badly across the arm and face before Sarthos reeled away, blood streaming from his wounds. The bladesinger pressed his attack, stretching for his last reserves of strength as his blade glittered and flew, weaving in the complex and perfect patterns taught by the swordmasters of Evermeet.

But Sarthos was almost as skilled as Daried in bladework. He matched Daried's attacks for five heartbeats, steel leaping to meet steel, and Daried managed a quick spiraling riposte that caught the moonblade in the human's hands and sent it spinning through the air. It landed point-down in the forest loam and stuck there, quivering.

The Chondathan lord fell back from Daried's attack and cried out in a harsh, hissing language that brought stabbing pain to the elf's ears. "Nevarhem! Sheor! Aid me!" he shrieked.

In the space of an instant, two more barbed devils appeared in clouds of brimstone smoke, displacing the air in twin thunderclaps as they teleported to their master's aid.

The bladesinger eyed his new adversaries without fear. He had no strength to meet them, but he would try anyway, and death came to everyone in time, didn't it? He could only meet it as best he could. He turned back to Sarthos and smiled coldly through his pain and exhaustion.

"It seems that we have determined who is the better swordsman," he remarked.

"You'll find that little comfort when you're dead!" the Chondathan snarled. He motioned to the devils, and the creatures advanced on Daried, claws and spikes reaching for him.

"You'll precede him, murderer!" Nilsa called.

She stood near the Morvaeril moonblade, drew her bowstring to her ear, and took aim at the warlord. But the barbed devils stalking Daried leaped for her so swiftly that she couldn't take the shot. She whirled and buried her white arrow feather-deep in the chest of the first monster, staggering it in its tracks. Then, out of arrows, she dropped her bow and seized the hilt of the sword in the ground before her.

The instant her hand touched the hilt, the Morvaeril moonblade flared to life. A shock of brilliant white light flashed from the ancient elven steel, and a row of incandescent runes marking the blade flared so brightly that Daried had to look away.

"Impossible," he breathed. "That moonblade was dead. Dead!"

Sarthos and the remaining devil hesitated, blinded and astonished as much as Daried himself. For that matter, Nilsa herself stood staring dumbly at the sword in her hand, struck senseless in amazement. But then the last of the devils recovered from its surprise. With a shrill screech, it hurled itself against Nilsa, talons and spikes reaching for her heart.

"Nilsa, the devil!" the bladesinger cried.

The girl glanced up just in time to bring the sword-point up. The hamatula halted its mad rush and tried to leap around the blade, but with one efficient turn and cut Nilsa took its foul head clean off its shoulders. The moonblade's white fire seared through its infernal flesh like sunshine burning through a mist. The first hamatula, the one that she had shot, scrambled to its feet and surged at her, but Nilsa backed away two quick steps and slashed its foul talon off its arm as it reached for her. The monster shrieked and stumbled. She stabbed the moonblade through the devil's heart, and sent it back to the foul hell it had been summoned from.

Sarthos paled, then he started to speak the words of a deadly spell against her. But Daried found the strength for one final leap of his own. Spinning through a low crouch he cut Sarthos's legs out from under him, and sent the Chondathan warlord to the ground. The wizard gaped at him in shock and astonishment—and Daried's thinblade pinned him to the ground.

"That was for Nilsa's father," the bladesinger said.

Sarthos gaped up at him, blood starting from his mouth. Then, to Daried's surprise, his features seemed to melt and shift, becoming leaner, more angular. Black-ribbed wings grew from the dying wizard's shoulders, and his pockmarked human face became scarlet and flecked with fine scales. His ears changed from rounded to pointed, and his eyes took on an elf's slant.

"I'll be damned," Daried muttered. "You're a fey'ri."

No wonder Sarthos had shown such skill with both blade and spell. He was likely as much a bladesinger as Daried himself, for the fey'ri were ancient sun elves touched by demonic blood. They wielded magic and blades with the same skill and traditions as Daried or any other son of Evermeet.

“Daried!” Nilsa hurried to his side. “You’re wounded.”

“It’s nothing,” the bladesinger said. “Go aid your folk, if you can.”

He stood over his foe, watching the fey’ri lord die. Then his own strength gave out too, and he toppled to the ground an arm’s reach from his adversary.

The last thing Daried saw of the battle was Nilsa raising the Morvaeril moonblade to the setting sun, as the Chondathans staggered away from the deadly woods.

At daybreak of the second day following the Battle of Glen, Daried and his surviving warriors rode slowly out of the town. Only eleven of his small company remained. Hycellyn lived, but Daried’s friend Teriandyln had fallen in the fighting along the ridge, killed by the fey’ri’s devils while he flung spell after spell with the last of his strength.

The elves found Nilsa and Earek waiting by the White Horse, standing alongside the road to see them off. Nilsa wore a plain blue dress, looking for all the world like a simple village girl instead of a skilled warrior and the heroine of her people. She stood stiffly, her back straight as an iron—beneath her blouse she was bandaged tightly around her ribs, where she’d taken a bad sword-cut during the fighting in the woods. But other than a faint wince of discomfort, she did not let her pain show.

“So that’s it?” she asked Daried as he rode past. “You’re just going to leave?”

Daried reined in his mount. The rest of his company halted as well, waiting on him. “Yes, I am afraid so,” he said. “Vesilde Gaerth is drawing back from Ashabenford. We must rejoin the Crusade.”

Earek stepped forward and met Daried’s eyes. “Lord Selsherryn, I don’t know how to say this, but I’ll try: Thank you for helping us against the Chondathans. There is no way we can repay you for the lives of your comrades, other than to promise that we will honor their sacrifice for as long as we and our descendants live in this place."

"We were glad to help. And we will not forget the valor of the folk of Glen, Earek. I am sorry that I did not think better of your people before I had the honor to fight alongside them."

"It's never too late to make a fresh start," the tall innkeeper said with a smile. "Or a first impression."

What a uniquely human way of seeing the world, Daried thought. He shook his head. "One of many things I've learned in the last few days, I think. Good luck to you, Earek."

He picked up his reins again and started to urge his horse forward, but Nilsa held up her hand and stopped him.

"There is something else," she said. She picked up a long, thin bundle from the ground by her feet, and offered it to Daried. "The moonblade of your House."

The bladesinger stopped and stared at the girl for a long moment. Moving slowly and stiffly himself—he had more injuries than he could count, it seemed—he slid out of the saddle and faced her. He accepted the sword from her, but then he gravely bowed and placed it back in her hands.

"It is not mine now, Nilsa," he told her. "The moonblade answered to your hand. For hundreds of years it recognized no elf as a suitable heir to the Morvaerils. But it knew you when you set your hand on it, and it accepted you. Carry the Morvaeril blade for the rest of your days, Nilsa Harvalmeer. Raise your children to be true and strong, so that they will be worthy of it too."

"I can't accept this, Daried. I am not an elf!"

"It's not a question of whether you accept the blade, Nilsa. It's whether the blade accepts you." Daried smiled. "As for whether you are an elf, well, you are clearly elf enough. Perhaps there is more to being *Tel'Quessir* than an accident of heritage, and this moonblade intends to show us that."

Nilsa snorted, and wrapped the moonblade back in its blanket. "If you have that much faith in the sword's judgment, I guess I do too," she said. Then she leaned forward and kissed Daried on the cheek. "Take care of yourself, bladesinger. Sweet water and light laughter until we meet again."

"Sweet water and light laughter, Nilsa," Daried answered. "I hope we meet again in better times." Moving carefully, the bladesinger climbed back into the saddle, and tapped his heels against the horse's flanks. He waved once in the human manner, and he turned his face to the west and led his comrades into the shadows of morning.

About the Authors

Richard Lee Byers is the author of over twenty novels, including the Forgotten Realms® titles *The Shattered Mask, Dissolution, The Black Bouquet, Queen of the Depths, The Rage, The Rite,* and *The Ruin.* A resident of the Tampa Bay area, he spends much of his leisure time fencing, shooting pool, playing poker, and dreading hurricanes.

Philip Athans is the managing editor for Wizards of the Coast's book publishing team and the author of seven published novels. He lives in the Seattle, Washington area and like everyone else there, drinks way too much coffee. "The Staff of Valmaxian" was originally written for the ill-fated *Neverwinter Nights* anthology.

Lisa Smedman is the author of more than a dozen novels, and has designed a number of role-playing game products. She's been a journalist for more than twenty years, a gamer for more than thirty years, and a mom for a little more than three years. Find out more at www.lisasmedman.topcities.com.

The life of **Erik Scott de Bie** is best summed up thus: a blurred frenzy of soul-burning work, energetic writing, flashing swords, cats named for Greek deities, and beautiful women (well, just one, really), punctuated by occasional moments of wit-based levity and sleep-based clarity.

R.A. Salvatore has spent so many years winding himself into fantasy worlds that he's still trying to figure out how to unwind. He is the author of more than forty novels and more than a dozen *New York Times* best sellers, including *The Two Swords,* which debuted at or near the top of many best seller lists.

Ed Greenwood is the stout, bearded, jolly Canadian librarian who created the FORGOTTEN REALMS® (Elminster, the Seven Sisters, liches, long-missing elf sorceresses, and all) and unleashed them on an unsuspecting world. The world seems, hundreds of novels and game products later, to have largely forgiven him for it.

Richard Baker has been a game designer since 1991. He has written or contributed to more than sixty game products, including 3rd Edition DUNGEONS & DRAGONS®. He is the author of six FORGOTTEN REALMS® novels, including *The New York Times* best seller *Condemnation* and the acclaimed Last Mythal trilogy. Rich lives in Washington state with his wife Kim Rohrbach and daughters Alex and Hannah.

FROM *NEW YORK TIMES*

BEST-SELLING AUTHOR

R.A. SALVATORE

In taverns, around campfires, and in the loftiest council chambers of Faerûn, people whisper the tales of a lone dark elf who stumbled out of the merciless Underdark to the no less unforgiving wilderness of the World Above and carved a life for himself, then lived a legend...

THE LEGEND OF DRIZZT

For the first time in deluxe hardcover editions, all three volumes of the Dark Elf Trilogy take their rightful place at the beginning of one of the greatest fantasy epics of all time. Each title contains striking new cover art and portions of an all-new author interview, with the questions posed by none other than the readers themselves.

HOMELAND

Being born in Menzoberranzan means a hard life surrounded by evil.

EXILE

But the only thing worse is being driven from the city with hunters on your trail.

SOJOURN

Unless you can find your way out, never to return.

Ed Greenwood

THE CREATOR OF THE FORGOTTEN REALMS WORLD

BRINGS YOU THE STORY OF

SHANDRIL OF HIGHMOON

Shandril's Saga

SPELLFIRE
Book I

Powerful enough to lay low a dragon or heal a wounded warrior, spellfire is the most sought after power in all of Faerûn. And it is in the reluctant hand of Shandril of Highmoon, a young, orphaned kitchen-lass.

CROWN OF FIRE
Book II

Shandril has grown to become one of the most powerful magic-users in the land. The powerful Cult of the Dragon and the evil Zhentarim want her spellfire, and they will kill whoever they must to possess it.

HAND OF FIRE
Book III

Shandril has spellfire, a weapon capable of destroying the world, and now she's fleeing for her life across Faerûn, searching for somewhere to hide. Her last desperate hope is to take refuge in the sheltered city of Silverymoon. If she can make it.

www.wizards.com

Dragons are descending on the Forgotten Realms!

THE RAGE

The Year of Rogue Dragons, Book I

Richard Lee Byers

Renegade dragon hunter Dorn hates dragons with a passion few can believe, let alone match. He has devoted his entire life to killing every dragon he can find, but as a feral madness begins to overtake the dragons of Faerûn, civilization's only hope may lie in the last alliance Dorn would ever accept.

THE RITE

The Year of Rogue Dragons, Book II

Richard Lee Byers

Dragons war with dragons in the cold steppes of the Bloodstone Lands, and the secret of the ancient curse gives a small band of determined heroes hope that the madness might be brought to an end.

REALMS OF THE DRAGONS

Book I

Edited by Philip Athans

This anthology features all-new stories by R.A. Salvatore, Ed Greenwood, Elaine Cunningham, and the authors of the R.A. Salvatore's War of the Spider Queen series. It fleshes out many of the details from the current Year of Rogue Dragons trilogy by Richard Lee Byers and includes a short story by Byers.

REALMS OF THE DRAGONS

Book II

Edited by Philip Athans

A new breed of Forgotten Realms authors bring a fresh approach to new stories of mighty dragons and the unfortunate humans who cross their paths.

NEW YORK TIMES BESTSELLING SERIES

R.A. SALVATORE'S
WAR OF THE SPIDER QUEEN

The epic saga of the dark elves concludes!

EXTINCTION
Book IV

LISA SMEDMAN

For even a small group of drow, trust is the rarest commodity of all. When the expedition prepares for a return to the Abyss, what little trust there is crumbles under a rival goddess's hand.

ANNIHILATION
Book V

PHILIP ATHANS

Old alliances have been broken, and new bonds have been formed. While some finally embark for the Abyss itself, other stay behind to serve a new mistress—a goddess with plans of her own.

RESURRECTION
Book VI

PAUL S. KEMP

The Spider Queen has been asleep for a long time, leaving the Underdark to suffer war and ruin. But if she finally returns, will things get better...or worse?

www.wizards.com